IN BALANCE

IN BALANCE

Peter Gillman

Twenty years of
mountaineering
journalism

Hodder & Stoughton

LONDON SYDNEY AUCKLAND TORONTO

British Library Cataloguing in Publication Data
Gillman, Peter
  In balance: twenty years of mountaineering
  journalism.
  1. Mountaineering history. Reporting
  I. Title
  070.4′497965′22

  ISBN 0-340-50294-0

Published by Hodder and Stoughton,
a division of Hodder and Stoughton Limited,
Mill Road, Dunton Green, Sevenoaks, Kent TN13 2YA.
Editorial Office: 47 Bedford Square, London WC1B 3DP.

Photoset by Rowland Phototypesetting Limited,
Bury St Edmunds, Suffolk

Printed in Great Britain by St Edmundsbury Press Limited,
Bury St Edmunds, Suffolk

To Dave Condict

CONTENTS

Author's Note

1 An Innocent Abroad   13

Climber killed on Eiger
Daily Telegraph, 1966
The worst mountain wins again
Sunday Times, 1968

2 Climbs and Climbers   40
A promise kept
Scotsman, 1967
The show must go up
Sunday Times Magazine, 1973
The Challenge of Changabang
Sunday Times Magazine, 1978
The peak of a career
Financial Times, 1987
The Himalayan year
Financial Times, 1988
Cut off on the top of the world
Sunday Times Magazine, 1988

3 Fingers on the Rock   90
A dinosaur in Wales
Sunday Times, 1967
TV circus goes up the Old Man of Hoy
Sunday Times, 1967
Forty years old and still the greatest
Radio Times, 1970
The fingertip phenomenon
Sunday Times, 1982
The peak of endeavour
Daily Telegraph, 1986

Conquest of the impossible
  Sunday Times, 1988
Traverse of the gods
  Climbers' Club Journal, 1967

4 MYSTERIES AND ROWS   119
  Cerro Torre, the cheated summit
    Sunday Times Magazine, 1972
  A Walter Mitty on Craig Gogarth
    Sunday Times, 1969
  Backtracking on Everest
    Sunday Times, 1981
  The Everest enigma
    Financial Times, 1986
  Measuring mountains
    Daily Telegraph, 1987

5 ACCIDENT AND RISK   143
  The fifty-fifty risk
    Sunday Times, 1968
  It's not going to happen to me
    Sunday Times, 1967
  Red tape halts rescue radio switch
    Sunday Telegraph, 1986
  The end of hope
    Radio Times, 1970
  The best days of my life
    Sunday Times, 1970
  Mick's own Everest
    Listener, 1975
  Avalanche on K2
    Sunday Times, 1978
  Two extraordinarily gallant men
    Sunday Times, 1982
  Climbing towards catastrophe
    The Times, 1987

6 MIXED GROUND   183
  Tales from the hills
    Radio Times, 1979
  Could a man do the job?
    Sunday Times Magazine, 1968

Up the walls
    Scanorama, 1984
Buildering
    Sunday Times, 1978
Book reviews
Down and out in Derbyshire
    Financial Times, 1988
Where on earth is Alex Pitcher?
    Sunday Times Magazine, 1988

7 SCOTLAND IN WINTER   231
Cold, hard, dangerous – and fun
    Sunday Times Magazine, 1969
The lure of the Ben
    Sunday Times, 1982
Climb every mountain
    Financial Times, 1987
Small hill, big triumph
    Sunday Times, 1988

INDEX   249

Illustrations

(*between pages 128 and 129*)

Chris Bonington[1]
John Harlin[2]
Dougal Haston[2]
The Old Man of Hoy team[2]
Haston on the South-East Arête
Cerro Torre
West Face of Fitzroy
The Cerro Torre team[3]
Mick Burke[4]
Nick Estcourt[2]
Joe Tasker and Pete Boardman[1]
Tom Patey and friends[2]
Julie Tullis and Kurt Diemberger[5]
Stephen Venables[6]
Dave Condict
Author at Swanage[2]
Author and family in the Glyders[7]
Danny Gillman on Blaven
Author on Beinn Narnain[8]

PHOTOGRAPHIC CREDITS
1 Chris Bonington
2 John Cleare/Mountain Camera
3 Ken Wilson
4 Doug Scott
5 Josema Casimiro
6 Ed Webster/Mountain Imagery
7 Chris Smith
8 Danny Gillman

Author's Note

Most of my articles about mountaineering appeared in the *Sunday Times*, both its news pages and its colour magazine, between 1968–88. After contributing to the *Sunday Times* for five years as a freelance I joined its staff in 1971 and remained there until 1983, leaving shortly after the arrival of Rupert Murdoch and happily before the onset of the Wapping dispute. I resumed writing for the *Sunday Times* in 1987. I have also written about mountaineering for *The Times*, *Observer*, *Financial Times*, *Daily* and *Sunday Telegraph*, *Scotsman*, *Listener*, *Radio Times*, *Climbers' Club Journal* and *Scanorama*, and I gratefully acknowledge all of these, together with the *Sunday Times*, as the sources of the articles in this collection. Some of the original headlines have been changed.

I also gratefully acknowledge the newspaper and magazine editors who have tolerated and even encouraged my private passion over the years, among them Peter Crookston, John Lovesey, Magnus Linklater, Don Berry, Philip Clarke, Will Ellsworth-Jones, John Davies and J. D. F. Jones. I owe particular thanks to two people who have been an unfailing source of information and advice, Audrey Salkeld and Ken Wilson, and, for his assistance over K2, Xavier Eguskitza.

Finally, most important of all, is my debt to my family, both to my children, Danny and Seth, who have allowed themselves to be written about and photographed without complaint, and to my wife and partner Leni, who encouraged me to go climbing in the first place and whose support has sustained me not only on the hill but also through those dark moments all writers know.

1

AN INNOCENT ABROAD

I knew that climbers hated journalists. It was only when I covered the Eiger Direct ascent in 1966 that I discovered how justified that hatred to be.

It was mid-March, and the attempt had been in train for three weeks. John Harlin, drawing on his meteorological experience with the US air force, had predicted a spell of fifteen days of perfect weather but this had failed to materialise. Instead the climb had been interrupted by a succession of storms which left the face looking, in Chris Bonington's facetious phrase, 'like a great big white Christmas tree'.

At dusk on 10 March John and Chris, together with Dougal Haston and Layton Kor, had finally reached the Death Bivouac. There they excavated a snowhole in a bulging cornice at the precise place where, as they discovered with chill fascination the next morning, Sedlmayer and Mehringer had died of exhaustion and hypothermia in 1935. That day Layton and Dougal pushed the route through the Third Icefield to the foot of what became known as the Central Pillar. The eight-man German team also attempting the route was at roughly the same level. Then another storm arrived.

Chris and Layton decided to return to the comforts of Kleine Scheidegg while John and Dougal sat out the storm at the Death Bivouac. They had food and fuel for about five days and felt that they would be best placed to continue the climb when the storm lifted. Although the word 'competition' was taboo in the British-American team, their judgment was certainly influenced by the fact that five German climbers had also bivouacked on the face and would undoubtedly be eager to start climbing as soon as possible. Meanwhile Chris and Layton, together with Don Whillans and myself as the *Daily Telegraph*'s reporter, languished at the Kleine Scheidegg Hotel, consuming as much food and alcohol as we could on the *Telegraph*'s expense account. The three remaining German climbers, backed by the Belser publishing company, did likewise.

For the next five days, as the storm raged outside their snowhole and spindrift avalanches coursed almost continuously down the face, John and Dougal radioed laconic messages to the hotel, which I did my best to convert into enthralling dispatches for the following day. Their comments on the prevailing weather conditions and climbing prospects usually made the newspaper; Dougal's uncharacteristically forthright description of being covered 'with a mixture of Scots-American excrement' did not. Even with such imaginative headlines as 'Storms batter Eiger men' and 'Blizzard pins Eiger teams in snowholes' my reports occupied an ever-decreasing space in the newspaper. As a condition of his contract with the *Telegraph*, which guaranteed him £1500 on a sliding scale (£500 for starting, £1000 for reaching the Death Bivouac, £1500 for the summit) Harlin had asked that the coverage should be 'accurate and without contrived sensationalism' and to the *Telegraph*'s enormous credit it never put pressure on me to do otherwise.

Hugo Kuranda evidently felt no such constraints. An elderly and tight-lipped Austrian, given to wearing foppish alpine-style tweed suits, he was the Geneva correspondent of Associated Newspapers, the London company which published the *Daily Sketch* (now defunct), the London *Evening News* (ditto) and the *Daily Mail* (extant). Today I have become less shocked that newspapers should publish stories that have been conjured out of the air. But this was, after all, my first reporting assignment. Looking at that absurdly youthful figure pictured on the back of *Eiger Direct*, the book I wrote with Dougal Haston, I feel that I appear like some journalistic Candide, an ingénu abroad. I was therefore quite unprepared for Kuranda's story in the *Daily Sketch* on Wednesday, 16 March. (It appeared under the by-line Arthur Durman, presumably because the *Sketch* considered that his real name had an unsavoury foreign flavour.)

It began as a light-hearted race, almost in the mood of a boyish escapade. But there was no laughter on the Eiger today and no dancing in the valley below, where the wives and sweethearts of the climbers wait. For sheltered in a tiny snowhole, 11,200 feet up the wall, Dougal Haston (24) from Edinburgh, and John Harlin, a 30-year-old American, have sent a walkie-talkie message to their three comrades: 'It is terribly grim up here. Can't you help us?' They have been marooned on the mountain since digging in last Thursday.

This afternoon Britain's Chris Bonington and the German leader Jörg Lehne led a combined rescue party up the Eiger. They ignored the warnings of the Swiss professional guides: 'Don't go yet. There are avalanches waiting to kill you. 'Even the vibrations caused by your climbing boots may cause some of them.'

Those happy hours seem so far away, when Marilyn Harlin, pig-tailed Wendy Bonington, and Audrey Whillans would take turns at the big telescope on their hotel roof and tell each other what grand chaps they were.

Today the adventure has gone sour.

I was already aware of Fleet Street's concentration on the most sensational aspects of mountaineering, coupled with the uncomprehending inaccuracies which permeated its reports. But never before had I encountered invention on this breathtaking level. Quite apart from its nauseatingly sugary tone, Kuranda's story contained at least six major inaccuracies.

First, neither Marilyn Harlin nor Audrey Whillans was at Kleine Scheidegg (although pig-tailed Wendy Bonington was). Second, John and Dougal had radioed no plea for help or anything remotely similar. Third, no Swiss guides had warned Chris about avalanches. Fourth, far from being trapped, John and Dougal could have descended the fixed ropes to Kleine Scheidegg at any time. Fifth, Chris and Jörg Lehne did not lead a combined rescue party up the Eiger.

Here Kuranda had been caught in the familiar trap of filing a story containing news which had not yet happened. The truth was that Chris, Lehne et al had *intended* to climb up to the Death Bivouac with fresh supplies that day. At lunchtime, presumably after Kuranda had telephoned his story to the *Daily Sketch*, they changed their minds. Instead they skied to the foot of the face and dumped their loads there, planning to return the following morning. In no circumstances, in any case, could this be called a rescue party.

Several days passed before this report reached us, by which time John and Dougal had descended to Kleine Scheidegg and then returned to the face. When John heard about it he asked me to get hold of Kuranda and 'straighten him out', while Dougal said he wanted to kill him. I decided to leave any straightening out to John and Dougal. Not for the only time a journalist was to be spared the wrath of climbers through the unfolding of events. For me it served as a brusque introduction into the ways of Fleet Street, before that concept, too, was overtaken by its technological nemesis.

At the time of the Eiger ascent I had been a journalist and climber for just two years. After writing for school and university magazines, I obtained my first job on *Town*, a glossy magazine that aimed itself at the proto-Yuppies of the early 1960s. I was sacked after a year (the proprietor explained that I did not represent a sound short-term investment) and progressed to the *Weekend Telegraph*, the colour magazine published at that time in conjunction with the Friday edition of the *Daily Telegraph*. I began climbing the year I started work. One summer's evening I was sitting outside a pub near King's Cross with a former schoolfriend, Dave Condict, who was off to Snowdonia for the weekend. My wife Leni suggested that I went too on the grounds that it would do me good. I followed Dave up those classic novitiates' routes, Amphitheatre Buttress on Craig yr Ysfa followed by Lockwood's Chimney, and despite my fear – perhaps because of it – I was hooked.

I soon discerned the abysmal manner in which climbing was reported. My feeling of how far climbing was traduced made me reluctant to write about it until I had fathomed more of its mysteries and appeal. But when I learned that the *Telegraph* had agreed to sponsor Harlin's attempt on the Eiger the opportunity was too good to miss. I asked if I could write an article on the preparations for the climb and was duly dispatched to Switzerland. To my delight I was accompanied by John Cleare, whose photographs, which I had seen in Walt Unsworth's book *The English Outcrops*, conveyed the sense of drama and revelation in climbing that I had come to know.

My first problem, as I embarked on my career as mountaineering journalist, was that I could not help regarding many of the climbers as gods. The first time I met Joe Brown I hardly dared speak; Harlin left me in awe. In retrospect he appears as a typical Californian of the 1960s, blond and muscular, and given to an introspective wordiness which the more pragmatic British members of the entourage (Don Whillans springs to mind) termed 'bullshit'. At the same time, once having absolved me of collective guilt for the debased standards of contemporary journalism, John showed me unstinting generosity and warmth.

It may have been those qualities which so beguiled me. John's mountaineering record was impressive, of course: first US ascent of the Eiger North Face, first ascent of the South Face of the Fou, first ascent of the Hidden Pillar of Frêney. His aura gained lustre from his reputation as some latterday renaissance man: air-force pilot, world-ranked skier, champion US footballer, *haute couture* fashion designer. All these I dutifully listed in my articles in the *Weekend Telegraph* and later in *Eiger Direct*. Only later did I discover the extent to which I had been misled.

Two years after *Eiger Direct*, Jim Ullman's biography of Harlin, entitled *Straight Up*, was published. Ullman, a veteran mountaineering writer whose most celebrated book was his account of the US ascent of the West Face of Everest in 1963, paid me the compliment of calling me a 'sensitive, strictly non-ballyhoo-type' of journalist. At the same time he enquired into the more colourful items on Harlin's curriculum vitae.

I had written that John had worked for Pierre Balmain in Paris one summer. Ullman discovered that he had in fact spent a weekend as a guest at one of Balmain's house parties, and had not worked for him at all. I had written that John had played for the all-US services football team. Ullman revealed that his career as services football-player extended to nothing more than captaining one of the internal teams at his USAF base in Germany.

As for the champion skier, I had written that John had come twenty-fifth in the world *Langlauf* championships six months after taking up the sport. Ullman discovered that the climax of John's international skiing career had been as a member of a four-man US services team competing in the European military ski championships. It had also met an ignominious end, for John had been compelled to withdraw from the race upon being inflicted with an embarrassing attack of diarrhoea. Ullman's demolition job, presented with admirable courtesy and restraint, proved a salutary lesson, and I hope I have never been quite so credulous again.

After my article appeared in the magazine, I was assigned to cover the ascent for the newspaper. Here I indulged in a minor subterfuge which showed that I had at least a modicum of the ratlike cunning which Nicholas Tomalin, the *Sunday Times* reporter killed during the 1973 Arab-Israeli war, asserted that all journalists require. The *Telegraph*'s news editor asked me if I had ever done any reporting before. At that time I had written

precisely one article for a newspaper, an account of an internal
Labour party row which appeared in the *Observer*. The report
contained the foolhardy allegation that one of the cliques involved was Trotskyist and it was only because I knew some of
its members that I managed to avert a libel writ. However, this
article enabled me to reply 'Yes' to the news editor with a
technically clear conscience.

My first real reporting assignment made an unpromising start.
John and his team had already been at Kleine Scheidegg for two
weeks, waiting for John's predicted spell of clear weather. On
the day I arrived John attempted a bravura one-legged ski
manoeuvre and dislocated his shoulder. He went home to
Leysin on the other side of Switzerland and I was summoned
back to London. By the time I returned to Kleine Scheidegg Jörg
Lehne's German team was halfway up the First Band and Dougal
and John – his shoulder sore but repaired – were about to set
off in pursuit. I felt a frisson of excitement which I now recognise
as the journalist's sense of a newsworthy story but which is also
strikingly similar to the rapture that overtakes climbers at key
moments on their routes.

It also seems to me now that I had little awareness of the
enormity of what was unfolding before me. I had never even
seen an alpine route before, let alone one of the scale and
renown of the Eiger. I did not appreciate how remarkable it was
to be watching those tiny figures etched against the face through
the telescopes at Kleine Scheidegg. Nor did I have more than a
glimmering of the rampant paradoxes involved. Having previously forsworn writing about climbing because of the media's
excesses, I was now pitched into what became perhaps the most
excessive mountaineering spectacular in the history of the sport.
Yet I did my best to observe the terms of John's request over
the tone of the coverage and my dutifully restrained reports
appeared in the *Telegraph* day after day: 'Eiger Teams Plan Big
Push Today'; 'Germans 150ft Ahead in Eiger Climb'; 'Eiger
Teams at Same Height'.

Although I perceived little of it at the time, Chris Bonington
was going through an early example of the vacillation and
self-doubt that were to recur during his career. Aged thirty-two
to my twenty-four, he appeared to be as mature, confident and
accomplished as could be, particularly in view of the renown
stemming from his remarkable list of first ascents, from Lakeland
to Patagonia via the Central Pillar of Frêney and the Eiger North

Face itself. He was also unfailingly kind and encouraging to me.

In *The Next Horizon* Chris tells how he first conceived of attempting an Eiger Direct almost the moment he came down from completing the first British ascent of the *voie normale* with Ian Clough in 1962. John Harlin had been thinking along the same lines, and Chris accepted John's suggestion that they should combine forces for an attempt. That was in the summer of 1965. Thereafter Chris succumbed to increasing doubts about the venture, never having previously attempted a major alpine route in winter, but he did not discuss them with John. Only when I read *The Next Horizon* did I realise that I had been the catalyst for his change of mind, when I telephoned him in the Lake District to ask if I could interview him for my preliminary article for the *Weekend Telegraph*. The prospect of talking about the attempt so alarmed him that he not only declined to be interviewed but also wrote to John to tell him he was pulling out of the team.

Shortly afterwards the *Telegraph* asked Chris if he would photograph the ascent instead. For Chris, the request arrived at a perfect moment, as he was still struggling to establish his career as professional climber and he accepted with alacrity. But once at Kleine Scheidegg he found himself swayed by John's blandishments and, far from hanging back as photographer, became fully committed to the route, culminating in his brilliant lead on the ice-gully beside the Central Pillar which proved to be one of the key pitches of the ascent.

This was the highest Chris reached on the face. Thereafter he recoiled from this degree of involvement and reverted to his role as photographer. Chris told me that he felt his principal responsibility was now to the *Telegraph*, since they and not John were his employers. He has since said that he also became anxious about the gladiatorial aspect of the attempt, the notion that here were climbers enacting life-and-death struggles in a public arena, which at first impinged so little on me.

Chris's forebodings came all too true three days later when the fixed rope John Harlin was ascending broke. John's death also brought home to me aspects both of mountaineering and of journalism in a manner for which I was quite unprepared. That may also explain why it was only some time afterwards that I was able to piece together the causes of the accident. Chris himself has said that accidents are rarely random occurrences but the culmination of a long sequence of events. Nowhere was that more true, I now feel, than on the Eiger.

As John had told me the first time we met, his strategy for the climb was to make a traditional alpine-style ascent. For this he needed the spell of settled weather he had so confidently predicted. But when the German team arrived at Kleine Scheidegg it was clear they had other ideas, pursuing Himalayan siege tactics which entailed climbing between storms and retreating when necessary down fixed ropes. As I observed, the two teams at first remained fastidiously apart, equally reluctant to be the first to cross the invisible line separating them with the consequent risk of loss of face.

It was Chris who broke the impasse by asking the Germans if he could borrow a shovel in order to excavate a snowhole below the Rock Band. I certainly did not realise then that so straightforward a request could have such momentous import: but the Germans were at first astounded at his presumption and John himself was manifestly uneasy. John was still less happy when Chris made the key decision which led to the two teams climbing together as well.

After the five-day storm, Chris and Layton Kor had taken over from John and Dougal on the face. While Chris and Layton forced the route to the left of the Central Pillar – Layton with his three-hour bolt traverse, Chris with his audacious and poorly-protected ice lead – the Germans met a dead end in a gully to the pillar's right. The next morning Jörg Lehne proposed that Layton and the amiable Karl Golikow should climb to the top of the Central Pillar. Chris agreed at once.

I can still see the chagrin on John's face when Chris radioed down to Kleine Scheidegg with the news. I passed John the radio handset and he told Chris, with impressive restraint, that he considered the decision somewhat premature. John was frank enough to admit that he had wanted to suggest an amalgamation from a position of strength, i.e. *after* Chris and Layton had pushed their route to the top of the Central Pillar. With equal frankness, Chris later told me that his prime motive had been to enable himself to take photographs while the others climbed.

It was therefore by the most savage irony that the rope that was fixed up the Central Pillar was one of the first fruits of the co-operation between the two teams. Supplied by the Germans, fixed in place by Layton Kor and Karl Golikow, it was a 100-metre length of 7mm perlon secured by pitons and dropped over the edge of an angled slab. No one at the time – and certainly not

me – appeared to appreciate the danger of making repeated
ascents on so thin a rope.

What I saw when I trained the Kleine Scheidegg telescope on
the face at 3.15 p.m. on 22 March will stay with me for ever.
Just before midday I had radioed to John and Dougal that a
German climber had reached the Fly, the satellite snowfield
above the Spider that led into the summit headwall. I also passed
on an optimistic weather forecast which suggested that John's
spell of clear weather was about to begin at last. John and Dougal
headed for the Spider at once, Dougal going first up the fixed
rope beside the Central Pillar, followed at around 3 p.m. by
John.

As I peered through the telescope, following the line of fixed
ropes up the face, I knew at once, beyond any conceivable
doubt, that I had seen a man falling to his death. I saw a figure
dressed in red, limbs outstretched, turning over slowly, finally,
in the air clear of the face. I tried to follow the figure but it
disappeared behind a buttress and all I saw were chunks of
snow tumbling out of a couloir by the Death Bivouac and another
climber standing nearby, presumably transfixed by what he too
had seen. I gave an involuntary shout and the others who
crowded round the telescope tried to suggest that I had seen a
rucksack or an anorak. I wanted so much to agree but I knew it
was not so.

I called Chris down from his room. I asked him to look through
the telescope and as he did so I told him what I had seen. He
too asked if it could have been a rucksack. I knew it wasn't but
said it might have been. Chris and Layton set off on skis towards
a patch of debris which we had located below the face, while I
guided them with the telescope and a radio. At 4.35 p.m. Chris
radioed: 'It's John. He's dead.'

There can be few climbers who have not encountered death
in the mountains. Perhaps I had some protection from its impact
at Kleine Scheidegg because I had seen both my parents die
from cancer. I am also now ready to accept that death is an
inescapable part of a risk sport. But I never quite made sense of
that figure falling through the frame of the telescope, unless it
was as an image of human mortality, an intimation of the fate
that awaits us all.

One of the people on the terrace at the moment I was scanning
the face was Hugo Kuranda. After I recoiled from the telescope
he bent down to take a look and then strolled away. It was on

that brief look, presumably, that he based his story which appeared on the front page of the *Daily Mail*, under the headline 'Eiger Man Falls to Death', the next day.

John Harlin, leader of the Anglo-American team of super-mountaineers, plunged 4000 ft to his death today down the Eiger North Wall, the Alps' greatest killer.

I was peering at Harlin, 30-year-old American, through a powerful telescope. It had just focussed on his solitary figure in a bright red climbing suit with a huge blue rucksack on his back. He was in a very steep gully on his way to the White Spider glacier 11,620 ft up.

Suddenly I saw the little figure throw up its arms. A split second later it sailed through the air, bouncing again and again against razor edged rocks, releasing a train of avalanches.

It seemed to me a horrible eternity before the body landed 4000 ft lower down, on a snowfield at the foot of the North Wall. I was watching from the roof of the hotel on the 7000 ft high pass at Kleine Scheidegg, Switzerland.

The American was climbing on one of the ropes fixed on the face by advance parties. It was believed that he was changing ropes when he fell.

Harlin, married with two children, had been a dress designer for Paris couturier Pierre Balmain . . .

By the time I read Kuranda's story in Switzerland I believe that I was impervious to further shocks. John's funeral was held at Leysin on the very day Dougal and four of the German climbers reached the summit after three days battling through a climactic storm. The fixed ropes had been pulled down behind them as they had proved to be as frayed as the rope which had killed John; the way out, as Dougal put it in *Eiger Direct*, was up. It was when I considered Kuranda's account in detail I realised that not only he but the *Daily Mail* was at fault. Kuranda could not of course have seen what he said he saw as I was looking through the one telescope on the hotel terrace at the time. But surely someone at the *Mail* should have realised that it would have been quite impossible to follow the path of a body tumbling down the face through a high-powered telescope as Kuranda described?

Kuranda's articles for the *Daily Mail* continued to appear.

Mine did not. The editor of the *Weekend Telegraph* was one of those characters who have favourites and scapegoats without apparent rhyme or reason. I was briefly the favourite when I returned to London, having led the front page of the *Telegraph* three times in four days. Then I became the scapegoat, and the editor did not address another word to me over the next five months. When I went on holiday he sent me a letter giving me the sack.

*   *   *

A year after the Eiger, I found myself in Patagonia. Whereas I accepted all that occurred on the Eiger with unquestioning credulity, in Patagonia I succumbed to a sense of wonder that can stir me now. I remember most of all the titanic storms that raged across the Patagonian ice cap to sweep down on our encampment in the trees at the foot of the Cerro Torre glacier. Great gusts of wind, sounding like an express train roaring out of a tunnel, shuddered our tents as if they were about to be lifted into the air. At times the ground reverberated with shock-waves as giant séracs toppled from the glacier into the lake above our camp, so that it felt as if we had been caught in an earthquake.

I also remember the utter contrast of the few precious days when the air became still and the sun blazed down from a cobalt sky. On one of these I stood on the gently sloping icefield beside our Advance Base Camp and gazed at the gigantic West Face of Fitzroy, tier upon tier rising 8000 feet to the summit, and reflected that perhaps no more than a dozen people had seen what I saw that day. Its dazzling clarity made me feel that I could almost reach across to touch it, and that climbing it would present no greater problems than the peaks of the far north-west of Scotland which by then I had come to love.

To set beside such transcendental moments are the weeks of ennui and animosity that beset the British Cerro Torre Expedition of 1967–8 as it laboured to make the first undisputed ascent of that extraordinary mountain. I owed my presence to the *Sunday Times*, which had dubbed it the Worst Mountain in the World. This time the entrepreneurial thrust had come from Dougal Haston. We had stayed in touch after writing *Eiger Direct* and in the autumn of 1967 Dougal told me that he, Mick Burke, Martin Boysen and Pete Crew had formed the British Cerro Torre Expedition which was to begin its attempt in December that year. I had never heard of Cerro Torre and guessed that it was in Italy. Even when Dougal told me that it was near the southern end of the Patagonian ice cap, on the border between Argentina and Chile 350 miles north of Cape Horn, my enthusiasm remained undiminished.

Although my contract with the *Sunday Times* was principally with its colour magazine, I wrote between times for its news pages. Dougal asked me if the *Sunday Times* would be willing to sponsor the expedition and so I put this proposition to the news editor. He took us to lunch at the Savoy where, over the mixed grill, Dougal produced his masterstroke, a photograph showing Cerro Torre at its most dramatic, a thrusting granite spire capped with the overhanging ice confections that are its hallmark.

The news editor saw the point at once. He formulated the six-word headline, 'The Worst Mountain in the World', soon to be shortened to the more economical version, 'The Worst Mountain', and the venture was on. Just as on the Eiger, I now feel that I had little sense of what lay in store. But whereas the complications of covering the Eiger ascent largely stemmed from the fact that the climbers were acting out their struggles in a public arena, in Patagonia they were quite the opposite – and rather fundamental at that. Just how do you get your reports back from the edge of a glacier in one of the most remote corners of the world?

Following Dougal's coup at the Savoy, the *Sunday Times* agreed to pay the expedition £1500. But there were complications. Pete Crew, who was acting as expedition quartermaster, persuaded British Caledonian Airlines to provide flights for himself, Martin Boysen and some freight at half the usual price. (Dougal, Mick and the rest of the equipment were to travel by boat.) In return, Pete promised that the *Sunday Times* would publish copious mentions of British Caledonian Airlines.

The game of plugging, as it is known, can be a delicate one. On one hand newspapers like to take a stern line over the ethics of confusing editorial and advertising matter. This line is likely to become progressively less stern in proportion to the benefits that may accrue to the newspaper's budget. In this instance, in any case, the venality of mentioning British Caledonian appeared minor enough; the problem for journalists becomes that of weaving the expected plugs into their prose as unobtrusively as possible. I accordingly constructed the following inoffensive paragraph: 'Burke and Haston sail for Buenos Aires with ¾-ton of baggage on November 3, and Crew, Boysen and myself fly out by British Caledonian three weeks later.'

I had not reckoned with the vagaries of the *Sunday Times* printers, then at the zenith of their power in Fleet Street. What appeared in the newspaper that Sunday ran as follows: 'Burke and Haston sail for Buenos Aires with ¾-ton of baggage on November 3, and Crew, Boysen and myself fly practicable but microfilm might be the answer.' I never discovered if an article about microfilm contained a plug for British Caledonian; but I did discover that there is no greater wrath than that of a public relations officer denied his plug. The British Caledonian man complained to Pete Crew, who referred him to me. I passed him on to the news editor who said that there was nothing he could do about what was patently a printer's error and referred him back to Crew. It is a tribute to Crew's powers of diplomacy that he dissuaded British Caledonian from charging the expedition the full fare, even if this was based on a promise of boundless plugs to come.

Meanwhile I too was encountering problems with the news editor. It had by then dawned on me that in comparison with Kleine Scheidegg, where in order to dispatch my reports to London I had merely to lift the telephone, communicating from the fastnesses of the Fitzroy massif would prove more difficult. The news editor was unperturbed. He ruled out the idea of taking radios on grounds of cost and told me: 'Play it by ear when you get out there.'

My first inkling of what 'out there' meant came when I flew from Buenos Aires to Rio Gallegos, fifty miles north of the Magellan Strait. The climbers had gone on ahead, Pete having persuaded one of Shell's Latin American outposts to lend the expedition a pick-up truck for the 250-mile journey across the pampas to the Fitzroy range. He had directed me to call at the headquarters of the Club Andino de Rio Gallegos where, he assured me, I would be able to arrange a lift for myself.

Rio Gallegos proved to be a desolate frontier town with duck-board shop fronts lining the rutted main street. It was assailed by the wind, with sage-bushes bowling in from the pampas to lodge against the wooden walls of the buildings. It had a public radio system consisting of loudspeakers which blared out a mixture of news, music and advertisements from which there was no escape. While trying to find the Club Andino de Rio Gallegos I found myself at the Rio Gallegos British Club, where a handful of second-generation ex-patriates, their faces cracked and leathery from the unforgiving climate, shook my hand and showed me the fading coronation photograph of Queen Elizabeth that hung over the club's venerable upright piano.

The headquarters of the Club Andino was an electrician's shop. Its name was Electricidad Pinguino – only later did I discover why – and its proprietor, who doubled as president of the Club Andino, was a Russian from the Ukraine. He was coy over why he had come to Rio Gallegos, but when he showed me a lapel badge which was a memento of his service with a special anti-Soviet brigade in the German army during the Second World War, I deduced that Rio Gallegos offered probably the furthest sanctuary he could find when the war ended. I never found out if the Club Andino had any other members; but I did discover that its principal occupation, rather than climbing the Andes, appeared to consist of visiting the Magellan Strait to kill penguins.

Despite the shop's name, I had been puzzled at seeing a stuffed penguin in the window. That evening I could not help noticing the pungent aroma that permeated the building. I traced it to its source: the bathroom, where a dead penguin, manifestly in early stages of decomposition, lay prostrate in the bath. That evening the president of the Club Andino showed me his colour slides: groups of curious penguins beside the Magellan Strait; the corpse of a penguin he had just battered to death; a series of dead penguins which he had stuffed. He had invited me to stay with him while he secured me a lift into the mountains but at this point, in the time-honoured Fleet Street phrase, I made my excuses and left. I found a bed at the grimy rooming-house that passed as Rio Gallegos's solitary hotel.

My lift drew up outside the hotel four days later. It consisted of a battered lorry loaded with building equipment destined for a construction site beside the Rio Fitzroy which emanates from the Fitzroy range. I tossed my rucksack into the back and clambered into the cab. I spent the next two and a half days in exquisite discomfort, jammed between the driver and his mate, as the lorry bounced and rattled its way across the pampas. There was little enough to divert my interest, beyond the armadillos that courted death on the road, the timid guanacos – a kind of llama – that bounded away at our approach, and the occasional sheep-farming estancia.

I had no idea the journey would last so long and had brought very little food. The driver and his mate allowed me to gnaw at their supply of dried meat and plied me with maté, the South American tea, which they brewed in a tiny pot over wood fires by the side of the road. At nightfall the driver stopped the lorry, rested his head on the steering wheel, and fell asleep. I made myself as comfortable as possible in a nearby ditch. In the morning the driver woke me with the call, 'Vamos, Ingles', and on we went. As we pressed on across the pampas the road became less and less defined until it finally disappeared. On the third morning we reached the Rio Fitzroy, where a rickety wooden bridge was due to be replaced. While there were some civilian contractors, the work-force mostly consisted of conscripts in the Argentine army, overseen by their officers who gave me food and maté and offered me a tent. When I said I wanted to press on they took courtesy too far.

Following a week of rain, the Rio Fitzroy had burst its banks and the bridge rose as if marooned from the flood waters some fifty yards away. After bidding the officers goodbye I began to remove my boots in order to wade to the bridge. Evidently feeling that it was his duty to spare me this inconvenience, an officer waved forward a young soldier and ordered him to carry me. I protested that I was perfectly capable of reaching the bridge under my own steam but the officer insisted. As the soldier bent down so that I could clamber on to his back, I could not help noticing that a large number of his comrades had gathered to watch. Inevitably, halfway to the bridge, he stumbled and fell, to rapturous cheers from the bank. We were both completely immersed. Summoning whatever vestige of dignity remained, I picked myself up and waded the rest of the way to the bridge.

I joined up with the British Cerro Torre Expedition that night. On the far side of the river a farmer gave me a lift to the end of the track some eight miles further on. There I found Mick Burke sitting in an orange igloo. This was another of Pete Crew's wheezes: a modification of the Whillans box, in effect a tent with plastic walls, that was to be installed at the foot of the route. However it proved too cumbersome to carry and so never left the place beside the track where it had been dumped. Mick, whom I had first met at the Eiger, gave me his usual cheerful welcome and guided me along the three-hour walk through trees and alongside rivers to the Base Camp. It seemed a homely place: a cluster of tents beside a stream, with the climbers busying themselves around a camp fire or relaxing with books. Together with Pete, Martin and Dougal there was an Argentine climber, José Fonrouge, whom they had invited to join them for diplomatic reasons, in particular to thank the Argentine Alpine Club for its help in setting up the expedition. But where was Cerro Torre?

Mick led me on to a ridge that protruded from the trees. Some five miles away, at the head of a long, featureless glacier, was a shroud of angry clouds. Somewhere inside was Cerro Torre. During the previous week the climbers had battled through wind, rain and snow to establish a camp in an ice-cave some 1000 feet above the glacier and a further 1000 feet below the true start of the climb. But they had found further progress impossible and so retreated to Base Camp. When I saw the mountain for myself a day or so later I gasped. The clouds parted to reveal a shimmering granite spire, glistening with fresh snow and capped with a grotesque mushroom of ice. Mick called it the most unclimbable mountain he had ever seen.

Base Camp became home for the next ten weeks. Since no more than two weeks of that time was spent climbing, life became a round of eating, sleeping, reading and playing cards. Real time – as measured by the BBC World Service, with its concerts, sports reports and news from the real world – gave way to camp time, so that if a game of bridge lasted until 6.00 a.m. we would simply sleep throughout the following day. Pete compiled a Dictionary of Mountaineering, I taught myself Spanish from a manual, and we all read the same books and passed them around. There were intense discussions over the true worth of *The Tin Drum* and I managed to persuade Dougal that Graham Greene was not merely a Catholic novelist but expressed wider concerns. Martin, listening to World Service concerts as they waxed and waned on the ether, sang along with the tunes he had learned from his father, a music teacher. José Fonrouge largely kept himself to himself, emerging from his tent to eat the meals the others prepared and doing little, it appeared to me, by way of communal chores. It would, I suppose, have been an acceptably indolent life, at least to begin with, were it not for the requirement to communicate with the *Sunday Times*.

After the paper had refused to supply radios, Pete Crew consoled me by telling me that I could transmit my dispatches from a weather station close to the camp. If the weather station existed, I never found it. My only recourse was to embark on the six-hour walk to Rio Fitzroy, negotiate the bridge, collect Shell's pick-up truck, and drive to the nearest telegraph office some 200 miles back across the pampas, at a coastal town named Santa Cruz. It seemed straightforward enough. But I had not reckoned with the tendency of anything mechanical to stop working as soon as I went near it. Shell's pick-up truck had functioned perfectly when the expedition drove into the mountains, and indeed was to do so when it left. Between those two events it broke down virtually every time I used it – and usually in the middle of the pampas. Each time I was saved by the extraordinary generosity of the estancieros and/or the Argentine army.

On my very first journey, the pick-up ground to a halt at a point almost precisely mid-way between Rio Fitzroy and Santa Cruz. Ahead the track snaked its way across the pampas towards a seemingly limitless horizon; there was an identical prospect behind. Staring under the bonnet made no difference, and I could think of nothing to do save to sit on a rock beside the track and hope that something or someone would turn up. Two hours later, as if alerted by the Patagonian equivalent of the bush telegraph, a farmer pulled up in his truck. 'No marcha,' I said elementally, pointing to the pick-up. The farmer towed me to his estancia and gave me food and a bed. In the morning he repaired the pick-up (I have no idea how) and sent me on my way.

On a later trip, when I was heading back into the mountains in the evening, I was so blinded by the setting sun that I drove off the road and broke both the pick-up's rear shock-absorbers. Bouncing insanely, it took me three hours to drive the last fifteen miles to Rio Fitzroy. The pick-up was now all but useless, both for my trips and for the expedition's eventual departure. But an army officer who was just ending his tour of duty in Patagonia wrote down the part numbers of the shock-absorber, bought replacements in Buenos Aires and dispatched them to the site. Another officer had them fitted to the pick-up by the time I was due to make my next journey out.

These mishaps apart, the trips to the coast presented a welcome release from life at Base Camp, where the monotony was becoming enervating. Santa Cruz was, if anything, more desolate than Rio Gallegos. But it did have a rooming-house with a restaurant with tables and chairs, a bedroom with sheets, and a bath. I pictured myself as the intrepid foreign correspondent as I sat on my bed and compiled my report. I handed it in at Santa Cruz's post office, proferring my Western Union credit card to forestall any demand for money. I also brought film, most of it taken by Pete Crew and myself, and air-freighted it to London from Santa Cruz's diminutive air-strip. Whether it actually reached the *Sunday Times*, and in what form it might have been published, I had no idea.

The biggest burst of activity on the mountain came when the winds eased in early January, bringing ten successive days of clear weather, almost unprecedented in the Fitzroy range. The climbers reached the snow-covered platform at mid-height which Pete Crew named the Col of Patience and pushed on up the steepening granite pillar above. I was now alone in the Base Camp, with no way of finding out what was happening. Each morning I climbed on to the ridge above the camp to look at the sky above the continental ice cap; after nine days I saw high cirrus obscuring the sun, followed by darkening tracers of cloud that heralded the return of the storms. The next day the climbers stomped back into the camp to report that they had come within 700 feet of the summit ice cap. The climbing was progressively harder, with the rock becoming more smooth and compact, and they had no clear idea how they were going to overcome the ice mushrooms above. But they had left fixed ropes in place above the col and appeared confident of success when the next spell of clear weather arrived.

We were to wait for another five weeks. They were not the most pleasant five weeks I have ever spent, for under the stress of boredom and frustration the group dynamics of the expedition took an interesting turn. Perhaps inevitably, in view of my excursions to the outside world, I became the outcast, or so it seemed to me. Dougal was the most ruthless in treating me that way, usually ensuring that I was excluded from the sessions of bridge. Mick said afterwards that I should have stood up for myself but at the time I did not have the assurance to do so. That stemmed in part from the ambiguity of my role, given that I was not really a full team member but was supposed to be preserving a degree of journalistic neutrality.

Far more serious than the matter of whose turn it was to play cards was the question of the expedition's food. Quite simply, it was running out. The expedition had miscalculated how much it would need to sustain what had essentially become a siege, especially since – as Mick admitted later – the climbers tended to eat merely for something to do. Here too I felt vulnerable: was I the supernumerary who was wasting their vital supplies? Mick seemed to raise the question when he asked me how much I was being paid. The answer was £60 a week – scarcely a fortune, even in 1967. But I felt so sensitive on this issue that I refused to reply, which did nothing to help.

As stocks dwindled, relationships plummeted. Much as in the Caine Mutiny, the worst crisis occurred over a can of fruit. These were now strictly rationed, with every mouthful counted. Then came the Affair of the Apricots (in the Caine Mutiny it was pineapple). An empty can was discovered near my tent, and in what came uncomfortably close to a kangaroo court I was accused of having consumed its entire contents. I said that if I had done any such thing I would scarcely have left the tin in such an incriminating place. After the expedition, when sanity was restored, Mick concluded that Fonrouge was the culprit, and I agreed, particularly as he had been my main accuser. At the time, when paranoia reigned, I hid two oranges I had been saving in a cave 200 yards from the camp. To their credit, the climbers also realised that things could not go on like this. A crisis conference was called which swiftly concluded that the expedition would have to give up its attempt unless it could buy more food. Since the expedition had also run out of money this presented certain practical difficulties. I was deputed to drive to Rio Gallegos where I was (a) to ask the *Sunday Times* to send more money and (b) to use it to buy more food.

After the customary tribulations on the road I spent five joyous days in Rio Gallegos. By now the dusty frontier town had assumed the éclat of the Kings Road. The rooming-house was full but an official of the local bank invited me to sleep on his sofa, and the overriding memory of my stay is of *Sergeant Pepper*, which my host had just received from Buenos Aires. Its bittersweet mix of celebration and nostalgia precisely suited my own mood and I played it day after day. It inspires the same distant longings in me now; while 'Lucy in the Sky with Diamonds', whatever else the letters LSD are supposed to stand for, means only one thing: that impossible spire of Cerro Torre shimmering through the clouds, 'repulsive yet beckoning', as Martin Boysen put it, like a Patagonian siren.

The money to bail out the expedition presented little problem. After waiting for a day to get through, I phoned the *Sunday*

Times' news editor and passed on the expedition's request. He asked how the climbers intended to repay the money; I said I had no idea, but that if the *Sunday Times* did not stump up, the expedition was at an end. A telegraphed money order arrived at the bank three days later. Laden with food, I headed back to the mountains, and for once the pick-up performed perfectly. The climbers fell on the supplies like wolves. The fresh food brought some relief of tension and a day or so later the skies cleared. On 11 February, Mick, Dougal, Pete and José Fonrouge set off for the mountain, leaving Martin to curse the bad luck that was to occur throughout his career: this time he had twisted his knee while trying to see who could jump furthest across the river and could barely walk.

12 February dawned brilliantly clear, so that Martin and I dared to hope that the summit was within the expedition's grasp. But on the mountain the climbers' hopes were being rapidly dashed. Instead of the three hours they reckoned to climb from the ice cave to the Col of Patience it took them twelve, mostly spent battling through thigh-deep powder snow. Mick was hit by a falling stone, Dougal and Pete fell into crevasses, and all four had a narrow escape from a windslab avalanche. The final blow came when they reached the Col that night and discovered, as they had increasingly feared, that their fixed ropes were tangled and frayed beyond repair. They excavated the best shelter they could in the unconsolidated snow and in the morning awoke to a raging storm. Retreat became a matter of survival and it was late the following afternoon, 13 February, before they stumbled back into the camp. Their disappointment was manifest in their faces; Dougal, economical as ever, said: 'It's all over.'

In the morning I sat down with each of the climbers to note down their accounts. There was a relaxed end-of-term atmosphere which I at first shared. It was Wednesday: plenty of time, I thought, to compose my story and to drive back to Rio Gallegos with the climbers in order to dispatch it to London by the weekend. But that afternoon a demonic homing urge overtook me. I collected my belongings and hurried down to the road-head. Although it was almost dark I hammered on the door of a nearby estancia and said I had to get to the bridge at once. The farmer took me without demur and when I reached the army camp I placed further demands on the officers' hospitality. I told them that, as a vital press matter, I had to get to

Buenos Aires at once. They gave me a driver and a mechanic to take me to the nearest airstrip in the Shell pick-up. We left at dawn and by the afternoon were at Calafate, a tiny mining settlement which was serviced by a DC-3 twice a week. There was a flight to the oil town of Comodoro Rivadavia the next morning and from there I could fly on to Buenos Aires. The one problem was that no one knew if there would be room on the DC-3 until it arrived; I decided to take the chance and sent the soldiers back to Rio Fitzroy. After spending twenty-four hours in an agony of suspense I got the last seat on the plane. I reached Buenos Aires that night and sent my last dispatch to London in the morning. Two days later I was home.

Although some clippings from the *Sunday Times* had reached us via the Patagonian mail system, usually arriving at the bridge around three weeks after being posted in Britain, it was only when I returned that I could check how my reports had been handled. By the time of Cerro Torre I had become more aware of the problems of catering simultaneously for two audiences, namely the informed mountaineering readership, familiar with the concepts and terminology of the sport, and the lay public who had scant acquaintance with either. I felt I had achieved a judicious balance and was disappointed when the news editor told me that some of my dispatches had been rather 'spare'. On only one occasion, however, had he been tempted to inject what he considered the necessary vitalising note, inserting the hideous phrase: 'the five climbers struggled literally inch by inch up the icy slopes.' Otherwise the *Sunday Times* respected my judgment as to how the reporting should be pitched.

To my immense pleasure and gratification, the *Sunday Times* continued to do so for the next twenty years. So, by and large, did the other newspapers and magazines for whom I have written about mountaineering. In retrospect it is surprising that for much of that time I was one of the few national newspaper journalists to take a consistent interest in the subject, as opposed to writers in the mountaineering press. I was undoubtedly fortunate to work for the *Sunday Times* for much of that period, both as part of what now appears as a golden age of British journalism, and for the opportunities it gave me to write about my particular passion. I was also fortunate in being able to do so as a complement to my other work, which ranged from overseas reporting to five years with the Insight team. I was thus able, I feel, to avoid the dangers faced by specialist writers of becoming part of the world they are covering, so that they become beholden to the system of privileges and favours by which such groups maintain their cohesion, as well as to the friendships that naturally arise.

Despite the ambiguities I sensed in Patagonia, that is not to deny the strength of those friendships. Nor is it to deny the fact that the most distressing aspect of mountaineering is the manner and frequency with which such friendships are broken. Even though they acknowledged the risk themselves, and talked of balancing it against the rewards, I find little consolation in the deaths of so many of the mountaineers I came to know and remember. Yet there is consolation for the writer in being able to help keep such memories alive.

Climber killed on Eiger

Daily Telegraph, 1966

John Harlin, thirty, the American leader of the Anglo-American team attempting the unclimbed 'direct' route on the North Face of the Eiger, was killed in a 4000-foot fall from the face at 3.20 p.m. today.

He was climbing the last section of the fixed ropes below the Spider icefield. Peter Haag, co-leader of the eight-man German team attempting the same route, radioed from the face tonight that Rolf Rosenzopf, a member of his team, reported that a falling stone had cut Harlin's rope. Both teams were using fixed ropes to progress from one bivouac site to another. While making their way on these ropes climbers are never roped together.

Harlin had not intended to climb today because of a bad weather forecast last night. Perfect weather this morning caused him to change his mind. He and Dougal Haston decided to carry equipment to the Spider 750 feet above Death Bivouac and 3750 feet up the face. By mid-afternoon Haston had reached the Spider.

Harlin was climbing the fixed ropes below. At 3.20 p.m. I happened to look through the telescope at Kleine Scheidegg at the last section of rope beneath the Spider. Suddenly I saw a figure in red cartwheeling downwards. It fell too fast for me to follow it. I saw snow knocked from the face in the region of

Death Bivouac. A climber who turned out to be Rolf Rosenzopf, of the German team, saw the figure fall past him.

Five minutes later I saw a figure lying in the snow below the face. Scattered around were a rucksack and clothing.

Layton Kor of the Anglo-American team, who had come down from the face on Monday because of the bad weather forecast, left Kleine Scheidegg on skis with Chris Bonington at 3.45. At 4.30 they reached the body. Bonington radioed that it was Harlin's.

Haston radioed from the face at 8 p.m. that he and the Germans had decided to join together to climb to the summit. They will form an international rope and the climb will be known as the John Harlin Route.

There are precedents for the climb continuing despite the death of one of its members. In particular, Himalayan expeditions have continued although one of the members of their team has died. Layton Kor will leave Kleine Scheidegg to join the combined climb.

John Harlin said during his last radio call from the face made at 11.45 a.m.: 'We might be able to climb all the way up to the summit tomorrow. But the bad weather makes it a very difficult decision.'

He had originally hoped to make a ten-day push for the summit, carrying all his equipment with him. Unsettled weather dictated otherwise.

The team is sponsored by the *Sunday Telegraph* and *Weekend Telegraph*. The German team is backed by Christian Belser, publishers, of Stuttgart.

Harlin was a Californian. He went to Stanford University and then served five years as a pilot in the United States air force. It was while serving in Europe that he started climbing in the Alps. When he left the air force he came to Switzerland to teach skiing and climbing at the American School at Leysin.

Last summer he started the International School of Modern Mountaineering with Beverley Clark who runs the Glencoe Climbing School, Argyll.

He had a son aged twelve and a daughter of ten. His wife, Marilyn, teaches science at the Leysin School.

Harlin is the twenty-seventh climber to die on the North Wall. A descent by Harlin and Kor six days ago, risking death in an avalanche, was described by one of the Germans as 'an absolute miracle'.

In the last four years Harlin had established himself as one of Europe's leading alpinists. In 1962 he climbed the North Face of the 13,025-foot Eiger by the existing route. He spent two days fighting his way up from the Spider in a bad storm, saving two Swiss climbers in severe difficulties.

He had made three previous attempts on the direct route on the North Face of the Eiger, recognised as the greatest unclimbed problem in the Alps.

In 1965 he climbed a new direct route on the South-West Face of the Dru.

Beverley Clark flew to Leysin last night. He said that John Harlin, with whom he formed the mountaineering school at Leysin, was an 'extremely fine' climber.

'From a physical point of view he was massive, and it seemed that the Eiger would break before John.'

The manager of the German expedition in Stuttgart last night expressed the deep sorrow felt by German friends of John Harlin. 'He was one of the world's best mountaineers whose example was inspiring,' he said. 'We are mourning for this courageous and gallant man.'

The worst mountain wins again

Sunday Times, 1968

The end of all hope for the British Cerro Torre expedition came 100 feet below the snow col to which they had been struggling all day. For the first time they could see all 1500 feet of the fixed ropes leading from the col to the expedition's highpoint 700 feet below the summit.

'They were like a jigsaw puzzle with the pieces missing,' said Dougal Haston. One rope, which they had tied tightly between two pitons, had stretched so much in the wind that it was now hooked over a flake of rock thirty feet away. Another was draped like a cat's cradle between two pinnacles.

The nagging fear the climbers had lived with during the thirty-five days of waiting out the bad weather in Base Camp had come true. 'I'd always wondered about fixed ropes breaking, but I just didn't think it could happen to us,' said Mick Burke.

To drive the point home they now saw the last fixed rope up to the col was itself partially cut through, its yellow nylon core showing clearly through its protective red sheath. 'One man on that and it would have worn through like butter,' said Haston. With resignation, he climbed the pitch without the rope and Crew and Burke followed him.

They had planned to reach the col in three hours and it had taken them twelve. The good weather which had enticed them on to the mountain was now quickly disappearing as the clouds over the continental ice cap darkly thickened. They looked for the snowhole they had dug six weeks previously but it had vanished under six feet of fresh snow. It contained their ice-climbing equipment and bivouac gear but the most they could find after digging in three separate places were some tea leaves and a chocolate wrapper.

Darkness hurried towards them along the Adela Ridge as they hastily dug a new hole for the night. Mingling insidiously with their cold and fatigue was an awareness that two months of waiting and climbing had ended in failure. 'I didn't come here to climb two-thirds of the mountain,' said Mick Burke. 'I came here to sit on top.'

Although they professed to each other satisfaction at having made a good attempt, the inescapable fact was that it was all over and they had lost.

February 12 had begun with a clear dawn and high hopes. Haston, Burke and Crew had climbed up to the ice cave at the foot of the route the previous evening, leaving Boysen in the Base Camp resting a twisted knee. That day, they planned to reclimb the fixed ropes to their highpoint – the last time, this had taken them six hours – bolt their way across the smooth wall where their last summit attempt had ended, and bivouac at the beginning of the large icefield on the other side.

The next day they would cross the snowfield to the ice gullies in which they hoped to thread a way through the Torre's grotesque mushroom-shaped ice cap to the summit. They left the ice cave below the Torre at 8 a.m., their earliest start ever. The air was still and the weather perfect.

Perhaps it was too perfect to be true. The first blow, sickening and unforeseen, came as they made their way up the fixed ropes on the first of the two buttresses below the col. A stone the size of a man's fist fell and hit Burke on the head. Dazed, he stared, at first uncomprehendingly, at the blood pouring from his face and staining the snow around him. He packed snow on to the wound until the bleeding stopped.

Weakly, he said that he would carry on. Crew was staying back to take photographs and Haston was now faced with the exhausting responsibility of leading every pitch from there to the col.

Above the first buttress the route slanted across a steep ice-field. That day it glittered in the sun but was also laden with menace. The wind had hardened it to the avalanche-prone condition known as windslab, with a surface crust lying insecurely on deep powder snow.

With his extensive winter experience, Haston was fully aware of the danger as he set off across the icefield and, after eighty feet of climbing, his fears appeared on the point of realisation. There was a dull thud and, with horror, he saw a zigzag crack snake away from his feet. 'Watch the rope, Mick,' he yelled.

Burke, directly in the path of any avalanche, knew what Haston meant. 'I didn't think about anything. It was completely beyond my control.' For some reason the surface slab held. 'I don't know why I didn't go,' said Burke. 'We must just have been lucky.'

Gingerly, Haston crossed to the rock buttress at the far side of the icefield. At the foot of the second rock buttress was a bergschrund, the gap where the ice ends and rock begins. Previously they had crossed this by a snowbridge but now the gap seemed to have been completely filled by a huge powder snow avalanche.

Haston crossed safely but Burke fell through the snow's surface up to his neck and when Crew tried to follow at a different place, he disappeared completely. Twenty feet down, he was held by the rope and, bridging his feet on each side of the crevasse, he inched his way laboriously back to safety.

With fatigue already wearing them down, the climbers now had to battle their way up the fixed ropes in the worst snow conditions any of them had experienced. A cloying mixture of wet and powder snow clung to their feet, weighing them down as if they wore diver's boots. To accentuate an encroaching feeling of unreality, they saw huge transparent plates of ice that must have fallen from far above, skimming silently through the air hundreds of feet away.

They arrived on the snow col, utterly exhausted – so much so that even the awareness of failure came almost as an anticlimax.

The one relief that night as they lay in their hastily dug snowhole, watching spindrift spurting past the anorak blocking the entrance, was that they now knew the outcome of the months of waiting. 'I'd much prefer to have it happen this way than to sit in the Base Camp until the end of March,' said Mick Burke. 'The worst thing was not knowing, going to look at the weather every hour and wondering whether it was going to change.'

The next morning a full storm was raging. With the wind continually threatening to hurl them bodily into the void, they crept back along the col and climbed down to the ice cave. Inside were huddled three members of the Argentinian Cerro Torre expedition whose own summit attempt had literally not left the ground. Together, all six climbers stumbled back down the Torre's glacier and through the unstable boulders of its moraine, arriving in the British Base Camp at eight that evening.

'I knew from their faces that there had been a catastrophe, an accident or something,' said Martin Boysen. Haston spoke the three fateful words: 'It's all over.'

It was the end of one of the most brilliant assaults in mountain-eering history – an assault that served only to confirm Cerro Torre's reputation as 'the most unclimbable mountain'.

It was this reputation that brought the four climbers to the Torre in the beginning. They met at a dinner of the Alpha Climbing Club in Manchester in November 1966, spent the summer months organising and left for Patagonia in November. Burke and Haston sailed with three-quarters of a ton of equipment and Crew and Boysen flew out three weeks later.

They arrived in the Fitzroy area at the beginning of December. To the left of the granite monolith of Fitzroy rose the steep, slender spire of the Torre. 'I just laughed every time I looked at it,' said Boysen. 'It was an unbelievable mountain, something out of a fairy tale.'

Will the climbers ever return to Patagonia to complete their self-imposed task?

'I need time to sit and forget about it for a bit,' says Dougal Haston.

'I don't know,' says Mick Burke, 'but after a time, I might think about coming back.'

2

Climbs and Climbers

The short profile of Dougal Haston, with which this section begins, appeared between the Eiger Direct ascent and the Cerro Torre expedition. After the Eiger I felt I had got to know Dougal well and enjoyed his company, and I was confident enough to speculate on his motivation for returning to the North Face of the Matterhorn following his earlier winter failure with Robin Smith. When Dougal complimented me on the piece I concluded I had come somewhere near the truth. Cerro Torre showed me a harder Haston: the ruthless, self-centred figure, often impassive and opaque, who was not prepared to compromise towards his colleagues in his single-minded pursuit of summits. He also told me he did not actually like *Eiger Direct* and he criticised an article I wrote when Dave Condict, the friend who introduced me to climbing, was killed in the Alps, saying that my overwrought reaction showed that I did not understand the true nature of the sport, of which risk was an inseparable part. His words sharpened the irony of his death in Switzerland in 1977: the man who had survived the Eiger, Annapurna and Everest, killed by a tiny avalanche while skiing close to his home at Leysin in Switzerland.

Chris Bonington and I had words, too, after my first profile of him was published in the *Sunday Times* magazine. Chris himself had suggested that I should write it, and since it was a time when the disagreements in the climbing world over his pioneering role as mountaineering entrepreneur were at their most acute, it was natural for me to home in on these. Chris complained that the article made him appear unduly mercenary by ignoring mountaineering's less material rewards, the challenges and the fulfilment that all climbers know. In retrospect I concluded that Chris was right. I attempted to redress the balance in a second profile in the *Financial Times*, although since that appeared almost twenty years later, Chris could be forgiven for considering it a somewhat tardy response.

It was partly in the light of Chris's complaint that I attempted to convey far more of the philosophy and techniques of mountaineering when describing the epic ascent of Changabang by Joe Tasker and Pete Boardman. That presented the usual dilemmas: how to render mountaineering comprehensible to the lay reader without patronising the mountaineers themselves; and how to convey its excitement without descending into sensationalism. When I wrote the profile of Stephen Venables, following his astonishing ascent of Everest via the Kangshung Face, I learned that since he was writing a book about the expedition he faced the same dilemmas. My limited climbing experience makes it difficult to imagine myself in the position of someone like Stephen, in this case alone on Everest's summit ridge. The best I can do is to recall the worst conditions I have known – a winter gale in the Cairngorms, perhaps – and try to extrapolate from there. But since I knew about the problems of writing I felt that here at least I understood Stephen's difficulties. He said afterwards that I had got it about right, too.

A promise kept

Scotsman, 1967

I n making the first British winter ascent of the 4000-foot North Face of the Matterhorn Dougal Haston has firmly established himself as Scotland's foremost alpinist. In 1963 he made the second British ascent of the Eiger and last March was one of the five climbers who reached the summit after the international month-long siege of the new direct route. His success on the Matterhorn with the English climber, Mick Burke, makes him the only man to have climbed both these massive north faces in winter. His reputation in Europe is immense.

What are the qualities that have enabled Dougal Haston, still only twenty-six, to achieve such a position? Born in Currie, the son of a baker, his first climbing was on the brickwork of local railway bridges. At sixteen he joined the Junior Mountaineering Club of Scotland and came under the influence of Jimmy Marshall, one of the pioneers of modern Scottish climbing.

He formed a partnership with Robin Smith, the brilliant young climber who was to die in a fall in the Pamirs in 1962. The pair were among the group of Scottish climbers advancing standards on rock to the level already reached in Wales and putting up snow and ice routes of greater and greater steepness.

Their life was bohemian, even irresponsible, and alienated some of the older Scottish climbers. In 1959 Haston and Smith went to the Alps and started up the North Face of the Matterhorn wearing only jeans and sweaters. But they were turned back by oncoming bad weather after covering the first 1200 feet in an hour. They attempted the Eiger the same year, with the same inadequate equipment: long gaps showed between the seams of Haston's boots. Their overconfidence became almost fool-hardiness, as Haston now concedes. 'We had this primitive urge for big routes. But we just didn't understand big mountains.'

It was inevitable that, given the urge, when the understanding came, all things would be possible. The bitter cold and ferocious winds of winter seasons in Scotland taught Haston not to under-estimate the mountains. In 1963 he paired up with the Rhodesian, Rusty Baillie, and climbed the *voie normale* on the North Face of the Eiger. They had to contend with verglas and black water-ice, but reached the summit in two and a half days.

For the Eiger Direct last March Haston had to draw on the last reserves of his hard-won experience. His very first bivouac was beset by 100 mph winds and constant powder snow avalanches. Later he weathered the five-day storm in a snow-hole halfway up the face. Much of the climbing was in steep ice gullies which Haston relished, although the leader of the German team at that time, climbing parallel, thought them 'impossible'.

The supreme test came on 22 March. When the American, John Harlin, fell 4000 feet to his death the immediate thoughts of the climbers on the face were to renounce the attempt. It was Haston who voiced what at first seemed unthinkable: that the climb should continue. If they gave up then, 1000 feet below the summit, Harlin's death and the month's endeavours would have been in vain. In cold retrospect the decision seemed the only one possible. Four hours after Harlin's death it needed a man of steel nerves to make it.

On the face Haston remained in control of himself, knowing that an immense effort would be needed if he and the other climbers were to battle their way through the approaching storm to the summit. The next three days were a trauma of wind and cold and at times Haston had to prise open his frozen eyelids with a piton. Only after the climb was over and he visited

Harlin's grave did he allow himself to be affected by his death.

Haston spent a month in hospital recovering from frostbitten fingers, an agony of inactivity. He realised, he said, that only climbing brought him more than momentary satisfaction in life. He longed to be delighting again in the freedom of decision and action that climbing entails.

He returned to Switzerland in the summer as a director and instructor at what was formerly John Harlin's climbing school in Leysin. He has effectively become a professional climber, determined to make a living from the sport that has become for him a way of life.

The Eiger Direct had been in Haston's mind since he climbed the *voie normale* in 1963. The North Face of the Matterhorn had been an objective for far longer – ever since the first attempt with Robin Smith in 1959. They tried it twice more before Smith died. The guarded way Haston used to parry questions about it led one to suspect that it remained a deeply cherished ambition, a debt to Smith's memory that had to be fulfilled. The successful attempt with Mick Burke last week was steady and assured, and again demonstrates the maturity of approach Haston has achieved.

Haston is planning to climb next winter in Patagonia, a region notorious for its vicious weather. The climbing problems will be equally fierce. But everything in Haston's history indicates that they, too, will be overcome.

The show must go up

Sunday Times Magazine, 1973

Mick Burke waltzed through the door beside the stage, saw the Festival Hall's terraces of waiting seats, and staggered back in mock amazement. Then he called 'Right on, brothers' and gave a clenched-fist salute.

He and six other climbers from the 1972 British Everest team, already buoyed by a long lunch, were inspecting the venue for the largest lecture of the post-expedition circuit. 'How many does it hold?' he asked Chris Bonington, who had strolled to the centre aisle. 'Two and a half thousand?'

'Mmm,' said Bonington.

'Two four one nine,' said the mountaineering sales director

of Pindisports, the climbing equipment firm, who organised the
lecture.

Bonington, Burke, and Dougal Haston were the original
speakers but Bonington, leader of the expedition, had made a
typically late decision to bring in three other members of the
team. He wanted to make sure the new speakers knew their
cues. 'I'd like you,' he told Doug Scott, 'to take it from the
leeches.'

At seven, an hour before the lecture was to start, Bonington
had disappeared. Most of the climbers were gaining strength at
the hall's main bar; discussion dwelt for a time on the fact that
Bonington would be delivering more lectures, and therefore
receiving more appearance money, than anyone else. Bonington
had defended himself by saying that many places had asked for
him personally, but Mick Burke said they should have been told
to take who they got.

'Let's forget it,' said one climber.

'Let's not forget it,' said Burke.

A Wigan man, accustomed to speaking his mind, Burke had
instantly protested to Pindisports when he saw the lecture
posters, headed 'Bonington on Everest'. Convinced this was
Bonington's work, he had been nonplussed to find the wording
had been chosen by the man he was complaining to.

Not that any of this affected the audience's enjoyment of the
lecture that night. All tickets had been sold a week before, and
the speakers' dry jokes were willingly laughed at. The climbers,
who had not reached the previous highpoint on the unclimbed
South Face, being turned back by the cold and appalling post-
monsoon winds they had always expected, were a little surprised to find such ready audiences; and it was perhaps
inevitable that there should be the occasional argument over the
division of the spoils.

At least half the Everest team could be accounted professional
mountaineers. Among them Burke had just won a prize for the
best TV sports film of the year, with his sequences shot at 27,000
feet; Haston, whose autobiography had been published the
week of his summit bid, had since been commissioned to write
a book about the Eiger.

But ahead of them all was Bonington himself, that figure in a
brown suit with pointed lapels, who stood on the Festival Hall
stage to direct the technicians' spotlights: the most successful
entrepreneur of present-day British mountaineering.

He is one of Britain's most accomplished climbers, with a list of achievements that includes the first British ascent of the notorious North Face of the Eiger in 1962, and leading the successful Annapurna South Face expedition in 1970, as well as the Everest expedition from which he had just returned. But his position derives also from the zeal with which, since the Eiger, he has pursued the goals of making enough money from climbing to continue the sport, and to live comfortably and securely as well. Others have since followed the course he plotted and, like him, have been subject to pressures earlier generations of climbers did not know. In climbing, as in many other sports, the gentlemen have given way to the players.

There have always been rows on expeditions; and mountaineers have always been strongly motivated, highly individual people. But today's disputes have a keener edge. Since mountaineering became a professional sport, they are more likely to concern money than before; and since mountaineering came to depend on press and TV backing, they have been more public than before. And the need to secure media backing has led some climbers to accuse others that they have allowed their sport to be misrepresented and, worse, sensationalised. Bonington has been at the centre of such rows. Says Martin Boysen, who has climbed with him for ten years: 'He's the biggest wheel, the most obvious target.'

Bonington had the personality to capitalise on the opportunities climbing offered; and, because of this, climbers' attitudes towards him have been ambivalent. 'Chris and I are rather similar,' says Mick Burke; 'grasping, selfish, and self-centred. That's probably why we argue so much.' Says another climber: 'He's a nice guy with two eyes for the main chance.'

Successful Bonington may now be; but in his ten-year career as professional mountaineer he has been beset by doubts, indecision and periods of depression which his fluent and articulate public exterior does not betray. Yet he has a trait, which disarms his critics, of admitting to his own weaknesses; his two volumes of autobiography are larded with such confessional insights. Yes, he is indecisive, and can sell himself on a course of action only to convince himself of the opposite a short while later; yes, he is readily swayed by other people and yes, he has constantly sought security and self-confidence. Even though he recognised this need, he abandoned a conventional career in 1962 to 'plunge into the unknown'. Ten years later the gamble has evidently succeeded, for he is more comfortable, more busy and more secure than at any time in his life.

He lives with his wife Wendy and their two young sons, Daniel and Rupert, in a tall Victorian house in the Manchester satellite of Bowden. His study is lined with mountaineering books and photographs, records of mountains climbed.

The telephone rings regularly. Yes, he would like to take part in a Canadian TV chat show. No, he didn't have time to take a magazine writer climbing – why didn't they try Doug Scott? Yes, he could supply photographs taken on Everest. He plugs the telephone into his new answering machine and plays the calls back later. Mick Burke can't make one of his lectures. An Italian going to Everest this spring would like to talk to him about oxygen. Could he ring Arabella at *Vogue*?

And yet he still has doubts. Things are all right now, he concedes – but who knows what could happen next year, or the year after?

The insecurity, he supposes, has much to do with his early life: his father left home when he was one and at five, when the war began, he went to a succession of boarding schools. 'I was very lonely and I found it difficult to make relationships with other kids. I was just too shy and introverted.' His mother, an advertising copywriter, took him home to Hampstead and he settled in at a public day school.

He first went climbing at sixteen, having been caught by a book of Scottish mountain photographs he picked up visiting an aunt. In two years he became a very good natural rock climber. He lost a place at London University through exam nerves and, attracted by the institutional security of the forces, applied for a commission in the RAF when he was called up in 1953. But at Cranwell, displaying no mechanical aptitude whatsoever, he failed to qualify as a pilot. He transferred to Sandhurst.

At first he was totally committed. 'He believed he was all set to be a general,' says Mike Thompson, who met and climbed with him there, and was in Bonington's Annapurna team in 1970. Thompson was to join the Cavalry, who formed, with the Guards, Sandhurst's social élite. 'They believed in spending lots of money, whistling up to London, going to debs' balls, riding horses,' says Thompson, 'and people down the ladder believed this was the way to behave too.'

'I did try to ape this upper crust,' admits Bonington. But in

Germany, where he was to command a tank crew, he found his Sandhurst style a hindrance. 'By expecting to be treated as a little tin god I did damage in the first few weeks that took me a year to repair.'

Bonington had started climbing with Thompson on the steep, loose limestone walls of the Avon Gorge. Limestone was then held to be treacherous, and Bonington's bold new routes were a breakthrough. But in Germany, in contrast with Thompson, who was able to borrow money from his regiment's polo pony fund to climb in the Himalaya, Bonington found it hard to get away. He transferred to the Army Outward Bound school at Towyn in central Wales. He was now steadily building his reputation with early repeats of many of the hard new routes Joe Brown and Don Whillans had been putting up in Snowdonia; and he took part in two important first British ascents in the Alps.

Yet in the aggressive, sometimes uncouth and often jealous climbing world, his background and his growing reputation sometimes proved a handicap. Several groups of climbers from the industrial cities thrived on notoriety, on stories of drunkenness and fighting. It is told how Bonington arrived at a hovel (once a sheep-pen) in Glencoe, used by the Creag Dhu boys from Glasgow, to ask for a climber called John McLean.

'You've been recommended to climb with me,' Bonington is supposed to have said, in nasal Sandhurst tones. (He was known elsewhere as 'the big plumb'.) McLean, who was sitting in Y-fronts frying eggs, saw Bonington off, and the younger climbers in the hut laughed at his discomfort.

Bonington, who was undoubtedly vulnerable to rejection of this kind, thinks the story sad. He had climbed with the Creag Dhu several years before and had simply wanted to renew the contact; and it shows him how ready some climbers have always been to want to knock him down. But ironically he was experiencing discomfort in the army too. 'There was antagonism between him and the Brigadier commanding the school,' says Mike Thompson. 'He used to get very worked up about Chris's vagueness, and ignored his very good instructing work.'

He had climbed Annapurna II with a services expedition and when the opportunity came to go on a civilian expedition to Nuptse, one of the peaks adjoining Everest, Bonington decided to leave the army.

Now came another of the 'lurches' (his word) his career has

been subject to. He joined a Unilever margarine company as a management trainee. Mike Thompson remembers, again, his initial enthusiasm. 'He had completely convinced himself that he would become a high-powered executive and was talking about sales and promotions all the time. Sometimes he even missed a weekend climbing.'

Wearing his army-issue civilian suit, a stiff white collar and his regimental tie, Bonington sought orders for margarine in the groceries of Hampstead. But in six months he closed six accounts without opening a single new one.

'He used to get tremendously depressed,' says Thompson. 'He thought he would be the greatest executive in the world, but he also wanted to climb the Eiger and other great routes. He couldn't see that it was impossible to achieve all this simultaneously.'

Bonington started taking time off to climb and then asked for leave to go on an expedition to Patagonia. Unilever told him to choose between mountaineering and margarine.

He had married several months before and Wendy Bonington – then an illustrator of children's books – remembers a walk across Hampstead Heath. 'It was agonising. His mother was very security-minded. He said he thought he should stick to a career. I felt this was so wrong for him . . .' Bonington finally chose mountaineering.

He had already begun a partnership, at first sight unlikely, with the practical Lancashire ex-plumber, Don Whillans. In 1961 they had attempted the North Face of the Eiger, which no British team had climbed; but the weather was poor so they moved to Mont Blanc and snatched the Central Pillar of Frêney from the Italian and French alpinists who regarded it as their own.

They returned to the Eiger in 1962. As they camped in the meadows of Alpiglen, the conversation often turned to methods of earning a living from mountaineering. A year earlier they had somewhat innocently promised their story to the *Daily Mail* in return for the food they needed during their wait for good weather. 'He was thrown into a world he hadn't ever known before,' says Whillans. 'The rat race. The discussion always came round to him and his problems.'

Their first attempt in 1962 ended when they had to rescue a British climber, Brian Nally, whose partner had been hit by a stonefall and fell to his death from the steep Second Icefield. It took great courage and mountaineering sense to reach Nally on the vast face and bring him to safety as stones whistled down and a storm broke about them.

But afterwards, wrote Bonington, 'the nightmare reached its climax'. Cold, soaked, exhausted, the three men were surrounded by journalists who had hired a train to the point where they came off the face; the train sat stationary for an hour while Nally, who did not think to ask for a fee, was pumped for his story. This event is described as having hardened many climbers' attitudes towards the press.

Shortly afterwards Whillans had to return to Britain. Bonington teamed up with Ian Clough to climb the Walker Spur on the Grandes Jorasses, a route as formidable as the Eiger though less notorious. As the good weather held, Bonington returned with Clough to the Eiger and made the first British ascent.

It is said that Whillans was bitter that Bonington climbed the Eiger without him after so many attempts together. 'You did feel a slight sense of guilt that you were grabbing it with someone else,' says Bonington. 'But you knew that Don would have done exactly the same thing.'

Whillans wrote to Bonington complaining at the 'commercialisation' of the climb. It was a legitimate attack, says Bonington. 'We were whipped away by the *Daily Express*, who paid us about £500, I think, and it was projected in about as tasteless a way as possible.'

Nonetheless, Bonington saw that money was there. Mike Thompson remembers helping to arrange a lecture for weekend climbers at Keswick, a new and speculative venture. 'We just hired a hall and wondered what would happen. But it was a sell-out and we made about £70. I remember how we stared at all that money in amazement.'

Bonington lectured about the Eiger at luncheon clubs, tea clubs, evening lecture societies – and did so with greater determination and efficiency than anyone before. Other climbers emulated him. But Bonington acquired a reputation for single-minded, acquisitive zeal which led the Scottish climber Tom Patey to compose a sardonic song about him. One verse, repeated in Patey's book, *One Man's Mountains*, runs:

> He has climbed the Eigerward,
> He has climbed the Dru,
> For a mere ten thousand francs,
> He will climb with you.

Then the opportunity came for Bonington to broaden his activities. In the Alps he had met the American John Harlin, whose ambition was to put a new 'direct' route on the North Face of the Eiger and who had secured backing from the *Weekend Telegraph* for his attempt. It was another time for indecision for Bonington. He agreed to join Harlin's team; then changed his mind and withdrew, torturing himself with the fear that he would be missing out on a major and historical climb.

But then the *Telegraph* asked him to cover the climb as their photographer. He went so far as to meet the successful climbers on the Eiger's summit in a raging winter storm, three days after Harlin himself had fallen to his death.

Other commissions followed, although his first assignment ended tragically when he had to hurry back from Ecuador after his first son Conrad was drowned.

But in 1969 he was greatly disenchanted by his experiences on the Blue Nile, where he came close to death from both shooting and drowning.

'I was shaken rigid on that trip. In this kind of adventure journalism you're putting yourself in the hands of other people and being exposed to risks over which you have very little control. I don't think I have a power complex, but I think I know how I like to have things done. I don't think I'm really happy about something now unless I have actually got overall command of the situation.'

With Boysen, Haston and Nick Estcourt, Bonington began looking for a mountain to climb in the spring of 1970. When they heard that Nepal was relaxing its four-year ban on expeditions they decided to aim for one of the huge unclimbed faces of the Himalayas, the South Face of Annapurna. The team were joined by Whillans, Burke, Thompson, Ian Clough, and the American Tom Frost. (Bonington's agent George Greenfield told him an American in the team would make it easier to sell the expedition in the USA.)

After six weeks of some of the most difficult high-altitude climbing ever accomplished, Whillans and Haston reached the summit the day before the monsoon storms arrived. It was a superb achievement by a basically contented expedition. But one major row took place which catalysed many of the opinions about Bonington, and which was to lead to the final break with Whillans.

Each of the four pairs of climbers were to take turns at leading

– always the most attractive role – while the others rested or carried loads. Burke and Frost had been leading up the Rock Band, the last main obstacle before the summit, when Bonington decided to move Haston and Whillans forward out of turn, arguing that they were the strongest pair remaining. A week later, they reached the summit.

There had been bitter argument over the expedition radios when Bonington made his decision, and later Frost told him he had 'destroyed the spirit of the expedition'. Burke especially felt that Bonington had simply fallen in with Whillans's desire to move through into the lead when the summit came within reach. 'We were going faster than expected but he fell in with Don's suggestion that we were too slow. He protected Don and Dougal at the expense of everyone else because Don is a stronger character than Chris.'

Martin Boysen, who would otherwise have moved to the front, says: 'Chris was not leading, he was being led. Don and Dougal were going up, and that was it.'

Mike Thompson believes that the row could have been avoided. 'It was Chris's fault. He changed his mind six or seven times during his process of thinking aloud.'

Whillans denies any undue influence over Bonington. 'Chris and I were in complete agreement. I thought he was right. There was no decision. It was obvious.'

And Haston: 'Chris felt badly that he couldn't make the decision democratically. But he pushed Don and myself through because we were the strongest pair at that time.'

For a time, the argument was to remain academic. International expeditions were planned to the unclimbed South-West Face of Everest in 1971 and spring 1972. Bonington was invited on both, and changed his mind five times about going. Although the process of indecision greatly entertained his friends, Bonington was deeply depressed by it. He wanted a new goal but couldn't convince himself that Everest was the right one; yet he was racked once again by the fear that he was opting out of a major event.

'There's a mixture of impulsiveness and caution in my make-up,' is how he explains his volatility. 'I tend to plunge into a decision and then the cautious side of me starts totting up all the points against. I kind of yo-yo – but in the big decisions of my life I think I've almost always, actually, yo-yoed back to the right decision.'

His track record bears him out. Including Annapurna he had been on four expeditions, all of which succeeded. And then the two international expeditions to Everest, both of which featured full-scale rows between different national groups, failed at the Rock Band, the 1000-foot rock wall beginning at 27,000 feet.

Bonington had forsworn large, expensive expeditions after his return from Annapurna; he was talking of returning to the purer and more romantic notion of small, light teams, and he started trying to raise the backing for a four-man party to attempt Everest by the South Col route. But then he decided to launch a full-scale attack on the South-West Face himself. 'I can't help feeling,' says Martin Boysen, 'that commercial reasons weighed in his decision. It was a saleable commodity.'

However, Bonington took the risk of committing himself to the attempt before trying to raise the necessary £60,000 from commercial and media sponsors and the Mount Everest Foundation. It's a tribute to the pulling power of his name that the gamble succeeded.

For his team, he kept the nucleus of the Annapurna expedition. But he did not ask Don Whillans, even though he had twice been high on the South-West Face. The reasons, for Bonington, go back to the row on Annapurna. He still believes his decision to move Whillans and Haston through out of turn was correct. 'I think I could be accused of having been weak with Don on Annapurna. But I think if I had been anything else we might not have climbed it. I think I probably handled that situation not absolutely fairly. I think I was over-malleable. But I think if I had been less malleable the situation might have been very much worse. But I would never repeat that situation. I think my own style of leadership . . . I think I am good at working with people and getting people to work with each other. I need a group of people who are prepared to put up with my weaknesses and each other's to work together. You need everybody to be prepared to give and I don't think Don is prepared to give.'

Some climbers, including Whillans himself, believe that the main factor in Bonington's decision was commercial competition between the two men.

'Chris has been completely carried away in trying to establish himself as the number one, the only number one,' says Whillans. Another climber, friendly towards Bonington, contends: 'Chris was absolutely against having Don on Everest because Don is his nearest rival as a professional mountaineer.'

To suggest that this was Bonington's prime consideration is to ascribe some fairly base motives to him; and it's significant that this is what some climbers do believe. But Bonington did ask the other Everest invitees, including those who went on the two international expeditions with Whillans, whether they were in favour of him: they divided roughly two to one against.

It's asking a great deal of your fellow men, says Bonington, to help push two men to the summit of Everest who will then receive rewards far above the rest of the team: 'Riches,' says Mick Burke, 'beyond the dreams of even Chris Bonington.' In contrast to Annapurna, Bonington argues, on Everest his decision to move Haston and MacInnes through out of turn for a summit attempt was accepted without ill-feeling. 'You wouldn't have got half the team I chose working their guts out to get Don to the top.'

The British expedition, like the two before it, failed at the Rock Band. 'If they *had* got up,' says Whillans, 'it would have been Bonington for breakfast, lunch, tea, and supper.'

There has been a continuing debate in the mountaineering world in the last three years on the consequences of depending on money from press and TV to finance expeditions. There was criticism of the BBC's film of Everest, 1971, for example, when it blamed the expedition's failure on the row between the 'Latin' climbers and the rest, although bad weather and illness were the principal causes. Bonington is seen by some climbers as one of the men who have led climbing into this vulnerable position. The British Everest expedition met criticism, too, the nub of which is made by Ian McNaught-Davis, himself a former star of BBC climbing broadcasts.

'Everest was a very pushy attempt by a strong team. But they were there at the wrong time of year and they didn't achieve anything, and the story of the attempt is very boring. The problem is that if you're going on an expedition and you pump it up before you go to raise the money, then you're obliged to make it into that when you get back . . . You're involved in sensationalism . . . you have to grind up the importance of the mountain to achieve maximum publicity whether or not it has any intrinsic merit. But people still go and listen to the lectures just because it's Everest . . . in a way Everest itself is a fraud.'

'I don't think I've ever done a climb just for money,' Bonington replies. 'This is something that people like Mac don't understand. I've done things that I've really wanted to do and I've made this possible by making money around them. You'll always get resentment from climbers. One's just got to live with the fact that because you do something successfully in the public eye you'll inevitably get a certain number of bricks chucked your way. I've never promoted something that I didn't believe in and as far as Everest is concerned I don't think that myself or any member of the team have exaggerated what we did. I think this is unbalanced criticism.'

The climbers agree that Bonington's leadership on Everest was excellent. 'I can't think of any way he can be faulted,' says Mick Burke. There's a greater maturity to him now – and not just on the mountain, says Wendy Bonington. 'He's gradually become much more aware of other people. He has learnt more about himself, too, more about his depressions. He's able to sort himself out now.'

He has been busier than ever before since Everest, even though it was the first expedition he's been on which failed. But Bowden remains his base. He has a circle of climbing friends nearby, including Martin Boysen and Nick Estcourt, and together they climb as many weekends and summer evenings as they can. For climbers, who remember the freezing bivouacs together, the shared moments of danger and exhilaration, the fact that he still climbs hard counts for a great deal.

'He can be selfish and greedy, but his redeeming factors overcome his faults,' says Martin Boysen. 'He's still a very keen climber and he's very dynamic and forceful and competitive.'

'When he gets on the crag,' says Mick Burke, 'all the arguments about money disappear.'

Although Everest is booked up by other countries until 1978, Bonington, now thirty-nine, would like to make another attempt. He knows that his gymnastic ability on rock will diminish in his forties but reckons that, like Eric Shipton or Bill Tilman, he'll be able to go on expeditions until he's sixty. He plans to launch a business scheme this year to give himself the 'solid background' he has always wanted. He hopes to go on writing and taking photographs.

Some climbers have devised a scenario for him whereby he becomes Lord Bonington, succeeding Lord Hunt at the head of the climbing establishment. In one way he already fulfils the role, fluently answering broadcasters' questions on subjects from patriotism in mountaineering to the Cairngorms schoolchildren tragedy. But a peerage is not really on; Lord Hunt's position results more from his public work than from mountaineering, anyway.

'No,' says Bonington, although the possibility has clearly occurred to him. 'That's completely . . . I mean, I wouldn't want . . . it's interesting, but I'm not terribly worried . . .'

He orders his thoughts. 'I reckon I've got six years' very hard climbing and I want to utilise this, and I think this is genuine, not for the reputation it gets me but just for the personal experience. There's nothing like climbing hard and while I've got full control over my physique I would like to push it to the ultimate.

'I'm too much of an individual . . . I've got a sense of responsibility to the climbing world but I'm not a committee man. I want to go on doing the things I like doing. I've no great desire to educate and I don't think I'm particularly a do-gooder.

'I'm doing the things I'm doing because I want to do them.'

The challenge of Changabang

Sunday Times Magazine, 1978

Everest, even though he reached the summit, left Pete Boardman dissatisfied. There had been the long periods of inactivity, waiting for others to perform their tasks – like watching a pyramid being built and then being allowed to fit the top piece yourself.

There was also the death of Mick Burke, who had disappeared after Pete had met him close to the summit. 'Because of Mick, what I had done was shrouded in a mess,' says Pete. 'After all that I wanted to do something that was completely me – something where everything was mine.' When Joe Tasker asked him to go to Changabang he agreed at once.

Changabang is a 22,250-foot peak in the Garhwal Himalaya, thirty miles from India's border with Tibet. Other mountains nearby are higher and have more illustrious names – Nanda Devi, Kamet – but none have struck such thrilling chords among Himalayan climbers as Changabang. It is a cone-shaped mountain of soaring granite precipices streaked with ice and snow; in its symmetry, and isolation, it resembles the Matterhorn. Eric

Shipton sat at its foot and stared at it for an hour, spellbound. The Victorian mountaineer Tom Longstaff said it was the most beautiful mountain he had ever seen.

Changabang was not climbed until 1974, when a strong party of six, led by Chris Bonington, took it by its line of least resistance, the East Face. A year later another British team was climbing the neighbouring peak of Dunagiri, 23,180 feet high. The climbers were two young Yorkshiremen, Joe Tasker and Dick Renshaw. For six days they had watched Changabang as they climbed, and were captivated by its beauty and its challenge. Tasker was enthralled by its immensely steep West Face, rising almost 5000 feet to the summit, which had been the Bonington team's original objective. Bonington had found it 'preposterous' and searched for an easier line. The idea of attempting the West Face lay in Tasker's mind, growing stronger through the autumn. His partner Dick Renshaw was recovering from frostbite sustained during a desperate descent from Dunagiri. Tasker met Boardman, whom he barely knew, at Christmas 1975, and put the idea to him. The West Wall was immense, he conceded; but he thought there was a line.

'He said yes right away,' says Tasker. 'I was a bit surprised that he was so keen.'

Tasker was entitled to be surprised. But it was another month before Boardman realised just what he had agreed to. Tasker showed him photographs of the West Face which left him somewhat subdued. 'Where *is* your line, then?' he asked Tasker.

The task they set themselves was indeed enormous. Most Himalayan peaks have been climbed by teams of men sharing the burdens of load-carrying and the responsibility of lead climbing. In case of accidents or emergency they have men in reserve. Boardman and Tasker were proposing to tackle a 4500-foot face – at altitude, and as technically difficult as the hardest alpine routes – utterly alone. If they had an accident, or were hit by a storm, they would be able to turn to no one for help.

Martin Boysen, one of Bonington's team, said that the West Face looked 'quite impossible'. Bonington himself said that anyone climbing it would have made the hardest ascent ever in the Himalaya.

It was also unusual that a team to attempt such a peak should be formed so casually. The tensions on a Himalayan expedition prise at the weaknesses in a relationship, exposing hostilities, sometimes creating permanent animosities. In this partnership there was one immediate potential for division – Everest itself.

Boardman, an official of the British Mountaineering Council, was twenty-four when he stood on the summit of Everest. As the youngest member of Bonington's party he was a little surprised, even embarrassed, to find himself there. His achievement gave him the instant public status, and the chance to make a permanent living from climbing, that many other climbers coveted.

Tasker, a teacher, two years older than Boardman, had almost no public name at all. But in the climbing world his reputation was high. He had a long list of impressive alpine climbs to his name, including, with Dick Renshaw, the third winter ascent of the notorious North Face of the Eiger – the first in winter by a team of only two men. Respect among climbers is hard-won: the ballyhoo surrounding Everest or the Eiger is discounted. Soon after agreeing to join forces on Changabang, Boardman and Tasker went climbing together in North Wales. It was Tasker who found himself embarrassed. 'I knew that Pete was interested in seeing how I would perform. I don't know why – perhaps I wasn't really fit – but I was climbing really badly. Pete must have been thinking, "Who is this bloke? He's all bullshit."'

But as preparations for the expedition proceeded, and excitement grew keener, the relationship hardened. Both men now believed strongly that theirs should be an expedition as unlike Everest, with its enormous marshalling of men and resources, as possible. As Pete had said, they wanted the achievement to be theirs alone. This is in fact the coming thing among mountaineers of the 1970s: an application of the light, fast style of alpine climbing to the world's greater ranges, and a return to the self-sufficiency, the ethical purity, that are supposed to be climbing's rationale.

They flew to Delhi on 22 August, 1976, then rode by train and local bus, their packing cases and rucksacks loaded on top, to the Rishi Gorge on the edge of the Garhwal Himalaya. A four-day approach march, aided by fifteen porters, took them to the site of their Base Camp by the moraine of Changabang's glacier, at 15,000 feet.

They were now quite alone. Soon afterwards they made their first reconnaissance of the vast West Face, soaring above them. As they gazed at its steep, smooth walls, the daunting descriptions plied them by other British climbers no longer seemed exaggerated. 'All our optimism,' says Tasker, 'drained away.'

There is a dictum with which climbers try to encourage themselves when their task seems, from a moderate distance, beyond them. Tom Longstaff had once declared: 'You must go and rub your nose in a place before being certain that it won't go.' This they now repeated to each other, rather than the doubts each felt, as they spent six laborious days lugging supplies to establish a Base Camp on the glacier at 17,000 feet.

From there a further 1000 feet of rock and ice took them across the foot of the face to a buttress where they had decided their route should start. At 18,000 feet they excavated a ledge on which to perch their tent to form Camp 1, anchoring it with ice-axes against the bitter thirty mph wind which streamed across the face. Above them lay 700 feet of 'mixed' ground, alternate rock and ice; then the true rock difficulties would begin. They were heartened by a system of cracks that seemed to offer a chance of progress in the rock, although this line appeared to fade into a barrier of dark overhangs.

They started to climb on 17 September. That first day, up the mixed ground, was straightforward; but then their pace slowed. A private vocabulary describes the qualities of rock, reflecting both its aesthetic qualities and the purchase it offers. 'The granite of Changabang,' explains Joe Tasker, 'was good granite. But it didn't give you delicate climbing, like North Wales. It was *wild* climbing. There were long, ragged cracks, ending in overhangs. The route-finding was very difficult. There were blank slabs and we found ourselves pushed off our line several times. It was as hard as anything I'd done in the Alps.'

They took it in turns to lead, allotting themselves four pitches at a time. Each night they returned to Camp 1 by abseiling – the method of sliding down the climbing rope at a speed controlled by a friction device at the climber's waist. In the morning, they would reclimb the ropes they had left in place on jumar clamps – these can be pushed up the rope, but do not slide down again. It's a laborious process, and one fraught with danger. As they crept up the route, they found that they were not reaching new ground until midday.

It fell to Pete Boardman to tackle the dark line of overhangs 1200 feet or so above Camp 1. It was a major barrier, and the first climbing problem which could prove insuperable. The overhangs were intricate, the rock around them very steep and plastered with ice. It was almost impossible to hammer in pitons: the rock-cracks were blocked with ice; the ice itself was not thick enough for pitons either. 'It was very exhausting and *committing*,' says Pete. If he had fallen off he would have hung free on the rope over several thousand feet of space, and faced with great problems in getting back in contact with the rock again.

It took Pete three hours to inch his way through the overhangs, while Joe watched shivering from the shade. That night in their tent they knew they had made an important breach in the mountain's defences, and allowed themselves to hope that their task might not after all be beyond them.

In the camp Joe would prepare the evening meal, Pete the breakfast. It took two hours each time to melt enough ice on their stove to make hot drinks and to mix with their American freeze-dried food. Like a newly married couple they were discovering more about each other. There was the question of conversation, for example. In his work for the British Mountaineering Council Pete attended numerous meetings and functions. 'I think I'm more used to getting on with people. I go to all these meetings and utter platitudes and that sort of thing. In the tent I would chatter away and I used to get annoyed because Joe wouldn't respond.'

'It was a big question,' agrees Joe, 'how well we would get on with each other. We were both able to speak our minds. When we had an argument we were very blunt with each other. But apart from that I didn't like making small talk. Pete sits on all these committees and I felt he was just trying to be polite, treating me as if I was one of them. If there's nothing important to say I prefer to keep my brain ticking over in neutral.'

They were gradually coming to judgments about each other's abilities. 'As a climber,' says Pete, 'Joe is not fantastic technically but he's got great determination and endurance. Because he and Dick Renshaw climb rather slowly he's had more experience of bivouacs than me and he's masterly at looking after himself. He'll always ease himself into a comfortable position. He always takes a pillow with him – he's obsessed by pillows. He's not a sufferer at all.'

'Pete's climbing,' says Joe, 'is impeccable. I was amazed at his ability to perform. But there was a complete disparity between that and his inability to function in a bivouac. He'd lose everything – even the matches. He's got this thing about me being a slower climber and therefore I've had more experience of bivouacs. But in bivouacs himself – well, he's hopeless.'

By 26 September they had reached the foot of a steep icefield above the line of overhangs. Having accomplished 2500 feet in nine days they decided that they deserved a rest, and they abseiled back to their Base Camp. Two days' recuperation were almost outweighed by renewed doubts over the almost feature-less upper section of the climb: the principal obstacle seemed to be a towering pillar perhaps 1000 feet high. Now came the most serious disagreement of the expedition. As they trudged back up the moraine it started to snow; Pete wanted to carry on, Joe to retreat. Such arguments are always difficult to resolve. 'If you want to go back down,' says Joe, 'you're never sure whether you're arguing from a balanced evaluation of the circumstances – or simply out of fear and weakness.' Pete's morally stronger position prevailed.

They hoped to start to bivouac in hammocks, saving the time spent climbing between their camps and their highpoints each day. That night they slung the hammocks from pitons ham-mered into the rock some way below the icefield. But the weather worsened; the wind tore at their hammocks and spin-drift avalanches poured over them.

In the morning the wind was gusting around fifty mph; the landscape was uniformly white. The hammocks were only ten feet apart but it was impossible to talk to each other. Pete climbed out to put on his boots and in ten minutes in the lashing wind his fingers froze, turning numb and white.

'I've got frostnip,' he announced.

'What's that?'

'Don't worry – it won't stop me.'

Later Pete's fingertips turned black and dead, and tasks such as tying boots and lighting the stove became very awkward. Joe meanwhile had been dressing inside his hammock, his feet lifted high above his head. They struggled up to the icefield, and there spent a further two hours making a lukewarm brew. It was pointless trying to climb any further; they harnessed their hammocks and crept into them. Joe appeared surprisingly tolerant about the decision to return to the mountain. Says Pete: 'He didn't complain to me at all.'

On the third morning the storm showed no signs of abating, and they returned to Base Camp once more. It was now 2 October, and timing was becoming critical. 'We knew we had time for only one more go,' says Pete. 'Joe said that the year before the weather had broken on 15 October and climbing would be out of the question after that.'

In Base Camp they were visited by several members of an American expedition attempting Dunagiri – the first people they had met in four weeks. As they returned to the mountain the omens hardly seemed favourable. A violent storm crashed around them in Camp 1. But suddenly the clouds pulled apart to reveal Changabang's upper section swathed in a golden evening sun.

On 9 October, thirty-two days after first leaving Base Camp, they set up Camp 2 at the top of the icefield at 20,000 feet. The term 'camp' was an overstatement: they hacked away enough ice to form a ledge large enough for the inner portion of their tent, and pinned it down with ice pitons. If the man on the outside bent his legs, his knees hung over a drop of 5000 feet.

A week remained to climb the final 2500 feet. Of this, 1500 feet was up steep rock, including the formidable rock pillar. Only in the final 1000 feet of snow and ice did the angle appear to relent. The two climbers found that they were now well acclimatised; but they also knew that the cold, the altitude and the mental effort would eventually take their toll.

The strain was testing the relationship. Joe thought that Pete complained too much. 'He used to go on about how he wished he could see Nanda Devi from where we were. I got really depressed because I felt it was all my fault.'

Pete, however, was reconciled to the lack of small-talk. 'We got to the point where we understood each other so well that we hardly needed to talk anyway. Our decisions kind of evolved and emerged.' On Everest Pete had felt in awe of men such as Haston, Scott and Burke, and hesitated to express a point of view. On Changabang it was a partnership of equals. 'Sometimes when Joe said something I was thinking it already. We developed an intensity that became almost frightening. We were so united trying to get up the climb.' Their shared determination became the most important sustaining factor. 'It was as if we were trying to cheat someone – we were trying to climb it *despite* everything. We were fighting our way up the thing – and there was a thrill which in retrospect can seem almost unhealthy. The great thing, though, was that on Changabang we were never over the line.'

'The line' is the climber's metaphor for judging whether or not a situation is in control. The thrill of climbing comes from seeing how close you can go to the line without crossing it; if you do cross it you must get back as quickly as you can. Pete and Joe both knew what it was like to go up to, and over, the line. Pete had been right *on* the line on Everest, descending from the summit after Mick Burke had disappeared in a storm, and finding the fixed ropes leading to Camp 6 just as night fell. He had gone over the line when he tackled a 3000-foot face in the Hindu Kush in 1972 without adequate equipment or supplies. He had been four days without food and then had to walk fifty miles back to Base Camp after descending the mountain on the wrong side.

Joe, with Dick Renshaw, had gone way over the line while coming down Dunagiri in 1975. They had spent four days without food *or* water. 'I was just convinced we were going to die. I just thought, you keep on until you drop. It was only through Dick's determination that we kept going even though we thought there was no point.' There *were* moments on Changabang when each man did lose control. Both came when they were on the rope in the evening, a time of danger when tiredness leads to carelessness. Once Joe found he was hanging on to the rope by just one jumar clamp. 'I just thought – is this it? Am I going to leave Pete in the lurch?' He wrapped his other arm round the rope in desperation and managed to fasten his second clamp back to the rope.

Pete's crisis was similar. He, too, miscalculated the sequence of moves while descending, had one foot in a sling attached to the rope, and was toppling over backwards when he grabbed at the rope with one hand. He tried to close his mind to the incident. 'If you think the risk is very great you just turn your mind off. There's nothing else you can do.' Towards the end of the climb, too, a sense of euphoria settled over them. 'Things were going so well it almost made the drop seem meaningless. You almost felt that if you fell off, you'd float . . . It was very, very beautiful in the evenings. The valley was in darkness below and we were right up there on this beautiful rock which had turned golden in the last of the evening sun.'

The climbing up the rock pillar was of sustained steepness and difficulty. One pitch took Pete across a booming flake – a slice of rock that gave hollow, metallic reverberations, indicating that its attachment to the mountain was far from secure. Joe's hardest climbing came near the top of the pillar. Rock alternated with ice, which meant climbing in crampons, then removing them, then putting them back on. On a blank slab he had to resort to the extreme manoeuvre known as a tension traverse.

When there are virtually no holds a climber can sometimes move *sideways* by using the pull of his rope against him. Out of sight of Pete, Joe strained to reach a crack at the corner of the slab. He could just touch it with his fingertips – but not insert them. Balanced on tiny footholds he flicked at the crack with a sling of rope threaded with a metal nut. Finally the nut slid into the crack. He pulled down the sling, swung his weight on to it, clipped into it at his waist, then hammered a piton into the crack above.

Even on the final rock pitch the difficulties did not ease. It was as steep as ever: a groove capped by an overhanging block. As Pete laboured up it, they wondered how they would pass that block – surely, after thirty-seven days, they could not be defeated now? Relief flooded over them when they found, almost miraculously, a hole behind the block that they could scramble through, taking them on to the summit icefield. They were certain now they would make it.

As night approached, they dug out a ledge on the summit slopes and huddled into their sleeping bags. It was 14 October, one day before their deadline. Pete was now suffering from the climber's affliction, piles; Joe was coughing blood, although he kept it secret until later. That night the temperature fell to around −40°C. Pete awoke in darkness to discover that he could no longer feel his feet. He took off his boots and massaged them until the circulation returned.

In the morning they waited until the sun reached them before daring to move. They left the bivouac site at noon and after two hours' steady climbing reached the summit – a heavily corniced rise in a sharp ridge. Pete was disappointed that Joe showed little emotion. 'I thought he would at least have shaken hands but he was very matter of fact.'

'I felt satisfied,' says Joe. 'It meant that all our efforts had been justified. I also knew we couldn't relax as we still had to get back down. But I was pleased that we could see Nanda Devi at last. It was there for about five minutes before the clouds closed over. If Pete hadn't seen Nanda Devi he'd have been shattered.'

They reached Camp 2 after dark, and laughed unashamedly at the terrible warnings other climbers had given them. They had two more nights on the mountain before reaching the glacier moraine. As they trudged back to Base Camp they heard voices and saw smoke. 'We thought, great – some people to talk to,' says Joe. 'We arrived at the camp and there were some Italian climbers there and a woman from the American expedition on Dunagiri.'

Gradually the woman's words penetrated their tiredness and their elation. There had been an accident on Dunagiri. Four men had been killed. One of them was her husband. She had arrived at their tent only an hour before.

Joe went to the door of the tent. 'It was something we really couldn't comprehend. We were so pleased with ourselves – then faced with that.'

They left the camp at six the next morning to climb back up to 20,000 feet on Dunagiri. They buried the four bodies by pushing them into a crevasse. On Everest Pete's achievement had been sullied by the death of Mick Burke. Once again the feeling of satisfaction had lost its edge.

Back in England, Pete returned to the committee work of the British Mountaineering Council in Manchester; Joe became the English representative of an Irish boot company. The authoritative magazine *Mountain* said that their ascent was 'the most advanced lightweight Himalayan climb so far achieved'. Joe felt that his ability had been confirmed. He had wondered if Dunagiri had just been luck. 'Changabang showed that it wasn't just a flash in the pan. I may die but it will show that I had the ability and it wasn't just a fluke.'

'I feel reasonably satisfied,' says Pete. 'I don't think I'd like to do anything that technically hard again. It does put things in a different perspective. It has made me more confident. But then it wears off again. That's the trouble.'

The peak of a career

Financial Times, 1987

Chris Bonington embarks today on his latest and perhaps most enticing venture. Last night Britain's foremost mountaineer arrived in Oslo to renew an intriguing alliance with some of Norway's leading climbers. This morning he and his colleagues fly on to China, and within two weeks will be gazing at Menlungtse, an unclimbed peak close to Everest which is regarded as one of mountaineering's most glittering prizes. It is, says Bonington, 'a magnificent mountain'.

The impish adventurer Eric Shipton first revealed Menlungtse's delights in 1951, while making the reconnaissance of
Everest that led to its triumphal ascent two years later. Shipton
made an illicit foray across the Himalayan watershed from Nepal
into Tibet, then closed to Western mountaineers. He came across
an isolated peak rising almost sheer from a glacier, 'its colossal
granite walls pale and smooth as polished marble – every evening they glowed as coral.'

The British climber Peter Boardman obtained an even better
vantage point from the neighbouring summit of Gauri Sankar
in 1979. He saw 'a mighty white obelisk of snow and pale pink
granite, whose shape matched that of the Matterhorn.' Of all
the peaks around, Menlungtse 'was the nearest and loveliest
vision of all'.

In the quest for virgin peaks, no mountaineer could want a
better recommendation. In 1984 Bonington, who had glimpsed
Menlungtse during his successive attempts on Everest in the
1970s, sent a somewhat speculative letter to the Chinese government, seeking permission to mount an expedition.

The first reply was hardly encouraging: the Chinese said they
had never heard of Menlungtse. In fact, Bonington had offended
the Chinese preference for local names rather than those be-
stowed by Westerners. Shipton had christened the peak Menlungtse, after the nearby Menlung pass, whereas the Chinese
knew it as Qiao Ge Ru. Bonington therefore made a second
application to climb Qiao Ge Ru and, with the diplomatic niceties
restored, the Chinese agreed. Bonington's surprise was matched
only by his delight. 'I am as excited about this as I have been
for any previous expedition,' he says.

For Bonington, fifty-two, the Menlungtse expedition comes at
a juncture when most mere earthbound mortals are considering
how to bring their careers to a close in the most comfortable
manner. He looks rudely fit, with bright eyes and a sporting
beard, and has been at the forefront of British mountaineering
for twenty-five years.

In his twenties, Bonington helped set new rock-climbing
standards in Snowdonia and Lakeland in partnership with the
legendary Don Whillans. He next turned to the Alps and made
the first British ascent of the North Face of the Eiger, a mountain
made notorious by a series of gruesome accidents in full view
of the media watching through the telescopes of the Kleine
Scheidegg Hotel.

Bonington then looked to the Himalaya, and has now led three expeditions to Everest and others to K2 and Annapurna. His parties forged audacious new routes on the mountains' most intimidating faces, such as the South-West Face of Everest and the South Face of Annapurna. Yet his duties as leader meant that he was never able to join the final assault teams, and the world's highest summit eluded him until he climbed Everest by the traditional South Col route in 1985 – at that time the oldest person ever to do so.

Bonington has been a pioneer for British mountaineers in other ways, setting an example through his skill at financing what is hardly a profit-based activity. After a spell as an army officer, Bonington worked for a time as a margarine salesman, but found that when the mountains beckoned his sales quotas suffered.

He resolved to become a full-time mountaineer, gleaning a living from whatever spin-offs he could devise. Since then he has become an accomplished and fluent author with nine books to his name, including several bestsellers; his lectures are invariably packed; and he has made rewarding forays in television and films. 'I've been fairly successful,' he says discreetly, 'and I earn a reasonable amount of money.'

Bonington's entrepreneurial activities at first aroused the enmity of other climbers, who found him defensive and edgy where money was concerned and wondered if it was distorting his goals. He has become visibly more relaxed and is today universally respected by his peers, both for his achievements and the image of the sport that he portrays.

He and his family – his wife Wendy, and their two teenage sons – live in a converted shepherd's cottage on the northern edge of the Lake District. Wendy has grown as accustomed as she will ever be to his absences, which he calculates at four or five months each year.

Bonington's greatest unease comes from the guilt he feels at exposing his family to the undeniable risks of his profession. All too often Bonington has had to convey the news of the death of a companion: Ian Clough on Annapurna; Mick Burke, Joe Tasker, Peter Boardman on Everest. 'It's a risk game. And in that sense I can't justify putting Wendy at risk. Yet I love climbing so much I couldn't give it up.'

Those reservations apart, Bonington professes to being as keen on climbing as ever. 'I used to worry whether my stamina would go, but it hasn't. I'm climbing as well as I have ever done. I've learned from what's happened in the past, I enjoy doing what I'm doing now and I'm excited by what is in prospect for the future.'

The Menlungtse expedition illustrates Bonington's attractive ability to find friends in the competitive world of élite international mountaineers. The friendships in question were struck during the Norwegian bid to climb Everest in 1985.

Since the Norwegians had never attempted Everest before, they invited Bonington for the experience he would contribute. Bonington hesitated, for his own previous attempt in 1982 had seen the deaths of Boardman and Tasker, who vanished high on the North-East Ridge in circumstances chillingly reminiscent of the disappearance of Mallory and Irvine in 1924.

But Bonington's natural and deep-seated desire to reach the ultimate summit won and in the end he had much to thank the Norwegians for. He was at least ten years older than most of his companions and found himself lagging behind on the final summit approach, and at one point collapsed in the snow.

The Norwegian Odd Eliassen, a carpenter, encouraged Bonington to his feet and promised to stay with him for the rest of the way. Bonington retains the warmest feeling for Eliassen: 'He is one of the kindest, nicest people I've ever climbed with.'

When Bonington received permission to attempt Menlungtse, it was natural for him to reciprocate. He invited two Norwegians to join him: Eliassen, and Bjorn Myhrer-Lund, a nurse from Oslo, who is probably Norway's best all-round mountaineer and, Bonington says, 'a very modest and self-deprecating man'.

The fourth climber in what is a comparatively small team is Jim Fotheringham, a dentist who lives near Bonington in the Lake District and has climbed with him in the Alps and Himalaya. Two other Norwegians have been enlisted as support climbers: Torgeir Fosse and Helge Ringdal, both businessmen who joined a trek to the Everest base camp during the Norwegians' 1985 ascent and leapt at the chance of returning to the region.

The Norwegian alliance has also helped to solve the problem of how to finance the expedition which will cost £45,000. Bonington has been adept in the past at attracting top-flight British companies to sponsor his ventures but even his name proves less seductive for a lesser peak such as Menlungtse – 23,564 feet high, against Everest's 29,028 feet.

For a time Bonington contemplated selling places on the expedition for trekkers who could accompany them to Base Camp and might even be prevailed upon to help carry their loads. In the end Helge Ringdal found the neatest solution. He canvassed his business contacts until he had enlisted a consortium of Norwegian companies with interests or ambitions in China to underwrite the expedition. They include the Bergen Bank, which has an office in Beijing; the China-Geco Geophysical Company, a joint Norwegian and Chinese seismic company; Norsk Hydro Power; and the '17 Group' which sells ships' gear to China.

Ringdal also wooed a variety of marine, export and exploration companies, among them Fjellstrand, Osco Shipping, the Skele group, Stord Bartz, and the Ulstein group; banks and finance groups, such as the Christiana Bank and Eksportfinans; and the airline SAS. He even persuaded Europe's business newspaper to become involved, and Bonington's reports on the expedition will appear exclusively in the *Financial Times*.

Bonington, meanwhile, was lobbying his own business acquaintances, and the British companies who have agreed to supply goods and services range from Dan Air and the Newcastle equipment company, Berghaus, to the Lake District manufacturers of Calthwaite fudge and the local farmhouse which makes its own Cheddar cheese.

Even for a man of Bonington's experience, the days before departing on an expedition are invariably hectic. Bonington was in London last week to complete a last-minute deal with ITN, and his time was further circumscribed by taking part in a lecture tour to help raise money for an alpine climbing hut that will serve as a memorial to Don Whillans, who died in 1985. But once the team arrives beneath the mountain it will be able to concentrate on the task in hand.

Since no one has attempted Menlungtse before, it remains something of an unknown proposition. The first goal will be to establish Base Camp in a yak pasture at the foot of Menlungtse's West Ridge. The team will spend ten days acclimatising to the altitude and conducting a reconnaissance of the mountain's southern and northern flanks. From poring over photographs taken by expeditions to neighbouring peaks, Bonington believes that the most promising route could lie up a slender arête or ridge in the centre of the mountain's South Face.

The arête looks formidably steep. But Bonington recalls the

climber's adage that 'you can never tell how difficult a route is until you are rubbing your nose against it.' 'It is likely to present around 5000 feet of climbing on both rock and ice and will require a high degree of technical expertise. But it has one overwhelming advantage. It is, says Bonington, 'reasonably safe'.

What climbers and non-climbers imply by 'safe' are of course two different things. In this context it means that the climbers should not be in danger of avalanches, since the arête stands clear of the snowslopes and there are no overhanging ice pinnacles above. As Bonington concedes, no Himalayan expedition is ever risk-free. 'But in this case,' he says, 'the risks seem reasonable and acceptable.'

The main obstacle may lie in the strong, cold winds that could greet them at this early stage in the pre-monsoon season. Bonington draws consolation from the fact that they will not be venturing into the so-called 'death zone' that supposedly lies above 26,000 feet, where the lack of oxygen causes an inexorable physiological decline. With due caution, however, Bonington points out that while their chances must be rated as fair-to-good, 'success, especially in the Himalayas, is never guaranteed.'

The expedition has one further objective to give it spice. The glacier close to Menlungtse was where Eric Shipton took his celebrated photograph of a yeti footprint in 1951. It remains the single most important item of evidence for the existence of the Yeti, supposedly half-man, half-beast. Recently, some authorities have expressed doubts over the footprint, wondering whether it could have been a combination of several paws or feet, or even – in view of Shipton's puckish sense of humour – a fake.

Bonington is not among the sceptics. 'I am sure there is something there,' he says, and he and his colleagues will be keeping an eye open for further evidence. But Bonington admits that if he did see a Yeti he would be presented with a 'terrible ethical dilemma'.

Should you broadcast the fact to the world, he asks? 'Or should you leave the poor old Yeti to live in peace?'

The Himalayan year

Financial Times, 1988

One is not supposed to be patriotic about such things; but it has been a terribly good year for the British in the Himalaya. Last week's news that two UK mountaineers had climbed the North-East Ridge of Everest – although the precise status of their achievement remains a matter of controversy – crowns a formidable list of achievements among the world's highest peaks.

In contrast to 1987, when storms of almost unprecedented ferocity pinned most expeditions in their Base Camps, this year's climbers have been blessed with the fortune of good weather. But luck is not the only commodity required to climb mountains: it has to be accompanied by sound planning, good leadership, technical prowess, virtuosity and imagination. All of these qualities – in differing proportions – have featured in the British expeditions which have reached their summits. With the mountaineering season not yet over, there could be further triumphs to come.

Somewhat perversely, the account of the British year begins with a failure. That is because the international expedition which attempted a winter ascent of K2 – at 8611 metres, the world's second highest peak – did so in the wake of last year's appalling weather. It is safe to say that the British members, John Barry and Roger Mear, came home awestruck at the weather they had encountered. For Mear, who previously had retraced Captain Scott's footsteps to the South Pole, enduring ferocious Antarctic blizzards en route, that is no casual statement. 'It was worse than the worst weather in the Antarctic,' he says, 'and it just went on and on. We lay in our tents day after day, listening to the rumbling of the wind. It was the sheer power that was so formidable.'

Barry was compelled to return to Britain after succumbing to a virus infection while Mear remained to take part in what became a campaign of attrition. In three months of waiting and climbing, he, with Polish and Canadian colleagues, reached just below the Shoulder, the snow platform where the fearful dramas of 1986, including the deaths of Britain's Julie Tullis and Alan Rouse, were played out. That was the limit of the expedition's endeavours and, with food and supplies dwindling, it was compelled to withdraw. It was, all in all, a relieved as well as an impressed Mear who returned in the spring. 'To be honest, I was quite scared about the whole business,' he says. In such circumstances, mere survival can be considered a victory on its own.

Mear's home-coming coincided almost precisely with the return of Chris Bonington to Menlungtse. Bonington, it might be recalled, made his first attempt on this shimmering coral-coloured peak, close to Everest, in 1987. He, too, was defeated by the outrageous weather. This year's second bid proved something of a watershed. He failed to reach the summit and now, at fifty-four, says: 'I don't think I've got the application to go for these big, hard, technical climbs.' In future he would prefer trips that combine climbing with exploration in lesser-known regions: 'If you like,' he says, 'to do a Shipton.'

There was a curious outcome to the expedition, for media attention focused almost exclusively on the animal remains it brought back, with the *Daily Mail* claiming that they constituted evidence for the existence of the yeti (the Natural History Museum, called on to adjudicate on the outcome of bets placed with bookmaker William Hill at 66–1, concluded that they did not). It passed almost unnoticed that, at the tail-end of the expedition, its youngest member, Andy Fanshawe, teamed up with the *Daily Mail*'s news runner to climb the mountain.

After his colleagues had given up, Fanshawe, an official of the British Mountaineering Council, and Alan Hinkes, an accomplished climber in his own right, embarked on an audacious attempt in the modern lightweight fashion, carrying minimal supplies and staking all on a dash for the summit. They succeeded brilliantly after a four-day ascent capped by fourteen hours of grappling with a 300-metre head wall that reminded Fanshawe of climbing in the Cairngorms. They reached the 7181-metre West Summit after nightfall on 23 April; climbing in the dark, Fanshawe observes drily, 'was a bit unnerving'. (The East Summit, two kilometres away and 158 metres higher, remains an unclaimed prize.)

The same month saw an ascent of Cho Oyu, at 8153 metres the world's eighth highest peak and one of the very few of the fourteen 8000-metre peaks the British had not climbed previously. The expedition had hoped to employ ski-mountaineering techniques, bringing the bonus of a luxurious descent from the summit. The conditions defeated those plans, for scouring winds had left their route up Cho Oyu's West Ridge almost bare of snow above 7500 metres. In the event, only one man reached the summit: climbing instructor Dave Walsh, who, at forty-four, proved that the experience and sagacity of middle age are at least equal to the exuberance of youth. His partner, Dave Morris, turned back 200 metres below the top and suffered frostbitten toes.

And so to Everest. In 1987, the weather defeated all but one of the dozen or more expeditions laying siege to it by a variety of routes. However, in the past decade there have been several notable ascents of Everest, representing the latest advance in mountaineering standards.

Once, climbers spoke in awe of the 'death zone' above 8000 metres where no one could survive without carrying oxygen sets. But in 1980 the Austrian Reinhold Messner made an astonishing solo ascent without oxygen and there have been similar climbs since, the most remarkable that of the French and Swiss pair who reached the summit without oxygen in just twenty-six hours in 1986. These precedents helped to inspire the first British mountaineer to succeed on Everest this year, Stephen Venables, a writer and lecturer aged thirty-four.

Venables, the one British member of a small American party attempting Everest's unclimbed East Face, made a fast ascent to the South Col and embarked on the final 850-metre stretch to the summit on 12 May. His two companions turned back at the subsidiary South Summit but Venables pressed on to become only the eighth British climber – in a list now standing at 204 – to reach the world's highest peak. He survived a bivouac in the open during his descent at the eventual cost, through frostbite, of three toes – a price he considers worthwhile.

Venables's triumph was followed by news of the most recent British success, on Everest's North-East Ridge, which was doubly satisfying since it climaxed a prolonged series of attempts by British teams. The route, reached via Tibet, follows an immensely long outlying ridge that merges eventually with the mountain's North Col route, scene of the heroic failures by the pre-war British expeditions.

The North-East Ridge acquired a rather sinister reputation when the first British attempt, led by Chris Bonington, ended in the disappearance of Joe Tasker and Peter Boardman in circumstances chillingly reminiscent of that of Mallory and Irvine fifty-seven years before. The main stumbling block, and the point where Tasker and Boardman were last seen, proved to be a line of jagged pinnacles shortly below the junction with the North Col route.

The challenge was taken up by a highly experienced group of climbers, including the venerable Joe Brown, reinforced intriguingly by a detachment of former members of the SAS. On their first attempt, in 1986, they barely reached the pinnacles; on the second, last year, they passed the first pinnacle before being driven back by a hurricane. It could, therefore, be regarded as a considerable act of faith that they should have returned for a third attempt.

There was an early setback when their leader, Brummie Stokes, had to be flown home after succumbing to the high-altitude ailment, cerebral oedema. For Stokes, it was a disappointing end to what had become something of an obsession. He had climbed Everest with the SAS but resigned from the regiment when it refused to let him make another try. Thereafter, he had pursued his ambitions as a civilian instead.

Under the new leadership of Paul Moores, a member of the Glencoe Mountain Rescue team, the expedition persevered and, on 6 August, New Zealander Russell Brice and Harry Taylor, another ex-SAS alumnus, overcame the last of the four pinnacles. They had to spend a night in the open, during which a foot of snow fell. They told their colleagues later that the climbing had been 'like walking a tight-rope'.

What ensued after they had overcome the pinnacles has spurred controversy in the mountaineering world, for Moores felt that the weather presented an unjustifiable risk and told them to descend via the North Col rather than continue for the summit. The question posed among climbing cognoscenti, therefore, is whether this constituted a true ascent. It was a question of immediate concern to Bonington, since he was already preparing an expedition to the North-East Ridge in 1989. The ascent, he says, 'was a bold, necky push and a fine piece of mountaineering. But they haven't climbed the North-East Ridge because you've got to get to the summit to do that.' Nonetheless, Bonington has decided to abandon next year's attempt. 'With the pinnacles climbed there would be no mystery in it, and I personally don't think all the effort would be worthwhile.'

Bonington now has offered his permit for 1989 to Doug Scott, who took part in one of the previous attempts on the pinnacles and was planning his own expedition to the North-East Ridge in 1990. Scott's response is not yet known as he is engaged in an attempt on Makalu, a majestic peak twelve miles south-east of Everest; at 8481 metres, it is the fifth highest in the world and has not yet had a British ascent. But that is not for want of trying, either, as Scott already has made three attempts. In 1984, he came within 100 metres of the summit and undoubtedly would have reached it if one of his companions had not been suffering from an oedema and unable to walk another step.

This time, Scott is doubling his chances by leading an expedition preparing to make two attempts. One group in his party will be following a couloir on the edge of Makalu's West Face while Scott will be leading a team on the West Face itself, so far unclimbed. This will present probably the hardest technical climbing ever attempted at high altitude: a 750-metre rock band starting at 7500 metres which defeated the only previous expedition to try after just one rope length.

Scott scrutinised the face from Everest last year and believes he discerned a feasible line. He was, thus, moderately hopeful about the expedition's chances of succeeding on at least one of the routes. 'We've got a good chance of climbing the mountain, one way or the other,' he said before leaving.

Cut off on the top of the world

Sunday Times Magazine, 1988

With impressive detachment, Stephen Venables was contemplating the toes of his right foot. He had just returned from the Royal United Hospital in Bath but already the bandage protecting them was coming loose. Protruding from its folds was a gleaming black digit that had clearly once been a big toe but was now – in the renowned words of the *Monty Python* parrot sketch – no more.

Venables eased his foot on to his parents' sofa and pulled away more of the bandage to reveal the rest of his toes. The second and third were equally black and defunct and he could wobble them back and forth on their stumps like loose teeth. The fourth and fifth bore a closer resemblance to what toes are supposed to look like, with patches of pink indicating flesh that the frostbite had spared. While Venables readily conceded that it was not a pretty sight, it was also a sight that he would not have to endure for much longer. In ten days' time he was due to return to Bath Hospital to have the three most damaged toes excised.

'I hope it won't be too painful,' he says. 'I'm a terrible wimp.'

Some wimp. Two months before – to be precise, from 3.40 to 3.50 p.m. on Thursday, 12 May – Stephen Venables had stood on the summit of Everest. Those climbers who have reached the world's highest peak can no longer be considered a particularly exclusive group, for they now number 204. But Venables was only the eighth British climber to do so.

By some quirk, his ascent received virtually no coverage in the media, normally so ready to bestow patriotic superlatives on any British triumph. Yet in mountaineering terms it was a truly astounding feat. None of Venables's seven British predecessors had climbed Everest without oxygen. With the probable exception of Mick Burke, who disappeared near the summit while making a solo attempt, none had reached the top alone.

What was more, Venables had helped forge a new route up what had long been considered Everest's most dangerous side, the East or Kangshung Face. Chris Bonington calls his ascent 'absolutely brilliant – a superb, fabulous achievement'.

It was not free of risk or cost. Venables admits that his survival during the descent was by the narrowest of margins, while its aftermath was all too visible in his doomed toes. Yet, if it all sounds tremendously heroic, that is a notion Venables rejects. When the media caught up with him in Kathmandu he gave one of the most anti-heroic interviews ever recorded. Climbing Everest, he told a BBC reporter, was 'a bit of a cliché'.

If so, it is a cliché he will have to invest with meaning for, having retreated to his parents' home near Bath to convalesce, he has been writing a book about the ascent. It has been eagerly awaited by cognoscenti since he won the annual Boardman-Tasker prize for mountaineering literature in 1986 – and some parts are awaited no less eagerly by the author himself.

It is not just that he has found it hard remembering just what did occur in the extremity of struggling for his life above 28,000 feet: he has also, given his dislike of the stereotypes of mountaineering, found it hard to decide precisely what *stance* – the mock heroic? the coolly ironic? – to adopt.

He faces a similar decision over his doomed toes: will he be able to carry on climbing? Plenty of mountaineers have continued after suffering the same fate, says Venables: 'I feel sad about losing part of my body. But I intend to carry on. There's so much left I want to do.'

Venables is thirty-four. Those meeting him outside the mountains find him a considerate and sensible man, modest and self-deprecating. If this makes him an unlikely celebrity in an activity where it is often the most ruthless and self-centred individuals who reach the top, Venables insists that he has those characteristics, too. 'All mountaineers are selfish,' he says.

Those qualities must nevertheless lie some way below an accomplished middle-class veneer. Both his parents went to Oxford in the forties. His father, now retired, was in advertising, ending his career as chairman of Ogilvy and Mather; his mother is a teacher and psychologist. Venables grew up in Surrey, the eldest of five children. He was educated at Charterhouse and Oxford, where he read English.

He was introduced to the mountains at an early age. His parents took him walking and skiing and he began climbing as a teenager on the sandstone outcrops of Kent and Surrey. He took up the sport seriously at Oxford, going on summer visits to the Alps with the university mountaineering club.

Over the next fifteen years he built up a priceless backlog of experience, ranging through Scottish winter climbing, the Eiger and other major alpine routes, and expeditions to the greater ranges. With it came a hardening of the psyche acquired through experiences like the Christmas night he spent bivouacked on Mont Blanc in temperatures of $-30°C$, cowering from the wind and continuous spindrift avalanches: 'That was the worst ever.'

He tested himself in a variety of jobs, including teaching, furniture making, decorating and stage management. But mountaineering and travelling, complemented by lecturing and writing, took over his life. He followed the path pioneered by Chris Bonington, who showed that it was possible to earn enough from climbing to finance its pursuit. But he was far from attaining Bonington's exalted level; nor had he entered the realms where the professionals may be accused of choosing climbs according to the commercial prospects they offer.

Among climbers his reputation was as an accomplished mountaineer rather than as a skilled rock technician. Early in his career he tended to defer to his partners' judgment, especially when it came to turning back. Now he is more single-minded about backing his own instincts and pressing on, even if it means defying bad weather or continuing alone – a violation, he says, of the 'perceived norms' of mountaineering. 'You're brought up to follow the wisdom, "when in doubt, turn back". It's rather a British thing, especially in the Alps.'

The British would once have argued that team spirit was the paramount virtue on expeditions, too; now it is accepted that the best recipe for success is a group of highly motivated individuals. 'In the end, however selfless you are, you've got to have a lot of personal motivation and you've got to be very competitive' – though not, Venables hopes, 'in the sense of being unpleasant to other people.'

So why does Venables climb? Why is he competitive and selfish – if he really is – and why does he indulge in such manifest risk? These matters puzzle Venables himself. None of his brothers and sisters climbs: 'Perhaps they've got better things to do.' On the other hand, his mother brought him up to consider it a 'normal and sensible' pursuit.

He adds that he has always liked to 'stretch' himself but does not feel particularly brave. In any case, risk has a deceptive habit of coming up unawares. 'You're there and it's the thing to do. Once you're involved, I don't think you worry too much. You feel you've just got to get on with it and you have a gut feeling that you will carry it off.'

Even so, Venables acknowledges that a degree of apparent insanity may be a useful commodity for mountaineers. He talks of climbing's 'wonderful irrationality' and adds that it is often 'the very absurdity of a particular situation that makes it so appealing'. What, after all, could be more wonderfully absurd than risking your life to stand on the highest point on earth for just ten minutes?

Venables was not particularly surprised when he found a message on his answering machine a year ago, relayed by his mother, that an American expedition had invited him to join it on Everest the following spring. 'There was a sort of inevitability about it,' he says.

Venables had always savoured the mythic nature of his sport, drawing inspiration from the epic accounts of predecessors such as Bonatti, Haston and Buhl. Now that he was following, sometimes literally, in their footsteps, it was as if Everest was somehow preordained – an essential part of the script, perhaps, or an indispensable item in the curriculum vitae of the modern mountaineer.

At first Venables assumed that the attempt would be by way of the South Col, the classic ascent route on the Nepalese side forged by the British in 1953. He was therefore taken aback to learn that it was to be via the East or Kangshung Face, on the Tibetan side, renowned as the most difficult and hazardous approach of all.

Since the first ascent in 1953 the routes on Everest had proliferated. But the East Face had remained taboo, a series of monumental ice terraces swept by avalanches that appeared to transform any bid into an elaborate version of Russian roulette. In 1983 an American expedition finally climbed an immensely demanding buttress at the centre of the face. It was a vast endeavour, with equipment including rocket launchers to set up aerial ropeways for load-hauling and oxygen equipment for the summit bids.

The 1988 expedition believed it had found another feasible route on the left-hand edge of the face. For the first 3500 feet it, too, followed the crest of a buttress that rose above the avalanche runnels. But the buttress was obviously hideously difficult, with vertical granite and overhanging ice on the scale of a major alpine face. Beyond it lay 7500 feet of climbing: 4500 feet up terraced snowslopes to the South Col, then 3000 feet up the South-East Ridge to the summit.

As if the route was not intimidating enough, the expedition had decided to impose upon itself a number of handicaps that appeared to fall under Venables's rubric of 'wonderful irrationality'. The first concerned its size. The other expeditions who would be attempting Everest by different routes that year ranged from twenty to 250 members. The Kangshung Face team, by contrast, numbered just four.

Besides Venables, there was the leader, Bob Anderson, who had previously been to within 800 feet of Everest's summit; Ed Webster, a rock-climbing expert; and Paul Teare, a devotee of winter climbing. There would be just four people in support: a doctor and photographer; and a Nepalese cook and his assistant.

Venables thoroughly approved. Like many of today's mountaineers he looked askance at vast, military-scale expeditions which create logistic pyramids to deposit their lead climbers on the summit. Far better to make what is termed an alpine-style ascent, a romantic or even existential approach whereby climbers rely as far as possible on their own resources. But the penalties of this style are severe. There are no support climbers to help stock the camps that must be established up the route; and, crucially, nobody to mount a rescue attempt should things go wrong.

The second handicap the expedition faced related to the use of supplementary oxygen. Quite simply, it decided to do without it. Although, in any case, it would not have the resources to stockpile oxygen cylinders up the route, that too accorded with its members' preferences.

The use of oxygen has been central to the apparently arcane debates that mountaineers conduct over the ethics of their sport. Venables regards carrying supplementary oxygen as close to cheating, 'an unacceptable level of artificiality', since it effectively lowers the height of the mountain, and he has never used an oxygen set himself.

Yet to attempt Everest without supplementary oxygen is to defy medical evidence about the risks climbers face at high altitudes. To compensate for the lack of oxygen, the blood produces extra red corpuscles and becomes increasingly viscous, impairing the circulation and making the body more vulnerable to cold and thrombosis, reducing the muscle function and leading eventually to death.

In addition, the vastly increased breathing rate of a climber without extra oxygen dehydrates the body by up to eight litres a day, causing acute wasting. That too has potentially lethal effects, for in an attempt to protect itself the brain accumulates extra liquid, which can lead to a form of stroke known as an oedema. High-altitude climbers may also suffer disturbances of consciousness and orientation and make poor decisions as a result; they may experience psychotic episodes, exaggerated fears and hallucinations; they may even suffer permanent brain damage.

The most poignant example of these dangers was provided by the disasters on K2 in 1986. Several climbers fell to their deaths after making mistakes almost certainly caused by poor judgment at altitude. In the culminating horror, a storm which raged for five days pinned down seven climbers at 26,000 feet; five of the seven died, including Britain's Julie Tullis and Alan Rouse.

'Wonderfully irrational' may therefore appear a minimal description of any attempt on Everest without oxygen. The fact remains that it has been done. The first were Reinhold Messner and Peter Habeler, who were determined to climb Everest in as 'pure' a style as possible, Messner as part of his successful campaign to climb all fourteen of the world's 8000-metre peaks. They made their ascent in 1978 by climbing to the summit from the South Col in eight hours, returning in a helter-skelter descent of little more than an hour. There have since been some twenty ascents of Everest without oxygen.

The British mountaineer Doug Scott has coined a term to describe the way in which the laws of physiology have apparently been defied. He calls it 'flashing' – the art of making the quickest possible dash for the summit and descending to safety before damage can occur. It is, none the less, a high-risk approach, as Venables was the first to acknowledge.

'To make a serious attempt on what we were trying to do, sooner or later you were going to have to put your head on the block. I don't like the idea of dying, and I don't like the idea of a lonely unnatural death. But I have to accept that possibility. When I went on the Everest trip I was more conscious than ever before that I might not come back.'

When Venables and his colleagues first looked up at the Kangshung Face from the Base Camp beside the Kangshung Glacier in March they felt strangely reassured. While the buttress at the front of the face seemed dauntingly technical, it had the merit of being at reasonably low altitude compared to the rest of the face. Beyond it, the snowslopes leading to the South Col seemed relatively easy and should take no more than a day and a half to climb.

Once on the South Col the concept of 'flashing' would apply. After a few hours' rest they would head for the summit via the South-East Ridge, giving them no more than twenty-four hours above 26,000 feet and enabling them to be well on their way back before damage could set in. 'At least,' says Venables, 'that was the idea.'

Having established an Advance Base Camp at the foot of the buttress, they began climbing on 3 April. Fixing ropes in place as they progressed, they spent the next six days edging their way up polished granite and green ice, steering their way among tottering ice pinnacles and overhangs, climbing which Venables regards as among the most exhilarating of his life. On 8 April they set up Camp 1 near the top of the buttress and believed that the way to the summit was clear. 'We thought we had cracked it,' Venables says.

Another month was to pass before they could embark on their summit attempt. At the head of the buttress they encountered a vast crevasse which took them three days to overcome. Then the weather broke, bringing storms and avalanches which drove them back to Advance Base. During a lull they climbed back up the fixed ropes and reached a height of 24,500 feet, setting up Camp 2, equipped with food, stoves and fuel, before having to retreat once more to the Advance Base Camp.

On 8 May the weather cleared at last. With the frustrations of the previous month spurring them on, they made an excellent start and reached Camp 1 that afternoon. Their plan was to make the South Col by midday on 10 May and then, says Venables, 'blast for the summit from there'. But the morning brought the first of a series of setbacks. It was snowing heavily, filling in their previous tracks, and it took fourteen hours to reach Camp 2. 'It was very tiring,' says Venables, 'and fourteen hours was too long to be out.'

They had intended to make an early start the next day but they were too weary from their previous exertions; and when they did set off the weather was against them once again. This time the sun was beating down so that it felt, says Venables, 'like climbing in a furnace'. They had to strip off their high-altitude clothing and carry it in their rucksacks, which now topped forty pounds in weight, while they kept sinking up to their knees in fresh snow. 'Totally knackered', as Venables says, they reached the South Col at 6.30 p.m.

Venables had been looking forward to seeing the South Col, one of the mythic sites of mountaineering. Previous climbers had warned how inhospitable it could be, a wasteland of rock and ice, and Venables found it 'just as bad as all the books said. There were horrendous winds blasting across. We had quite a battle to get the tents up. It was a very nasty place.'

Their original schedule called for them to head for the summit that night. But the wind made it almost impossible to stand upright and they were, in any case, far too tired. As they huddled in their tents that night all four suffered frightening bouts of breathlessness, aggravated for Venables by attacks of claustrophobia which made him want to leap out of his sleeping bag and rip open the tent door.

In the morning the wind was blowing as hard as ever, ruling out any question of a summit attempt. Paul Teare said that he was feeling dizzy, the sign of an incipient oedema. The only cure is to lose height and so Teare set off for Base Camp at once. (He reached it the following morning and made a full recovery.) Meanwhile Venables, Anderson and Webster decided that they could wait at the South Col for twenty-four hours before the altitude compelled them to retreat. In a despondent mood, they spent the day brewing drinks from melted snow. But that evening, says Venables, 'the wind miraculously died down'. They decided to head for the summit that night.

They calculated that it would take them twelve hours to reach the summit and a further three to four hours to return. That would get them back to the South Col the following afternoon and enable them to begin their descent towards Base Camp before night fell. Since speed was of the essence, they decided to climb as light as possible, leaving their rucksacks behind at the South Col. That meant that they would have no bivouac equipment if they were benighted high on the mountain or if the weather broke. 'I felt it *was* a gamble,' says Venables. 'But only a slight one.'

They set off at 11 p.m., their head-torches lighting the way across the initial stretches of the South Col. From there, the route follows a broad snow-filled couloir leading to the crest of the ridge at around 27,000 feet. Rather to his surprise, Venables found that he was forging ahead: he supposed he must be the fittest, and perhaps most determined, of the three. But he found it strenuous work breaking the trail and although he had emerged from the couloir when dawn broke at 6 a.m. he was still far lower than he had hoped.

He could see Anderson and Webster some way below but decided to carry on ahead for the time being in the hope that they would eventually catch him up. 'I realised I was going too slowly at that stage. I knew it was a question of packing it in or getting my finger out.'

Above the couloir the route follows the line of the South-East Ridge, with most climbers choosing to keep to the snowfield just below the shattered rock which forms its crest. At first Venables managed to increase his pace but as the morning wore on found himself going more and more slowly. Lower down he had been able to climb for twenty steps before taking a rest, taking one breath to each step. Now he was reduced to one step at a time between rests, up to five breaths for each step. Finally, at around 28,250 feet, he ground to a halt.

It was 11 a.m., the time he should have been on the summit.

Ahead was a steepening snowslope that culminates in the South Summit at 28,750 feet; beyond that lay the final 250-foot stretch to the summit itself. Feeling desperately tired, and still hoping that Webster and Anderson would join him to help break the trail, he sat down in the snow and promptly fell asleep.

Venables woke an hour later to find that Webster had pulled ahead of Anderson and almost caught him up. It is an indication of the increasing effects of altitude on him that he now finds it hard to recall what happened next. 'I remember some sort of exchange, with him saying his brain was hurting and he wasn't going to come up and break trail,' Venables says. He also recalls shouting down that Webster was 'a bloody nuisance' as he had just wasted an hour waiting for him.

It was now that Venables made the first of two crucial decisions. It is a moment that comes to most mountaineers, when they must choose between continuing in the face of risk or turning back. It was the decision made by Scott and Haston at almost the same place in 1975 when they knew that if they went on they would have to bivouac without equipment close to the summit, placing them in extreme peril if the weather broke; they reached the summit and survived.

It was the decision made by Mick Burke a day or so later, heading for the summit alone after his partner, Martin Boysen, was forced to turn back. Storm clouds closed around him and he was never seen again, almost certainly killed by walking through a cornice and falling down the Kangshung Face.

Hours behind schedule and close to exhaustion, Venables knew that the odds against him were multiplying. He also knew that he was increasing the risk by continuing alone, since he would not be able to rope up on the most exposed sections ahead. In the end he decided on a compromise: he would aim to reach the South Summit by 1 p.m. and, if successful, make a further decision there.

Venables remembers that he was carrying two caffeine pills and swallowed them as he set off. He was gratified to find that he could now take four steps at a time between rests. Climbing steadily, he reached the South Summit at 1.30 p.m. – only half an hour behind schedule, or the revised schedule, he was pleased to note.

That brought the second moment of decision. There could be no doubt that the dangers were accumulating: the weather was deteriorating, with clouds forming over the South Col and the light becoming a uniform grey. This time it was the mountain's history which willed Venables on.

From the South Summit the ridge dropped eighty feet to a dip. Beyond it Venables could see the final fluted section leading to the summit, a jagged stretch of rock and ice with giant cornices soaring out over the Kangshung Face like fangs. It was the view first obtained by Bourdillon and Evans in 1953: their photograph became one of the icons of mountaineering.

'It was like going on to the North Face of the Eiger, this famous place you've read so much about. I really thought, I've got to do this.'

After descending to the dip, Venables was carried forward on a surge of excitement and adrenalin. Shortly above the dip came the notorious forty-foot buttress known as Hillary's Horror or the Hillary Step, on the very edge of the Kangshung Face. Conditions on the step vary considerably from year to year: in 1975 Haston and Scott had found it encased in ice and tackled it like a winter climb on Ben Nevis. Venables was relieved to find it as Hillary had described, with a layer of snow adhering to the rock. Like Hillary, he eased his way up by bridging between the two, conscious all the time of the 11,000-foot drop.

Above the step, Venables knew that the way was clear. He climbed a series of snowy hummocks, wondering if each would be the last. Finally he stepped on to a tiny, triangular plateau that fell away on all sides and knew that he had only a few more steps to climb. 'There was this wonderful feeling – I've done it, I'm going to make it.'

The summit was marked by a pile of oxygen bottles left by Japanese climbers a week before. Venables stood beside it and saw Everest's three main ridges, South-East, West and North-East, each redolent of past struggles and triumphs, disappearing downwards into the clouds.

'I had this feeling of disbelief and a very great feeling of privilege just being there. I was also very glad to sit down and have a rest.'

Venables is proud that despite his fatigue he remembered some important tasks. He deposited some dried flowers at the summit which some friends in India had given him and retrieved a small collection of rocks as souvenirs. (To his immense chagrin, they were lost during the return trek to Kathmandu.) He also attempted to take the all-important summit photograph but somehow failed to set the delayed action mechanism, obtaining a picture of the ground instead. He would have loved to linger, but after ten minutes knew that it was time to head back down.

His predicament was now acute. He was alone on the highest point on earth with clouds closing around him. He knew that having been at 26,000 feet or above for forty-eight hours it was vital to make it back to the South Col by nightfall. But he suddenly felt immensely tired; he also felt lost. As he picked his way down the ridge he found himself veering on to the cornices overhanging the Kangshung Face and told himself: 'Don't do a Mick Burke.'

The Hillary Step brought a moment of utmost peril. He descended it by abseiling down a rope left behind by the Japanese but found the manoeuvre far more demanding than the ascent. To unclip from the rope at the bottom he had to remove his gloves: knowing that frostbite would take hold within seconds, he was seized with panic that he would be unable to get them back on. He seemed to have been drained of his last reserves of strength and heard himself taking huge, draining gasps of breath.

'At that point I almost collapsed. I thought, It'll be easy to give up, I'll die very quickly, but I think the fear was stronger.' He was also impelled by the notion of how ridiculous his death would seem. 'You're going to look so bloody stupid, climbing Everest and not getting back down.'

The next crisis came on the eighty-foot reascent to the South Summit. He reached the top on all fours and once again almost collapsed. By now his fatigue was compounded by a sense of unreality, 'a great aura', that stemmed from his awareness that he, too, had become part of mountaineering history. 'There was this feeling of disbelief because of all the historical associations. It was hard to assess what was really going on.'

As he descended the snowslope below the South Summit Venables was overcome by the absolute conviction that he was no longer alone. One of the first characters to appear was an old man who, after a particularly arduous section, told him to sit down on a rock for a rest. Then, attempting to glissade down a snowslope, Venables found himself being carried towards the edge of the Kangshung Face.

'I stopped in a panic and was suddenly desperate to have a pee. The old man said, "Well pee in your pants then, it'll keep you warm." And so I did.'

For a while the old man disappeared; then he returned,

together with other characters, some familiar to Venables, others not. The Everest pioneer Eric Shipton was there, together with Doug Scott's son Mike, whom Venables had never met, and 'lots of other people I didn't know'.

Most disconcerting was the fact that he found himself switching continuously between waking and his dream-like state. 'I was chopping and changing between hallucinating and realising I was hallucinating. I would become part of it all, believing it all, and then suddenly it would click and I would realise this isn't real, I'm actually the only person here.'

At 7 p.m. Venables was still less than halfway back to the South Col. With darkness gathering he knew that he would have to stop for the night. Since he had no bivouac equipment – no tent, stove, or shovel to excavate a snowhole – all he could do was to dig out a ledge with his ice-axe and trust that his four layers of down and fibre-pile clothing would enable him to survive until dawn. Mercifully, the night was still and the cold, between −20 and −25°C, did not seem unbearable.

'I didn't think I was in danger of getting hypothermia,' says Venables. 'I didn't think I was going to die.'

But he did think he was going to suffer frostbite. Eric Shipton seemed to be taking care of his hands, protected by three pairs of gloves, and Venables felt reasonably sure they would remain intact. 'But I knew there was a fair chance I would lose some toes. I'd read the books.'

At dawn Venables resumed his descent. He caught up with Anderson and Webster, who had turned back from the South Summit and had found shelter in an abandoned tent. Venables has no idea how they greeted him: whether they congratulated him, embraced him, or shook his hand. 'I do remember that it was a sunny morning and they said, "Hey, come on, we'd better rope up," and the three of us went down together which was quite symbolic.'

The three reached the South Col in mid-afternoon and collapsed in their tents. Only now did they receive an intimation of the injuries they had suffered. Venables removed his boots and saw that his first three toes were slightly discoloured, with a demarcation line between the sound and damaged flesh. For the moment he was not unduly concerned. 'I'd had frostbite once before in my fingers and they had recovered, so at that stage I was fairly optimistic.'

Anderson had frostbitten toes too, but by far the worst affected was Webster: when he took off his gloves he saw that his fingers had turned white and wooden. 'He hadn't realised before,' says Venables. 'That's the awful thing, because they just go numb and you don't really notice.'

The most immediate danger stemmed from the fact they had now been at 26,000 feet or above for seventy-two hours. But one of the consequences of altitude is to induce an illusion of well-being and that night, says Venables, they succumbed to 'a false sense of security', accentuated by the euphoria of having reached the summit. Another consequence is an overwhelming lethargy that makes the slightest task appear a monumental ordeal. 'It took an enormous mental effort just to lean on one elbow to light the stove,' Venables says. 'The rot had really set in.'

From this point the struggle to descend the mountain became a struggle for their lives. In the morning they lay in their tents unable to face the series of basic chores, such as donning their boots and crampons, which they needed to undertake before they could descend. They abandoned their sleeping bags because they simply could not face packing them into their rucksacks.

It was 3 p.m. before they were ready to leave and even then Venables sat on the ground outside his tent for another hour before starting down. Their original plan had been to descend all the way to Advance Base but they were forced to stop for rest at frequent intervals and by nightfall had made only the 1500 feet to Camp 2.

In the morning their trials continued. Although they knew it was vital to make a prompt start they decided to brew a drink first. Because of the altitude the water came to the boil agonisingly slowly: just as it did so, they knocked the stove over. They brought the water to the boil for a second time and knocked it over again. Once again it was 3 p.m. before they were ready to leave. By then it was snowing heavily and after only a short distance they turned back to Camp 2.

Venables believes that the next day saw them closest to death. Webster seemed to have aged by ten years. 'He looked terrible. He normally had an intense light in his eyes which had completely faded. He kept saying, "Look, you guys, if we don't go down today we're going to die."'

Webster, says Venables, was right. It took him an hour to summon the energy merely to stand up, but all three managed to leave the camp by 10 a.m.

It was now that what Venables regards as the greatest horror unfolded: the point when selfishness, going beyond the instinct for self-preservation, took hold. Venables had been critical of the mountaineers who survived on K2 after abandoning companions who were still alive, especially the Polish climber, Dobroslawa Wolf, who was left behind descending the fixed ropes and was never seen again.

'I was shocked by K2. But having been through this I can see how it happens.'

After battling through deep snow for most of the morning Venables and Webster finally reached the fixed ropes at the top of the buttress. By then Anderson was some way behind. Webster shouted up to him: 'We're going all the way,' and he and Venables began to descend. But Anderson could not find the start of the ropes and so became marooned on the mountainside.

'We shouldn't have split up, we really shouldn't,' says Venables. 'We should have stayed together.'

As darkness fell Venables and Webster pressed on down the ropes. Towards midnight they began shouting for help but their cries fell on deaf ears. At the Advance Base Camp Paul Teare and the doctor, Mimi Ziehman, had given them up for dead. To assuage their grief they had taken sleeping pills and so did not stir until Venables and Webster stumbled into the camp at 4 a.m. 'They were absolutely delighted to see us,' says Venables. 'It was a very emotional moment.'

Ziehman began treating their frostbite at once, immersing their hands and feet in warm water in the hope of reviving the frozen flesh. In the morning, to their immense relief, they could see that Anderson had found the ropes and was on his way down. He arrived that afternoon. So far as Venables can recall, there were no recriminations. 'He was very good-natured about it,' Venables says. 'He didn't seem to mind.'

When Venables returned to Britain at the end of May, specialists warned him he would lose his big toe. As his second and third toes blackened he realised that they, too, were doomed. All three were amputated at Bath Hospital on 2 August. Venables returned to his parents' home on crutches, relieved that it had not hurt as much as his mother had predicted, and pleased to be rid of the smell.

His foot, he said, 'looked as though someone has taken a huge bite from it. I'm sad about it, but compared to a road accident it's pretty minor.' He had also fared far better than Webster, who lost parts of seven of his fingers.

During his convalescence Venables began to write his book, *Everest, Kangshung Face*, knowing that he would have to solve the problems not only of recalling what happened but of making sense of it. He had been appalled by a headline, 'Briton conquers Everest', and an article calling him a hero.

Jingoism apart, he says, heroes are those who risk their lives for others; and mountains are not adversaries but strictly neutral. Yet he still had to place himself centre-stage if the narrative was to succeed, and answer questions about himself. Were the hallucinations merely the result of physiology, or something more? Had he revealed a dark side of his nature under pressure? Would his readers think he was mad?

'I've tried to describe exactly what happened, or as closely as I can remember,' he says. 'In the chapters concerning the summit and the descent, I've done a fairly unabashed personal account.

'I've tried to give an accurate impression of what was going on in my mind – perhaps I should say spirit, but I don't know about that. It's difficult to know if the hallucinations are chemical, psychological, spiritual or what. There's no doubt that the effects of exhaustion, hypoxia and cold do extreme things to your brain, but maybe it goes beyond that.

'I've tried to be honest. The thing I feel ashamed about is that on the final day we didn't stay together. I think I knew that Robert was going to get down okay but really we should have waited. It reinforces this business about the selfishness – when you're really stretched you do tend to look after number one.

'However hard you try to explain the compulsion of it I think in the end the layman will think you must be crazy. But I have tried to show the enjoyment and exhilaration of it too.'

Venables has also been conducting a series of lectures on his ascent. Inspired by the example of Reinhold Messner, he hopes to be climbing again by the summer. Messner, he recalls, lost six toes while climbing Nanga Parbat. He had a pair of boots made to fit his truncated feet and went on to climb thirteen more 8000-metre peaks.

Venables is already mentally drawing up plans to climb in the fastnesses of Patagonia and the hitherto closed regions of the Chinese Himalaya. And he would like to return to Everest: 'It would be nice to go back and do it again and soak it up and find out exactly what it was like.'

3

FINGERS ON THE ROCK

If Pete Crew worshipped Joe Brown, so did I: and, as I observed in my opening chapter, the awe in which I held some climbers was quite inappropriate for a journalist assigned to write about them in a dispassionate and objective manner. It was the same when I first met Tom Patey: I can still see his embarrassment as I struggled to ask him questions. My confidence had improved when I met Joe again for the second piece in 1970 and by the time I interviewed Ron Fawcett and Mark Leach in the 1980s I realised that I was far older than most of the climbers I was writing about, and did my best to assume a suitable *gravitas*.

I should point out that any illusions about my climbing abilities will be dispelled by my description of Traverse of the Gods at Swanage. I undertook it at the behest of John Cleare, who took a generously paternal view of my early climbing career. He took me in hand, and led me on climbs from Swanage to the Highlands, so that I owe my first intoxicating taste of the Scottish winter to him too. John's recompense may in part have been the pictures he took of my failure to accomplish a pendule at Swanage.

A dinosaur in Wales

Sunday Times, 1967

'It's great climbing with Pete,' says Joe Brown. 'I don't have to worry whether he's going to be able to follow me.'

'I worship Joe,' says Pete Crew. 'He's the best climber in the world.'

After years of keeping warily apart, the two best rock-climbers in Britain, representatives each of the two generations of modern climbing, have come together. Since last June Joe Brown, thirty-six, the ex-plumber who burst in on the middle-class world of climbing with a series of brilliant climbs in the early 1950s, and Pete Crew, twenty-three, a computer programmer and the most forceful of the new 'hard men', have climbed seven new routes together on Craig Gogarth, a 500-foot sea cliff in Anglesey.

They have immediately set new standards of climbing diffi-culty, putting up for the first time 'extreme' climbs on rock which is not only vertical or overhanging but also very loose. To combat this looseness Brown and Crew have had to relearn their climbing techniques, avoiding pulling up on handholds where possible and reverting to the classical principle of moving up in balance on footholds.

'Techniques such as bridging are ideal,' says Crew: 'anything which keeps the rock pressed in place instead of pulling it out. To keep in balance on overhanging rock you must press yourself flush against the rock, arch your body, and bridge as far out behind you as possible so that your feet are outside your centre of gravity,' he explains. 'Though first of all you must learn to relax. You're all gripped up at first because of the loose rock.'

Placing pitons – to limit a leader's possible fall – was a major problem. Brown and Crew have established high ethical stan-dards at Gogarth, keeping pitons to a minimum. 'Though actu-ally,' says Brown, 'it was very difficult to get them in. We could have done with a few more.'

Craig Gogarth itself is an important find, and was not climbed on extensively until last year. But whereas it took twenty years for forty new routes to be climbed on Clogwyn Du'r Arddu, a comparable discovery on Snowdon, last year fifty new routes were put up on Gogarth. Virgin rock in Wales is rare indeed.

The stories of Gogarth and the Brown/Crew partnership gradually converge. Two of Crew's friends, Martin Boysen and Bas Ingle, discovered the cliff in 1964, and the three put up seven new routes on it that year.

'These were all routes which looked fairly easy but we had epics on every one,' says Crew. 'We were very frightened by the cliff, and thought that was all we'd be able to do.'

Climbing a major cliff over the sea was a new experience, and the loose rock, the danger of being cut off by the tide, and attacks from birds in the spring, all made Gogarth a formidable place.

The cliff was left untouched in 1965, but in 1966 two climbers revisited it. Crew went back himself the following week, climbed a new route, and in a month had added three more.

By now Brown had heard of the doings of the younger generation and went to look for himself. But he confused Gogarth with a nearby cliff called Red Wall (later climbed for BBC television). It looked steep and holdless, and Brown was shaken: 'I thought this time I'd really been left behind.'

But someone put him right and he found Gogarth. Typically, he chose to do his first new route in an area until then untouched: a 400-foot white slab with a thin crack running down its centre. Crew watched from a cliff opposite. 'It's grotty rock,' Brown yelled to him as he hurled handfuls of it down into the sea.

But the problems of climbing on loose rock fascinated Brown and he returned. His third new route, climbed in June, he called Winking Crack – 'every time I walked underneath, it winked at me.' By then Crew had done ten new routes himself but although he and Brown visited Gogarth in the same group they had still never climbed together.

In the early 1960s, when Crew and Brown were both trying to climb Master's Wall on Clogwyn Du'r Arddu – so named from Brown's numerous attempts on it – they and their camps had kept their distance from each other. Crew, the son of a Barnsley railwayman, had renounced an Oxford maths scholarship after a term and lived in a cottage below Clogwyn Du'r Arddu. Tense and competitive, he was visibly obsessed by the crag.

Brown, then an instructor at the Whitehall outdoor pursuits centre in Derbyshire, disliked the eminence others had thrust upon him, but was none the less aware that his position was being challenged. The rapprochement began in 1965, as a commercial deal: Crew began taping conversations with Brown for a biography, to be published by Gollancz.

In June 1966, the biggest wall on Gogarth was still unclimbed: Brown had tried it but had retreated below an overhanging wall at the top of the first pitch. In the pub one evening Crew decided to ask Brown to try it with him. He excitedly rushed down to Brown's house, and Brown agreed.

The 400-foot climb took eight hours, and they shared the lead. They took two hours to pass the overhang on the first pitch, but the crux of the climb turned out to be the beginning of the second pitch, an overhanging crack line.

'Joe thought it was too loose, so I had a go,' said Crew. He used three pegs and two slings for aid in the first twenty feet. 'They were enough to keep me in balance but they'd never have held if I'd come off, and I was fighting to get up. Joe was really gripped up about this.'

It was while watching Crew on this pitch that Brown decided on the name of the climb: Dinosaur. 'It needed,' he said, 'few brains but a long neck.' It remains the hardest climb on Gogarth and has not been climbed since.

Crew and Brown did not climb together for another month. Then Brown was making his third attempt on a line which had already repulsed more than twenty climbers, including Chris Bonington. Twice Brown had been forced to retreat when his partner had been unable to follow him. It happened again but this time Brown called to Crew, already on the cliff, to join him. Again they were successful, and called the route The Rat Race to commemorate the competition there had been to make the first ascent. By the end of the year they had put up another five new routes together, all in the highest extreme category and all still unrepeated.

It has been a good year in many ways for Brown. He moved to Wales a year ago and last Easter successfully opened a climbing shop in Llanberis. He takes people climbing for £5 a day. (The official guiding rate is £2 10s: 'I could make twice that plumbing.')

As a climbing partner he ranks Crew with Don Whillans, the fellow plumber from Manchester with whom he made his brilliant climbs of the 1950s. 'With this sort of partnership the leader can go all out: he can afford to knacker himself making the pitch safe and the second can follow using a tenth of the energy.'

He climbed fifteen new routes on Gogarth last year, including the seven with Crew. His previous best year was six, on Clogwyn Du'r Arddu in 1952. 'I'm always happiest when I'm doing something new.' He considers that he is climbing as hard as ever, and has no idea when he will stop. 'When I'm climbing badly it's usually for a reason, like drink or not enough sleep. I'm not getting stiff at all.'

Crew's best partnership until Brown was with Bas Ingle. 'We complemented each other perfectly. With Joe it's different: he's obviously the dominating figure.'

He is getting married next month and is taking a regular

job working on the Bangor University computer in March. He recognises that Brown has influenced not only his climbing: 'Joe has tended to quieten me down. I'm pretty impulsive and Joe is exactly the opposite. I'm learning a hell of a lot.'

There are still perhaps fifty new routes to be climbed on Gogarth and the neighbouring cliffs, but Crew and Brown are talking about climbing together in Norway or the Alps. Their one definite objective, once they can get access permits, is the Trango Tower in the Karakoram, in Kashmir. 'It's this perfect rock spire, going straight up for 5000 feet,' says Crew. 'It's a natural.'

TV circus goes up the Old Man of Hoy

Sunday Times, 1967

If a carefully planned schedule works out, viewers will today see the climax of the BBC's most ambitious outside broadcast – the arrival on the summit of six climbers attacking by three routes a crumbling sea-stack in the Orkneys known as the Old Man of Hoy.

This, say the telly climbers, is the biggest ever climbing extravaganza, bigger than the Red Wall programme from Anglesey last year, bigger than the Dru rescue, bigger even than the fabulous Eiger Direct. Assembled to perform in front of seven cameras and ten million viewers are six of Britain's finest climbers, with another four working as mobile, climbing cameramen. They include all four British Eiger men and the ageless, immaculate Joe Brown.

The clifftop opposite the Old Man, a 450-foot stack of crumbling standstone, is now a muddy site covered with a tangle of aerials, scanners, cameras and cables. Three marquees have been pitched for the BBC as a training exercise by a platoon of Scots Guards.

Climbers have been working on the Old Man himself for two weeks, preparing mobile camera positions and bivouac sites, festooning it with ropes, and hammering into it bolts and pitons. A brown scar marks the trail to the main campsite at Rackwick (population five) three miles away, where the climbers live in tents. 'It's not a climb any more,' said Hamish MacInnes, a mobile cameraman, 'it's a circus.'

The 500 inhabitants of the Island of Hoy are watching with fascination. 'People only usually come when there's a war,' says Isaac Moar – Hoy is one of the bastions of Scapa Flow. Mr Moar has been for thirty years the island's county councillor, postmaster, and taxi-driver, and is known uncompromisingly as the King of Hoy.

The programme is the most ambitious outside broadcast the BBC has attempted. They have been quoting an above-the-line budget figure of £22,000 although in the planning stage an estimate of £50,000 was made.

Climbers and mobile cameramen are receiving a basic rate of £125 with an extra £25 for those who have been here two weeks, and a further £25 for taking part in a film shown last Friday evening.

The Sherpas – climbers acting as porters – are getting a basic £30. Last Thursday the BBC agreed to give them a further £12 10s for each day spent on the rock. All climbers, cameramen and Sherpas are insured for £25,000.

Most of the climbers, naturally, have a hard-headed attitude. Four have sold stories or pictures to newspapers. 'Hey, Chris,' yelled one to Bonington. 'The *Daily Record* say the piece you promised is three days late.'

Bonington, at that precise moment writing an article for the *Daily Telegraph*, promptly subcontracted the piece.

There have been keen discussions among the climbers on the terms in which the BBC planned to present the climb.

Three routes are being attempted. That by Bonington and Tom Patey on the East Face was the line taken on the first ascent of the pillar last year. Those by Joe Brown and Ian McNaught-Davis on the South Face, and by Pete Crew and Dougal Haston the South-East Arête, both immensely difficult, are new. The East Face line has become the trade route, with climbers and Sherpas taking equipment up and down it all day.

'I just don't see,' said one climber, 'how the BBC can maintain that the second attempt on the East Face is unrehearsed.' The East Face route had featured in a run-through on Thursday night.

On the pillar itself the sole preoccupation was the task in hand. Haston and Crew started their route on Tuesday and it is so difficult that they will be lucky to reach the top by to-night.

'I'm about to take one of the great decisions of my life,' yelled Haston to Crew as he swung in the slings below an overhang. 'Whether to put a peg in this or not. There's a hairline crack all round it and I think the whole thing is detached.'

Away to the left Joe Brown was prospecting his South Face route. 'What's it like? It looks really easy,' said Crew when he returned.

'I was frightened to death,' said Brown.

The man most worried about communications was Tom Patey, who had to make a frightening swing into space on a fixed rope. 'If I do it before you're ready,' he said to Bonington, 'I'll fall 120 feet and you'll fall 220 feet. "Please do not adjust your set. What you have just seen did not happen."'

A stretcher and pulley equipment are ready on the clifftop and an RAF helicopter is standing by at Lossiemouth in case. Joe Brown had a narrow escape when a huge block grazed past his shoulder. Eric Beard, a Sherpa, was even luckier: he was standing below the pillar when a large rock fell past his head and hit his hand. One of the climbers is a doctor. 'But if anything does go wrong,' said a climber, 'the only medical equipment we'll need is a spade.'

Pictures coming back in rehearsals have been superb. 'The trouble is,' said Ian McNaught-Davis, 'that climbing has romantic and aesthetic attractions but television doesn't present them at all. All it gets across is the "grip" – "kicks".'

Fortunately for the climbers' own peace of mind, they are able to absorb themselves in the climbing. 'When it comes to it,' said McNaught-Davis, 'you just don't think about the ten million people wondering if you're going to fall off.'

Forty years old and still the greatest

Radio Times, 1970

Without much enthusiasm, Joe Brown was preparing to leave for the Andes. The advance party of the eight-man expedition which he was to lead had left several weeks previously and was heading for unclimbed 19,400-foot Mount El Toro – in the centre of the area of disaster wrought by Peru's most destructive earthquake during this century.

'The way I'm feeling now,' Joe said, 'I'd be prepared to spend

a month doing relief work.' There were newspaper reports that
the expedition had offered its services and supplies but that the
Peruvian army had said it was getting the situation in hand. 'So
perhaps it would be best to make the climb after all,' pondered
Joe, 'to show everyone that things are returning to normal.'

There was another reason for Joe Brown's momentary apathy
towards his sport. A week previously, Tom Patey had been
killed in a fall after making the first ascent of a sea-stack off
the coast of Sutherland. Patey was one of Scotland's greatest
climbers. BBC viewers saw him on the epic broadcast climb of
the Old Man of Hoy in the Orkneys, of which Patey had schemed
the first ascent, and it was with Patey that Brown climbed the
Mustagh Tower in the Karakoram.

It is this climb that Brown rates the most dangerous he
ever undertook – 'we were trogging around in thigh-deep
snow which could have avalanched at any time' – and Patey's
death had affected him deeply. 'It is,' Joe admitted, ' a bad
period.'

Joe Brown is forty next month. He occupies a place in the
climbing world much like that of Bobby Charlton in soccer or
Henry Cooper in boxing.

Twenty years ago he began to put up the new routes that
have become the climber's classic tests and he has continued to
do so ever since. Forty is the age beyond which only the greatest
sportsmen hope to continue; but the climbing world is still
waiting for some evidence that Joe Brown's powers are now on
the wane.

'It's not the actual technique – that's easy to keep hold of,'
says Joe; 'though I do get the odd bloody creaking joint. The
hard thing is to keep the enthusiasm to drive with. If you get
pressure on you it does affect you. But it's not quite as simple
as that – you can just go off for no apparent reason at all.'

The talk in Snowdonia this summer has been of the growing
band of climbers who have been climbing solo up the routes
that ten years ago or less were regarded as the hardest tests –
Brown's own classics Cenotaph Corner and Cemetery Gate in
Llanberis Pass fell long ago, and so have many of his routes on
Clogwyn Du'r Arddu, the dark crag on the North-West Face of
Snowdon.

Solo climbing has, say the men who do it, the greatest sense
of achievement – but it also holds the greatest risk. A climber
who falls while leading has, he reckons, every chance of being

held on his rope by the second man below him; a solo climber has no such margin of error, and one who fell 150 feet after slipping on one of the hardest climbs in Llanberis Pass in May was lucky to escape with broken limbs.

'I'm glad I'm not with them,' says Joe. 'I'm glad I'm not climbing with the same drive as they are. It's absolutely logical to me that if you make a mistake it could easily be your last. Solo climbing must have something but I don't know what it is – because I don't do it. But in an area like ours where things have been worked out so much, for someone wanting to make a mark it's the only way to do it.'

One brilliant nineteen-year-old had just soloed a climb called Boulder Direct, one of the dozen hardest in North Wales. 'The trouble is,' said Joe, 'he's got no fear.'

Joe Brown says that he certainly still knows fear. 'If I thought I was going to fall off, I would certainly be afraid.' And when, I asked Joe, did you last fall off? 'About fifteen years ago.'

Monday's televised climbs will be on Craig Gogarth, a formidable sea-cliff on Holy Island on the north-west tip of Anglesey. It was discovered as a climbing ground only five years ago – and it has been Joe Brown, who, some had whispered, was beginning to fade, who has put up many of the hardest new routes. He climbed a number with Pete Crew, who some climbers had considered Brown's main rival.

The most difficult climb of Monday's three is Spider's Web, which Joe climbed with Crew in 1968, and which has not been repeated since. 'The hardest pitch,' says Joe, 'is the first.'

The most spectacular is decidedly the second, and it is this which has dissuaded aspirants from making the second ascent. The leader has to abseil thirty feet down a rope and swing like a pendulum to reach the lip of an arch fifty feet above the glaucous sea.

'Rock,' explains Joe, 'is stable. A rope isn't. You have to work out what you're going to do very carefully.'

Such complicated tactics are a feature of Craig Gogarth's specialised, technical climbing, particularly on the traverses now popular amongst climbers who have conquered all the more obvious vertical lines.

In winter Gogarth is a chilling place, with boiling seas which sometimes launch spray 200 feet to the clifftop; however on a fine summer's day it is idyllic. The scent of wild flowers merges with the sea air, gull chicks nestle on every ledge that gives them purchase, and seals basking inshore stare insolently at the climbers' strivings.

'It's terrific here,' says Joe. 'You've usually got fine weather, there's no crowds, and the rock generally is really superb.'

Climbing, decides Joe, still holds the same pleasure it did twenty years ago. 'But the degree is different – it's very hard to bubble over the way I did then.'

He still experiences the same sensations as the weekend climber, too; even Joe Brown admits that when he and his friends set out to climb in the morning, 'quite often we're hoping we're not going to climb anything at all. It's so easy to just sit down and do nothing. But then you go home at night and think what a waste of a day it's been. But if you put a lot of effort into something, you go home and think what a fantastic day you've had.'

The fingertip phenomenon

Sunday Times, 1982

One day last week Ron Fawcett stood at the bottom of a climb named Downhill Racer on Froggatt Edge in the Peak District of Derbyshire. Downhill Racer, forty feet high and graded 6B, is one of the hardest rock routes in Britain, requiring a long reach and immense finger strength. Even good climbers take anything up to an hour to reach the top – if they can climb it at all. Fawcett climbed it without hesitation or apparent effort in just two minutes. 'It's quite straightforward really,' he said apologetically.

Rock-climbing in Britain has always progressed in phases, with each generation dutifully impressed by what its successors achieve. This time the advance seems truly awesome. 'It's astronomic,' says Ian McNaught-Davis, a prominent member of the Brown/Whillans generation of the 1950s. 'They are on a different planet.'

But among today's élite, even his peers agree that Ron Fawcett is something special. Geoff Birtles, editor of *High* magazine, who has partnered Fawcett on a number of climbs, says: 'Ron is the biggest thing since Joe Brown. He is the Seb Coe of the rock-climbing world.'

The object of this adulation is a surprisingly shy man of

twenty-six who lives with his wife Gill in a chilly stone house near Buxton. Over six feet tall, with a powerful, lean physique, he has dark blue eyes set in an Edwardian face, with high cheekbones and a trim moustache.

Most noticeable of all are his fingers, battered and scarred and so developed through their constant fight to grasp minute holds that they bulge like a bunch of bananas. They are already something of a myth in the rock-climbing world, where it is widely related that to save their skin going soft, Fawcett wears rubber gloves in the bath. 'It's true,' he admits.

Fawcett's devotion to rock-climbing is further illustrated by a daily training schedule that would make members of any previous generation wince. He may solo thirty routes like Downhill Racer on Froggatt, and then run to a neighbouring crag to repeat the process there. If the weather is too poor to climb, he starts the day with a circuit consisting of 200 press-ups, twenty-five pull-ups, and fifty sit-ups, repeated four times, which he follows with a seven-mile run. Then he goes for a two-hour work-out on Buxton's indoor climbing wall and does four more circuits when he gets home.

Old sweats like McNaught-Davis – who tells proudly how he once managed ten pull-ups – would regard all this as close to fanaticism, but Fawcett doesn't mind. 'Before this period, training was taboo – it was all beer and cigarettes,' he says. 'But if you want to stay at the top in any sport you have to put in the hours.'

There is evidence, however, that even his friends thought at one point he had gone too far. 'He once gave up drinking altogether – that was really boring,' says Geoff Birtles. 'He will at least have half a pint with you now,' he adds, with relief.

Fawcett burst on the climbing scene with the éclat of a naïve artist who has just discovered paint. The son of a lorry driver in the Yorkshire Dales, he started climbing at fifteen and within a year had climbed most of the classic 'extreme' routes in Britain. 'They seemed quite easy, really,' Fawcett says.

Next, Fawcett set his sights on the routes of Pete Livesey, the pace-setter of the early 1970s. Fawcett repeated most of them, and then he and Livesey – like Joe Brown and Pete Crew in the sixties – joined forces. Opinions about the partnership still differ among the climbing fraternity; some hold that Fawcett benefited from it enormously, others that it held him back. It was certainly tense at times, with the two men competing to take the most challenging leads. In the end, after a semi-public row over Livesey's use of a piton at the crux of a climb, they split up.

Since then, Fawcett has had two principal partners, neither nurturing any ambition to oust him from the lead. The first was a retiring young man named Chris Gibb, a self-employed electrician; the second, his wife Gill, a maths student at Bangor when they met. They were married in 1981, and for their honeymoon they went climbing in Derbyshire. 'He said we couldn't afford anything else,' says Gill.

For several years after the break with Livesey, Fawcett made steady if unspectacular progress. Then, in early 1980, came a series of dramatic routes in Snowdonia which won him the headline in a climbing magazine: 'Fawcett blitzes Wales'. Most were graded 6B and 6C, the highest available. Soon even this classification was not to prove enough. In April that year, Fawcett climbed a new route at Tremadoc up an eighty-foot overhanging wall with minute fingerholds. Even Fawcett was impressed ('it was incredibly hard') and it won the unprecedented grading of 7A.

Since then, three more 7As have been put up, two by Fawcett. As well as immense finger strength, they require no little nerve, and here too Fawcett's boldness astonishes earlier generations. He appears to think nothing of jumping twenty feet or more off a climb if the going gets too tough. However, he has by now broken each of his heels, ankles and wrists. (Last time he was back climbing, with his wrist in plaster, inside two weeks.)

Like others before him, Fawcett's natural aim is to make enough money from the sport to carry on pursuing it. But whereas climbers like Chris Bonington have largely made their names on overseas expeditions, such jaunts are not for Fawcett: 'I couldn't stand all that hanging around, doing nothing.'

Instead, he would like to be known as Britain's first professional rock-climber. He made a dramatic appearance in the BBC TV series *Rock Athlete*, and is a consultant to the Troll equipment company. So far it has all amounted to no more than a bare living, although a useful windfall came his way last week when the film maker Leo Dickinson asked him to take the part of Dougal Haston in a documentary about the Eiger.

This summer he aims to spend three months with Gill in the United States: 'We'll start in the east, work our way west and do all the hardest routes on the way.' Much nearer home, he is working on a route that could make the climbing world's next headlines. He won't say where it is, but it can confidently be predicted that the first 7B in British rock-climbing is on its way.

The peak of endeavour

Daily Telegraph, 1986

T he sport of rock-climbing is 100 years old today. On 28 June 1886, Walter Haskett Smith scaled the alluring granite pillar in the Lake District known as Napes Needle, thereby making the ascent which is generally accounted the first modern rock-climb.

His feat is being celebrated this weekend with festivities which include a champagne picnic on the Needle itself. But if Haskett Smith were to return to the Lake District today, some developments in the sport would undoubtedly leave him shaking his head.

Haskett Smith – Eton, Oxford and Lincoln's Inn – was one of a group of leisured climbers (although a member of the Bar, he never deigned to practise) who spent whole summers at the Wasdale Head Inn near Wast Water. Until then, the Victorian mountaineers had looked principally to the Alps: the Wasdale group aimed to explore the delights available nearer home.

Haskett Smith first noticed Napes Needle, a seventy-five-foot pinnacle on the flank of Great Gable, when bright sunlight picked it out against a background of clearing mist. Then he approached it, to discover its steep and lichenous sides: 'The prospect,' he later wrote, 'was not encouraging.'

Haskett Smith thrust and levered his way via a series of cracks and ledges to an airy stance fifteen feet below the top. There he lobbed a stone on to the summit to establish that it was flat and then completed the ascent. With the yawning drop beneath, he found it all 'rather a nervy proceeding'; before descending he tied his handkerchief to a rock so that it would be seen by possibly sceptical colleagues from below.

The ascent was a landmark for its risk and audacity and marked the birth of British rock-climbing as such. No longer was it a subsidiary activity, mere practice for the Alps, but could be relished on its own account.

Previously, too, information about new ascents had been passed on by word of mouth; in another pioneering move,

Haskett Smith compiled a guidebook that helped popularise the sport. As he observed, his ascent had been followed 'by a remarkably rapid increase in the number of men who climb for climbing's sake'. (Women, even though one made an early repeat ascent of the Needle in 1890, were still accorded little credit.)

Haskett Smith, who made his last ascent of the Needle at the age of seventy-four, would be astonished if he returned to the Lake District today. Last weekend the crags around Scafell and Scafell Pike were draped with climbers apparently defying gravity to glide up routes he would have thought utterly impossible.

Haskett Smith took a stern attitude towards what he termed 'mechanical aids'; he considered even ropes 'illegitimate' and climbed Napes Needle alone, although a fall would probably have proved fatal. Today's climbers are festooned with equipment, from protective helmets to lightweight rubber-soled boots, to improve both adhesion and safety.

The consequences of accidents have been mitigated too. When a climber fell from Mickledore, the cliff below Scafell, Haskett Smith helped push the injured man to Wasdale Head in a wheelbarrow. Last weekend, after an accident in precisely the same place, an RAF helicopter clattered in to whisk the two victims to hospital in Whitehaven.

A further sign of the popularity mountain activities have attained – there are reckoned to be half a million hill-walkers in Britain and 50,000 pure rock-climbers – can be seen in the scar in the hillside leading to Scafell and the eroded scree below Mickledore. Although the damage has not yet reached the level of Snowdonia, where the most popular paths have to be shored up, such measures may be needed soon.

Among the current celebrations, the Fell and Rock Climbing Club, of which Haskett Smith was a founding member, is dining at the Wasdale Head Inn tonight, and staging an exhibition there of climbing memorabilia, which includes Haskett Smith's original guidebooks and a reprint of his account of the Napes Needle climb. A club member also plans to dress like Haskett Smith, including Norfolk jacket and shepherd's boots, to make the Needle's centennial ascent.

Last Sunday, a firm of caterers held a dinner, with chefs and waiters, near the summit of Scafell Pike; this weekend a local guide will reward successful clients on the Needle with champagne. Since Haskett Smith enjoyed his evenings at the Wasdale Head Inn as much as his outings on the hills, it can be taken that where these more sybaritic activities are concerned, he would almost certainly approve.

Conquest of the impossible

Sunday Times, 1988

The Kilnsey Overhang is one of the mythic sites of British rock-climbing. With the extraordinary 'free' ascent this month by a Lancashire climber, it has become the scene of the latest, and perhaps most dramatic, watershed of the sport.

Deep in the Yorkshire Dales near Grassington, Kilnsey Crag consists of a forbidding limestone buttress whose top extends some sixty feet beyond its base. At its most extreme section, ninety feet above the ground, the overhang is almost horizontal, like the underside of a shelf.

In the 1960s the overhang was considered the test piece of what is termed artificial climbing – the technique of ascending via a system of slings suspended from pitons hammered into the rock. The notion of climbing it 'free' (by sheer unaided muscle power) was unthinkable, and in 1975 the definitive guidebook, *Hard Rock*, declared that it could never be done. Now Mark Leach, a twenty-three-year-old climber from Rossendale, Lancashire, has achieved just that.

Ever since Walter Haskett Smith reached the top of Napes Needle in 1886, rock-climbing has advanced in generational stages. In the 1950s the legendary Joe Brown and Don Whillans astonished fellow climbers with new standards of audacity and technical prowess; ten years ago Ron Fawcett led the next surge. This time it is Leach who has rendered his contemporaries, in his triumphal phrase, 'gob smacked'.

Leach is one of a tiny élite of rock-climbers dedicated as never before to their sport. Of dauntingly muscular build, at five feet ten inches tall, he became a full-time climber last summer after emerging jobless from an engineering course at Bolton Institute of Technology. He receives a modest income as an adviser to Asolo, the boot manufacturer, and Edelweiss, the rope-maker.

If they trained at all, climbers of the Brown/Whillans era performed the occasional set of press-ups. Leach, by contrast, does more training than climbing: running and stretching, and weight training to build strength and endurance.

He finds indoor climbing walls too easy and practises instead on the ceiling of a garage, owned by a Rossendale friend, the photographer Ian Horrocks, where a series of minute wooden niches recreates the gravity-defying ambience of modern rock-climbs. Leach's language would mystify his predecessors, too: once the hardest routes were described as 'thin' and 'desperate'; now they are 'wild', 'outrageous', and – invoking body-building jargon – 'the ultimate pump'.

Most traditional climbers regard rock-climbing as one aspect of mountaineering, which involves reaching summits rather than merely ascending rock faces. Not Leach. 'Although I like the mountains, I like them to look at, not to climb.'

Leach first considered tackling the overhang last year. At the time, he said, it seemed 'too futuristic – people said maybe it would go free in ten years' time.' He nonetheless decided to train for an attempt and by July felt it might be feasible after all.

Leach climbed up to the main overhang a number of times to try out key moves and to perform the chore of 'cleaning' the route – removing pitons left from previous artificial ascents and replacing them with six neatly spaced 'bolts', a form of piton that is drilled into the rock. However – and the distinction is crucial – he would not be using the bolts to climb on but as 'protection', namely to hold him on his rope should he fall.

The attempt was delayed by the wet summer. On 16 September, Leach and three companions arrived at the foot of the crag. Leach faced a difficult tactical decision over how fast to climb. On the one hand, he could not afford to linger. 'As soon as you start, you go – if you don't, you're going to pump out, you're not even going to make it halfway.' On the other, there were two crucial moves that could not be rushed. 'The sequence is quite complicated and you can blow a move by climbing too fast.'

It took Leach little more than a minute to climb up to the main overhang. There, he launched himself across and in another minute reached the two vital moves. The first was a 'crucifix' whereby he had to grip two tiny fingerholds with both arms extended horizontally, his back to the ground ninety feet below, and his toes pressed against minute blades of rock.

Next came a 'cross-through', which entailed passing one arm under the other to reach for a hold, requiring the control of an

Olympic gymnast to prevent himself from twisting off the rock. 'It was quite strenuous,' Leach admits. When Ian Horrocks, suspended on an abseil rope at the edge of the overhang, saw the holds, he was 'amazed at how bad they were. It looked touch and go.'

With his strength draining fast, Leach surmounted the lip of the overhang and embarked on the brief final vertical section. The entire ascent took no more than five minutes and at the top Leach let out a yell of triumph. 'I was obviously very pleased,' he says. 'And quite relieved.'

The response in the climbing world has been one of awe. 'People are quite stunned,' says Leach. 'Nobody realised it would go quite so soon.'

He has graded the climb as E8 6C, representing an almost unique combination of exposure and technical difficulty. There is in fact one climb graded even higher, at E9 7A, which Leach put up himself and no one has managed to repeat. But even that, says Leach, is not 'such a wild proposition as the overhang – it's really out of it and mentally it feels a lot further than ninety feet off the ground.'

Leach has now departed to climb in France but intends to search for new challenges on the Yorkshire and Derbyshire gritstone this winter. He is duly modest about his new place in the history of the sport. 'I went out to push climbing to my own limit,' he says. 'Now I find I'm pushing rock-climbing's limit too.'

Traverse of the gods

Climbers' Club Journal, 1967

For Londoners, the great advantage of the limestone cliffs of Swanage is that they are only 135 miles away and thus within reach for a day's climbing. Unlike the sandstone outcrops, they have a definite feeling of the wild. They are steep, between forty and 130 feet high, and on a clear day you can see boats far out in the English Channel, with the sea and sky bringing a feeling of spaciousness and freedom. On a rough day in winter spray bursts over the top of the cliff and it becomes a very intimidating place.

The cliffs have been unevenly developed. The most popular

area is just west of Durleston Lighthouse, known as Subliminal
Ledge. Here much of the loose rock has been cleared away –
elsewhere new climbs tend to finish up in substantial rubble or
even holdless earth. For that reason traversing climbs are popular and sensible, particularly as the cliffs are mostly overhanging
and traverse lines are well protected from falling rocks.

There are a number of good routes east of the lighthouse.
Until recently climbing was forbidden here, but new access
agreements have been worked out. The physical access to the
climbs can be difficult. Last summer Layton Kor, Bev Clark and
I had a mad scramble among boulders dodging waves to reach
the foot of a climb. We remained dry until the last dash of all,
when to the others' delight I was stranded yards from safety
with a wave bearing down on me. It was so big that I crouched
behind the nearest boulder instead of on top of it so that I
wouldn't be taken out to sea when the wave bounced back off
the cliff. Fortunately the day was hot and I steamed dry during
the climb.

In between these two areas, and directly below the lighthouse,
is a 1500-foot stretch of cliff with only one route up it, and that
can only be reached by climbing down it first. From the sea
there is an obvious traverse line that is just at the point reached
by a high high tide. The ledge has been scoured out of the cliff
by the sea and is extensively overhung. The cliff itself is pierced
by zawns and swings in and out dramatically.

In 1963, John Cleare, Rusty Baillie and Ian Martin came home
from the Alps where Rusty had just made the second British
ascent of the Eiger Nordwand with Dougal Haston. The cliff
below the lighthouse was then totally unknown ground – no
one had even made a reconnaissance by boat. The three reached
sea level east of the lighthouse, climbed westwards for seven
hours, and were finally stopped by a wide zawn which they
called the Black Zawn from the colour of the rock. Fortunately
it was no later in the year than September so Rusty took his
clothes off, tied on a 150-foot rope, and swam across, landing
near the easy way down to Subluminal Ledge. They rigged up
a rope pulley and hauled their gear across, John following in
the sea. Ian Martin had left the climb at the one possible escape
route halfway along, a chimney now known as Scotsman's
Retreat. John and Rusty named the climb Traverse of the Gods,
partly in Rusty's honour and partly because John said 'it was a
hell of a traverse.' They reckoned it had 3000 feet of climbing

and was XS and A2. Since then it has been climbed perhaps eight or nine times, and has been downgraded to 2000 feet, HVS – the vertical artificial pitch can be avoided by a very thin traverse.

I became a journalist in August 1964 and started climbing in May 1965. As I enjoyed climbing I naturally enjoyed writing about it. In November John Cleare and I went to Switzerland to do a 'background' feature for the coming attempt on the Eiger Nordwand Direct. In February and March I reported the climb for the *Daily Telegraph*. 'Now that you're writing about climbing we'd better get you up some climbs,' said John when I came home. 'We'll start with Traverse of the Gods. It's the longest serious climb in southern England.' John has always taken an avuncular interest in my climbing, and his eyes lit up as he described the pendule, the tyrolean traverse, the irreversible bridging move across a zawn, and finally the swimming pitch. To add to the enticements he declared he would photograph every inch of the climb.

It was to be another Cleare climbing extravaganza, with death-defying ropework and using all conceivable items of modern American equipment, for the sake of some passing glory in the *CCJ*.

We were to spend the whole summer on the climb, finally completing it on 12 December, and ending with what can only be described as an epic, due largely to my own inexperience.

In the summer Dougal Haston, Mick Burke and Layton Kor all said they wanted to do the climb. The first party actually to arrive on the clifftop comprised John, myself, Royal Robbins and Tom Patey. Tom was nursing the hand he had impaled on an ice-axe in the Alps and was to provide musical accompaniment only. But as we walked past the way down Subluminal Ledge a girl ran up to us and said: 'There's someone shouting down there.' At sea level we found a boy unconscious, half in the water. His partner was supporting his head. He had been climbing a difficult crack with no protection and had fallen thirty feet. It was the end of our day's climbing. We eventually evacuated him by rubber dinghy and then the Swanage lifeboat. By the time we got back to the cliff it was too late to start the climb.

We came down again a month later. This time John and I had with us Roy Smith, just home from the British Andes expedition, and Dave Condict, who climbed Rondoy with the 1963 LSE

Andes expedition. Roy had with him Barry Cliff, but Barry didn't think he would climb as he was still nursing the back he broke in a flying accident in 1964.

We arrived at the eastern end of the cliff at one o'clock. John looked like an over-decorated Christmas tree, laden with his hardware and cameras. The London Sub-Aqua Club were sunning themselves on the rocks and, seeing us uncoil our ropes, some came across. 'Rescued a climber from the sea here two weeks ago,' said one. 'More dead than alive when we got him out.' We thanked him for his kind thoughts.

The first obstacle was a vertical wall undercut by the sea. Halfway along the wall was a nose which jutted out above a zawn. Roy, who was leading, had to climb free to the nose, fix a rope there, and then continue to a wide ledge on the far side. The rest of us were to pendule across the zawn.

Roy, climbing in a vest, white trousers which looked like long johns, and boots, appeared contemptuous of the problem. The traverse line followed very thin cracks high on the wall and climbing delicately he reached the nose quickly, and then continued to the ledge. Dave said he would prefer to climb free too but John instructed us to pendule for the sake of the photographs.

The traverse line to the hanging rope was just above the waves. Dave never really had much chance. John told him to tie a loop in the rope for a foot and to attach a hero loop with a prusik knot to the rope for a hand. Dave did so and swung. But with his foot in the loop he could not jump for the ledge and went straight into the water up to his waist to cheers from the skin-divers. He untangled himself from the rope and ignominiously climbed on the ledge. He found a place in the sun and took off his masters and socks to dry them out.

John went next, using only the hero loop for his hand and just caught the ledge with his feet at full stretch. 'Okay, Pete, you come next,' John shouted. I was annoyed already because before even trying the first of John's rope manoeuvres I had been soaked by a large wave as I stood innocently on the first stance.

I advanced along the base of the wall. The situation was like a whirlpool, drawing you further and further into its clutches so that any retreat became more and more impossible. At the edge of the zawn you had to lean out and clutch the rope. From that moment you were committed. The holds were precarious, forcing you to turn to the greater insecurity of the rope itself. I stopped thinking about the problem, grabbed for the rope, and swung. For a moment, as the ledge came near, I thought I had made it. But my flailing foot just failed to get a hold and, like Dave, I subsided into the water. From the ledge Roy hauled me in on the climbing rope and I grounded gratefully. Barry decided not to follow on account of his back.

Chuckling happily, John continued ahead with Roy, climbing unroped. The ledge now ran round the back of two cavernous zawns – 'the sort of place you expect to find a dead sailor washed up, lashed to a spar,' said John. Water dripped from the roof and the rock was black and wet. Dave and I roped up and I led round the first cave on to the nose separating it from the next. Dave followed and I led again into the back of the second cave and out again. The handholds on the ledge were good and there were usually good footholds below it, although they were sometimes wet. There followed a third cave. We came out into sunlight on a wide ledge at the back of which was an overhanging crack.

The traverse line petered out here and we had to go up the crack and strike along higher up. A fine bridging move on small holds took you off the ground and then by placing your left foot up near your ear you were on top of a large block – a mild VS move that gave a peculiarly strong feeling of achievement after the continual sideways scuttling of the traversing thus far.

Having gained height, we now had to lose it again. We walked along a ledge for several yards and then traversed gently down a slab to below the original line we were on and perched on a nose. Roy now had to lead up a crack in a corner, hand traverse along the top of the left-hand side of the corner, and slide on to yet another nose, offering a very constricted stance which, to compound our difficulties, was covered with guano.

Roy climbed the pitch successfully and ensconced himself away from the mess with his legs dangling over the edge. I followed. The crack offered narrow finger jams but I followed a natural tendency to back up the left-hand wall of the corner. At the top I found out why this was the wrong thing to do: I now had my back to the holds I was to use next. I turned round precariously and launched myself off on the hand traverse. When I arrived at the stance I found that there was only two feet of space between it and the roof that overhung it.

'You've got to sort of back in head first,' said Roy. 'There are some holds on the roof.' I did as I was told and slithered on to the stance through the biggest and most nauseous pool on the ledge. 'Smells a bit, doesn't it, Pete?' said Roy. I sat in that pool for the next two hours.

There was no room for anyone else on the ledge, or so we thought, and Roy set off on the next pitch. The obstacle was another zawn about twenty feet across, with wave-swept rocks at the bottom. The idea was that Roy should perform a diagonal abseil on to a block halfway down the back of the zawn, do an unpleasant stomach traverse along a guano ledge running along the opposite wall, and thus gain a substantial ledge on the far side.

There were two ropes to manage – the climbing rope and the abseil rope – as well as the one I had climbed on. Roy set off on the abseil but came back after a long time saying that the rope was jamming. He thought he would try a hand traverse along the continuation of the ledge we were on and climb down the back of the zawn on to the block. Eventually he came back from that line too. 'You'll have to do it, John,' he called.

John came round and joined us on the stance, a heap of tangled ropes and bodies. I moved away from the scene of action while John and Roy sorted things out. Roy muttered to John: 'I thought I was going to come off then.'

'What was that, Roy?' I asked.

'Nothing, Pete,' said Roy.

It was nearly half an hour before John was ready to set off. He did the abseil and remained on the block while Roy followed him and led through. John wanted to be in a good position to photograph the next piece of circus tomfoolery.

Roy had by now reached the far nose and was securing the end of the rope he had climbed on. Dave and I, squashed on to our stance, passed the other end through a rusty ring piton, coiled it, and threw it across the zawn to Roy. 'Okay, Pete, that's it, across you come.'

'You're joking,' I told him. 'On that?' I refused to contemplate a tyrolean traverse – whatever it eventually turned out to be – until the rope was fixed to a newer-looking piton. Everything had to be undone and Dave fixed the rope to another piton round the corner of the nose.

'Right, Pete, it's quite easy. Just hang on to the rope with your hands and hang your feet round it as well.' John gave his instructions from the block at the back of the zawn, his vantage point for taking pictures of terrified climbers silhouetted against the sky. Dave belayed me and I set off.

At first it was easy – the rope sloped downwards towards Roy's ledge. But as I passed the halfway mark the rope sagged more and more, and so the last few feet were uphill. To make things more difficult for myself I had wrapped my feet too tightly round the rope and this counteracted the pull of my hands. Roy strained a hand out, I managed to hunch myself forward into a semi-sitting position and grabbed his hand, and he pulled me in.

John wound his film on happily. 'You . . . rotten . . . swine,' I yelled at him. 'You . . .'

'Great action shot, Pete,' said John.

Dave, on the wrong side of the zawn, admitted he wasn't looking forward to the acrobatics, but came across none the less. Roy and I had managed to tighten the rope and gaining the ledge was rather easier for him.

We now tried to pull the rope across. It had, of course, stuck.

It was six o'clock and it would be dark in under an hour. There were still three to four hours' climbing and Dave and I had to return to London that night. John and Roy were staying overnight and John said they would come back for the rope the next morning. We were now just below Scotsman's Pinnacle. Two escape routes lay on either side of this: one, Scotsman's Retreat, on the far end of a hard severe pitch; the other, Rhodesian's Retreat, on our side of the pitch. The two routes meet halfway up the cliff. We took Rhodesian's Retreat.

The Swanage rock lived up to its reputation. John hurled down a few boulders as he went up and Dave, who came last, was narrowly missed by one which the rope dislodged. It was half past six when we were all up. It had remained perfectly fine all day and there was a red sunset.

The months passed. We made plans to return to complete the climb on several occasions, but they were always thwarted by pressures of work or bad weather forecasts. 'We can't let it run into next year,' said John. At the end of the first week in December the forecasts were still consistently bad. But on Saturday, 10 December, a partial clearing was forecast and we arranged to meet at Swanage the next morning.

I travelled down with Dave, and John brought Ian Howell, fit and enthusiastic from the Andes and Yosemite, and his friend Adrian Lang. We went down Scotsman's Retreat at eleven o'clock. The sea was calm but the sky in the west was dark. By coming down the wrong chimney we had missed out a pitch so Ian led across it followed by myself and Dave and we then climbed it back again. It was a pitch typical of Swanage – a deep recess for your hands and a sloping ledge for your feet. John said that on the first ascent Rusty had so disliked the look of it that he had climbed down on to the ledge below it, run across dodging the waves, and climbed up at the other end. He had been put off by a formidable bulge halfway along but as it turned out it was reasonably easy to balance past this. John stood below us on Rusty's ledge to take his pictures. Since our last visit he had got married and his wife had kicked £800 worth of Nikon cameras over an 800-foot cliff in Sutherland. He now had the latest waterproof Nikon, designed – unlike our crabs, pegs, and peg hammers – to withstand the corrosive action of salt.

We now approached what John said was the hardest pitch on the whole climb – the one that he and Rusty had avoided at first with an artificial pitch of A2. The barrier, as usual, was a zawn. Ian climbed down to a block at the back of the zawn followed by Adrian and myself – the principle being to pack as many people on to the stances as we could to provide front and back belays wherever possible. John looked into the back of the zawn and laughed: we were crushed together like rush-hour passengers on the London Underground.

The hard pitch followed. As usual, there was a recess for hand jams but this time literally nothing for your feet. Two-thirds of the way along the pitch was a corner which would provide rest. Ian climbed up out of the back of the zawn to the traverse line and placed a runner high up. He stuffed his arm into the recess, pulled his legs up to almost the same level, and monkeyed his way leftwards, pausing in the corner and then pushing on to the nose that formed the next stance. Once again its height was severely limited by an overhang. Adrian went next, tackling the pitch differently: he jammed as far out along the crack as he could and then pendulumed on his arms, just reaching the first foothold.

John arrived in the back of the zawn, told me to wait until he had his camera ready, and then sent me off. 'It's easy for the first move,' he said, with his usual bonhomie. I had to bridge across the corner to unclip from the runner. Adrian's method seemed to be the better one. The jams were poor and the rugosities all sloped the wrong way. But brooding on the problem only wasted strength and I swung. My left foot hooked on to the first foothold and I gained enough purchase to bring my arms across. Another move and I was into the corner. It wasn't very restful as there were no footholds there either. 'You've done it once you're in the corner,' lied John. The overhang above the stance prevented me from pulling straight over and I had to move out round to the point of the nose. Ian looked blandly at my hands as they scrabbled for a hold among the coils of rope and his feet. I failed to find one, sank back, and then heaved over the edge.

Dave chuntered round next, finding the same difficulty in finishing while Ian and Adrian continued ahead. The next pitch was a wider zawn which looked easier than it actually was. The holds were good but awkwardly spaced and the shelving ledge that provided footholds was wet from the water trickling down the cliff wall. The pitch was probably just VS.

It ended on yet another nose, after which came a longer pitch of some sixty feet. When I arrived Ian and Adrian were already at the far end and I waited as Dave and John came round. The pitch consisted of three typical recesses and should have been much easier climbing than I made of it. You can practically walk into the first recess but I mistakenly traversed with my hands where my feet should have been. I baulked the last move long enough for John to tell one of his interminable jokes about the Pope. I decided to go just as he came to the punchline, which I missed, thus inflicting the whole joke on the party again at the other end of the pitch.

The end was in sight from the next stance. An easy ledge led to a narrow zawn just beyond which was a rope hanging down the cliff face. It had been drizzling earlier but we had been sheltered by the overhangs. Although it was dry now the sky was darkening. The tide was coming in. Fortunately I did not realise it would be another four hours before I was at the top of the cliff.

John explained that we had now come to the irreversible move. 'Alvarez had to be hauled across but he's short. Ha ha!' he said. The zawn was about five feet wide. 'You just fall over until your hands can reach the opposite wall, then you bridge across, move your hands down and jam them into the crack, bring your back foot over, monkey round into balance, and then hand traverse to the end,' he said proudly. 'It's very simple,' he added, with the confidence of a man who knew he was big enough to make the initial move.

I only arrived in time to see Ian flexing his drained hand

muscles at the far end of the pitch. Adrian fell across the gap, found he had his feet wrong, came back, and then bridged across at full stretch. He pulled across successfully, extended himself on the hand traverse, and then flexed his muscles too.

Now my turn. I didn't so much fall across to the opposite wall as make a reluctant flop. I found myself staring at the waves that were tumbling into the back of the zawn twenty feet below. I brought my foot across. It was a good twelve inches short of the foothold just below the crack where I was to jam my hands. I came back. 'It won't reach, John,' I said.

'Step a bit lower down this side,' said John. I did, and strained across, thigh muscles aching. 'Put the back of your heel on that nick just below where your foot is now,' said John.

I did so, an act of utter faith. Poised above the sea, my stomach level with my chin, my left foot pawed for the hold. One lunge, two, and then it touched. 'I've got it, John,' I shouted. 'I've got it.'

My moment of glory lasted perhaps half a second. There was a baffling hiatus and I found myself five feet below the traverse line suspended above the sea by the ropes. 'For God's sake don't pull me back,' I thought. But Ian and Adrian won the tug of war and I got a hold on the rock on the other side of the zawn. I climbed up to the traverse line, did the hand traverse, and pulled over on to the ledge. 'I hope you got that,' I shouted back to John.

'I was too busy hanging on to you,' John shouted.

'Perhaps it's just as well,' I said.

Dave arrived next. 'I thought if Gillman can reach it I'll be all right,' he said – he is four inches taller than me. 'But it was full stretch.' John, last across, was delighted with the way things had gone.

It was 3.30 and we had come to the end of the climb. In summer you follow a ledge system for about twenty-five feet until it arrives at water level, strip down to your masters, and then swim across the Black Zawn. The first man takes a rope to haul everybody's gear across. The way up the other side is easy.

But this was December. Ian said he'd do the swims so that John could take a picture but we managed to talk him out of it. 'The way out,' as Dougal Haston says in *Eiger Direct*, 'was up.'

John produced from his rucksack his pair of magic jumars, souvenir of the Red Wall television extravaganza. Only Ian had used them before. I had never used hiebelers or prusik loops before either. I assumed it was like standing in slings – all right once you got used to it.

The rope hung down from an overhang above us. John went first, steadily but rather slowly. It was about seventy feet to the top of the cliff. The rope was laid, not as easy for jumaring on as perlon, and the clamps did not appear to slide up the rope very easily. John rested a number of times and negotiated the overhang by reaching up over it, clipping a hiebeler on to the rope, and pulling up on that. He disappeared.

By now it was half light and had begun to rain. The wind was blowing up and waves were sweeping powerfully into the Black Zawn to our left. Ian gave me a lesson in the essentials of jumaring – weight on one sling while you push up on the other clamp. I had the usual total confidence that anything an experienced climber told me to do would work.

I made progress at first, although it was very slow and I was obviously using too much arm strength. The rope swung about and the clamps seemed very hard to push up. Then my foot came out of one of the slings and it was difficult to tie it on again. The rain was heavy now and the rocks glistened in the light of the head-torch shone from below. The waves were lashing against the cliff. I had swung away from our ledge and was now dangling free above the irreversible zawn.

It would be tedious to detail the way I gradually lost control of the situation. My feet started to splay outwards and I danced on the rope as if it was being shaken violently from above. I got a foothold on the rock face and stood there only just in balance. I had a sling between the top jumar and my waist which was meant to allow me to rest but it was too loose. I knew I had to get off the rock face and in trying to get back into position on the rope I flipped upside down.

I had only shouted 'Help' twice before in my life, both times when I thought I was drowning. Once was in heavy seas during a regatta off the Isle of Wight, the other when I got mixed up with the breakers at Sunset Beach in Hawaii. I knew the moment I shouted it this time that it was a pointless thing to say, as I was the only person who could get myself out of trouble.

There should now follow the story of how I fought with myself, forcing myself to balance upright in the slings, painfully relearning the technique of jumaring, and pushing myself inexorably up the rope to safety. I pulled myself upright and looked up. The top twenty-five feet of the cliff were smooth, with no holds for rests anywhere. I knew that once I had left the ledge I was now on I was deeply committed. I had used up a great deal of strength already.

The others on the ledge below were yelling encouragement, whatever they may have been thinking. John was invisible above. I did a simple sum in my head. Surely four of them could pull me up? And that is why the story that should follow does not. I shouted up to John: 'Let me down on the safety rope.'

The three below shouted, 'If you come down you'll only have to get back up again.'

I didn't tell them what I had decided. 'I'll swim,' I shouted back.

'You can't,' they shouted, and they were quite right. The waves were now pouring in like tanks.

John did not seem to have heard me. 'Let me down on the safety rope,' I yelled into the wind.

His voice drifted back: 'I have.'

I found that I was still clipped into a jumar with a sling. I hauled myself up on it three times before I got enough weight off it to release the crab. I had just time to think, This shouldn't be happening, as I plummeted down, and then I felt the beautiful deceleration of the rope. I was dangling over the irreversible zawn – John must have paid out the safety rope in response to my demands until there were twenty feet of slack. The others pulled me on to the ledge with the back rope and I sprawled there apologising.

Ian at once took control. He climbed up to where I had left the jumars – I had thought of bringing them down with me but decided not to in case I dropped them. Ian came back down with them and sent Adrian off. He made very good progress. As he climbed I asked Ian: 'Do you think four of you would be able to pull me up?'

'I don't know, Pete,' he said, rather disconcertingly.

I looked at the white-streaked waves pounding at the cliff below us. 'We should have a couple of hours before the tide reaches us, shouldn't we?'

'I don't know,' said Ian again.

I wished he wouldn't keep saying that.

As Adrian reached the top he gave a thumbs-up sign in the light of the head-torch we were shining from below. Now it was Dave's turn. He received his instructions and set off. He had a chest harness for safety and an abseil sling to sit in, whereas I had tried to stand up in both slings. He went very slowly at first and then came back to sort out his slings and start again. He set off and this time his progress was slow but steady. He took long pauses in between pulls but eventually disappeared over the top.

Ian told me that if they were going to try to pull me up they would take the climbing rope in slowly and give several yells. I was to try to help them by climbing on the jumar rope. I told Ian I would be able to climb on the cliff until those last twenty-five feet. 'Good luck,' he said as he set off.

'Good luck to you,' I replied, though aware I was not in a strong position for saying it. I shone the torch on him, sometimes swinging it down to look at the sea. Occasional waves were now throwing spray up on to the ledge where I stood.

Ian disappeared over the edge of the cliff and I was alone. I started thinking about my children and told myself to stop being morbid. I kept looking at the rope to see if it was being pulled in. At least six times I decided to give up climbing.

After about twenty minutes the rope started to snake upwards. I made sure the two ropes were free from each other. There was a tug at my waist and I started off up the wall facing me. I had made only three moves when the pull of the rope swung me off the holds and round over the zawn again, where I dangled free. But the steady pulls from above continued and I managed to kick up on holds on the wall.

About two-thirds of the way up the pulling stopped and I managed to stand precariously on a ledge, the rope tugging so hard at my waist that my head began to swim. I made a little height and yelled: 'I won't be able to help you much above here. Pull when you're ready.' I gripped the rope and tried to walk up the wall. But in no time I was over the top, gasping for breath like a stranded fish. Facing me were John, Dave and Ian who were pulling on the rope. Further up the cliff Adrian was acting as brake man.

I didn't know whether to make jokes or appear contrite. There was a fierce wind and driving rain but the others seemed cheerful enough. 'Thank you very much,' I said.

'That's okay,' said John. Ian said he had enjoyed himself, as he had never been on an epic in England before. Sodden, we stumbled to the cars. To complete our day, both had to be pushed out of the mud.

The first moral is, with hindsight, banal: a stormy December night at Swanage is no place to learn how to prusik. The second is more general: simply that Swanage is a serious place.

4

MYSTERIES AND ROWS

In 1972 I returned to Cerro Torre: not to the mountain itself, but to the vexed question of the first ascent claimed by Cesare Maestri in 1959. The article was a joint venture with Ken Wilson, then editing *Mountain* magazine at a time when it represented the best journalism any specialist climbing magazine has produced. Ken faced a difficulty which the second article in this section, 'A Walter Mitty on Craig Gogarth', shows at its most acute: how to tackle a contentious subject without the resources to defend any subsequent legal action. We joined forces for the Cerro Torre article, although the interview and article in *Mountain* was not much less explicit than mine in the *Sunday Times*. The Craig Gogarth article *was* far more forthright than anything that appeared in the climbing press, which confined itself to warning against the guide book descriptions of the disputed routes. It also followed the standard approach of newspaper investigations, particularly in the *Sunday Times* of the Harold Evans era. No legal actions ensued.

The *Financial Times* article was the last in a series I had written over a period of fifteen years, tracking Tom Holzel's obsession to prove that Mallory and Irvine could have reached the summit of Everest after all. In that time I found myself curiously persuaded by the ingenuity of Holzel's arguments, although I never quite plumbed the passion with which he presented them. I now accept Audrey Salkeld's judgment that Odell must have seen Mallory and Irvine on the Second Step, not the First, but I am happy, like her, to leave the matter unresolved.

*   *   *

Cerro Torre, the cheated summit

Sunday Times Magazine, 1972

E ric Jones came to the line of bolts first, the metal rings that formed their heads sitting squatly against the rock, eighteen inches apart. Hammered into holes made by a compressed-air drill, they provided a virtual ladder that slanted upwards across the vast granite slab at Jones's right and disappeared into the wraiths of cloud that the Patagonian wind was coiling about the mountain. Jones had reached this point on New Year's Eve, three weeks after the expedition had first set foot on Cerro Torre; they had climbed 4500 feet; 1500 feet remained. They had known that the Italian climber Cesare Maestri had used bolts, perhaps hundreds, when he had climbed the mountain a year before: but they had thought they were all in the almost sheer 500-foot headwall immediately below the summit. Darkness was already falling, and chunks of ice were tumbling down the wall crossed by the bolts. Jones and his partner Gordon Hibberd decided to retreat to the ice cave they had excavated on the steeply angled snow col at mid-height.

Leo Dickinson, who had spent the day in the Advance Base Camp at the foot of the mountain, decided late that afternoon to join them. As he reached the col the moon shone with such brilliance that it cast his shadow on the snow. He neared the cave moments before midnight and heard hoarse strains of 'Auld Lang Syne'. A cup of tea, laced with whisky, was thrust into his hand as he crawled into the cave. Soon they were discussing the day's climbing. 'What's going to happen,' asked Dickinson, 'when we come to Maestri's bolts on the headwall?' Jones answered him: 'It's already happened.'

A strict ethic governs the use of what climbers call artificial aids. Pitons are spikes which they drive into cracks with a hammer to enable them to advance up otherwise impossible rock. Where there's no crack, no chance of finding an alternative route, of lassooing a spike of rock, of using devices such as the skyhook, which can catch on the smallest flake of rock – where there's no other way of making progress at all, a climber, in the last resort, places a bolt. A bolt has a circular blade and a smaller eye than a piton – and the crucial difference is that the climber has to drill a hole in the rock for it first. It takes fifteen strenuous minutes, using a masonry bit and a piton hammer, but if it were any easier, climbers feel, there would be too much of a temptation to use them, and it would somehow be unfair to the mountain besides; some climbers still feel that the use of bolts can *never* be justified.

So when in 1970 the Italian mountaineer Cesare Maestri took to Cerro Torre a compressed-air drill which enabled him to place fifteen bolts an hour, most climbers saw a difference only of degree between doing this and landing on the summit by helicopter.

Before they left for Patagonia in November 1971, the British expedition were in no doubt about what they thought of Maestri's methods. 'Ridiculous and senseless,' said Cliff Phillips, a twenty-six-year-old professional mountaineer from Snowdonia. 'It would be nice to climb the mountain without bolts,' said Leo Dickinson, a twenty-five-year-old photographer from Blackpool who was the prime mover behind the expedition, 'to give it back its good name.' And the British climbers decided that they would not use Maestri's bolts.

They had originally planned to take the route attempted by the previous British expedition in 1968, following the mountain's South-East Ridge from the col into the ice towers some 800 feet below the summit, and then moving left to look for a way through the ice to the top.

But now this way seemed impossible: the ridge above seemed plastered with a sugary snow, loose and untrustworthy. The only alternative, it seemed, was across the wall where Maestri had placed his bolts. 'After a lot of soul-searching,' said Dickinson, dictating his thoughts at the time into a portable tape-recorder, 'we have decided we would climb up these bolts. It's a question not of black and white but what degree of grey is acceptable. People who criticise us should come out here and see for themselves the conditions – the wind, the ice, the tremendous exposure. It's very, very hard not to be human and fall for the temptation. We have completely changed our minds and we're not going to hide anything. But it's impossible to climb this ridge without involving yourself in Maestri's efforts. If you use one bolt, you might as well use ten, and if you use ten, you might as well use 300. But we are not very happy at all.'

All the same, the expedition did decide that they would make their stand at the foot of the 500-foot headwall leading to the summit. 'We're not going to use his bolts there,' Dickinson declared, 'even though it might be hypocritical in that we've used them already. We're going to use the crack system we think we can see, and either climb it or fail.'

Throughout the discussions that still continued, one thing was agreed. Maestri had ruined their expedition, and he had ruined – despoiled, violated – the mountain they had come 8000 miles to climb.

Cerro Torre is a granite spire near the southern tip of Patagonia whose beguiling beauty has beckoned the world's best climbers for nearly twenty years. Comparatively low – 10,280 feet – it is in one of the most inhospitable regions of the world, 125 miles north of the Strait of Magellan, and the first peak in the Fitzroy group of the Andes to face the 100 mph Pacific storms that blast in across the continental ice cap. Its summit is a fantastic confection of ice, with enormous overhangs formed by the wind. Good weather – clear skies, light winds – comes perhaps two or three days a month.

One of the first expeditions to attempt the mountain was led by the great Italian Walter Bonatti in 1958. He failed. Cesare Maestri, whose name dominates the controversial history of Cerro Torre, failed in the same year. He returned in 1959 with the Austrian alpinist Toni Egger. By late January they had reached the mountain's North Col, and then started up the 2500-foot ice-plastered East Face. 'At each step,' wrote Maestri afterwards, 'the whole crust made a dull noise like a low whistle; it cracked and broke and large pieces fell off. The ice pegs went in like butter and gave us only an illusion of security. At the end of each pitch we made a small platform so that we could drill through to the rock, where we found not the slightest trace of a crack; so we had to drill holes for bolts, and each hole needed 500 hammer blows.'

The next day, they climbed up walls 'plastered with snow and ice'; after bivouacking 450 feet from the summit in an ice hole, they reached the top on the fourth morning. But now the weather broke, and Maestri and Egger began a desperate retreat. Snow and ice were avalanching down the route – and on the sixth night Egger was swept to his death. Maestri was rescued, semi-conscious and delirious, by the third member of the ex-pedition. The French alpinist Lionel Terray, who had seen Cerro Torre from the summit of Fitzroy seven years earlier, described their ascent as 'the greatest mountaineering feat of all time'.

It was some time before anyone perceived possible irony in Terray's words. But then some of the more puzzling aspects of

Maestri's account began to obtrude. He had no summit pictures – Egger had been carrying the camera, he said; and his colourful description of the ascent contained few technical details. How, for example, had they penetrated the enormous summit cornices? And how had it been possible to climb 2500 feet of such appalling difficulty, placing pitons and bolts, in only three days?

In 1968 the first British expedition, with Dougal Haston, Mick Burke, Martin Boysen and Peter Crew visited Cerro Torre. I went with them, to report on their attempt. They followed the mountain's steep, smooth South-East Ridge and came to within 1000 feet of the summit. But then we spent thirty-five days sheltering in our Base Camp from the wind which hurtled through the trees like an express train. When the climbers returned to the mountain, they found that the fixed ropes they had left in place had been impossibly twisted and torn. But they had been able to scrutinise Maestri's East Face, extremely steep and still coated with ice – and where they had been open-minded before, several went home sceptical about Maestri's claim. An Argentinian expedition failed at the same time, as did a later Japanese attempt.

In 1970 Carlo Mauri, an Italian who had been with Bonatti in 1958, led a strong team for his second attempt. He attacked from the west again, reached the bulging ice 500 feet below the summit, before retreating once more in bad weather.

Now, in the same year, Maestri announced he was going to attempt Torre Egger, the spire next to Cerro Torre, named after Maestri's companion of 1959. But in Patagonia, even though it was July – the Patagonian winter – he turned to Cerro Torre again. He had with him a compressed-air drill with which to place the 1000 bolts he expected to have to use. The effort needed just to take it on to the mountain was extraordinary: together with the motor, fuel, tubing, and a winch to haul it up the mountain, it weighed perhaps 400 pounds. Maestri spent two months following the South-East Ridge, and in that time reached little higher than the British had done. Maestri waited in Iturbe for four months, returned south in November, and completed his route, bolting his way up the headwall to the summit plateau – although he did not try to climb the 200-foot mound of ice that constitutes the mountain's highest point.

When the news of his ascent broke, it was heralded as a triumph of tenacity and endurance in the Italian press – and greeted with criticism and scorn by climbing magazines. 'Maestri rapes Cerro Torre', said Britain's *Mountain*.

In the USA, *Ascent* asked why, if Maestri had made such a brilliant ascent of Cerro Torre in 1959, should he want to return 'to blast his way up the same mountain in this most technologically absurd and questionable style?' Instead of confirming Maestri's estimation that he was capable of having climbed the mountain, his ascent only served to raise even more doubts that he had done so in 1959.

The British expedition, sponsored by John Player Ltd, which flew to Argentina last November, was stronger even than the 1968 team. Dickinson, Jones, Phillips, and Peter Minks, a twenty-four-year-old plumber from Birkenhead, had climbed the North Face of the Eiger together in 1970, and Dickinson's film of the ascent was shown on Yorkshire TV. Dickinson also filmed on Cerro Torre. The fifth man was Gordon Hibberd, thirty-four, an electrician from Barnsley, who climbed the Fortress with Ian Clough's expedition to Chilean Patagonia in 1968; the sixth, the Swiss Hans-Peter Trachsel, who had climbed the North Face of the Eiger three times.

They arrived in their Base Camp in the forest below the Torre's glacier lake on 30 November, and began climbing the mountain on 6 December, reaching the snow col on 23 December. On 28 December they started up the mountain's 2500-foot summit spire. On only two or three days was the weather perfect; on the others the wind gusted coldly, cloud churned about them, and slabs of ice slid down the mountain. They encountered clusters of Maestri's bolts at his stopping points between each 100- or 150-foot pitch, but these they regarded not as immoral, simply unnecessary. 'All around,' says Dickinson, 'were cracks that would have taken normal pegs. It looked as though someone had let fly with a heavy machine-gun.'

But then came the bolt ladder itself, which was to cause them so much soul-searching. On 3 January, Trachsel led across it, with Jones following. 'The man is a fool,' he called back to Jones, when he came to a fifteen-foot ledge he could walk along – but where the line of bolts continued none the less.

After some very hard climbing without bolts, Jones and Trachsel spent the night perched on a three-foot ledge, but in the morning Jones, who had twisted his left knee, found he could put no weight on it at all. 'In frustration, anger, and almost crying,' he says, 'I had to explain I couldn't go on.'

Phillips and Hibberd took over the lead, and on 7 January reached the strange ice towers at the foot of the final headwall. 'They were like huge, mushroom-shaped domes,' says Hibberd. 'Not hard ice, but very soft and sugary – you could push your arm right into them.'

The expedition's decision that they would climb the headwall without Maestri's bolts or fail in the attempt proved unnecessary: for the point that Hibberd and Phillips reached was the highest point the expedition was to attain. The storms returned – and the climbers were to wait forty days for good weather again.

On 16 February they climbed back up to the snow col. But, like the British in 1968, they found their fixed ropes worn and frayed; and there was real danger from ice cascading down the mountain. 'There was nothing for it,' says Jones, 'but to go home.'

All climbers have to come to terms with failure, and the expedition had made a strong attempt. But there was something more to contend with – a bitter after-taste, the frustration of travelling to one of the most beautiful, most perfect mountains in the world, and finding it full of bolts.

'That particular ridge,' says Eric Jones, 'is the best ridge on the mountain, and he's ruined it.' And had he climbed the mountain in 1959? 'I can't see it,' says Hibberd.

Cesare Maestri lives in a spacious third-floor apartment in the mountain resort of Madonna di Campiglio, in the Dolomites. Four of us met him there: Leo Dickinson, Ken Wilson – editor of *Mountain* – myself, and an interpreter. He greeted us warmly, and offered us coffee and schnapps in his study; pictures of Cerro Torre, and himself, hung on the walls. Still very fit at forty-three, he exercises with weights on his balcony overlooking Madonna's main street. He has just written a book about his ascent of Cerro Torre, which is on sale in his sports equipment shop 100 yards up the street. But he has little contact with Italy's leading alpinists, and chooses his expedition members from local climbers. All accept that Maestri will do all the lead climbing; that they will literally stay in second place.

'My friends know the score,' said Maestri. 'It's one of the conditions imposed at the start. Cerro Torre in 1959 was the one and only exception. Right from the start we had agreed that Egger would lead the ice pitches. He was a brilliant ice climber and just as good on rock, and our speed was due to his brilliance.

He could get up in an hour what other climbers would have taken two days to do. I wish more people could have seen him climb.'

On leaving Cerro Torre, deeply affected by Egger's death, Maestri decided he would never return, and even gave up climbing altogether. But then, he states in his book, his wife Fernanda persuaded him to climb again – although he did promise not to take part in any more expeditions. So why had he returned to Cerro Torre? Was it to meet the doubts about his climb in 1959?

'Suppose,' said Maestri, 'you worked in a bank and, just before you were to retire, you heard a rumour that you had walked off with £10,000 of the bank's money. What would you do? Would you go to court and try to prove your innocence? Or, if you could clear your name by one theatrical gesture, would you choose that? Even if it involved danger, wouldn't you take the latter course?'

In fact, said Maestri, the gesture continues, for he deliberately took no pictures on the summit plateau in 1970. 'There *is* proof of our ascent, but it's up on the mountain. If any doubters want to know, let them go and find out for themselves. Just below the summit they will find our compressor. It's up to anyone who repeats the route to prove to *me* that *he* reached the summit. But I don't mind how he gets there. You'll never find me criticising another climber for the techniques he uses.'

The winter expedition cost £13,000 and the return in the summer a further £6500. Atlas Copco, a Swedish building equipment firm, whose Italian headquarters are in Milan, made the compressor especially, contributed to the cost of the expedition, and issued publicity pictures of Maestri practising with the drill. 'I would accept money from anyone,' said Maestri. But taking the compressor, he explained, was in keeping with his character: 'I have spent most of my life trying to push forward the limits of climbing, and climbing technique in general . . . When all these other expeditions started failing on the South-East Ridge although they were composed of good climbers, it seemed to me that the route must be impossible by normal means.

'I calculated that up to 1000 bolts would be required, and I decided to try the compressor as a possible way of overcoming this problem. I don't care much for ethics, and I don't believe they exist in climbing. I have always been right at the forefront of the development of techniques and I'll use whatever technique is necessary to get up a given piece of rock. One day they will invent a glue that is adhesive enough to support me, and I'll be quite ready to use that.'

Actually, said Maestri, he wasn't sure that the compressor was worth all the trouble. 'It's just too heavy – the time you save drilling holes is wasted pulling the compressor up.' He placed some 300 bolts, he estimated – the British thought there were more – as well as those at the stances, or stopping places. He didn't really want to take it when he returned in November. 'But seeing that Atlas had paid me I thought that I'd better. They did pretty well out of it. They got lots of publicity. I reckon that Atlas started a lot of the controversy so as to get more publicity.' He is planning to return to Patagonia to attempt Torre Egger. 'I won't take another compressor then, but I'll still be able to get money out of Atlas because they know that their name will be bandied about.'

We talked of Maestri's other climbing in the Alps, and then returned to 1959: could he give us more details of his ascent? 'I wonder why it is that I am the only one who has to supply proof of his ascent. What about Terray on Fitzroy, or Messner on Nanga Parbat? Is there any proof that they were successful? It is said that a person who is always thinking about theft is really a thief himself.'

We asked Maestri if he could mark the line of his climb on a photograph. 'You must be joking. I can't remember the exact line after all this time, but I can tell you that where we went up it wasn't all that difficult. It was just very dangerous. On the descent we made a mistake and went down the wrong gully.'

Could he give more details? 'Are you saying that I didn't get to the summit? What details do you want? What details are there? I'm perfectly willing to answer any questions, but I don't understand why you have left this to the end of the interview. It's rather impolite, I think. How many cases can you remember where routes have been done very quickly when snow conditions were favourable, while repeat ascent parties have blown their minds? How can I give you this detail? Where am I going to get it from? Let me ask Leo how long he has been climbing. Ten years? How much can you remember about routes you did ten years ago? I can't even remember the details of routes I did five years ago. I wrote it all down at the time. There are a number of articles, and there is an account in my book. Suppose I had something to hide; do you imagine that I couldn't have perfected my story in the past thirteen years? The fact is that it has all slipped my mind. I don't know how many pegs I put in, and that sort of thing. Why don't you read the accounts I wrote at the time?'

During the later stages of the interview, Maestri had been scribbling notes in a notebook, then screwing up the pages and throwing them away. Now he tore out a sheet and handed it to me. It said: *'Tione Brescia Est. Autostrada per Milano'* – the instructions for driving back to Milan. After a few more questions we left. As we drove to catch our plane, we listened to the tapes of the interview. 'When you left Cerro Torre in 1959 did you think you would ever return?' I had asked.

'I never expected to go back,' Maestri had replied. 'I know looking back over my life that I don't really feel regret about anything except one thing, and that was going to Cerro Torre in 1959. It has given me a great deal of satisfaction but it has also caused me more anguish than anything else. If I could wave a magic wand and lay Cerro Torre flat across the pampas I would do so.'

A Walter Mitty on Craig Gogarth

Sunday Times, 1969

On Tuesday last week Pete Crew, one of Britain's top dozen rock-climbers, stood beneath a seventy-foot overhanging crack known as Gael's Wall on Craig Gogarth, a sea cliff in Anglesey, and pronounced it 'a chop route', a killer.

To the left of the crack was Crew's own route, Fail Safe, which followed a narrow ramp to a line of overhangs. 'We thought it looked easy,' said Crew, 'but it was far steeper than we thought. On Gael's Wall you'd just flake out after twenty feet.'

A few days before this incident, and seemingly unconnected, *Mountain*, Britain's leading climbing magazine, printed an unprecedented statement from the Apollo Mountaineering Club in the Midlands disowning one of its former members.

But these were the final moves in a controversy which has preoccupied the climbing world for over a year, and which amounts to nothing less than one of the biggest sensations in the history of British climbing. For nearly a year, its central figure had led many leading British climbers, including Crew himself, to believe that he ranked among them.

EIGER DIRECT, 1966. *Above left,* the youthful Chris Bonington, embarking on his career as photo-journalist.

Above right, John Harlin, the blond Californian god.

Below, Dougal Haston, watchful and brooding.

HOY, 1967. Convocation of the gods: *(left to right)*, Brown, Haston, Bonington, McNaught-Davis, Patey, Crew.

Haston at work on the Old Man's South-East Arête, belayed by Crew.

CERRO TORRE, 1967-68. The beckoning spire.

Left, the 8000-ft West Face of Fitzroy, seen by so few.

Below, the team assembles; Burke, Boysen, Haston and Crew plus *(left)* Gillman – the supernumerary?

FALLEN HEROES. *Above left,* Mick Burke, on Everest, 1975. *Above right,* Nick Estcourt. *Below,* Joe Tasker *(left)* and Pete Boardman on K2 in 1978. *Opposite,* Tom Patey on a magical day in GlenLair, 1969; with him, Mary Ann Hudson and Jim McArtney, killed on Ben Nevis in 1970; beyond, Allen Fyffe and would-be photographer Gillman.

RUNNING RISKS. Julie Tullis with Kurt Diemberger *(right)* and Spanish climber Mari Abrego, shortly before her fatal attempt on K2.

Stephen Venables, in mortal peril on the South Col shortly after climbing Everest.

PERSONAL NOTES. *Above left,* Dave Condict poses on the author's first climb, Amphitheatre Buttress in Snowdonia. *Above right,* author fails on pendule move on Traverse of the Gods, Swanage.

Author with family – Seth, Leni, Danny – in the Glyders in 1978, with the Carneddau behind.

SCOTTISH DELIGHTS. Danny Gillman on a transcendental evening ascent of Blaven on Skye.

Peter Gillman triumphant on Beinn Narnain in the Southern Highlands.

The controversy had small beginnings. In 1961, Keith McCallum founded the Apollo Mountaineering Club, the same club that was eventually to shun him. Few of the members at first had much climbing experience, and McCallum emerged naturally as the club's dominant personality.

'He was like a god almost,' says Ron Brownley, the club's present treasurer. 'He told us he'd been to the Alps and the Dollies, and once said a German had asked him to go on the North Face of the Eiger.'

McCallum produced the first issue of the club's magazine in 1964, when it contained five articles he had written himself, including an account of an ascent of the Comici Route, a long and serious climb in the Dolomites. The same issue, and later ones, also contained articles signed 'J. S. Martin', 'J. Irvine', and 'J. McLean'.

In January 1967, Ken Wilson, a friend of Pete Crew, a member of the Climbers' Club and the present editor of *Mountain*, gave an illustrated talk to the club. Wilson found McCallum knowledgeable and keen to help with guidebooks, so he gave his name to Tony Moulam, who was editing a guide to the Snowdon East area.

Climbs in Wales are graded into one of seven categories: easy, moderate, difficult, very difficult, severe, very severe, and extreme. 'Easy' climbs are little more than a scramble; the harder 'extremes' represent the physical limits of adhesion and nerve. Guidebook writers carry out the laborious task of checking the climbs in their area in their spare time and receive offers of help enthusiastically.

McCallum was soon writing to Tony Moulam with details of the existing routes he had checked and new routes he said he was putting up on several smaller crags in the area. He also wrote to Wilson about the work he was doing, and in July mentioned a new route called Samurai Groove on Carreg Hyll-Drem. It was, he said, 'pretty desperate – I've still got the shakes.'

At the same time he was writing about his new routes to Nigel Rogers, a doctor in chemistry at Lancaster University and editor of the Climbers' Club annual publication *New Climbs*, and to Pete Crew in Llanberis, resident expert on climbing developments in Snowdonia.

This was when Craig Gogarth, the most exciting discovery in Wales for over a decade, was still being developed by climbers eagerly snapping up the plethora of new lines still available. In

September, McCallum wrote to Crew telling him he had just put up three new routes there, which he called Tam Dubh, Hielan'man and A'Bhaisteir.

'I had a certain feeling of sickness that this guy was doing climbs which I had lined up as possible routes myself,' says Crew. 'But there was a feeling of discovery, too – we had come across an up-and-coming lad.' Crew visited the Apollo Club with Wilson to give a lecture in October 1967, and remembers being surprised to find that McCallum was in his mid-thirties. 'But we had no doubts at all that his climbs were genuine,' says Crew.

Exceptionally among sports, climbing relies on its participants to be utterly truthful about their achievements. Illustrating this was the first episode which only retrospectively was to cast doubt on McCallum's claims.

Les and Laurie Holliwell, two brothers among the climbers hard at work on Gogarth, had seen a line following a yellow groove on the Upper Tier. On 1 October, 1967, they climbed it, taking four hours. The following week at the Padarn Lake Hotel – the pub in Llanberis where climbers congregate on Saturday nights – they told Pete Crew of their new route. 'Pete said McCallum had claimed to have climbed it a month previously,' says Laurie Holliwell. 'I must admit we were rather surprised.'

McCallum had in fact called the climb A'Bhaisteir. The Holliwell brothers wrote to McCallum saying they had encountered immense quantities of loose rock, and asking how he had avoided it. McCallum replied that he and McLean had been unable to throw down the loose rock because there were too many people watching from beneath.

Soon afterwards McCallum told Wilson about a further new route: Gael's Wall, just to the right of Crew's line Fail Safe. It was, McCallum said, 'continually hard and poorly protected – the hardest thing I have done at Anglesey.'

In April 1968 the new edition of *New Climbs* was published, containing descriptions of twelve new routes on Craig Gogarth, including no fewer than five by McCallum and his partner J. McLean. *New Climbs* also had twenty-eight other climbs led by McCallum partnered by McLean, Martin, and Irvine. The new routes came as a bombshell to the Apollo Climbing Club.

If his climbs were genuine McCallum would have a right to be ranked among the leading climbers active in Wales at that time, and there was a natural curiosity about both McCallum and his partners. To try to satisfy this curiosity, Crew and

Wilson began to gather as much information as they could about the climbs – and some strange factors began to emerge. McCallum had claimed to have put up four new routes – including three 'hard very severes' – on one day. This, says Crew, was 'unlikely'.

Crew also discovered that on the day when McCallum said he had climbed Gael's Wall, the Holliwell brothers had been gardening a potential new route only fifty yards to its left – and they had not seen McCallum at all that day.

Several climbers told Crew that they had repeated, or tried to repeat, McCallum routes, and that the descriptions seemed inaccurate.

There was considerable consternation when Crew and Wilson reported their findings. 'We had really frantic discussions,' says Crew. 'Everybody realised how important it was to get at the truth.' Crew and Wilson decided to take a closer look at Gael's Wall, the hardest route McCallum had claimed to have done.

By chance, they met McCallum on their way to the clifftop and invited him to the Padarn that evening.

When Crew abseiled to the foot of Gael's Wall he discovered at the bottom that he hung almost ten feet clear of the rock. In addition to its angle, the crack that the route followed was broad and shallow, making it almost impossible to use hand jams; it was also 'blind', rendering it unreceptive to pitons. 'This for me was the clincher,' says Crew. 'I realised that the whole thing was ridiculous.'

McCallum did not go to the Padarn that night, and the situation had now become urgent: Crew and Wilson were strongly aware of the danger of allowing McCallum's published climbs to remain unchallenged.

'We tried to contact as many people as possible so that no one would get hurt trying to follow his descriptions,' says Crew. It was felt that the time had come to confront McCallum himself. And it was not long before the opportunity to do so was provided.

By chance, Ken Wilson met Ron Brownley in a pub on the A5 one Sunday evening on the way home from Wales, and questioned him closely about McCallum. Brownley told him that McLean, Martin and Irvine were unknown to anyone in the Apollo Club, and that the new routes that McCallum claimed represented climbing of a higher standard than any at which they had seen him perform.

This was all Wilson needed, and on 15 July 1968 in a letter to

McCallum, he said that after several months of uncertainty he was now in possession of sufficient evidence to lead him to the conclusion that many of the routes he claimed seemed in doubt. He asked McCallum to produce McLean or Martin as eyewitnesses to his new routes.

'My conscience is clear,' McCallum wrote back. 'If you choose to believe the routes do not exist that is up to you . . .'

At a meeting last week, *Sunday Times* reporters asked McCallum if he would bring forward his seconds, Martin, Irvine, and McLean. 'I don't see any reason why I should, frankly,' said McCallum.

After they had received McCallum's petulant and inconclusive letter, the problem preoccupying Crew and Wilson was what step to take next. Then the magazine *Rocksport* published an editorial in which it emphasised that theirs was a sport in which lives were at stake and warning of the necessity for accounts of routes to be absolutely reliable.

Yet in referring to unspecified 'rumours' in the climbing world *Rocksport* only deepened the mystery for many climbers, and Wilson took the chance to persuade Nigel Rogers to publish a statement in *Mountaincraft* (now *Mountain*). Rogers listed twenty-eight routes claimed by McCallum in *New Climbs 1968*, and concluded: 'It's emphasised that the greatest caution should be exercised by anyone attempting to repeat these routes.'

The Apollo Club took its own action when, on 31 October, its twenty-five members decided to 'terminate' McCallum's membership.

But perhaps the most disturbing aspect of the whole affair then ensued. The Apollo members discovered soon after Mc-Callum had left the club that he had published a guidebook to a number of crags in the Snowdon East area. The guide records sixteen first ascents by McCallum with Martin or Irvine.

When *Mountaincraft* finally published Nigel Rogers's statement, most climbers were satisfied that the controversy had been resolved. Further evidence to convince any still in doubt came last weekend, when the Holliwell brothers, previously cautious in their judgments, followed the line of McCallum's route, Hielan'man. 'This convinced me without any doubt at all that he hadn't done it,' says Laurie Holliwell. McCallum had claimed to have done Hielan'man and another first ascent on Craig Gogarth in one day – yet the Holliwells, two of the most skilled and forceful climbers now active, began the climb on

Saturday and finished it in darkness on Sunday evening.

Despite the furore that raged about him, McCallum today stands by his routes, and says that he is waiting for the 'other side' to make the next move. 'They started the whole bloody business and it's on their plates and that's the way I'm leaving it.' He seems, however, to have disappeared from the haunts of climbers.

'I don't derive the same pleasure from climbing that I used to,' he concedes. 'One got so terribly wrapped up in this thing. It became a little bit of an obsession. Then one began to see there were different values in climbing and that the hardest climbs weren't the be-all and end-all of climbing.

'I may start climbing again when I get back a bit of form.'

Backtracking on Everest

Sunday Times, 1981

Tucked away on page 353 of a new history of Mount Everest to be published this week* is a remarkable statement. 'There seems little doubt now,' writes the author, Walt Unsworth, 'that the Chinese did climb Everest in 1960.'

That judgment reflects a considerable volte-face in the mountaineering world. When the Chinese claimed their ascent twenty-one years ago they were greeted with widespread scepticism. Gradually, almost surreptitiously, that view has changed. When *Mountain* magazine published a complete list of Everest ascents last Christmas, it slipped in the names of the three Chinese summiteers. But Unsworth's assertion is the first explicit Western acceptance of the ascent.

First news of the Chinese claim to have climbed Everest – they used the pre-imperialist name Chomolungma, Goddess Mother of the Earth – came in May 1960. But when fuller accounts reached the West they were less than convincing. While the expedition's leader Shih Chan-Chun attributed success to 'the leadership of the Communist Party, the unrivalled superiority of the socialist' and 'the strategic thinking of Mao Tze-Tung', technical details were sparse. Most startling of all, the three-man summit party had supposedly reached the top in darkness after climbing the final fifty metres without oxygen, while a fourth support climber had bivouacked all night in the open.

* *Everest* by Walt Unsworth, Allen Lane, 1981.

The Chinese could offer no summit photographs and the expedition film, first shown in Britain in 1962, did not help their case, as the highest point shown appeared to be no more than 8500 metres, some way below the formidable rock barrier known as the Second Step. The Royal Geographical Society and the Alpine Club held meetings to scrutinise the evidence and those who said they did not believe the Chinese claim included the 1953 British expedition member George Lowe and the broadcaster and pre-war Everest veteran Jack Longland.

Later ascents of Everest, however, began to make the Chinese claim appear more credible. Other expeditions have reached the top in semi-darkness with their oxygen supplies exhausted; several climbers have survived bivouacs near the summit; and further analysis of the highest Chinese pictures suggested that it was taken at 8700 metres, and therefore *above* the Second Step, with the way to the summit clear.

The greatest shift in Western opinion came when British and American mountaineers recently received permission to climb in China and met some of the 1960 expedition members. Climber Chu Yin-hua told vividly of suffering frostbite after taking off his boots to gain a better grip on the Second Step – and displayed his toeless feet. Chris Bonington, who has just returned from climbing in China, talked at length with the 1960 leader Shih Chan-Chun: 'I got to know him pretty well. I have no shadow of doubt whatsoever.'

The Chinese, meanwhile, appear to have learned from the episode. In 1975 they made a second ascent of Everest, and defiantly titled their account 'Another climb of the world's highest peak'. Once again, their claim was received with scepticism – 'ridiculously far-fetched,' snorted *Mountain* magazine. Four months later the British expedition attacking the South-West Face arrived at the summit to find a six-foot metal tripod anchored there as evidence of China's success.

The Everest enigma

Financial Times, 1986

It has been a sad mountaineering season in the Himalaya. Not only was there the multiple disaster on K2, in which Britain's Julie Tullis and Alan Rouse perished, but the appalling post-monsoon weather, with incessant high winds, has defeated almost every other expedition in the region.

Among the teams now completing their retreats is the strong British group which had hoped to climb the virgin North-East Ridge of Everest but which barely reached the true climbing difficulties. It was just one of half a dozen expeditions attempting Everest by various routes; only one – a Franco-Swiss pair who made a dramatic two-day ascent in August – reached the summit.

Yet, one Everest party – mainly an American venture – has returned satisfied. Perhaps perversely, the summit was only its ancillary objective, for it also hoped to resolve one of the most intriguing mysteries in the history of exploration.

It concerns George Mallory and Andrew Irvine, two figures from the heroic age of Himalayan mountaineering when. climbers wore Norfolk jackets and puttees and inhaled oxygen from heavy and unreliable apparatus strapped to their backs. In 1924, while making one of the earliest attempts on Everest, Mallory and Irvine disappeared after being last seen less than 1000 feet below the 29,028-foot summit, leaving the perpetual enigma of whether they reached it.

One member of this year's US expedition, Tom Holzel, has long been convinced that they could have done so – and hoped, by his visit to the scene of the drama, to prove it. Another member, the British mountaineering historian Audrey Salkeld, although initially sceptical, now regards Holzel's case as highly plausible.

Their arguments are contained in a book,* completed before they left and published last week, which also helps to explain why the fate of the two mountaineers has proved so beguiling a controversy. What they found on Everest last month has strengthened their belief that it could have been Mallory and not Sir Edmund Hillary and Sherpa Tenzing twenty-nine years later, who made the first ascent.

It was early on the morning of 8 June, 1924, that George Mallory, a thirty-eight-year-old Charterhouse schoolmaster, and his twenty-two-year-old companion, Oxford undergraduate Andrew Irvine, left the tenuous shelter of Camp 6 at 26,800 feet. Half a mile along the mountain's North-East Ridge, Everest's

---

* *The Mystery of Mallory and Irvine,* Tom Holzel and Audrey Salkeld, Jonathan Cape, 1986.

summit was etched white against a clear sky. In his last note, Mallory observed that their oxygen sets were 'a bloody load for climbing' (an unduly sensitive *Alpine Journal* editor later rendered Mallory's epithet as 'beastly') but that they had 'perfect weather for the job'.

Some 2000 feet below, moving up in support of their summit bid, was geologist Noel Odell. In mid-morning clouds drifted across the North-East Ridge, but at 12.50 p.m. they suddenly cleared. Odell's description, contained in a dispatch to *The Times*, has become one of the classic texts of mountaineering.

'The entire summit ridge and final peak of Everest were unveiled,' Odell wrote. 'My eyes became fixed on one tiny black spot silhouetted on a small snow-crest beneath a rock-step in the ridge; the black spot moved. Another black spot became apparent and moved up the snow to join the other on the crest. The first then approached the great rock-step and shortly emerged at the top; the second did likewise. Then the whole fascinating vision vanished, enveloped in cloud once more.' Mallory and Irvine were never seen again.

Just what Odell's 'fascinating vision' signified has been minutely debated. At first, Odell believed he had seen his colleagues surmount a buttress at around 28,300 feet known as the Second Step. As it was the last major obstacle, Odell concluded there was 'a strong possibility' that they had reached the summit, presumably dying through some mishap during their descent.

Later, Odell changed his mind, for the next British expedition to Everest in 1933 found the Second Step a daunting obstacle: Percy Wyn Harris described it as a 'dark-grey precipice, smooth and holdless'. It seemed doubtful whether Mallory and Irvine could have climbed it at all, let alone in five minutes as Odell had described. When he learned of this, Odell supposed that he must have seen them on the First Step, a buttress 300 feet lower down.

That made it far less likely that Mallory and Irvine could have succeeded – and a further item of evidence seemed conclusive. Above Camp 6, the 1933 climbers came upon Irvine's ice-axe, and deduced that it marked the point of a fatal slip during the two men's descent. It seemed to follow that they must have failed. For if they had been on the First Step when last seen, they could not possibly have reached the summit and returned to the site of the ice-axe before nightfall. Nor, with their primitive equipment, could they have survived a night's bivouac so high. The British climbing world sadly concluded that Mallory and Irvine must have met their deaths in gallant defeat.

Enter, forty years later, Tom Holzel. A tall and blue-eyed electronics engineer from Massachusetts, Holzel finds it hard to explain why his obsession with the legend of Mallory and Irvine took root, except that it began when he came across an account of Odell's dramatic sighting while perusing books in a public library. Holzel soon learned of the conventional wisdom that Mallory and Irvine must have failed – but then, after reading every available account, became convinced that this was not necessarily so.

For Holzel, the crux of the matter was oxygen. There was considerable hostility among Mallory's colleagues towards their apparatus, which they regarded as burdensome, unreliable, and even unethical – an 'artificial aid' in the contest with the mountain. Holzel believed that the prejudice against oxygen had led the mountaineering world to underestimate what Mallory and Irvine could have achieved. He produced tables to show the ascent rate of later climbers using oxygen, and calculated that the summit was within reach for Mallory and Irvine after all.

Holzel's conclusion rested upon two controversial assumptions. The first was that Mallory and Irvine had been sighted at the Second Step, as Odell had first believed; and if Odell had considered it a 'strong possibility' that they reached the summit from there, Holzel argued that with oxygen the chances were even higher.

The second was that having reached the Second Step, Mallory and Irvine decided to split up. For, as Holzel conceded, they would have had only enough oxygen left between them for one person to make a summit bid. Holzel therefore proposed that Mallory instructed Irvine to return to Camp 6 while he took the remaining oxygen and pressed on alone.

Then, however, by Holzel's scenario, disaster struck. While descending to Camp 6, Irvine fell at the point where his ice-axe was found. Mallory meanwhile came close to the summit, and perhaps even reached it, before he also fell to his death. When Holzel expounded his arguments in the British climbing press they caused a furore.

As Holzel himself recognised, the supposition that Mallory

and Irvine were on the Second Step required a considerable act of faith. But it was his contention that the two men had then separated that aroused the greatest anger. Would Mallory really have dispatched his inexperienced partner to Camp 6 alone, ignoring what Percy Wyn Harris termed his 'overwhelming responsibility' towards him and thereby transgressing one of the gravest canons in the climber's code?

In fact, as Holzel was able to point out, the history of Everest provides several such transgressions, born of the climbers' drive for success. In 1924 Edward Norton left his colleague, Howard Somervell, on the North Face while he also made a solo summit attempt; and on the British expedition of 1975 Mick Burke went on alone when his partner's oxygen set malfunctioned, a decision that led indirectly to Burke's death.

These examples led Holzel to speculate further just why the climbing world was so enraged. He had enlisted the help of Audrey Salkeld, a British researcher who supplied much of the material for the definitive history of Everest by Walt Unsworth, published in 1981. After further foraging among Britain's mountaineering archives, she was able to account for the potency of the myth.

By the time of the 1924 expedition, Mallory had become one of the heroic figures of his age. The process had begun twenty years before when, as a Cambridge undergraduate, he was lionised by the Bloomsbury set, which fell upon him with uninhibited delight. Lytton Strachey wrote that he had 'the mystery of Botticelli, the refinement and delicacy of a Chinese print, the youth and piquancy of an unimaginable English boy'. Mallory's tutor, A. C. Benson, found him 'ingenuous, pure minded, beautiful, and finely proportioned'.

These effusions helped to shape Mallory's public role. In the aftermath of the First World War, when conventional images of gallantry had been so undermined by the slaughter, there was a renewed longing for heroes of an uncomplicated kind.

With reports and photographs of the early Everest attempts appearing in the British press – there were expeditions in 1921, 1922 and 1924, Mallory taking part in all three – the process had also begun whereby climbers play out their life-and-death struggles to the vicarious satisfaction of their audiences. It can even be argued that Mallory, as vicarious heroes are tempted to do, fulfilled the expectations others held of him by selecting Irvine as his climbing partner.

Noel Odell was fitter and more experienced and would have been a more suitable choice for the summit bid. But Irvine, an enthusiastic and athletic young man who had won an Oxford rowing blue the previous year, perfectly complemented Mallory as the idealised pairing of experience and youth.

It can also be argued that this was the raw nerve Holzel touched upon. By suggesting that Mallory and Irvine had split up, Holzel violated the sanctity of Odell's vision in which two men go bravely forward together to meet their destiny, be it death, glory, or both.

While the opposition Holzel encountered did nothing to dissuade him, his determination to seek conclusive proof grew, and he resolved to go to Everest himself. Further research yielded one possibility: both Mallory and Irvine were carrying cameras – the latest Kodak Vest Pocket model, with a concertina frame – on their summit attempt. Holzel reasoned that if he could find the bodies of either Mallory or Irvine, and *if* the cameras and film were intact, the photographs could show Mallory setting off from the Second Step or even – the ultimate grail – the view from the summit.

It looked like the longest of shots, but Holzel's determination was fired when he learned that a Chinese climber had reported that in 1975 he discovered a body on a snow terrace below the point where Irvine's ice-axe had been found (the Chinese died in an avalanche four years later). Holzel asked every expedition departing for Everest to take him, without success. Finally, and most audaciously, he decided to organise an expedition of his own and received permission from the Chinese government for the post-monsoon season of 1986.

Holzel's plans drew further expressions of outrage in Britain, which were not assuaged when Holzel combined forces with a strong American climbing team. Salkeld, although nurturing doubts about Holzel's thesis, was sufficiently won over to accept an invitation to go.

When Holzel and Salkeld arrived at Everest in mid-August, they did not find the smoking gun Holzel craved. But what they did see came as a revelation. Western expeditions have only recently been permitted to attempt Everest from the north, via Tibet, following the same route as the pre-war British attempts (the British triumph of 1953, and most Western expeditions since, have approached from the south, via Nepal).

Thus, when Salkeld reached Camp 3 at 21,300 feet she was one of the first informed observers to obtain the same perspective on the North-East Ridge as Odell. She found that the Second Step fitted his epic description perfectly – while the First Step was not even in sight. 'Mallory and Irvine *must* have been on the Second Step,' she says.

American climbers who went higher reported further significant discoveries. It was not even necessary to climb the First Step, as it could be bypassed with ease; and the daunting account of the Second Step given in 1933 applied only when viewed from below. When approached from the crest of the ridge, the Second Step appeared quite feasible – recent Western expeditions had found the same – and again matched the details given by Odell.

Salkeld remains unpersuaded that Mallory and Irvine would have split up, as Holzel argues; her own suspicion is that they would have continued together, despite their depleted oxygen. And then? With the summit tantalisingly close when their oxygen ran out they could have pressed on regardless, as other climbers using oxygen have done since. Even when night overtook them during their descent, they tried to reach the safety of Camp 6 – only to fall at the point where Irvine's ice-axe was found.

Salkeld admits that her scenario, like Holzel's, lacks absolute proof. She believes that the odds that Mallory and Irvine succeeded have increased considerably, but she admits that she is content for the enigma to remain unsolved. 'Of course I would like them to have climbed Everest,' she says. 'But I would hate it to be proved that they didn't.'

Measuring mountains

Daily Telegraph, 1987

It's official. Everest is, after all, the highest mountain in the world. The news follows last year's claims that K2 had moved into first place in the mountaineering league table, thereby threatening to rewrite mountaineering history. The renown of Edmund Hillary and Sherpa Tenzing, as first to reach the supreme summit, would have been usurped by two Italians, Achille Compagnoni and Lino Lacedelli. Now an Italian expedition has conducted a fresh round of measurements. Its findings, announced last weekend, mean that the height long attributed to Everest must be revised. But it has also confirmed that Everest remains the ultimate prize.

News of Everest's possible demotion came in the aftermath of last summer's disastrous events on K2 when thirteen mountaineers perished, including Britain's Julie Tullis and Alan Rouse. All were attempting K2 via Pakistan but at the same time an American expedition was making a bid from the Chinese side. Although the Americans failed, they brought home an astounding claim. After conducting measurements via a passing satellite, they asserted that K2 was not 8611 metres, as had previously been thought, but 8858 metres. Since Everest is 8848 metres, that made K2 the highest mountain in the world. Not only would Hillary and Tenzing be relegated to subordinate status, but Tullis and Rouse would posthumously become the highest ever British climbers.

While reactions among climbers ranged from dismay to delight – a forthcoming British-Polish winter expedition to K2 quickly proclaimed that it could now be climbing the world's highest mountain – among surveyors and cartographers there was considerable scepticism. Even using satellites, the calculation of distant isolated heights is immensely complex. It entails measuring signals transmitted by the satellites and it is customary to take the average of as many satellite passes as possible, with a dozen considered a respectable minimum. But the Americans' figure was based on just one reading. (It was rumoured that they had intended to make six readings but their receiver batteries ran out.)

The Italian expedition left for the Himalaya in July. Sponsored by a scientific institute in Padua, its leader was the remarkable Ardito Desio, a mountaineer with a clear proprietorial interest in the outcome. In 1954 he headed the Italian team which reached the summit of K2 a year after the British triumph on Everest. Now ninety, Desio led the new expedition as far as Islamabad, the capital of Pakistan. From there the Italians headed first for Everest, trekking in via Tibet. They deployed a combination of survey methods, using passes from no fewer than four satellites as well as more traditional theodolites, positioned at four different points. Their calculations produced a new height of 8872 metres, twenty-four metres above the accepted figure of 8848 metres, and equivalent to 29,108 feet –

thereby replacing the magic figure of 29,028 feet that school-children used to learn.

The Italians now returned to Pakistan, where they received a lavish send-off. Conscious that Pakistan could become the gateway to the world's highest mountain, the authorities provided extra climbers and a helicopter. But for those hoping that history might be rewritten, there was disappointment. Using the same techniques as on Everest, the Italians found that K2 was indeed higher than had been thought – but only by five metres. The revised figure was 8616 metres, or 28,268 feet – and with Everest's new height, the difference between the two summits had grown rather than shrunk.

What is notable about the Italian results is the extent to which they confirm the work of the original nineteenth-century surveyors. The officers who staffed the British survey teams would depart with theodolites, spirit levels and plumb lines, and contend with complications as diverse as the diffraction of light and gravitational pull. The first measurement for K2, obtained in 1858, was 28,278 feet – just ten feet more than the latest figure.

The Pakistan authorities have received the news that they do not, after all, have co-ownership of the world's highest mountain with stoical good humour. At the same time they have reopened another controversy. K2's curiously elliptical title also dates back to the 1850s, when a British surveyor listed the peaks in the Karakoram range, from K1 to K33. Although K2 was only a provisional name it stuck. For a time some geographers adopted Mount Godwin-Austen, after the British captain who came to within twenty miles of K2 in 1861, but this was never officially confirmed.

The fashion today is for local names to replace their colonial counterparts. Everest, named after the chief British surveyor, is now also known as Chomolungma, Tibetan for Goddess Mother of the Earth. But there has never been a consensus on an alternative to K2, with Chogori – the 'Great Mountain' – the most favoured candidate. Now new proposals are emanating from Pakistan. Henceforth, it is proposed, K2 should be known as Jinnah Peak, after Mohammed Ali Jinnah, the revered leader who was the founder of Pakistan.

5

ACCIDENT AND RISK

The most sensitive area of mountaineering writing, the one where you suspect that climbers are studying most fastidiously the nuances of your words, is that of accidents. When I started climbing I happily told myself – and my wife – that it was essentially *safe*: if you obeyed the rules, I intoned, there was almost nothing that could go wrong. I now know this to be a delusion: that climbing is a risk sport and no matter what precautions you take, an irreducible element of danger remains.

This of course was brought home most forcibly when Dave Condict, my former school-friend who first took me climbing, died in the Alps in 1968. It was Dougal Haston who provided the answer to my plea to know why he had died. As Dougal coldly observed, it was because he was not wearing a climbing harness. I nonetheless accepted that climbing entails taking risks, and further believe that enquiring into the nature of risk is a legitimate topic for mountaineering journalism. Climbers like Mick Burke were ready enough to talk about accidents and risk, although I now know that the statistic I quoted, that one in eight of all Himalayan climbers die, is a considerable exaggeration. The climber and computer expert John Town has recently demonstrated that the true figure for any one expedition is one in thirty.

I also felt that some of the accidents needed a better explanation than the rest of the national press had presented, even, in the case of the K2 disasters of 1986, than was to be found in the climbing press. There was such confusion over what proved a remarkably intricate set of events that I felt that only a detailed exposition could answer all the questions that mountaineers, far more than the general public, were asking. I should add that Kurt Diemberger, who appeared to be clinging to a particular view of a most distressing set of events, was at first most reluctant to help me, although I had access to an interview he had given to the *Sunday Times*. But when I heard his account of the accident at the Alpine Club this year I found that we hardly diverged at all, and Diemberger told me afterwards that he considered my account the most accurate he had read.

The fifty-fifty risk

Sunday Times, 1968

A t five in the evening on 13 August two British climbers, Dave Condict, twenty-six, a London lecturer, and David Charity, twenty-six, a solicitor, were 100 feet from the summit of the Aiguille du Peigne, one of the thrusting granite needles above Chamonix in the range of Mont Blanc.

They had already climbed 1900 feet of the Aiguille's North Ridge, a route graded as *Très Difficile*, the second most difficult of the French Alpine Club's six categories of difficulty.

But now, according to their guidebook, the difficulties had 'eased', and there was just one short fifty-foot pitch to climb before they reached a chimney that led easily to the summit. It was Condict's turn to lead. With slight difficulty he negotiated a minor overhang at the foot of the pitch and disappeared from Charity's view.

The rope snaked steadily up through Charity's hands for some minutes – but then abruptly stopped. Charity assumed that Condict, who could now be only a few feet from the top of the pitch, had paused to work out a move. But then he heard Condict yell the chilling words: 'Dave, get ready for a fall.'

'About five seconds later Dave fell past me a few feet to my left,' says Charity. 'I remember seeing the rope go slack and I braced myself for the jerk. I don't remember seeing him falling so I think I must have closed my eyes. Then there was a terrific blow but I managed to hold him.'

Condict was now hanging on the rope about forty feet below. As Charity could not see him, he called down: 'Shall I lower you, Dave?' But Condict called back: 'There's nowhere to lower me to.' He was, it turned out, swinging free in the air below another overhang, unable to reach the rock face to find a foothold, the rope round his waist a lethal, suffocating force.

In this situation only one solution remained for Condict: to climb back up the rope on slings tied in special 'prusik knots' (devised so that they can be pushed up the rope without slipping down again). Charity asked if he should slide a pair down the rope. 'It's no good,' Condict called back. 'I'm too tired.' They were the last words he ever spoke. 'He moaned a few times,' says Charity, 'and then he stopped.' Condict lost consciousness within five minutes of his fall, and died of suffocation probably not more than fifteen minutes later.

Charity himself was now in an appalling predicament, alone, with night and bad weather approaching, near the top of a 12,000-foot peak. He sat on a ledge for thirty-six hours and then, having failed to attract anyone's attention, climbed alone the by now snow-plastered pitch on which Condict had fallen.

The descent from the summit should normally have taken two or three hours; it took Charity, equipped only with a forty-foot length of rope and a dozen slings for abseiling from, ten hours.

On several occasions Charity came near to losing his own life. Once he was on the point of stepping backwards off a ledge to start an abseil when the nut securing his abseil sling came out of the crack it was jammed into – Charity just managed to remain in balance on the ledge. 'I was so lucky,' he says.

His long series of narrow escapes during his descent only make more acute the malignant, tragic unluckiness of Condict's own death, falling from not more than five feet below the top of a 2000-foot climb, and on a route that climbers consider comparatively safe.

Condict's body was recovered by guides from Chamonix, a week after his fall, and flown home. At his funeral on 2 September, I spoke a tribute to his memory.

For Dave Condict was my own climbing partner, and one of my closest friends. The first time I went climbing, four years ago in Snowdonia, was with him; and so was the last time, last summer, again in North Wales. (I haven't climbed this year because my climbing equipment has been delayed in Buenos Aires by customs problems since the end of the British Cerro Torre expedition last February.)

On that last occasion in Wales, on a crag called Castell Cidwm,

Dave fractured his wrist when the rope he was abseiling on broke. On the way to the crag we had carefully removed our boots and socks to cross a stream. On our way back, in pouring rain, I nursed Dave over some boulders and then when we came to the stream we uncaringly waded through without a pause.

When we took our boots off at Bangor Hospital, long puddles of water flooded the floor. Later, as Dave's wrist slowly mended, I asked him if he felt the accident, unpredictable and unforeseen, would affect his confidence. He said he just didn't know; and I believe that he preferred not to think about the episode's unsettling implications.

In 1967, I wrote in an article in the *Sunday Times*: 'There *is* danger in climbing, and it has to be faced.' I had already seen one man die, the American John Harlin, as he tumbled through the frame of my telescope as I peered at the North Face of the Eiger during the siege of the Direct Route in March 1966.

Climbers, I wrote, accept that they are putting themselves at risk, but balance this against climbing's varied, complex pleasures. They do, and I did.

Once, as we sat out the weeks of storms in the Advance Base Camp of the Cerro Torre Expedition in Patagonia, I asked Mick Burke, one of Britain's hardest alpine climbers, what odds on survival he would accept before embarking on the final traverse beneath the Torre's menace-laden overhanging summit ice cap. His answer was 'Fifty-fifty.'

It seems that climbers are able to protect themselves with a cloak of necessary self-deception. On another occasion Burke said: 'You never think it's going to happen to you.'

My palms still sweat with fear when I think back on the only time while climbing when I seriously thought I might die – a wild December night at Swanage when, due to my own inexperience and incompetence, I was unable to get off a ledge at sea level, with the tide coming in and a storm blowing up, and was hauled up the cliffs on a rope as the waves began to drench me with their spray.

As I waited alone on the ledge I thought morbidly of my children, and swore that if I reached the top of the cliff I would give up climbing for ever. Came the dawn, and the promise was safely forgotten.

Dave Condict was closely aware of the odds himself. He was one of the six men in the LSE expedition who reached the summit of the beautiful and dangerous virgin peak of Rondoy in the Cordillera Huayhuash in Peru in 1963 – when two of the successful climbers fell 4000 feet to their death during the descent. Dave went on accepting the gamble – but he lost.

It isn't worth it. I would forswear now the intense exhilaration climbing has given me in Snowdonia, in the snow-covered Cairngorms, in Switzerland, if Dave could be alive still. Real friends are too precious.

Dave's wife Diana, twenty-six – married for only two years, they had no children – refuses to become bitter about climbing. 'It was part of him when I first knew him, and I always knew it would be. I couldn't imagine him not climbing.'

His friends can perhaps be more detached. 'It's only when it happens to someone you know that you realise the terrible effect it has on the people left behind,' says Peter Westnidge, Dave's closest companion during the expedition to Peru. Westnidge is married himself – and now doubts whether he will ever climb again.

Will I ever go climbing again myself? Climbing in Britain is certainly far less dangerous than in the Alps – but how do I explain that to my wife, when confronted with an accident as rare and as unlucky as Dave's? And what did Dave die for? Why did he die?

It's not going to happen to me

Sunday Times, 1967

The odds are that the Glencoe Mountain Rescue team will be in action this weekend. 'If the weather's good, June's a busy month,' says Hamish MacInnes, the team's bearded, vastly experienced leader, who with 100 other searchers spent five days last month looking in vain for a nineteen-year-old boy who went climbing alone and disappeared. In North Wales and the Lake District, the two most popular mountain areas south of the border, the rescue teams will be standing by. They are at their most active on Bank Holiday weekends, the time of mass exodus from the cities. The Ogwen Cottage team in Snowdonia once went out five times on a single Easter Sunday. Accident figures have risen steadily in the last decade – from 54 (12 deaths) in 1957 to 186 (36 deaths) in 1966.

But, say rescuers, the increase is in proportion with the growing popularity of the sport. Because of the sport's inherent lack of organisation, overall figures are hard to come by. One estimate – lacking any scientific basis – is that there are 50,000 active rock-climbers, with perhaps ten times that number going in for the more innocuous scrambling and fell-walking. But equipment dealers are riding a continuing boom, the number of clubs belonging to the British Mountaineering Council has risen from forty-eight to 135 in ten years, and the major cliffs of North Wales and the Lakes are simply more and more crowded. One Sunday morning recently there were eighteen people queuing at the foot of a climb in Llanberis Pass, and the top climbers are turning away from the more popular crags in favour of such incredibly difficult – and hence less populated – recent discoveries as the sea cliffs of Anglesey.

Why has climbing, despite the accident figures, become so popular? One answer lies in the nature of modern industrialised society, in which too many people have too little say in the decisions affecting their lives. Poised on a nub of rock, caressing the face above to find the rugosity that will give him the purchase to advance, committing himself to his judgment that the next move is feasible, the climber is in a situation of which he alone is master. For a moment he is a free agent, making his own decisions and acting upon them.

Climbing's first major expansion came in the 1930s, when young men from Sheffield and Manchester escaped from the emasculating experiences of dole queues and short-time working to the gritstone edges of Derbyshire. 'I'm a wage slave on Monday, but I'm a rock-climber on Sunday' says Ewan McColl's song. Mick Burke, who climbed the North Face of the Matterhorn last winter with Dougal Haston, threw up a job as an insurance clerk after four years. 'Whether you enjoy your work or not, it's not what you choose to do,' he says.

But climbing need not be seen as simply an escape. In their paper, 'The Quest for Excitement in Unexciting Societies,' Professor Norbert Elias and Mr Eric Dunning of Leicester University argue that, 'unless the organism is intermittently flushed and stirred by some exciting experience . . . overall rationalisation and restraint are apt to engender a dryness of the emotions, a feeling of monotony . . .' Leisure pursuits have a function which is 'the restoration of that measure of tension which is an essential ingredient of mental health'.

In his quest for excitement, what are the dangers to which

the rock-climber exposes himself? There are three main types of mountain accident in Britain. The most shocking are those involving badly led, ill-equipped parties – often of school-children – who lose their way, are caught by bad weather, or benighted. Then there are the walkers or scramblers who tres-pass on to difficult ground and fall or get stuck. The most frequent actual rock-climbing accidents occur to inexperienced climbers leading beyond their capabilities. Sixty-nine of the 187 mountain accidents in 1965 involved people aged twenty-one or under. Like motor-cyclists, many young climbers go through a tearaway phase which persists until they are sobered by an accident or a near-miss. (A rather disturbing analogy used by some climbers when explaining the pleasures of the sport is that with driving a fast car.)

Older, more experienced climbers use the accident statistics to console themselves that their own chances of misfortune in Britain are slight.

Equipment and safety techniques have improved greatly; hemp ropes have been replaced by nylon and perlon; American high-strength steel pitons are growing in popularity against European soft steel pitons; and crash helmets which reduce injuries by as much as twenty per cent are being worn increas-ingly.

Attitudes to the classical precepts of climbing have changed; it is no longer considered ethically necessary to lead out 100 feet without placing any running belays to limit the possible fall.

'If you obey the rules there's very little that can go wrong,' says Hamish MacInnes. Ron James, leader of the Ogwen rescue team, puts the proportion of accidents to experienced rock-climbers in Wales at 'less than one per cent'.

A major attraction of climbing anyway lies in reducing an ostensibly dangerous situation to one that is under the climber's control. On the face of it there is something quite absurd about standing on a minute ledge hundreds of feet above the ground. But the climber knows what he is at – knows that the ledge is wide enough for him to stand in balance, and is pretty sure how to reach the top of the crag in safety.

'It's a kind of mental and physical chess,' says Chris Boning-ton. If there is an opponent, it is not the mountain, which remains blandly neutral, but the climber himself, as he fights to control the fear welling up in his stomach, making his fingers clammy with sweat.

For some climbers these sensations make the total experience more delectable. 'I enjoy watching other people – and myself – react under stress' says Dougal Haston, who on the Eiger Direct ascent in March last year endured frostbite, five days in a snowhole in a storm, and the death of fellow climber John Harlin. The quest for self-awareness is less common among older climbers. Joe Brown once said that he didn't need to prove himself because he knew exactly what he was already. Don Whillans climbs for 'the perfect moments that make the rest of the year worthwhile'.

But there *is* danger in climbing, and it has to be faced. It can come at the end of a long day, when a lapse in concentration is the ten per cent contributory cause to an accident that tips the scales. In the Alps objective dangers – those beyond a climber's control – are much greater: loose rock, stonefalls, or sudden changes in weather hours from a refuge hut. Death when it is encountered is stunning: a friend transformed, perhaps in seconds, to a distorted mass: a malleable personality snatched into lifeless anonymity. 'It's always shocking,' says Mick Burke, who took part in the spectacular rescue on the stormbound Dru last summer when two Germans were saved and one rescuer was killed. 'But you never think it's going to happen to you.'

Despite the press outcry at the time of the Dru rescue, climbers accept a responsibility to go to the help of others, reserving strongest criticism for inexperienced leaders taking parties on to the hills. They accept too that they are putting themselves at risk, but balance against this the exhilaration of wild mountain scenery, the sensuous delight of stretching for holds, the freedom of decision and action climbing entails. In accepting the risks for the sake of the pleasures the climber is making a choice that is entirely his own.

Red tape halts rescue radio switch

Sunday Telegraph, 1986

A bureaucratic muddle over emergency radio equipment is putting mountaineers' lives at risk, according to rescue teams in Scotland. The problem has arisen over the radio frequency allocated to the rescue teams which, they say, is inadequate.

Mr Hamish MacInnes, leader of the Glencoe team, says, 'We desperately need a solution but all we get is red tape. The problem is really urgent, because people are falling off all the time.'

He has asked Mrs Thatcher for her help before winter sets in. But the body which controls rescue radios says that change is not possible before 1995.

About twenty walkers and climbers die in the Scottish mountains each year and rescue teams answer several hundred emergency calls. The teams have been allocated what is termed a low-band frequency – 86.3215 Megahertz – for use with AM radio equipment.

But teams in the rugged Western Highlands find that their radios are limited in range and prone to interference. Mr Donald Watt, leader of the Lochaber team which covers Ben Nevis and is the busiest team in Scotland, says: 'Losing radio contact on a difficult rescue, which happened to us last winter, can be very dangerous indeed.'

The problem has come to a head because of the unorthodox solution adopted by Lochaber's neighbours at Glencoe, where several members of the rescue team are fishermen. Four years ago the team abandoned its AM sets and started using a VHF marine radio channel, which gave far better results – and also allowed it to communicate with RAF rescue helicopters.

However, as team members acknowledge, this also broke the rules of the Radio Regulatory Division of the Department of Trade and Industry.

Ironically, the DTI learned of Glencoe's unauthorised move after a team member radioed the Oban coastguards to offer his help when a quarry worker died in a fall above Loch Linnhe last March. Even though the team member was calling from his fishing boat, the coastguards reported him to the DTI.

After an investigator visited Glencoe, the DTI told Mr MacInnes that the team must revert to the correct frequency within two months. That deadline has now expired.

The Glencoe team is unwilling to return to its unsatisfactory AM sets and would prefer to use modern FM equipment and a new high-band frequency. The Japanese-made FM sets are also far cheaper – around £450 a set, against £850 – than the British AM models.

Now the Glencoe team has met a new obstacle in a body known as the National Controlling Committee for Search and

Rescue Radio Channel. It is largely composed of police and Whitehall representatives and meets infrequently.

It first received a request from Scottish teams to switch to FM equipment and a high-band frequency in August 1984. Nothing was done and the Scottish teams repeated their request at the next meeting, held at the Home Office on 5 June this year.

This time the committee suggested a working party 'to look at the whole subject of the future development of the search and rescue channel'. As the minutes record, 'some change was possible in the future' – which could occur 'around or after 1995'.

In trying to reverse the committee's decision, the rescue teams face further problems, including trying to discover who is responsible for the committee.

The DTI said that it believed that the committee came under the Home Office. The Home Office, while acknowledging that it had several members on the committee, referred inquiries to its chairman, Mr Ronald Broome, Chief Constable of Somerset and Avon. Through an aide, Mr Broome said that he was unsure of the committee's formal position as he had only been its chairman for eighteen months.

Despite its denial, the Scottish teams blame the Home Office for the delays. The British police are about to embark on a switch from AM to FM equipment, funded by the Home Office, and the Scottish teams believe they have simply been pushed to the back of the queue. They also suspect that the Home Office would like them to use the police's discarded AM sets.

The end of hope

Radio Times, 1970

Lt-Col Streather had just moved again. 'It's the fifth time,' he said, 'in three years.' Around the new house, a large red-brick semi, at the School of Infantry at Warminster, Wiltshire, were piled the wooden crates that had contained his belongings. 'We haven't even unpacked some from Berlin, and that was over six months ago.' Commanding Officer of the Gloucesters, he'd gone with them from Berlin to Londonderry, and then back to the regiment's base at Honiton in Devon. This autumn the Gloucesters are to amalgamate with the Royal

Hampshire Regiment; and Col Streather is now a chief instructor at the Infantry School.

In the garage were the last of the cases. In one were a rope, a long-handled ice-axe, and a pair of crampons – sets of metal spikes for climbing on ice. The ice-axe Streather took to the summit of the third highest mountain in the world, Kangchenjunga, 28,146 feet high in the Himalaya. The crampons he wore during one of the most agonising and drawn-out disasters ever to befall a Himalayan expedition – on Haramosh, a 24,270-foot peak in the Karakoram in Pakistan, two years later.

Streather joined the Indian army in 1943, at the age of seventeen. In 1947, when India was partitioned, he stayed in Pakistan. In 1950 he was asked to join a Norwegian expedition to the unclimbed peak Tirich Mir (25,264 feet). He went as transport officer, wore a golfing jacket, and found himself on the summit. It was the highest any British climber had been for fifteen years.

Streather was considered for the 1953 Everest expedition, but was turned down because of his lack of experience. He went instead on an American expedition to K2 – at 28,250 feet the second highest mountain in the world. On K2 Streather survived an episode that was a chilling forerunner of Haramosh itself.

The climbers were camped at 25,500 feet when a storm descended. For days they waited; climber Art Gilkey became seriously ill. Retreat, at the height of a Himalayan storm, was the only possibility.

Gilkey was bundled in a sleeping bag and lowered on ropes, but the expedition had descended less than 1000 feet when the accident happened. Climber George Bell slipped on a forty-five-degree ice slope, pulling Streather on the same rope with him. Their rope fouled another, and two other climbers started sliding too. They in turn pulled off a fifth climber who was attached to Gilkey's makeshift stretcher, at that moment held from the other end by Pete Schoening, the last man still on his feet.

'We were heading,' says Streather, 'for a drop I suppose of 8000 feet.' Clinging to an ice-axe driven into the snow, Schoening held them all. 'It really was,' says Streather, 'an extremely tense situation.'

Nor was that all. After the climbers had recovered, Gilkey was swept away by an avalanche. Brutally, it was the best thing for the other climbers that could have happened.

Streather says: 'If it hadn't, we probably wouldn't have got off. We were so exhausted, we just couldn't have carried him any more. What would have happened the next day, it's very difficult to hazard a guess.' As it was, the desperate descent – on which Streather emerged as one of the strongest figures – took three days.

In 1955 – undaunted – Streather joined the British expedition to Kangchenjunga. Streather was one of four men to reach the summit. It was the best moment of his climbing life. 'We sat there and looked right down over India and Tibet and Nepal,' he says.

Two years later came Haramosh. It was a small Oxford University expedition which Streather was invited to lead to an icy, elegant peak 100 miles west of K2. After bad weather the expedition modified its objective, finally aiming for the crest of a ridge leading to one of the mountain's subsidiary peaks.

The four climbers had set 15 September as their last day. On the ridge Streather was roped to New Zealander Rae Culbert; on the other rope were students John Emery and Bernard Jillott.

Suddenly the ridge avalanched and Jillott and Emery were carried 1000 feet into a snow basin.

To help them, Streather and Culbert climbed down into the basin themselves – and the efforts of the four climbers to climb out occupied the next three days. After several long falls, Jillott and Emery reached the ridge first. But Culbert lost a crampon and Streather climbed out alone on 18 September. He reached the camp expecting to find two fit climbers in the camp with whom he could return for Culbert. 'Instead I just found John Emery with his crampons on. He said: "Bernard's gone."' Jillott had walked over the edge of the ridge to his death.

It was the end of hope for Rae Culbert. The next morning Streather and Emery, frostbitten and near exhaustion, climbed on down the mountain. 'There was no choice,' wrote author Ralph Barker in his book *The Last Blue Mountain*. Streather agrees.

'There was no question of being able to go back,' he says. 'Thinking about it afterwards there is no doubt in my mind that Rae died while I was getting out that night. It's unfair to me or to John or to Rae to say that there was a *decision*. It wasn't an issue. There was absolutely nothing else we could have done and it would have been madness to have tried.'

Streather and Emery stumbled off the mountain, being aided from Camp 3 downwards by an American who'd accompanied the expedition, Scott Hamilton.

Emery later had fingers and toes amputated, but Streather recovered. Looking back, he's convinced that it was his army experience that enabled him to survive.

'The worse thing was the awful scabbing in our mouths and lips from trying to eat ice and snow. We were getting more and more tired and dehydrated and our hands and feet were getting frozen and our brains were getting numbed. But at no stage was there a fear that we might not get out, because by the time we were in that situation we were no longer able to realise it. We moved into a state of semi-dream. And that's where the army training counted. Tight corners – the frontier, Korea – were part of the normal pattern.'

Six years after Haramosh, John Emery, who'd learnt to climb again in specially shortened boots, was killed in the Alps. 'It brought it all back when John was killed. It upset me terribly.'

So he is relieved to find he can now discuss Haramosh dispassionately.

'It still plays a pretty dramatic part in my life – something which is a very large landmark. I've never had the desire to climb particularly high mountains, for the sake of it, afterwards. I've been more interested in passing my experiences on to others.' He has been on two youth club expeditions with Lord Hunt, and is still active in the Army Mountaineering Association.

How long Col Streather stays in the army depends, he says, on the politicians, but he expects to be there for another five or six years anyway.

He talks of the great days of the Gloucesters with regret, reeling off the countries they've served in since the Second World War without hesitation: 'But all that's come to an end, I'm afraid.' At least at Warminster the Streathers' porcelain will find a permanent home on the mantelpiece – he's proudest of the Meissen horse which he bought the last time he was in East Berlin. Life, he regretfully expects, will become more predictable. 'But I don't know whether I'll adjust to that,' he ponders, 'or whether I'll find something more to do.'

The best days of my life

'He was moaning and groaning and then he became unconscious. I said, "Are you okay?" but he very obviously
wasn't okay. The thing was, there was very little I could do. I
just thought he was going to die. Then I remembered he had
some nuts. It wasn't a case of getting the nuts off him before he
seized up – it was just that I felt like doing something while I
waited for him to die.'

These words of Mick Burke, interviewed at Annapurna Base
Camp at 14,000 feet, are part of an outstanding film, *The Hardest
Way Up*.

The incident Burke refers to took place at 22,500 feet on
the South Face of Annapurna, when climber Mike Thompson
collapsed below Camp 5, near the top of the most exhausting
carry of the 1970 British expedition. Back at sea level in London,
Burke doesn't withdraw a word of his interview.

'I suppose it seems funny now,' he says, 'but it was very
serious at the time, even the nuts. I was just suddenly sure Mike
was going to die in front of me. It didn't particularly bother me.
I was just upset that there was nothing I could do. It's just
nothing to do with you, this person having his own dying scene.
You can't give them your life. All I could do was to stay there
until he was dead.'

Thompson, climbing higher than he had done before on the
expedition, had driven himself almost beyond exhaustion. He
regained consciousness after ten minutes and managed to descend to Base Camp.

Burke, thirty, almost embarrassingly articulate about climbers'
attitudes towards themselves and the dangers of their sport, is
one of the strongest characters to emerge from Tuesday's film
– in more ways than one. Son of a Wigan baker, now a student
at the London Film School, he shot many of the high-altitude
sequences. 'Nearly everyone did some filming, but there were
so many problems. You're shaking all the time because you're
addled, you're never certain whether the focus and exposure
are right.'

Above the point where Mike Thompson collapsed was the
Rock Band, a 1000-foot near-vertical wall of rock. Burke and
American climber Tom Frost led up it for five days, fixing 1500

feet of rope and enabling Don Whillans and Dougal Haston to leapfrog over them to the summit. Chris Bonington, the expedition's leader, describes the lead in his forthcoming book, *Annapurna South Face*, as 'probably the hardest climbing ever attempted at altitude'.

'They were the best five days of my life,' says Burke. 'It was completely a world of my own. Nobody else existed. I'd left everything else behind, all the problems, all the mechanics. The only problem was one of survival.'

One in eight of all climbers who go to the Himalaya die. The expedition rode the odds until its very last day on the mountain. Then an ice sérac below Camp 2 collapsed, killing Ian Clough.

'The odds against Ian getting killed then were enormous,' says Burke. 'It was like a racing driver getting killed on the last lap. When anybody's killed you can't feel sorry for them – it's just a collection of skin and bones. I was very exhausted then, and I felt sorry for myself. And I felt tremendously sorry for Niki, Ian's wife.

'I was very surprised when Ian got killed because by then I'd been lulled into a false sense of security. I even thought everyone else was down off the mountain by then – and you never think it's going to be you.'

Burke is one of the few climbers who'll admit that the danger of climbing is one of its attractions. 'There's a line and you can go right up to it and you never go over it intentionally. But then you find you're on the other side accidentally. This is when your adrenalin starts pumping and you work as hard as you can to move back.

'If anything, it's more exciting if it's a little bit out of control. Though you don't think it's exciting at the time – only when you've got it back into control. Part of the thing is running as close to the line as you possibly can.

'But I know the appeal isn't suicidal – just from the number of times I've been up to the line and insisted on pulling myself back. There have been a number of times when it would have been the easiest thing in the world.'

It was with special interest that Burke waited for news last month of attempts to rescue French alpinists René Desmaison and Serge Gousseault, caught in a storm near the summit of the Grandes Jorasses. In 1966, Burke and Desmaison took part in one of the most audacious rescues of alpine history, when two German climbers were trapped on the West Face of the Dru.

American climber Gary Hemming – who later committed suicide – organised the rescue team. 'I was just leaving Chamonix,' says Burke, who doesn't believe in mock heroics, 'when Gary caught me and said, "What about the Germans?" I said I thought they were probably dead and he said, "Well, you'd better come."

'I still thought they'd die, but we climbed up in a storm for three days and they were still alive when we got there.'

The climbers now faced a terrifying first abseil which Burke, who had climbed the same route the year before, tackled first. 'You were twenty feet out with 2000 feet of space below, and you had to swing like a spider to get into a groove. Even Desmaison blew his mind on it – I was very chuffed about that.

'But I was very impressed with Desmaison. In a storm on the Dru your normal reaction is just to bale out, and it didn't faze him at all. I can see how he survived on the Grandes Jorasses. It's as if after five days Serge said, "I can't take any more of this," and he sat down on the ledge and died. But when Desmaison said, "I can't take any more of this," he sat down and worked out that he could. Serge was by far the fitter – he was twenty-four, Desmaison is forty – but Desmaison's got the mind. He just wouldn't give in.'

Burke believes that the Annapurna film is the best climbing film ever made – and not just because he shot much of it himself. There will be plenty of people to agree with him. 'I'd go back to the Himalaya – not on just another expedition, but if I could help make another film,' he says.

'There's something about the Himalaya, something weird. You're way out above the rest of the world. It's a thing, I suppose, of really feeling high.'

Mick's own Everest

Listener, 1975

Chris Bonington had always hoped that, on the 1975 expedition to the South-West Face of Everest, there should be more than one summit attempt. Having led two previous major Himalayan expeditions, he knew how important it was that his men should subordinate themselves to the overall goal; he also knew how much this was to ask of men who, by nature, were single-minded, competitive and personally ambitious. On Annapurna in 1970, there had been a bitter row when he had brought forward Dougal Haston and Don Whillans out of turn and allowed them the first – and as it turned out, the only – summit bid. On Everest in 1972, he had been more successful in creating a team of climbers prepared to work for each other. In 1975, he was determined that, for as many climbers as possible, the reward for team effort would be the chance of going for the top.

Bonington's attempt on the unclimbed South-West Face in the post-monsoon season of 1972 had been defeated by 100 mph winds and bitter cold. In 1975, he decided to make an earlier start, to try to take advantage of the periods of settled weather that sometimes occurred as the monsoon died away. The expedition made fast progress, establishing Base Camp beneath the Khumbu Icefall in late August, and arriving beneath the Rock Band, the slanting rock wall which seemed to bar all progress at 27,000 feet, a week ahead of Bonington's most optimistic schedule.

When, on 20 September, the climbers Nick Estcourt and Tut Braithwaite found a route through the Rock Band, the way to the summit was open. Dougal Haston and Doug Scott made Camp 6 at 27,600 feet on the fifty-degree slope of the Upper Ice Field on 22 September. They spent the next day fixing ropes across 1500 feet of the icefield and, on 24 September, went for the 29,028-foot summit, reaching it at 6 p.m. They spent the night in a snowhole at the South Summit at 28,750 feet, thus surviving the highest bivouac climbers have ever made, and began their descent to the Western Cwm the following morning. The ascent was the fastest ever, thirty-three days out of Base Camp, and Bonington had plenty of time in hand.

Bonington had already decided on the climbers who would form the next three summit parties. He had placed himself in the fourth; the second, who passed Haston and Scott as they made their way down the mountain, consisted of the youngest expedition member, Peter Boardman, who was twenty-four, and the best Sherpa climber, Pertemba; and the experienced pair, Martin Boysen and Mick Burke.

Burke was thirty-two. He came originally from Wigan, one of the tough and aggressive working-class climbers who had steadfastly made their way to the highest levels of the climbing world. He had early on become interested in photography and, on the expedition to the granite spire of Cerro Torre in Patagonia in 1967, had taken a picture which won the main prize for a still photograph at the mountaineering film festival at Trento in the Italian Dolomites. In 1970, he had been on Bonington's expedition to Annapurna, and had made the second but unsuccessful summit attempt. ITV had made a superb film of that expedition, for which Burke had shot much of the high-altitude footage. Once an insurance clerk, he then saw the possibilities of a career as a film cameraman. The BBC employed him first as a freelance, then took him on to their full-time staff.

By 1975, he had become less interested in climbing as such than in the opportunities it presented him to film. In 1968, he had married a bank manager's daughter; their first child, Sara, was born in 1973. Before he left for Everest in 1975, he told his wife, Beth, that he didn't really want to go through the rigours and hardship of a Himalayan expedition again, but he couldn't afford the risk of someone else obtaining the first moving pictures ever shot on Everest's summit. Beth Burke, a realist, knew then that to film on the summit was 'Mick's own Everest'.

The second summit party was due to leave Camp 6 on 26 September. That morning there were traces of high cirrus clouds in the sky, a hint of a possible change in the weather. But there had been such dawns before, and the cloud had disappeared; it was certainly not sufficient of an omen to postpone the attempt.

'An accident,' Chris Bonington was to comment after the expedition, 'is usually composed of several often unconnected incidents, which inexorably compound the final tragedy.' The first such incident involved Martin Boysen. Up to Camp 6, Boysen says, he had been climbing 'like a bomb'; he felt confident of reaching the summit, and was the first man to leave camp that morning, at 4.30 a.m. But now his oxygen set stopped working: 'I found that I couldn't go more than two or three paces without stopping for breath.'

The expedition had brought with it eighteen lightweight American Robertshaw Blume oxygen sets, chosen in the belief that they were the best available in the world. At the end of the expedition, only five of the eighteen were still working, and Bonington remarked that they had climbed Everest in spite of them and not because of them. Lower down the mountain, several climbers found that their demand valves would jam; during the first summit attempt, Haston's feeder tube had become blocked with ice, and it had taken Scott an hour and a half to diagnose and correct the fault.

For a time, Boysen struggled on without oxygen; both Boardman and Pertemba passed him. Then Boysen came to a short but steep wall of rock; in his flailing and unco-ordinated effort to climb it, he kicked off one of his crampons, and knew then he would have to turn back. Burke, the last to leave Camp 6 that morning, was now just behind, and said to Boysen: 'Bad luck, mate.' As to the question of whether Burke should have continued alone, Boysen says there was 'no decision' involved. 'We were all highly motivated, and anyone else would have gone on. There seemed little risk involved really. I think Mick would have wanted to catch the others up, but, unfortunately, he wasn't fast enough.'

It would, indeed, have been sensible – and safer – for Burke to join the pair ahead of him; but several factors now told against him. Although his camera equipment was very light, at such height every extra pound was a burden. Burke had also been at high altitude for more than a week and, Boysen believes, had begun to deteriorate physically. 'We were a bit concerned about him having been up there so long, but he was so determined, you couldn't tell him. Whatever you said, he would just have kept going.' So while Boysen retreated to Camp 6, suffering the 'torment' of seeing others go for the summit without him, Burke continued.

Boardman and Pertemba, in fact, now believed that they alone were going for the summit. As they made their way across the Upper Ice Field, they could see no other climbers. But, as they climbed the gully leading from the Upper Ice Field to the South Summit, Boardman happened to look back, and saw a stationary figure on the icefield below. He decided it must be Boysen, watching them for a while before he finally turned back. 'For some reason, I presumed that Mick had not set foot on the mountain at all that day. When we came over the top of the gully, we lost sight of the figure again.'

Boardman and Pertemba reached the South Summit at 10 a.m. There, Pertemba's oxygen tube iced up, and they spent over an hour unblocking it. Then they continued along the summit ridge and stepped on to the summit at 1 p.m. Haston and Scott had described an extraordinary sunset view of Tibet, but clouds now filled the valleys to within 2000 feet of Everest's summit; the morning's high cirrus had, indeed, presaged a change in the weather. Pertemba photographed Boardman wearing his Stockport climbing club tee-shirt; Boardman photographed Pertemba holding the flag of Nepal. They ate chocolate and Kendal mintcake, and set off back down shortly before 2 p.m., reckoning to reach Camp 6 just before nightfall.

Some ten to fifteen minutes below the summit, Boardman was amazed to come across Burke, sitting in the snow with his camera in his hands. Burke had been filming as he climbed, but had almost caught up with Boardman and Pertemba because of the time they had lost on the South Summit; it was a magnificent solo climb on Burke's part. He shook hands with Pertemba and congratulated both climbers on reaching the summit; then he asked if they would return with him to the top so that he could film them there.

Boardman's first concern was for Pertemba, who was moving cautiously and quite slowly along the summit ridge. He felt there was no danger in leaving Burke; he judged that he would have undertaken the same climb himself, and knew that Burke was a far more experienced climber. He decided that the most important thing was to lead Pertemba back to the South Summit. 'I said: "Oh, well, we'll go back up," but in such a way that showed I wasn't happy about it. Mick said: "Its okay, I'll be able to film on the summit, anyway." And he also borrowed Pertemba's still camera. We went back a few steps so that he could film us walking past him, and we agreed that we would wait for him at the South Summit.'

Boardman says that he is 'quite certain' that Burke reached the summit, for the remainder of the route from where they parted was straightforward; with this judgment, Chris Bonington agrees.

It was now, with the expedition at its most stretched, with three men on the summit ridge, one climbing alone, that the weather dealt the decisive blow. As Boardman and Pertemba, roped together, negotiated the toughest obstacle on the summit ridge, the pinnacle known as the Hillary Step, a white-out began: cloud and wind-blown snow enveloped them, and their tracks, which Burke would have hoped to follow, filled in rapidly. Climbing most carefully, they reached the South Summit at 2.45 p.m.

As they waited for Burke, the wind increased. Boardman, peering up the summit ridge, found that his goggles froze over; when he removed them, snow drove into his eyes, and he had to force his eyelids apart. Burke, who was quite short-sighted, must have been in an even worse position.

Earlier in the expedition, he had been wearing a pair of soft contact lenses, worth £300, that a manufacturer had donated; at altitude, they had misted over and Burke had reverted to wearing glasses. In the gathering storm, these would have been almost useless. Boardman and Bonington believe that Burke, tired from his long climb to the summit, in extreme difficulty trying to follow the route back down the summit ridge, walked over one of the monster snow cornices overhanging the Kangshung Face on the Tibetan side of Everest. The film he would have shot on the summit was, of course, lost with him.

On the South Summit, Boardman's own position was worsening each minute. The storm was strengthening; he now had no chance of reaching Camp 6 before nightfall. 'At ten to four, we decided we would give Mick another ten minutes, and, if he didn't come then, we would have to go. In a way, that made it a little easier. And then, as soon as we left, we started fighting the storm, and it was just us struggling to get down.'

At the press conference that followed the expedition's return to Britain, Lord Hunt paid tribute to Boardman's coolness and skill. He was not to be blamed for abandoning the wait for Burke; had he stayed any longer on the South Summit, not one but three climbers would have died. Boardman made a circular reconnaissance to find the top of the gully leading to the Upper Ice Field; at the bottom of the gully, his life and Pertemba's depended on their finding the line of fixed ropes that would lead them back to the refuge of Camp 6. 'I kept going left and down, and just hoped we would find them. Just as it got finally dark, I saw the two oxygen cylinders Doug and Dougal had left at the end of the ropes.'

Martin Boysen had been waiting in Camp 6 all day. As night fell and the storm crashed around his tent, he became more and more anxious. 'I just sat there in the dark, waiting and hoping. Finally, I heard voices and I knew someone was coming. I stuck my head out of the tent and asked: "How many are you?"'

Avalanche on K2

Sunday Times, 1978

C hris Bonington and Peter Boardman, advance guard of a
British expedition attempt to climb K2, the world's second
highest mountain, flew from London to Rawalpindi, Pakistan,
yesterday. They will be joined by the rest of the eight-man team
on Wednesday.

K2 is a spectacular and isolated peak in the Karakoram range
on Pakistan's border with China. At 28,740 feet, it is only 286
feet lower than Everest. Only two expeditions have reached its
summit and both took the straightforward route, up its East
Ridge.

The British team will tackle the mountain's awkward and
twisting West Ridge, which Bonington describes as 'every bit as
hard as the South-West Face of Everest'. It has never before
been attempted. In keeping with mountaineering trends of the
1970s, Bonington will take only a small compact team relying
largely on its own resources.

Two hundred Balti porters will carry five tons of equipment
and supplies on the fifteen-day approach march and Bonington
aims to set up Base Camp by the end of May at the junction of
the Godwin-Austen and Savoia glaciers. Just ten porters will
help establish Camp 1 at 19,000 feet at the foot of the ridge.
After that the climbers will be on their own.

The lower part of the route is at a variable angle, much of it
on snow. But above a possible Camp 5 at 25,000 feet it steepens
dramatically and follows mostly rock. It is there, Bonington
believes, that the greatest problems, and risks, will arise.

'We'd like to put the last camp around 26,500 feet but that
may be optimistic,' he says.

Inevitably, says Bonington, any pair making a summit bid
will have a long way to go and will have to spend one night in
the open, in sub-zero temperatures and exposed to the risk of
storms, during their descent.

The climbers are well aware of K2's awesome reputation. In
1939 a climber in an American expedition was marooned at
24,500 feet. He was not seen again – nor the three high-altitude
porters who set out to rescue him.

In 1953 seven climbers on an American expedition were hit
by a storm at 25,000 feet. One fell ill and the others tried to bring

him down. Another man slipped on the descent and, in a tangle of ropes, swept five others from their holds. The six, including the invalid, were sliding towards a 5000-foot drop when the last man managed to stand his ground and held the others on his rope. The drama was not yet over. That night the invalid climber was swept to his death in an avalanche. The others reached Base Camp safely although several were badly frostbitten.

Last year Bonington and three other members of the K2 team – Doug Scott, Nick Estcourt and Paul Braithwaite – made a harrowing ascent of the nearby Ogre, culminating in Scott's agonised retreat with two broken legs. The K2 team is completed by Peter Boardman, who, like Scott, climbed Everest by the South-West Face in 1975; Joe Tasker, who with Boardman made an audacious two-man ascent of Changabang, also in the Karakoram, last year; team doctor Jim Duff; and photographer Tony Riley.

K2 was first climbed by an Italian team in 1954. Six members of a forty-five-strong Japanese party reached the summit in 1977. Both followed the East Ridge.

Bonington first fancied K2 in the aftermath of the 1975 Everest expedition, and one of his original team members was to have been the late Dougal Haston, who wanted to make the attempt without oxygen. In fact the expedition will use a modest amount of oxygen above the last camp. Following prolonged trouble on Everest with the demand system which automatically adjusts the flow of oxygen, Bonington has reverted to the older and simpler fixed flow system.

Success would complete a remarkable decade for Bonington, with Everest in 1975 and his earlier triumph on the South Face of Annapurna in 1970. He accepts that on a small expedition his style of leadership will have to change. 'Your role is as a catalyst of ideas – you're not so much a leader as a chairman,' he says. He concedes that the restricted size of the team has reduced its chances, 'but if we are successful the satisfaction will be that much greater.'

It was on 7 June that the British K2 expedition first came upon the snow basin where Nick Estcourt was to die. That day, there were four climbers pushing the route forward on K2's unclimbed West Ridge.

They began by following a gully that led to the crest of the ridge. But Chris Bonington, the leader, was afraid the gully might be too steep for the expedition's Balti porters, and decided to cross the snow basin.

Bonington says: 'It was slightly convex, and at an easy angle. I have used far more dangerous slopes before. To me, this one looked quite safe.'

The four men did not bother to rope up to cross the basin, and when they reached the far side they were in good spirits. They found a good site for Camp 2 at 21,400 feet and were already ahead of schedule in their attempt on the 28,750-foot peak. Before them was a rock step – the first technical challenge of the climb.

That night, back in Camp 1, the climbers drew lots with matchsticks for the privilege of tackling the rock step. Joe Tasker and Pete Boardman won, consigning the others to the drudgery of load-carrying. On 9 June Tasker and Boardman embarked on the rock step while the others ferried supplies between Camps 1 and 2.

For the next two days, wind and snow confined the climbers to their tents. On 11 June they returned to their tasks. Doug Scott led a four-man team carrying loads from Camp 1. They found it hard work breaking a trail through the fresh snow.

At the edge of the snow basin, they stopped. They were tired, and Scott felt uneasy at venturing across a slope with so much loose snow. They dumped their loads and returned to Camp 1.

12 June dawned clear. Somewhere above Camp 2, Tasker and Boardman worked away at the rock step, while a three-man party left Camp 1 with more loads. Doug Scott led again, followed by Nick Estcourt, with the high-altitude Balti porter Kamajan in the rear. When they reached the snow basin they added the previous day's loads to their rucksacks, which now weighed about sixty pounds each.

To Scott, the snow basin seemed safe: the loose snow had either consolidated or blown away. As he led across the basin, however, he fastened a thin 5 mm rope in place as a route-marker and handrail. It would also protect the climbers against small snow slides.

'It was hard going, with the snow up around my knees,' says Scott. 'I had got to within thirty feet of Camp 2 when I heard and felt two cracking sounds.' When he looked back, Scott saw the entire surface of the basin moving, slowly at first, then gathering speed. Caught in the middle, some 300 feet behind Scott, was Estcourt.

Instinctively Scott drove in his ice-axe to try to secure himself. But he was still attached to the 5 mm rope. 'Immediately I was yanked down the slope, sliding, spinning round and round, choking, head covered in snow – and then I came upright and stopped.' The rope had snapped when Scott was within feet of being sucked into the avalanche. There was no sign of Estcourt.

As Scott made his way back up the slope, he yelled dementedly, 'Nick . . . Nick . . .' and swore violently. At Camp 2 he could see the extent of the avalanche. It was enormous: a slab of snow 750 feet across, 1000 feet long, and eight feet thick had slid away, carrying Estcourt over a 3000-foot drop. On the far side, Kamajan was nursing his hands, having seared his flesh in a vain effort to hold the rope.

Back at Camp 1, Bonington and the expedition doctor, Jim Duff, had watched the avalanche roar past. Bonington even photographed it, still believing the snow basin to be quite safe, and not dreaming that anyone could be caught up in it. But Duff heard Scott's wild shouts, and when Bonington called up by radio, Scott told him that Estcourt had been lost. Both men sat down in the snow and cried.

The climbers returned to Base Camp that night, and in the morning considered whether to carry on. Bonington says: 'We tried to approach the matter rationally. All but one of us thought we should give up.' The principal factor was the climbers' feeling that their chances of success were now virtually nil. Tut Braithwaite was already out of action with a chest infection, and the loss of Estcourt reduced the expedition to four main climbers. Bonington and Scott hurried back to Islamabad with the news of Estcourt's death, leaving the others to clear up. For Bonington in particular it was a sad end to a well-prepared expedition, backed by the London-based company, LRC International, and a further example of the tragedies that beset even successful expeditions to the Himalaya.

Ian Clough died under a falling ice-sérac on Annapurna in 1970; Mick Burke was lost in a storm near the summit of Everest in 1975. Bonington estimates that the avalanche that killed Estcourt was a 'one-in-five-year event'.

Estcourt and Bonington were very close friends. 'Nick was a perfectionist with a talent for making very dispassionate and balanced judgments,' Bonington says. 'He was an incredibly fine person who was underrated as a mountaineer.'

On the South-West Face of Everest in 1975 Estcourt and Braithwaite opened up the route through the rock band to the summit, and in 1977 Estcourt safeguarded the long, painful retreat by Bonington and Scott from the Ogre, after Scott had broken both his legs. Just before K2, Estcourt, thirty-five, had resigned as a full-time computer programmer to open an equipment shop in Manchester and to give himself more freedom to climb. He leaves a wife and three children.

Two extraordinarily gallant men

Sunday Times, 1982

Both Peter Boardman and Joe Tasker, the climbers whose deaths on Everest were announced yesterday, had been on the mountain before and knew the vicissitudes it could deliver.

Boardman climbed Everest via the South-West Face in 1975, a success marred by the death of Mick Burke. Tasker was a member of the 1980 winter expedition which was driven back by unrelenting winds and bitter cold. Yet each was determined to return.

Boardman was only twenty-four when he stood on the summit in 1975, yet his triumph left him strangely dissatisfied, and not only because he had been the last to see Burke alive. He felt guilty at having leapfrogged over other good climbers, and later described his feat as a 'hollow victory'.

He accepted that success on Everest could deliver the climber 'from the prison of his ambition'. He turned to smaller, lighter expeditions, and at the same time became an accomplished writer in the tradition of earlier scholar mountaineers. He also directed a climbing school in Switzerland, and was married in 1980.

Yet his thoughts kept returning to Everest, which he came to see as a metaphor for the pursuit of self-knowledge, 'like chasing after Moby Dick'. When Chris Bonington proposed a compact expedition to the mountain's unclimbed East-North-East Ridge, he unhesitatingly agreed.

Tasker, although more prosaic than Boardman, had similar

longings. Aged thirty-three, and unmarried, he owned a climbing shop in Sheffield, and had accumulated an impressive roster of alpine and Himalayan climbs.

He knew, when he attempted Everest in the winter of 1980, that the odds were stacked against the expedition, but relished the chance to come to grips with the most renowned mountain.

When Bonington invited him to join the new attempt, he was especially pleased that it was approaching the mountain from the north, through Tibet, scene of the epic endeavours of the pre-war British pioneers.

After the bitter experience of 1980, however, Tasker was cautious about the expedition's chances. He told me just before he left that the ridge seemed 'monstrously long' and that its main difficulties began very high, just before it joined the North Ridge proper (the route followed by successful postwar Chinese and Japanese attempts). At around 27,000 feet was a cluster of rock pinnacles which, he believed, seemed 'quite difficult and, at that altitude, the most problematic section'. He accepted Bonington's modest estimate that their prospects were 'about as high as for the pre-war expeditions'.

When the expedition set foot on the mountain, its gloomy assessments seemed borne out. After establishing Base Camp on 4 April, it had reached 25,600 feet by the end of the month, some 3400 feet below the summit. But the climbers were forced to retreat to Base by snowfalls and, more disturbingly, the fatigue from spending three weeks at high altitude.

In early May they returned to the ridge and reached a new highpoint of 26,400 feet, but suffered a new blow when climber Dick Renshaw had a mild stroke.

The notorious pinnacles, too, seemed as formidable as had been feared. As Bonington himself reported from the expedition: 'They could well give the hardest climbing ever encountered at that altitude. We are just hoping that they are going to be easier than they look.'

In mid-May Bonington, by now also feeling the effects of altitude, decided that Tasker and Boardman should make the expedition's single summit bid. Even so, he was optimistic when the pair, carrying enough food for three days, departed from the Advance Base Camp at 21,000 feet on 16 May. They climbed confidently and by the next day had reached almost 27,000 feet, ready to tackle the pinnacles.

What occurred next was to prove chillingly reminiscent of the disappearance of Mallory and Irvine, high on the North Ridge, fifty-eight years earlier.

Late that afternoon Bonington watched through the expedition's telescope as Boardman and Tasker appeared to search for a site where they could excavate a snowhole for the night's bivouac. The two men cautiously approached a pinnacle and then passed behind it. They were never seen again.

Bonington's fears were first aroused when Tasker and Boardman failed to make their scheduled radio contacts that evening or the next morning. Later that day Bonington and team member Adrian Gordon climbed some way up the ridge but could see nothing of either man. On 24 May, by then 'very frightened that something had gone wrong', Bonington and expedition doctor Charles Clarke made a vain search from the Kangshung Glacier.

Bonington concluded that Tasker and Boardman must have fallen from the ridge down the mountain's vast, 10,000-foot Kangshung Face. 'It was inconceivable that anyone could survive such a fall,' Bonington said.

The expedition was formally abandoned and the remaining team members returned to Peking, where Bonington announced yesterday that the two climbers were 'missing, presumed dead'. He paid tribute to their 'excellent mountain judgment' and said that 'while being bold and determined in concept they were also sensibly cautious. Their loss is an immense one for the entire world of mountaineering.'

Close to tears, Bonington added: 'They were both very good friends and extraordinarily gallant men.'

Climbing towards catastrophe

The Times, 1987

J ulie Tullis was entranced by K2 from the start. When she first saw its North Face soaring sheer from its glacier, she thought it the most beautiful mountain she had seen. Although her attempts in 1983 and 1984 failed by wide margins, she left no one in doubt that she intended to climb K2, the world's second highest peak, one day. She took to calling it 'my mountain' and 'the mountain of my dreams'.

She came to mountaineering late in life. Born in Croydon in

1939, she took up climbing at sixteen. After marrying at twenty, she and her husband Terry ran climbing courses and a shop near the sandstone outcrops around Tunbridge Wells. Terry was the breadwinner while she brought up their two children, Christopher and Lindsay. Their roles began to switch when Terry suffered a horrific gardening accident, impaling his thigh on the rotor arm of a mowing machine. She also took up the martial arts of karate and judo which gave her a new sense of purpose and control. They helped her climbing, and she especially recalled a day in Snowdonia when 'nothing seemed impossible – it was like flying'.

Her introduction to the world of international expeditions came when she met the Austrian mountaineer and film maker Kurt Diemberger. Seven years older than Julie, Diemberger was a senior figure in mountaineering. They first met in 1975 in Snowdonia; a strong-willed man, Diemberger became angry when Julie turned down an invitation to go on a sailing trip. Finally she agreed to go climbing with him in Salzburg.

It was the start of a friendship which for Julie held the key to a new life. Diemberger was captivated by her lively, ingenuous nature; she regarded him with something little short of veneration, and described him as 'the great man'.

Diemberger offered Julie a job as a sound-recordist and in 1982 they joined an expedition to Nanga Parbat. Julie was forty-three; it was her first visit to the Himalaya, and the two trips to K2, another to Everest, and a return to Nanga Parbat followed. When they climbed Broad Peak in 1984, Julie became the first British woman to ascend a 25,000-foot peak, although they were lucky to survive when they were avalanched over a 120-foot cliff.

Julie retained her implicit faith in Diemberger's judgment and was not deterred by the intimations of mortality the accident inspired. She later described thinking: 'I don't really mind dying this way.'

As her self-confidence grew, she took up photography and embarked on an autobiography. But her new career created undoubted strains. Her absences left Terry to tend their Sussex cottage and garden at Leyswood for six months or more each year. While Terry pledged Julie his support, he felt she could become involved in too many projects at once. For her part, Julie was troubled by feelings of guilt. 'Terry's absolutely fantastic,' she once said, 'and he gets such a bad deal.'

Yet Julie and Terry remained committed to one another, and there were always periods of retrenchment. One came in 1985, when Julie and Terry went to the United States together for Christmas and Terry felt that they were entering a period of stability at last. Then Julie told Terry that Diemberger had arranged for them to film an Italian expedition to K2. Terry last saw Julie at Eridge station on 20 March, 1986. 'We were always very emotional when we said goodbye,' Terry recalls. They both cried.

Before joining the Italian expedition, Julie and Diemberger flew to Nepal to complete another film. As usual, Julie began to compose a diary for Terry's benefit. She relished her surroundings, describing the 'towering granite cliffs, topped by snowcapped mountains', all around.

Julie and Diemberger joined the Italians in Pakistan on 15 May and ten days later began the long approach march to K2. The weather remained poor but on 8 June the clouds parted, and K2 rose before them against a brilliant blue sky. When they rounded the final bend and saw a line of tents on the glacier, Julie wrote, 'it felt like arriving at a second home'.

By mid-June no fewer then ten expeditions had assembled below K2. They contained climbers from a dozen countries and planned to attempt the mountain by four different routes. Four were bidding for the Abruzzi Ridge, named after the Italian duke who made one of the earliest attempts in 1909.

Four more – including the Italians – had their eyes on the South-West Ridge. An international expedition was trying the South Pillar and a strong British team was attempting the long North-West Ridge. Of the four routes, only the Abruzzi had been climbed before.

In the subsequent chain of disasters, the presence of so many expeditions, with the potential for discord and misunderstanding, was a potent factor. For the moment, there were happy reunions for Julie and Diemberger with climbers they had met elsewhere. Yet there was a certain chill undertone which the British were probably the first to sense.

According to Jim Curran, a British climber and cameraman, 'it was a thought that occurred to most of us. There were sixty-odd climbers and we would be remarkably lucky if there wasn't a death. It was as if we were waiting for the first one to happen.'

Most of the expeditions intended to follow the traditional

Himalayan method of establishing a line of camps up the mountain. The climbers would use the camps as staging posts and shelter in case of storms, and also hoped to fix ropes to safeguard the most difficult sections.

But the first week brought frustrating inactivity. That summer there were never more than five clear days of weather in a stretch, with storms and snow in between. Only on 19 June did the Italians embark on the South-West Ridge, while Julie and Diemberger filmed on the Abruzzi Ridge. The first deaths came two days later.

At 5.50 a.m. on 21 June the South-West Ridge was raked by a massive avalanche, the consequence of the heavy snowfall the previous week. The Italians escaped but two Americans were swept away. 'The glacier village is a mixture of emotions,' Julie wrote. 'Extreme sadness, and worry for those still up.'

Her anxieties proved justified. On 23 June, after the French team had reached the summit, the married couple Maurice and Liliane Barrard fell to their deaths. Julie was stunned: it was, she tautly recorded, 'a major tragedy'.

To outsiders with four deaths in three days, it might appear that the expeditions were playing an extravagant game of Russian roulette. But although climbers will admit theirs is a risk sport, they prefer to rationalise accidents as events which occur to other people and which are compounded by their mistakes.

It could therefore be argued that the Americans had erred in venturing on to their route before the fresh snow had consolidated. As for the Barrards, they were not in the top echelon of climbers and may have been out of their depth in attempting K2.

Thus it was only the surviving Americans who decided to renounce their attempt. The Italians switched to the Abruzzi Ridge. On 3 July, they launched their summit bid, with Julie and Diemberger filming from behind. On 5 July six of them reached the top.

At 6 a.m. next day, from a camp 2000 feet below, Julie and Diemberger embarked on their own summit attempt. It was, Julie admitted, 'a little cheeky', as they were not yet acclimatised to the altitude.

At first they made steady progress through a rock chimney known as the Bottleneck. They slowed on a difficult ice traverse above and it was 4 p.m. when they arrived at the final snowslope below the summit. It became bitterly cold, and they headed back down.

Julie and Diemberger waited for twenty-four hours in the hope of making a second attempt. But the settled weather came to an end and on 8 July it was their turn to fight for their lives. As they began their descent the storm threatened to hurl them into the air.

They were periodically enveloped in 'white-outs', when ground and sky merge in flying snow, and they huddled against the wind until they could locate the horizon again. It was almost dark when they reached Camp 3.

When a pale dawn broke the storm was still at full fury. The fixed ropes were encased in ice and as Julie tried to free them her fingers became 'worryingly numb'. Camp 2 was buried in snow but further down they came upon another tent and took refuge there.

Even now they were still in danger. The snow piling up outside was threatening to engulf them as well as creating an avalanche risk. But in the middle of the night, Julie later wrote, there was nothing to be done. 'There are certain points in mountaineering where all you can do is wait.'

The morning brought relief at last. The storm had subsided and outside lay a new world – 'calm, beautiful, quiet'. When they reached Base Camp climbers flooded out to greet them: 'A very warm home-coming,' Julie wrote. To her diary, Julie admitted that the descent had brought misgivings. There were moments 'when I convinced myself that that was it. I was not going all that way back up. Who really cared if I climbed 300 metres higher on K2 or not?'

Her doubts deepened when she learned of yet another death. On 8 July two Polish climbers had reached the summit via the South Pillar. But they were caught in the storm that had struck Julie and Diemberger. One man lost his crampons and slid over a 10,000-foot drop. 'Everyone was devastated,' Julie wrote.

That death could still be ascribed to inexperience or exhaustion, but six days later came the accident that confirmed the part of sheer, malevolent fate in determining who lived or died on K2 that year.

For the past month the Italian Renato Casarotto, accompanied in Base Camp by his wife Goretta, had been making his solo attempt on the South-West Ridge. On 12 July he set off for one last attempt, but on 16 July he decided to retreat and radioed that he expected to reach Base Camp that night.

At 7 p.m. Julie heard Goretta shouting hysterically. Casarotto had just radioed to say that he had fallen into a crevasse. Julie, Diemberger and five other climbers went to his aid. They found Casarotto forty feet down a crevasse with a serious head injury. He was barely conscious when he was pulled out and half an hour later he died.

It fell to Julie to try to console the grief-stricken Goretta. In her next letter she told Terry she would not be making another summit bid. 'To get three hours from the top and go down safely means more to me than standing on the summit,' she assured him. 'I have no more pleasure to climb my mountain of mountains.'

In late July the K2 Base Camp wore an end-of-term air. Bad weather had returned and a number of expeditions packed up to go home. Then the weather cleared dramatically. In evident haste, and making no reference to her earlier decision not to attempt the summit again, Julie addressed another letter to Terry. 'Chaos is reigning,' she wrote. 'We are rushing off for one more try.'

Five teams assembled for the new attempt, all but one trying for the Abruzzi Ridge. There were the South Koreans, who were using oxygen and high-altitude porters; the Austrians, taciturn and determined; and the Poles, who were attempting the South-West Ridge. There was an improvised partnership between the British climber, Alan Rouse, and the Polish woman Dobroslawa Wolf, nicknamed 'Mrufka', the ant. Aged thirty-four, an articulate and sensitive man, Rouse had a high standing in the mountaineering world. He had attempted K2 in 1983 and – like Julie – had sworn to return.

Finally there were Julie and Diemberger. Despite Julie's letter, they were coy about revealing their goal. Diemberger says now that they had a 'silent agreement' which neither dared articulate. 'We moved up with the equipment for filming,' Diemberger says, 'but also with the gear for a summit attempt.'

Most realistic of all was Terry. Only after Julie died did he receive her letter saying she was making another attempt. 'That was typical Kurt and Julie. There was always another corner for them to turn, another place to explore.'

Julie and Diemberger left Base Camp on 28 July. They made

steady progress and on 2 August headed for Camp 4, 600 metres below the summit. A shock awaited them.

On abandoning their first summit bid in July, they had deposited a rucksack between Camps 3 and 4 which contained vital equipment for any subsequent attempt.

But the rucksack had disappeared. They first supposed that it must have been buried by snow but after searching in vain with their ice-axes, Diemberger darkly wondered whether it had been removed by one of the Koreans' high-altitude porters.

Although the loss left them perilously short of supplies, they decided to continue to Camp 4. Precisely what occurred at Camp 4 and how far it bore on the subsequent tragedy was to become a matter of acute controversy. Inevitably, the accounts of the survivors differ, with each attempting to make sense of the harrowing events in which they were involved. Although it is possible to achieve a measure of consensus, irreconcilable discrepancies remain.

The dispute has its origins in the destruction wrought on K2 by the avalanches and storms. When the climbers left Base Camp, the Austrians forged ahead. But at Camp 3 they found that all but one tent had been swept away.

The remaining tent belonged to the Koreans. The next day the Austrians radioed to the Korean team below them on the ridge. According to the Koreans' leader, Chang Bong-Wan, 'they asked us, "if you lend us your tent at Camp 3 we will set it up at Camp 4. After we reach the summit we will leave the tent as it is."' The Koreans accepted the Austrians' offer.

When Julie and Diemberger arrived at Camp 4 on 2 August, they could see the three Austrians at work above, fixing ropes on the dangerous ice traverse above the Bottleneck. But the Austrians were forced to turn back 200 metres from the summit by waist-deep snow.

That night an extraordinary row broke out at Camp 4 over whether the Austrians were honour-bound to return the Koreans' tent. Diemberger's view – imparted with some force – was that the Austrians were 'under an obligation to bivouac in the open, or go down to Camp 3'.

The Austrian Willi Bauer denies that there was any argument. 'We discussed it,' he says. He also denies that the Austrians were obliged to descend to Camp 3. 'That would have made no sense.'

But Chang Bong-Wan confirms Diemberger's account. 'After

failing to reach the summit the Austrian team asked if they could sleep in our tent,' Chang says. 'We refused as we had to try to reach to the summit the following day. But they begged us. There was no way to escape so two Austrians slept in our tent. It was very overcrowded.'

While two Austrians – Bauer and Hannes Wieser – squeezed in with the Koreans, the third, Alfred Imitzer, asked Diemberger and Julie if he could stay with them. Diemberger said that the deal with the Koreans was nothing to do with them, and they refused. That left only the tent belonging to Rouse and Mrufka, the smallest of all. Rouse nonetheless took Imitzer in, later telling Julie he had spent a sleepless night.

How far these events contributed to the subsequent tragedy is a further matter of controversy. The Koreans planned to make their summit attempt the next morning and Julie and Diemberger intended to follow them.

According to Diemberger, the overcrowding delayed the Koreans' departure until eight o'clock. By then 'we decided the day was lost'. This time Chang Bong-Wan disputes Diemberger's account. While Chang agrees that the Koreans did fall behind schedule, he is emphatic that they left not at eight o'clock, but at six. The Koreans had been expecting Julie and Diemberger to follow – 'we didn't know why they did not'.

The loss of that day was to prove disastrous. If Julie and Diemberger had gone for the summit on 3 August, they would have been on their way down when the last, fatal storm struck.

There was another factor too. Afterwards Diemberger talked of spending 3 August as a 'rest day' when he and Julie brewed drinks and relaxed. But the notion of a rest day at 8000 metres is highly contentious. The height is sometimes called the 'death zone', and the term, if melodramatic, is accurate. To compensate for the lack of oxygen, the body generates extra red blood corpuscles. These cause the blood to thicken, clogging circulation while the brain accumulates liquid which can cause a form of stroke termed a cerebral oedema. Each day accelerates a physiological decline that leads only to death.

But the lack of oxygen has other effects that may help to explain why climbers may be reluctant to depart. It brings a sense of euphoria that one experienced mountaineer likens to 'being pleasantly drunk'. The greatest temptation is to remain at the same altitude.

At four o'clock that afternoon the three Koreans reached the summit, followed by three Poles on the South-West Ridge. As the six men descended, K2 saw its seventh death that summer, when a Pole slipped from the ice traverse above the Bottleneck.

Later a Korean climber fell behind and was forced to bivouac. But the arrival of four other climbers made Camp Four even more cramped. This time two climbers squeezed in with Rouse, so that he spent another wretched night.

At 6 a.m. on 4 August, Rouse and Mrufka left for the summit. They were followed by the Austrians Imitzer and Bauer – Wieser remained behind – with Julie and Diemberger last in line. The Austrians reached the summit at 3.30 p.m. followed by Rouse, while Mrufka turned back.

At 4.30 p.m. the successful climbers were descending when they met Julie and Diemberger some 100 metres below the summit, and they asked if they were sure they should carry on. The weather was deteriorating once more, and if they pressed on they would have to descend in the dark. By rights they should have turned back; but for most mountaineers there comes a moment when they face the ultimate gamble.

Doug Scott and Dougal Haston took the gamble when they decided to push on to the summit of Everest in 1975, even though they knew they would have to endure the highest bivouac ever made. The weather was merciful and they survived. It was the gamble made by Mick Burke on the same expedition, when he went for the summit in a gathering storm. He was never seen again.

As Diemberger recalls that moment, 'I said to Julie, "We are very close to the top. It's a question of one hour, shall we do it or shall we not?"' He adds: 'The summit was so close and we were feeling good and we went on.'

At 6 p.m. Julie and Diemberger stood on the summit of their dreams. 'We hugged each other,' Diemberger says. 'Both of us thought it was the most desired peak we could ever get to. We said it was "our K2".'

Julie and Diemberger were now at the absolute limit of their safety margins. Each decision they had made had eroded those margins. The dusk and weather were closing in around them; their safety limit was about to expire.

After their celebratory hug, Diemberger and Julie photographed each other by the tiny cairn of oxygen bottles that the Koreans had left at K2's summit the previous day. By now the light was fading fast and Julie told Diemberger: 'It's high time we started our descent.'

Two hundred metres below the summit came near-catastrophe. Diemberger was descending a patch of hard snow when he heard Julie shout, 'Oh, Kurt!' Diemberger believes that Julie slipped on a patch of ice; in the next moment she slid past him at gathering speed. He drove in his ice-axe but when the rope between them came taut he was wrenched from his stance. As they headed towards a 3000-metre drop Diemberger was convinced they were doomed. By some miracle they stopped, Diemberger sitting upright, Julie sprawled in the snow above. 'We were very relieved,' says Diemberger. 'It was almost death.'

Their predicament was acute. The weather was worsening, night was almost upon them, and they had left their bivouac equipment in a rucksack above the Bottleneck. They carved out a shallow snowhole at the edge of a crevasse with their ice-axes and passed an 'endless night', Diemberger says, sucking sweets and hugging each other in an attempt to stay warm.

When dawn broke, bringing with it clouds and a rising wind, Julie was suffering from frostbite on one hand and her nose. 'But she did not complain,' says Diemberger.

With considerable difficulty, in what soon became a complete white-out, Julie and Diemberger groped their way back to the fixed ropes and descended towards Camp 4. At the foot of the ropes they moved in zigzags to improve their chances of finding the camp. The Korean and Polish climbers who reached the summit on 3 August had left the next day. Rouse, Mrufka and the three Austrians had planned to start their descent on 5 August, but were unable to move in the storm.

By eleven o'clock that morning they had virtually given up Julie and Diemberger for dead. Then the Austrian Willi Bauer heard Diemberger's shouts and called out in response.

When he and Julie heard Bauer, says Diemberger, they were 'quite relieved'. Julie's eyesight seemed to be impaired and she crawled the last part of the way. Bauer helped Julie into his tent. 'Her fingers were frostbitten, as was her face,' Bauer says. 'We gave her hot drinks to try to get her going again.'

At the foot of K2, the climbers in Base Camp were increasingly alarmed. The weather had clearly broken and on 5 August, when four inches of snow fell on the glacier, the mountain disappeared from view. That night the most ferocious storm of the summer broke. As the wind roared from K2's higher reaches, the British climber/cameraman Jim Curran felt 'a well of sorrow' for his colleagues near the summit.

In Camp 4, the seven climbers were enduring the storm's fury. Julie rejoined Diemberger on the night of 5 August but seemed worried and distracted. They awoke to find their tent on the point of collapsing from the weight of snow. Yelling above the wind, they aroused Bauer and Rouse who helped them to struggle clear.

Julie returned to the Austrians' tent and Diemberger joined Rouse and Mrufka. Diemberger found the separation especially painful: the wind was so powerful, he says, 'that even by shouting you could not speak from tent to tent'. Later that day Julie struggled across to Rouse's tent. She told Diemberger she had come to say hello but added, 'I feel rather strange.'

Diemberger was unable to see Julie from inside the tent and asked her to bend down by the entrance. He could only glimpse her hair. 'Be strong,' he told her. 'I think of you.'

In the Austrians' tent, the weight of snow pressing from outside was restricting the space more and more. Bauer says that Julie was 'very undemanding' and lay quietly in her sleeping bag. But Bauer, who had trained as a nurse during military service, was only too aware how every hour they were pinned down was putting Julie above all at risk.

Weakened by the shock of her fall and the frostbite and hypothermia she had suffered during her enforced bivouac, Julie was the most vulnerable to the effects of high altitude – and Bauer knew that one of the symptoms was impaired eyesight. 'When we gave Julie drinks she kept missing the cup,' he says. 'We knew then she had no more chance.'

That evening Julie kept drifting asleep. Bauer was watching her and talked to her, he says, 'to try to perk her up'. At one point, when there was a brief lull in the storm, Julie asked if they could start to descend. Later, says Bauer, 'she asked me to make sure that Diemberger got down safely. An hour or so later I looked at her again and she had died.' Gently, Bauer closed her mouth and eyes.

For Diemberger, almost as distressing as Julie's death was the manner in which he learned of it. When morning came on 7 August, Bauer shouted from his tent: 'Kurt, Julie died last night.' The news struck Diemberger like a hammer-blow.

'It was totally unexpected for me. I couldn't understand that nobody had called me over. Maybe I couldn't have helped her. But when you have been with someone for so long, you can give her spiritual help.'

At ten o'clock the Austrians moved Julie's body into the collapsed tent she had originally shared with Diemberger. As the storm continued to rage, the six remaining climbers declined inexorably towards the same fate.

By 8 August, all supplies of food were exhausted. Worse still, there was no more cooking gas to melt snow for drinks, essential to counter the dehydrating effects of altitude. The most seriously affected, as a result of his lack of sleep and the energy he had expended going to the summit, appeared to be Rouse. At times he became delirious, beating his hands on his sleeping bag; at times, murmuring 'water, water', he lapsed into unconsciousness.

Mrufka, by contrast, closed in on herself, as if entering a state of near-hibernation. Diemberger, with his stocky, middle-aged frame, was also in better shape than Rouse to survive. In the Austrians' tent, Bauer observed with disquiet that his two companions were suffering from dizziness – a telling symptom.

Yet still the storm made it impossible to attempt to descend. 'Visibility was nil,' says Bauer. 'It was only on 10 August that we could see to go down.' According to Bauer, Rouse had lost either the strength or the will to move. Seemingly lost in fantasies, he told Bauer that he had a supply of water in his sleeping bag and had decided to stay in his tent.

Diemberger also tried to cajole Rouse into action, without success. Rouse asked him for water and Diemberger moistened his lips with snow. 'I had no choice but to leave him,' Diemberger says.

Imitzer and Wieser were also close to death. Bauer helped them to their feet and pushed them out of the tent. Then he set off, breaking the trail with Mrufka close behind. Imitzer and Wieser tried to follow but after struggling barely 100 metres they collapsed. Bauer and Mrufka attempted to support them but found they were unable to help themselves and so were forced to leave them behind.

Meanwhile Diemberger waited until the others had gone. Then he looked into Julie's tent for the last time. 'I could touch her,' he says, 'but I could not see her face.'

Soon after starting his descent Diemberger came upon Imitzer and Wieser lying in the snow. One was face down and motionless, the other on his back, his arms waving feebly. When Diemberger spoke to them they did not respond; concluding that they were beyond all help, Diemberger pressed on.

The three surviving climbers now headed for the safety of Base Camp. Bauer was still leading with Mrufka close behind, and she helped to extricate him when he sank into the snow, chest-deep at times. Then Diemberger caught up and all three shared the trail-breaking for a while.

Below Camp 3 many of the fixed ropes were encased with ice. It was Mrufka who found it hardest to cope and she gradually fell behind. That night Bauer and Diemberger reached Camp 2 to find supplies of food and gas at last. Mrufka did not arrive. In the morning Bauer and Diemberger waited until midday but she was never seen again. In Base Camp, Jim Curran was convinced that all seven climbers were dead. On 11 August he broke open the tent Julie and Diemberger had shared and found some lager that Diemberger had been brewing. Curran and the remaining climbers drank a sorrowful toast to absent friends.

As dusk fell on 11 August, a silhouette appeared on the glacier, stumbling towards Base Camp. It was Bauer, his hands and feet frostbitten, his clothing in tatters. He managed to convey the news that Mrufka was missing and that all other climbers save Diemberger were dead.

Curran and two Polish climbers left at once for the Abruzzi Ridge. Just before midnight they came upon Diemberger, moving down so slowly that he seemed to be barely alive. Curran told him that he was safe at last.

'I've lost Julie,' Diemberger replied.

6

MIXED GROUND

One of the delights of writing about mountaineering is the diversity it brings, from interviewing an author with the same passions, to meeting Captain John Noel, who died this year, and writing about climbing walls for a Scandinavian airlines magazine. The greatest diversity of all arose when the *Financial Times* induced me to go pot-holing. Like many mountaineers, I suspect, I regarded the activity with fascinated horror, but in the end curiosity overcame my fear. The experience also served as a taste, however brief, of the world I was to describe soon afterwards when trying to account for the baffling disappearance of the young pot-holer, Alex Pitcher, in the Gouffre Berger near Grenoble. I persuaded Maggie Body, my editor at Hodder and Stoughton, to include it in what was supposed to be a climbing anthology on the grounds that the gamut of experiences were sufficiently similar. The mystery of Alex Pitcher's fate was resolved after the article appeared, and the section ends with a coda the *Sunday Times* published which served to bring the story to its sad end.

Tales from the hills

Radio Times, 1979

When John Keay went fishing in Kashmir in 1965 it changed his life. He had left Oxford University with an indifferent history degree and for a career was contemplating such delights as demonstrating welding equipment or selling perfume. In Kashmir he found rushing hill-streams filled with fat brown trout, descendants of the stock introduced from Scotland a century before.

But his gaze was soon drawn from his rod to the soaring mountains behind – the enormous chain of the Himalaya, 1500 miles long and up to 400 miles wide, that presents one of its most awe-inspiring aspects in northern Kashmir.

Keay became captivated by the Himalaya and then intrigued by the nineteenth-century Europeans who were the first to travel widely among them. After extensive research and several return trips, Keay has written two books on the mountains and those men. The first forms the basis of the six-part radio series which starts this week. Keay – who also wrote the scripts – hopes they will convey his own sense of wonder at the Himalaya and his admiration for the pioneers who explored them.

A year after his fishing expedition Keay was back in Kashmir. He made a living by writing about the region first as a freelance, then as a correspondent for the *Economist*. As he journeyed in the foothills of the Himalaya he began to consider the obstacles and dangers his predecessors must have faced. Then a mission-ary doctor invited him on a trip to Srinagar, capital of Kashmir, and there he met refugees who had made the 400-mile trek through the mountains from the Sinkiang province of China.

'Until then,' says Keay, 'I had always thought of the Himalaya as forming an enormous political and topographical barrier, but talking to those people made me think a lot about the idea of travelling *across* the range.'

In 1970 Keay and a companion spent two months walking through an area of the mountains which few British had visited since the colonial days. Keay was fascinated by the relics of that era, such as the resthouses where early hill-trekkers stayed at night. His companion decided to open a travel agency for hill-walkers – while Keay embarked on full-time research about the European explorers.

Keay was surprised – and pleased – to discover that no single book had been published in English that attempted to tell the whole story. But among the voluminous and sometimes dusty records of the India Office in Blackfriars, he unearthed the papers and journals of many of the early travellers. Some had been stored among the secret and political files – an indication of the importance attached to them at a time when Britain was consolidating the boundaries of her empire, and was engaged in skirmishing and espionage against her principal rival in that part of the globe, Tsarist Russia.

Keay made several further trips to the Himalaya, and his book *When Men and Mountains Meet* (John Murray, £6.50) – the title is a quotation from William Blake – was published in 1977. He had originally intended to write only one volume, but he had gathered so much material that a second, *The Gilgit Game* (John Murray, £7.95), duly appeared this year.

For Radio 4's series Keay has selected six of the explorers he came most to admire. Foremost among them is William Moorcroft, a vet who joined the East India Company and was already in his fifties when, in 1819, he set off into the western Himalaya to seek supplies of livestock and to prospect for new trade routes. 'It was a time when virtually nothing was known about the region,' says Keay. 'He must have known it was a do-or-die effort.'

Moorcroft spent five years wandering over icy passes and through lush valleys before dying of fever. Although his journey was incomplete and his trade mission a failure, he bequeathed thousands of pages of detailed observations about the area and its potential. 'In stature and vision none of the others compares with him,' says Keay. 'Above all he was an enthusiast in a period when enthusiasm was hardly fashionable – he was a Magnus Pyke or Patrick Moore of his time.'

One of the first to follow Moorcroft was the Frenchman Victor Jacquemont, a botanist of dark good looks and a romantic disposition, who used his Byronic charm to ease his way through the territories of local rulers. Keay admires him for the honesty of his writings, for Jacquemont forswore the stiff upper lip of the British and described frankly the discomforts and hardship of the expeditionary life. At the age of thirty-one he, like Moorcroft, succumbed to fever, and developed a liver abscess which was to prove fatal. He was carried to Bombay where he continued to write, contemplating his approaching death with remarkable tranquillity.

In complete contrast to Jacquemont was the eccentric Joseph Wolff, a converted Jew who sought to preach Christianity to the people of the Himalaya, and who was attacked by brigands and forced to cross snow-covered ranges stark naked. Then came Godfrey Vigne, an Old Harrovian from a prosperous merchant family, whose accounts Keay regards as the most stylish and entertaining of all, even when Vigne is reporting a night spent on a glacier, cowering without shelter from a storm. Vigne is also the most mysterious, apparently involved in espionage – activities about which he drops the occasional clue.

Mystery also surrounds the American adventurer Alexander Gardiner, whose tales of gunfights and robbery would seem more in place in the Wild West. Early historians caught Gardiner out on points of detail, and harshly judged that his stories were fiction. But Keay discovered that Gardiner had been widely consulted by later travellers, including the distinguished surveyor Colonel Godwin-Austen, and concludes that his accounts contain a substantial kernel of truth.

Keay's sixth explorer is John Wood, a young British naval lieutenant who was despatched to find the source of the River Oxus. The journey, which Wood embarked on quite casually, ended at a frozen, wind-scoured lake at 15,000 feet; and Keay believes it irrevocably altered Wood's life. Wood graphically described the scene of desolation he found, and declared that man was a social animal whose true destiny was to live in the city. But when Wood himself returned to London he found he could not face city life again. He emigrated to Australia, moved on to New Zealand, and finally went back to India, where he spent the rest of his life in command of a flotilla of ferry boats.

Keay believes that once Wood had been lured into the mountains he remained for ever in their thrall. 'Mountains unsettle people and I think they had that effect on Wood. I love being in the mountains but they make me restless too.'

Like Wood, John Keay appears to have found the lure irresistible. In the middle of his research he and his wife Julie moved to a house in the Scottish Highlands, near the lowering peaks of Glen Coe, where they and their two children live now. There he felt more and more drawn to his explorers. 'The mountains seemed to inspire a kind of modesty in them which other explorers don't share; those who went to Africa are rather arrogant by comparison. Sometimes they seem even cowed by their surroundings.'

Keay reached some of his conclusions while striding out on long hill-walks near his home. 'I remain fascinated by the effects mountains have on people, having fallen in love with them myself.'

Could a man do the job?

Sunday Times Magazine, 1968

In 1913 John Noel was aged twenty-three and a junior officer in the Indian army in Calcutta; 350 miles to the north of him were the Himalaya, known to contain the highest mountain in the world . . . Everest. It was named after Sir George Everest, Surveyor General of India. On a clear winter's day in Darjeeling, near the closed Tibetan border, its top thousand feet could be seen over an intervening range of mountains – a tiny white pyramid well over 100 miles away.

Two and a half years at school in Switzerland had endowed Noel with a love of mountains – he had climbed many of the classic alpine routes. After leaving school he told his father, himself a professional soldier, that he wanted to be a hunter, 'to shoot crocodiles in India and walruses in the Arctic'. 'I think you'd just better join the army,' said his father tolerantly.

Before the First World War access into Tibet was forbidden and the approaches to Everest remained a mystery. This added to Noel's fascination. Northern India was hot and oppressive so British officers were given long summer leaves. 'I used to spend mine going up to the frontier to see if I could find a pass over the Himalaya that wasn't guarded,' says Noel. In 1913 he found the pass of Chorten Nyim in the Kanchenjunga massif, eighty miles west of Everest, and nearly 20,000 feet high. Noel and five Sherpas walked westwards through Tibet for two and a half weeks, before being intercepted by a party of Tibetan soldiers.

He was forced to return. Once back in India he discovered that he had been within forty miles of Everest, 'nearer at that time than any white man had been', he wrote in his book *Through Tibet to Everest* (1927). 'I leave you to imagine my chagrin and disappointment.'

Noel had overstayed his leave by two months. 'I told the Colonel we had been crossing a glacier river and had been swept off our feet. We lost all our baggage including my calendar and I didn't know what date it was. He just told me to take two calendars next time and said no more about it.'

The First World War prevented any further exploration; Noel fought with the infantry on the Western Front. At Mons 600 men in his battalion were killed in twenty minutes; Noel took part in hand-to-hand fighting. He escaped uninjured. 'Never a scratch,' he says. 'It was very exciting.'

In 1919 he lectured to the Royal Geographical Society about his Tibetan journey. 'Now that the North and South Poles have been conquered,' he said, 'it is generally felt that the next and most important task is Mount Everest.'

In 1921 a reconnaissance expedition left for Tibet. The Dalai Lama had given his permission; there was no need for Noel's earlier secrecy, and they crossed into Tibet by the Jelep Pass, to the east of Noel's higher route. One man in the party died of a heart attack, and a route-finding error cost them three months, but in September they reached Everest's North Col, at 22,900 feet, which was to become the starting point for every attempt until 1947.

In 1922 the Royal Geographical Society and the Alpine Club organised a full expedition. Noel was chosen as the official photographer, though not without opposition. 'They said they didn't want the climb to be vulgarised for the cinema,' says Noel. 'George Mallory said he was interested in climbing the mountain, not in being an actor in a film.'

The expedition began the 350-mile walk from Darjeeling in March, climbing to 16,000 feet before reaching the Tibetan plateau. 'You stand on the watershed and look over a vast plain that goes on and on to the horizon,' says Noel, 'just wild country, like the surface of the moon, with the thread of a river, swamps and lakes, and ranges and ranges of mountains beyond your ability to count.' At the end of April they reached the Rongbuk Monastery, and Noel at last had his first view of Everest. 'We all sat down and gazed and gazed. It was twenty-one miles distant and when I took a picture it filled the frame. We all asked, secretly, could a man do the job? We felt so small.'

Noel set up a darkroom in a tent in Base Camp at 16,000 feet. To dry his film away from the freezing, dust-laden wind, he heated the air in the tent with a stove, and filtered it through a muslin net with a hand-blower. Horsemen and runners carried his film and photographic plates back to Darjeeling, where they were shipped to England; Noel's pictures appeared in *The Times*.

Before the expedition, it was not known how high climbers would be able to go in the rarefied air, but Mallory, Norton and Somervell reached 27,000 feet on the North-East Ridge. The climbers wore Norfolk jackets and tweed trousers, and several suffered badly from frostbite. Under stress, tempers frayed. 'The too frequent sight of our companions' faces annoys us,' wrote Noel. 'We quarrel over the most trivial details.' The food was unappetising and unvarying, and one man hurled a plate of hot breakfast sausages into the Sherpa cook's face. The expedition ended when an avalanche killed seven Sherpas.

Back in England, distributors were unenthusiastic about

Noel's film. 'Wardour Street complained there was no love story in it,' says Noel. He hired the Philharmonic Hall for ten weeks and showed it himself. Bernard Shaw saw it, and was unimpressed: 'The Everest expedition was a picnic in Connemara surprised by a snowstorm,' he said, but he was almost alone in his judgment, and the film made a profit.

For the 1924 expedition Noel bought a piece of land in Darjeeling, levelled it, and built a wooden house where a photographic assistant was to process the film and send it back to England.

The expedition reached Base Camp at the end of April, but bad weather delayed the attempt, and two porters died. Noel felt isolated from the other expedition members: 'I felt I was there as a supernumerary – I was always afraid they thought I was there to make capital out of their climbing.' Mallory, who had relented on his earlier opinion about filming, showed Noel most consideration – one of his last two notes before he left Camp 6 told Noel where to look out for him.

On 4 June, Norton reached 28,124 feet without oxygen, and two days later Mallory and Irvine left on their own summit attempt. At 12.40 p.m. Odell saw two figures on the mountain, at first thought to be at around 28,400 feet, but now believed to be no higher than 28,000. Noel was in Camp 3 at 21,000 feet with his longest lens trained on the summit. He and three climbers waited there until 9 June, when a signal was relayed to them from Odell in Camp 6 that Mallory and Irvine had disappeared. 'We each looked through the telescope and tried to make the signal different,' says Noel. 'But we couldn't.' Nine years later, the 1933 expedition found an ice-axe 200 yards east of the First Step – almost certainly marking the spot of a fatal slip, and strongly suggesting that the pair had retreated without reaching the summit.

As the 1924 expedition withdrew, Noel believed that he would return. But in 1933, when the Dalai Lama next gave permission, Noel was forty-two, and Frank Smythe went as photographer instead.

Captain Noel lives today in a white weatherboard cottage at Brenzett, a village in the wide expanse of Romney Marsh in Kent. At seventy-nine, he remains fit and upright. 'He's never ill,' says Mrs Noel, a sturdy Irishwoman. Noel still gives lectures, his wife projecting his hand-coloured photographs on a spindly epidiascope which he made himself. 'He does everything,' says Mrs Noel. 'Plastering, carpentry, electricity.' When they moved into their present home six years ago, Captain Noel converted the two cottages into one.

His memories of his two Everest expeditions remain clear, but he talks reluctantly about himself. 'He's always telling you about what the others did,' says Mrs Noel. 'He won't tell you half of what he's done.'

He retains as his inspiration the seventy-two-year-old Swiss guide he met when he was twenty during a descent in bad weather from an alpine peak. 'He said to me: "Young man, if you are tired, lean on me, and I'll take you down." He has always been a model in my life. You should go on living until you die and that has always been my guiding principle.'

He was immensely proud when Everest was climbed in 1953. 'Mount Everest occupied such a large section of my life. The British started it and the British carried it through.'

Up the walls

Scanorama, 1984

I n the town of Ebbw Vale in South Wales, in a leisure centre, there is a wall that appears to be an audacious example of modern sculpture. Bricks project at odd angles, deep gashes indent it. Not meant as art, it is a climbing wall, an attempt to reproduce in brickwork one of the nearby rock faces where climbers delight in their skills.

A dozen miles away lie the Brecon Beacons, the most spectacular mountains of South Wales. To the west is the Pembrokeshire coast, whose limestone sea cliffs provide miles of climbing routes, and to the north is Snowdonia, containing the highest mountains in England or Wales, whose rough granite has been the joy of generations of climbers.

With nature providing such a magnificent wild environment so close at hand, what need is there of an artificial climbing wall?

The answer lies with Britain's climate. The notorious wind, cold and rain that can be the despair of overseas visitors present a serious handicap to rock-climbers, who prefer their sport most when the rocks are warm and dry. In its heated hall, illuminated at night, the Ebbw Vale wall provides a climbing playground where all such problems disappear.

The Ebbw Vale wall is far from unique. There are more than 350 climbing walls in Britain, a total that has been reached in a very short time, for the first was built only in 1965. They are to be found in sports halls, leisure centres, schools, colleges and training camps throughout Britain. Last year, it has been estimated, they had a total of 40,000 visits from climbers who ranged from outright novices to celebrated climbing figures.

Let's take a closer look at a wall, this time in the municipal sport centre in Bradford, in Yorkshire. The wall occupies the side of a room that is also used quite harmoniously by Bradford's bodybuilders, who come to tune up their muscles on an array of weight-training equipment. It differs from Ebbw Vale's in being more varied and also, in places, more realistic. It is 18 metres long and ranges from three to nine metres in height. One section consists of a vertical brick wall into which chunks of rock have been set or holds scooped out. But another section has been moulded to give a rough finish that is far closer in feel and appearance to a true rock face.

Waiting to demonstrate the wall's attributes is one of Britain's leading rock-climbers, twenty-eight-year-old Graham Desroy, a tall, lank figure, whose powerful forearms and calf muscles testify to the hours he spends reaching for or balancing on tiny holds. Desroy begins on an angled section of the wall that has been constructed to resemble what climbers term a 'slab', moving delicately upward by finding purchase on microscopic bumps and wafer-thin ledges.

Next to the slab is another angled section that leans out from the vertical to create an overhang. Desroy appears to defy gravity as he dangles from his arms and levers himself upwards with his feet. Then comes a 'chimney'. Desroy climbs it by the classic technique of bracing one foot on either side and edging his way up.

Finally he decides to climb to the top of the wall, nine metres above. He ponders his line of ascent like a chess player devising his strategy half a dozen moves ahead. Then he is off, stepping up briskly from hold to hold, a toe jammed into a crack here, pushing at a slanting rock there, with his hands caressing and testing the holds above before he commits himself to them, finally reaching the sanctuary of the top of the wall.

Desroy's performance has been deceptive: much of the rock-climber's skill lies in conserving energy and moving with as little apparent effort as possible, and Desroy has ably exemplified that. Once back on the ground, however, there is no doubt that he has undergone a very demanding workout. His forehead is beaded with sweat, he is breathing deeply, and he shakes his fingers and arms to relax their drained muscles.

'It's a very versatile wall,' he says. 'You can use it in so many ways and you can practise just about all your techniques. Even though I have climbed on it a lot, it still presents a very rewarding challenge.'

There are other people at Bradford who express their appreciation, not least the city authorities. Last year the wall attracted 5376 users, paying seventy-five pence a visit – a total of over £4000. As the wall cost £10,000 when it was built in 1978, it has now more than paid for itself and is bringing some very useful revenue to Bradford's city coffers.

Why did indoor climbing develop so fast? Climbers have little doubt who has played the principal role. He is a mild, bespectacled man named Don Robinson, who had been watching Desroy perform on the Bradford wall. Robinson is a fifty-six-year-old lecturer at Leeds University, ten miles east of Bradford. He designed the Bradford wall and some two dozen others that are widely reckoned to offer the best wall-climbing in Britain. Robinson also built Britain's first-ever brick climbing wall and effectively started the whole climbing-wall boom.

Robinson arrived at Leeds University in 1964 to take up a position as a lecturer in outdoor pursuits. He is an enthusiastic climber, backpacker and potholer. It is no secret that many climbers choose Leeds University because it is so close to the crags and cliffs of Yorkshire and Derbyshire.

Then Robinson came upon 'a nice big blank wall' that ran the length of a corridor in his department. Almost in a flash, the idea came to him that the wall, so enticingly virgin, could be made into a climbing wall.

There were a couple of climbing walls already in existence, but these were small wooden structures of limited appeal. 'So I began by analysing how climbers actually stay on the rock and what techniques they adopt. Then I tried to work out how to reproduce a rock face that would enable them to use and perfect all those techniques,' Robinson explains.

He toured the local climbing areas to garner suitable chunks of rock for the wall. Then, having obtained the permission of the somewhat sceptical university authorities, he enlisted the university's bricklayer. To Robinson's instructions the bricklayer hacked out holes in the corridor wall and inserted Robinson's rocks, firmly secured with cross ties and mortar. By the time it was finished, 102 rocks had been fixed in place. Puzzled passers-by assumed that Robinson was a sculptor at work on a mural, but the university's climbers showed no hesitation.

'They were on it almost before the cement was dry,' says Robinson. That winter the corridor was filled night after night with climbers eager to test their prowess and solve the problems Robinson had set.

The rest of the climbing world did not seem inclined to take the Leeds wall seriously – until its attractions were publicised in a sensational manner. A Leeds student who had never climbed before tried out the wall and discovered that he was a natural to the sport. 'He practised endlessly,' Robinson recalls, 'but it was a long time before he tried the real thing. Then he went to a rock outcrop and put up half a dozen new routes.' (In climbing parlance, new routes are first ascents.)

The university displayed a generous attitude toward its wall, allowing climbers from outside to use it. They were not the only visitors. Designers and architects came too, eager to introduce this novel feature to sport and leisure centres throughout Britain. At first Robinson gave his advice freely – 'and I must have spent hundreds of hours doing so' – but then, not unreasonably, decided to cash in on his expertise.

He formed a company, DR Climbing Walls, and acquired a workshop in one of the railway arches beneath Leeds station. Two years ago, Graham Desroy joined him to help handle the increasing flow of orders. Since the first wall at Leeds, Robinson has installed another twenty-five. They are divided, more or less equally, among schools, colleges and leisure centres, with two commissioned by the British army.

The average cost of a Robinson wall is now around £40,000, with Robinson's own charges about £10,000. If £40,000 seems a lot, Robinson points out that it is roughly the cost of one squash-court – which also needs far more maintenance. Robinson's current designs are notably more ambitious than his first effort at Leeds. The most remarkable is probably the one occupying a disused lift-shaft in the leisure centre at Darlington in north-east England. Eighteen metres high, it uses all four walls of the shaft and contains almost 1000 holds.

Robinson has also refined his construction techniques. He and Desroy now manufacture their own climbing bricks in their workshop, mixing the cement and pouring it into a mould. They then insert a rock selected from the considerable collection piled in one corner, which they replenish each time they visit a climbing area.

It is a matter of strenuous competition between them to see who can obtain a rock from the most outlandish source. Last year, Robinson triumphantly bore home two rocks he had picked up during a trekking holiday in the Peruvian Andes. Desroy has since retaliated by ordering two rocks from a friend working with a British survey team in the Antarctic.

To manufacture cracks, they use a similar technique, but insert into the cement a chunk of carved polystyrene. When the cement has set, they chip out the polystyrene, leaving a cavity of the desired configuration. They then prepare a minutely detailed chart for the building contractors, showing them exactly where to place each climbing 'brick'.

Robinson has also developed a process for reproducing the rock face in a more authentic manner, as illustrated by part of the Bradford wall. Robinson built that by preparing a series of far larger polystyrene moulds into which the concrete was tipped on the construction site itself. When the concrete had set, the moulds were peeled away, leaving a surface with much of the variety and subtlety of a true climbing crag.

That development has also assisted Robinson to carry through the most important principle behind the design of his walls. 'It is essential,' he explains, 'that they should offer something to everyone.' Walls made solely of vertical brickwork are daunting to beginners, whereas the angled slab at Bradford gives even a novice a sporting chance of getting off the ground. At the same time, Robinson is not without a certain mean streak, for he also insists that his walls have an element of what he terms 'fiendishness'.

Precisely what this meant, I discovered when I made my own consumer test of the Bradford wall. Once a keen if inexpert rock-climber, I have long since graduated to hill-walking, and it was disconcerting to find myself clinging to tiny holds once again, with the wall seeming determined to thrust me from my stance. Nonetheless, as I made a low-level traverse across the brick section of the wall, I felt I was making reasonable progress – until I groped for an enticing crack that appeared to offer the next handhold.

I was sadly wrong. The crack sloped away in the wrong

direction, and I was compelled to beat a hasty and awkward retreat. There came a chuckle from behind as Don Robinson witnessed my discomfort. He explained that I had fallen for one of his 'decoy' holds, and then pointed out the alternative hold, a little higher, that I should have aimed for.

How does the Bradford wall compare with the real thing? The previous evening I had visited the Roaches, one of the gaunt gritstone 'edges' to be found on the hillcrests of the Peak District south of Manchester. There I had climbed several of the easier routes that wind their way to the top of the seventeen-metre cliff, delighting in the natural feel of the rock, the sweep of the face and the shadowy evening landscape below.

The Bradford wall could scarcely offer these. On the other hand, it did permit me an undoubted sense of triumph at having solved one of its less demanding technical problems, coupled with the feeling of weary satisfaction that came from exercising my muscles to the full.

Not all walls have proved as successful as those of Don Robinson. Such is the controversy surrounding some of them, in fact, that the British Mountaineering Council (BMC) has recently become involved.

The problems arose, paradoxically, because of the very popularity of climbing walls following Don Robinson's initial success at Leeds. For some architects, the walls became the latest item of aesthetic fashion, and they paid little heed to the practical advice available from Robinson or experienced climbers.

The BMC has found basic design errors that render some walls inherently dangerous to use. Walls need a level surround so that climbers who decide to 'bail out' – jump off – have a safe landing. But some walls slope away at the foot, vastly increasing the likelihood of a climber jarring or breaking his heels. The first couple of feet of a climbing wall should be free of holds so that a climber who slips can slide smoothly back to the ground. And yet some have jagged projections just above ground level that, apart from being superfluous as holds, create the risk of broken ankles.

Among other faults, some walls are almost uniform in their design, offering no challenge or variety, and soon become quite monotonous for climbers. Still others have been finished in the wrong material, so that what should be a rough surface offering good friction is, instead, impossibly smooth. The most dramatic conflict between the aesthetic concerns of the architects and the practical needs of the climbers is exemplified by the wall that won a design award from Britain's brick manufacturers – and which climbers have rejected as virtually useless.

The BMC is now preparing guidance to offer architects who come to it seeking assistance and advice.

But it has a second problem to contend with: the attitude of local authorities toward walls. Too often they are weighed down by fears that climbers will have accidents and that officials will be held responsible. 'The result is that they impose all kinds of restrictions that destroy the whole ethos of climbing,' says Ken Wilson, chairman of the BMC committee that has been examining the use and misuse of climbing walls.

Wilson cites a wide range of regulations the BMC objects to. Some centres demand user certificates that they only issue to experienced climbers. Others permit only climbers who belong to official clubs. Some require climbers to wear various items of protective equipment, such as helmets. One painted a line across its wall four and a half metres above the ground and has banned climbers from passing it unless they are using safety ropes.

On the mountainside, climbers usually *do* use ropes, observing the complex procedures of 'belaying' to limit the length of a fall. On climbing walls they far prefer to climb 'solo', confident in their ability to retreat safely if they find themselves in difficulty.

Wilson explains: 'Of course climbing is a risk sport. But climbers know that better than anyone. They accept it and are entitled to weigh the risks for themselves.'

Wilson may seem unsympathetic to the anxieties of officials and administrators. Yet the facts are largely on his side. There has not been a serious injury, let alone a death, to anyone using a climbing wall in Britain. Nor has any local authority been sued for damages.

The clearest lesson comes from two walls in the suburbs of Manchester. At Altrincham, a wall that was opened in 1982 and has no restrictions had 10,000 users paying seventy-five pence each in its first year. At nearby Sale, a wall that both has severe design faults and is heavily regulated had just 114 users in the same period.

Wilson hopes that these examples carry their own moral, of which designers and planners will take heed. As for the future, both he and Robinson are looking ahead, curiously enough, to artificial walls that can be built out of doors. If that seems to contradict one of the central features of climbing walls, Robinson has already proved his point with an innovative wall at Liège University in Belgium, his first export order. It has *two* faces, one outside, for use when the weather is fine, one inside, for when it is not.

Wilson goes further: he believes that imaginative outdoor structures could help combat at least some of the problems of decaying inner-city areas. He has been working on an ambitious plan for a twenty-one-metre outdoor tower in the London borough of Islington. He also believes that climbing walls or towers are ideal to take advantage of city space otherwise regarded as dead, like the underside of motorway flyovers or disused railway bridges.

Other countries have taken up the climbing-wall idea. Robinson has built a second wall in Belgium, while others have been constructed in Germany, Japan and the US.

Robinson's latest idea is perhaps the boldest of all. Graham Desroy is a dedicated winter climber, one of the select band who venture into the mountains in conditions that drive most other people firmly indoors. Like other winter climbers, he holds that to climb in a snow-filled mountain gully or on a frozen rock face is a rare and rewarding experience, the ultimate the sport can offer. Now he and Robinson are wondering whether they could reproduce those conditions indoors.

There is of course a central irony in their proposal, for they will have come full circle from providing a summer environment for climbing during the winter, to recreating the worst of Britain's weather indoors.

'You'd need a sport centre that has a refrigeration plant already, or it would be too expensive,' he concedes. 'But apart from that, I don't see any great problems. After all it would only be like building an ice-rink – except that it would be tipped on its side.'

Buildering

Sunday Times, 1978

Before George Mallory left to attempt Everest, in 1924, never to return, he was asked why he wanted to climb the 29,000-foot mountain in the first place. His reply quickly became the most widely quoted aphorism of mountaineering: 'Because It Is There.'

In the same tradition is twenty-one-year-old shop assistant Steve Peake, who climbed the sheer 500-foot Birmingham Post Office tower last Tuesday. 'I just fancied it,' he says.

In the newly fashionable pursuit of buildering there are two strands: those who, like Peake, regard the activity as sufficient in itself; and those, like the two men who climbed Nelson's Column last month and unfurled a banner denouncing Barclays Bank, who believe that some extra rationale is required to justify behaviour that most of the public regard as daft. What unites the two groups is the immodest belief that virtually no building or skyscraper in the world is unconquerable.

Neither the Birmingham Post Office tower, nor Nelson's Column, in fact, were seen as presenting any great technical problems. 'I could see it from the shop every day,' says Steve Peake, 'and it didn't look difficult at all.' His eye quickly identified its line of weakness, an external lift running the height of the tower on two rails. An eight-inch gap between the rails and the tower was perfect for the climbing technique known as a layback and stanchions every ten feet or so afforded plenty of rest.

Peake had wanted to attempt the tower with a partner, which is preferred climbing practice. (It is safer to have a partner holding your rope while you are climbing.) When none was forthcoming – 'I asked one or two friends but they said we'd get into trouble' – he embarked alone.

Setting off at 7.30 in the morning he hoped to reach the summit platform before anyone noticed him. 'The trouble was I told my mother I might try it some time that week. I didn't know her office was close to the tower and when she saw me she called the police. She didn't realise how safe it was.'

At 1 p.m. Peake pulled over on to the summit platform to find police and firemen waiting for him. He was annoyed that they would not let him climb back down the last hundred feet to retrieve some equipment but that apart, he says, he enjoyed himself. 'It was great being up there in the early morning light. It was just like being on a big mountain wall. The Post Office seemed a bit cross at first, but in the end they were all right.'

Ed Drummond, who made the first ascent of Nelson's Column on 20 October, regards the Birmingham climb as an opportunity sadly wasted. 'I believe in making these climbs to some purpose,' he says.

A thirty-four-year-old Englishman who lives in California, he made two bold attempts to capture the headlines for political causes in San Francisco last year. He succeeded in nailing a flag denouncing investment in South Africa to the top of a 100-foot flagpole; but failed to climb the 853-foot Trans-America Building on behalf of Amnesty International, the San Francisco police intercepting him and hauling him in through a window on the twenty-first floor.

In comparison with these bids, Nelson's Column was simplicity itself. (In climbing parlance it was an 'artificial climb' of grade one severity. There are four artificial grades, the most difficult being a climb along a continuous overhang.) From the brackets that secure the column's lightning conductor, Drummond suspended webbing loops, known as etriers, that act like short rope ladders.

His greatest worry, in fact, concerned the pedestal at the top of the column that overhangs by several feet. In the event, he found it amply equipped with ornamental flourishes forming what climbers term 'jug-handles' or 'thank God holds'.

On top of the pedestal, Drummond and his twenty-two-year-old partner Colin Rowe triumphantly unfurled a banner announcing: 'Barclays profits from apartheid's coffins'. Then they abseiled down the column, dropping into the arms of the Metropolitan Police who arrested them and charged them with causing damage to the lightning conductor, later estimated at £500 plus VAT. (Drummond and Rowe, whose trial opens on 8 January, did not deny using the conductor, only that they damaged it.)

Both Drummond and Peake are staying silent about future projects for fear of alerting possible rivals. In London, however, there are several targets which builderers are known to covet. The most striking is the new National Westminster building, which at 600 feet will be the tallest office block in the City.

The most important item of equipment for these challenges will be a 'sky-hook'. In conventional climbing this was a hook some three inches long, but builderers have developed sky-hooks *twelve feet* long for hooking over ledges above their heads in the style of a grappling iron. When the sky-hook appears secure, the builderer climbs up a rope hanging down from it; in the dark, says Drummond, this can be 'quite exciting'.

Steve Peake sees no reason why he should not continue to climb buildings in solo fashion; but Drummond has plans to form perhaps the most formidable partnership in the brief history of the sport. He flew to New York last Friday and hoped to discuss joint ventures with George Willig, the twenty-eight-year-old American who climbed one of the 1350-foot towers of the New York Trade Center last year.

Like Drummond, Willig was led away from the climb by police, but in New York Willig's status as an instant hero ensured his prompt release. Even so, says Drummond, his climb was 'straightforward and quite safe'. Willig took just three and a half hours to make the ascent and the only ill-effects he suffered were sore hands.

Book reviews
Sunday Times, 1988

Feeding the Rat, Al Alvarez, Bloomsbury; *Nanda Devi*, John Roskelley, OUP; *Touching the Void*, Joe Simpson, Cape.

W ho are climbing books for? Members of the climbing world, or those outside? The question is prompted by three books which address the problems of communicating the mysteries of climbing in different ways.

Feeding the Rat by Al Alvarez is a fluid and affectionate portrait of Alvarez's long-time climbing partner, Mo Antoine, who although well-known in the mountaineering community as rock-climber, expedition member and equipment manufacturer, has achieved none of the media status of peers such as Chris Bonington and Doug Scott. Alvarez's admiration for Antoine stems in large part from that. He directs a series of barbs at Bonington for allowing his goals to be distorted through participating in the media circus, or so Alvarez suggests. It is through eschewing the limelight that Antoine has remained true to himself.

The antithesis is not quite so neat, however, for Alvarez's account fits a mountaineering genre which carries its own distortion, whereby Antoine is romantically portrayed as the anarchic, iconoclastic and immensely practical individualist, tough bordering on macho, a dispenser of gallows humour and a gambler for the highest stakes. The rat of the title is Antoine's metaphor for the alter ego that can only be satisfied by climbing. At the same time there are hints that Antoine represents Alvarez's own idealised other self.

The climax of the book is a tense set-piece account of Alvarez's last climb. On the verge of his sixties, Alvarez resolved to join Antoine in an ascent of the Old Man of Hoy, a daunting sea-stack in the Orkneys (which won its renown, ironically, through a televised ascent in the 1960s).

Impressive though the climb is, it is here that the book shifts most uneasily between the two audiences. Climbers may be unsympathetic towards Alvarez in his sub-Hemingway mode, the devotee of risk dipping into one more adrenalin-based experience. Non-climbers may fail to see the point of it all, even with the assistance of the rat. The fact that Alvarez defines some climbing terms for outsiders but leaves others unexplained illustrates the unresolved ambiguities of his approach.

It is plain to see for whom, first and foremost, *Nanda Devi* by John Roskelley was written. It was written for its author. Roskelley is a leading American mountaineer, Nanda Devi a shimmering peak, renowned as one of the most beautiful in the Himalaya, which Roskelley climbed in 1976. Roskelley's account of an expedition plagued by jealousy, bitterness and rows, mostly reads like an apologia for himself and a condemnation of his colleagues, variously presented as selfish, vacillating, disorganised and inadequate.

At the same time Roskelley shows himself to be self-centred, arrogant, abrasive, chauvinist and ethnocentric – which happen to represent qualities useful for climbing Himalayan peaks in the face of avalanches, frostbite, hunger, thirst and perpetual ailments. Roskelley faces the same difficulty as Alvarez. Mountaineers may recognise all of this as a truism, while outsiders may remain baffled as to why anyone should submit themselves to such an ordeal.

Near the end, however, the book shifts abruptly on to another plane, the litany of complaints being transformed into pure tragedy. Nanda Devi was the name not only of the mountain in question but also the daughter of the expedition leader, Willi Unsoeld, a choice inspired by his near-mystic vision of the peak some thirty years before. After Roskelley and a companion climb Nanda Devi, Unsoeld's desire that his daughter should follow them to 'her' summit culminates in her death while cradled in her father's arms at the highest camp.

The cause was an intestinal ailment which had been grumbling on throughout the expedition, and Roskelley was one of several climbers to warn Unsoeld that his daughter should descend, although he resists any temptation to say: 'I told you so.' At this point the climbers have become characters in a drama which leaves even Roskelley lost for words: 'It was our tragedy and none of us can explain why.'

The most successful resolution of the problem of the divided audience is achieved by Joe Simpson in *Touching the Void*. Simpson, a climber from Sheffield who is also a Greenpeace activist, was fortunate, if that is the right word, in having a ready-made plot for his first book. The result is a truly astounding account of suffering and fortitude.

Simpson and his partner, Simon Yates, had embarked on an ascent of a remote and difficult peak in the Peruvian Andes in 1985. They were making their attempt in the modern lightweight manner, forswearing the paraphernalia of a major expedition to climb with a modicum of equipment, giving them the advantage of speed but at risk of being beyond help in the event of an accident. Precisely such an accident occurred: having reached the summit via the mountain's ice-covered West Face they were descending through a storm when Simpson slipped on a crag and broke his leg.

Simpson's life now rested all too literally in Yates's hands. Yates secured Simpson to the end of their rope and began lowering him down the face, 300 feet at a time. They were approaching the bottom when they reached a position where Simpson was dangling over a crevasse so that it was impossible for Yates either to haul him back up or to lower him to safety. As he clung to the rope, Yates himself began to slide. Faced with a hideous dilemma whereby he was convinced that if he did nothing they would both die, Yates cut the rope and sent Simpson plunging to his presumed death in the depths of the crevasse.

By some fluke of fate Simpson landed on a platform of snow lodged between the sides of the crevasse. His account of how he managed to extricate himself and then crawl to the sanctuary of Base Camp, arriving after a three-day ordeal of pain, thirst and delirium, is among the most powerful passages in the canon of mountaineering literature. It gains further strength by being interspersed with Yates's description of his grief and guilt, heightened by his astonishment and relief when his partner returned from the dead.

I finished reading the book at 2 a.m. and found it so vivid and harrowing that it was another two hours before I could sleep. Chris Bonington (Alvarez's villain) was so moved that he supplied an introduction describing it as 'one of the most incredible survival stories I have ever read'. *Touching the Void* succeeds above all because it is more than just a climbing book. From the moment of Simpson's accident the narrative acquires an irresistible force, carrying all before it. The technicalities of climbing become incidental to the humanity and humility the two men displayed in confronting their own and each other's mortality.

The Guardian, 1986

One Man's Mountains, Tom Patey, Gollancz.

When Tom Patey was killed in an accident on a Sutherland sea-stack in May 1970, climbing lost not only one of its greatest performers but also one of its finest writers. In twenty years Patey had put up literally hundreds of new routes in Scotland – and had also written some twenty articles for climbing journals. These are now published together as *One Man's Mountains* and form the best collection of mountaineering writing to appear since the war.

Patey, who died at thirty-eight, was a GP with a practice in Ullapool in Wester Ross, an ideal base for climbing in the strange and desolate peaks of the North-West Highlands. The winter landscape has a rare beauty and Patey is best known for his superb succession of snow-and-ice climbs. Ten of the articles are about Scottish climbs, including the first winter ascent of Zero Gully on Ben Nevis, the first winter traverse of the Cuillin Ridge in Skye, and his last great winter route, a solo traverse of Creag Meagaidh, a plummeting cliff in the Central Highlands known to few outside the climbers' world.

His style of writing is very much that of the man: cool, direct, often very funny. He describes action with professional economy; there are few moments of lyricism and no attempts to advance 'reasons' for climbing. Instead, there's a continual strain of irony, anti-heroicism, even a sense of the basic absurdity of the whole enterprise. For Patey, climbing's rewards lay in the action itself, in moving across dangerous ground in complete control. Patey climbed more new routes alone than anyone else, believing that total self-reliance brought the greatest satisfaction.

Five more articles describe expeditions in the Alps and Himalaya, with a spare, black tale of a retreat from the Eiger with

Don Whillans. ('I was just beginning to enjoy myself, when I found the boot. "Somebody's left a boot here," I shouted to Don. He pricked up his ears. "Look and see if there's a foot in it," he said.') There are five incisive satirical pieces, and a collection of eighteen of the songs with which Patey delighted his friends on Scottish winter nights.

Sunday Times, 1989

All 14 Eight-Thousanders, Reinhold Messner, Crowood; *Climbing the Corbetts*, Hamish Brown, Gollancz; *The Island of Rhum*, Hamish Brown, Cicerone Press.

Mountaineering books are often about obsessions, and it would be hard to find two finer examples. The first is an Austrian's account of climbing every mountain above 8000 metres, the second a Scotsman's of ascending all the mountains in his country which stand between 2500 and 2999 feet high, known otherwise as the Corbetts. Those readers who are mountaineers or hill-walkers will probably need no explanation for behaviour that appears pointless or even perverse. Those who are not may simply ask: why?

In the case of Reinhold Messner, who comes from the South Tyrol, the answer is hard to find. He is truly the world's outstanding mountaineer who completed his self-imposed task of climbing the world's fourteen highest peaks, every single one without using supplementary oxygen equipment, within sixteen years. Yet his writing is sadly unable to rise to the same elevated heights.

It is drab and monotonous, matching the near-Nietzschean gloom that accompanies many of his ascents, like the 'negative blackness' he experienced on the summit of Dhaulagiri, number twelve on his list. Even after Lhotse, the fourteenth and final summit, he feels only 'the satisfaction of having realised a complex idea', coupled with a sense of relief at still being alive (understandable enough in all the circumstances) and at being free to do something else.

Virtually the only clue to his motivations appears in the chapter on his first peak, Nanga Parbat, which he climbed with his younger brother in 1970. His brother died in an avalanche during the descent and Messner himself lost six toes through frostbite. His ruminations make the subsequent enterprise (for which he wore a pair of specially truncated boots) appear as a form of penance, of self-testing to the edge of destruction, as if to redeem the horror of Nanga Parbat.

At this point even mountaineers may recoil from a man so grimly driven to achieve his goals. They may still want to own his book as it is a magnificent production in its own right, superbly printed and illustrated, interspersed with comments from other mountaineers and serving as the nearest equivalent to a history and gazetteer of the 8000-metre peaks at present available.

Hamish Brown, who comes from Fife, is the very opposite of Messner. True, they share an obsession, in Brown's case the consequence of having climbed all the 'Munros', the 276 Scottish peaks of 3000 feet or more, and looking for new goals. There are 223 Corbetts, named after the Bristol-based surveyor who compiled the list, first published following his death just after the war.

By contrast with Messner, Brown's account of completing his task is joyous and colourful. Of those Corbetts I have climbed, my favourite is Quinag, one of the isolated sandstone peaks to be found in the lunar landscape of the far north-west. My memories were perfectly roused by Brown's description of its 'intimidating, gully-riven barrel buttresses and jutting prows of bare rock' and the 'majestic openness' of the green terraces of its summit ridge.

Since it is hard to find new epithets for more than 200 mountains Brown often borrows from the Gaelic, deploying words like *slochd*, for a gash on the crest of a ridge, *dubh*, for the blackness of a crag or its reflection in water, and *meall*, for a bald or rounded mountain. (Just as there are supposed to be several dozen Eskimo words for ice, there are at least ten Gaelic words for mountain.)

Whereas Messner suggests little reason why anyone might want to emulate him, Brown has achieved the difficult technical feat of conveying his own sense of relish as well as providing accurate routes for others to follow. The illustrations are not particularly inspiring but the book's value is enhanced by its appendices listing all the Corbetts.

In the nature of obsessions, this is done in three different ways: alphabetically, geographically, and by order of height. Those completing the list be warned. After the Munros and the Corbetts, the Donalds, namely the Scottish Lowland hills between 2000 and 2499 feet, await.

There are two enticing Corbetts, incidentally, in Brown's useful individual guide ('for walkers, climbers and visitors') to the island of Rhum.

Down and out in Derbyshire

Financial Times, 1988

I should have kept quiet. But there was something beguiling about the way the editor of the *Weekend FT* leaned back in his chair and asked if there was any unfulfilled ambition I might care to undertake on the newspaper's behalf.

As a hill-walker used to savouring wide, open landscapes and the occasional *frisson* of space beneath my feet, I had long regarded the activity of caving with chill horror. Nothing, I felt, would ever lure me into that dank, claustrophobic world. And yet, like a sailor succumbing to the siren's thrall, I spoke the fatal words: 'I'd like to go pot-holing.'

Thus it was, one bleak day this winter, that I found myself shivering on a Derbyshire hillside as I struggled to pull on a wet-suit. Made of spongy rubber, it clung to my bare arms and legs, gripping my throat and crotch like a vice. I squeezed my feet into wellington boots and strapped a safety helmet to my head.

My partner in this enterprise was a boyhood friend, Gordon Parkin. An artist and illustrator (his latest book, *A Picture of the Peak District*, had just appeared) he spends his spare time pot-holing, with the special advantage of being (unlike me) short and slim. As I posed like the Michelin Man, Gordon fitted a light to my helmet, attached to a battery pack on my waist. There seemed to be special emphasis in his words when he explained that it was the most important item of the caver's equipment – just why I was soon to discover.

The cave Gordon had chosen was known as Giant's Pot. The entrance was a gash in the hillside, into which trickled a friendly-looking stream. Without ado Gordon set off, and we were soon following the stream through a rocky chasm with jagged walls and a high roof. I acquired the knack of directing my helmet to light the way and felt reassured that nothing more demanding was required.

My optimism was swiftly deflated. From ahead came an intimidating roar and we arrived at a narrow ledge. The friendly stream had been transformed into a torrent which plunged over the edge to tumble down a vertical circular shaft. Twenty feet below was a ghostly scene: a group of people, wreathed in clouds of their own breath, water spattering around them. Already on their way out, they silently ascended a flimsy wire ladder one by one and headed for the entrance.

When my turn came to descend, the ladder swayed alarmingly as I struggled to jam my feet between the aluminium rungs. Moments after I reached the bottom, Gordon was beside me. It became clear that nothing we had done thus far counted when he said: 'Now we'll start some pot-holing.'

The river disappeared into a narrow crack in the far wall of the chamber. Gordon disappeared after it and, as I followed, I found myself in a passage that twisted like a corkscrew, with the river coursing at my feet. It became so narrow at times that I could squeeze through only by breathing out to compress my chest.

As he watched my struggles, Gordon told me not to fight the rock but to try to ease myself through. 'It's important to conserve your energy,' he warned. I envied him his slender build even more, especially when I had to drop to the river bed and crawl along with the water swirling around me.

Although the water soon filled my wellington boots it did not seem cold; that, said Gordon, was because it was rapidly heated to my body temperature. At times he moved so fast that I lost sight of him ahead. 'You can't lose the way,' he said when I caught him up. 'There's nowhere else to go.'

We clambered along the passage for half an hour. The most startling moment came when we had to climb down through a waterfall, where the search for footholds became especially disconcerting. At last we emerged into a chamber where it was possible to walk normally again, bringing relief to my protesting back and knees.

Gordon was in raptures as he pointed out the intricate shapes the water had carved as it sliced its way through the limestone over the millennia. Banks of stalactites were glistening on the walls, soaring almost to the roof. 'They're called organ pipes,' Gordon said.

I glimpsed the sense of exploration and discovery that the sport brings – then Gordon announced that we were now

700 feet down. I tried to imagine the several million tons of mountainside above our head. Then I stopped trying to imagine them.

Gordon announced that for added interest on our return we would follow a new passage that rejoined our descent route halfway up. We had only climbed a short way when he pointed out a tunnel that led to a neighbouring cave known as Oxlow Cavern and proceeded to tell a story that explained the affection he had for his light.

Early in his pot-holing career Gordon was exploring Oxlow Cavern when he became separated from his partners and then broke his lamp. In utter darkness, he tried to find the way out but fell and hurt himself, whereupon he sat down to wait for help. Two days passed before it arrived, by which time he was suffering from hypothermia and hallucinating. 'In another six hours it would probably have been too late.'

I asked if we could leave. However, we had now reached what Gordon termed the crux of the route. Ahead the roof declined abruptly so that the passage was no more than two feet high. What was more, it was full almost to the roof with water.

'There's nothing to worry about,' said Gordon, which worried me intensely, as he had not said that before. I watched with trepidation as his feet disappeared along the tunnel. There was a long pause, then a muffled shout.

It seemed impossible to crawl and breathe at the same time. Each time I tried to move forward the water rose over my face, and I could take a breath only by turning my head on one side. In this manner I advanced, simultaneously fighting the crick in my neck and a mounting sense of panic.

The buoyancy of my wet-suit came to my rescue, enabling me to swim for a short way. By now I could see Gordon's light shining towards me, and I hauled myself ashore. As excitement mingled with relief I burst into laughter, and Gordon laughed with me. 'You'll be all right now,' he said.

That was not quite true, for there were two further ordeals ahead. The first consisted of a thirty-foot descent down a narrow chasm to the river bed. But after an initial shot of fear I found myself on familiar ground as I was able to use the mountaineering technique of bridging, whereby you brace yourself against the walls on either side, and reached the bottom without mishap.

Then came the moment I had been dreading most, the ascent

of the wire ladder we had left by the first waterfall. I was very tired by now and was convinced the ladder would be impossible to climb without losing my balance. But with Gordon calling reassurance from below, I was surprised at how quickly I reached the top.

We reached the cave entrance at dusk, after three hours underground. My knees were sore and my back ached but I felt elated, not so much for having survived but for having done so with my dignity reasonably intact – or so I thought.

An undignified scene ensued as I struggled to remove my wet-suit, which seemed to have shrunk by several sizes. In the end we repaired to the nearby farmhouse of my friends, John and Janet Stott, who combined forces to help peel it off. Then, after a blissful shower, we ate buttered crumpets and drank the Stotts' mulled wine.

'Would you go again?' Gordon asked.

'No,' I said. 'Well, maybe.'

Where on earth is Alex Pitcher?

Sunday Times Magazine, 1988

One of Europe's most mysterious landscapes is to be found on the high, isolated Vercors plateau above Grenoble. Gigantic cliffs tower out of the mists that linger even in summer, while the limestone terrain is full of pitfalls for the unwary. Ravaged by gashes and crevices, the French call it the *lapiaz*.

The *lapiaz* is created by the corrosive effect of rainwater which eats its way through the limestone. Sometimes larger apertures are formed, known as *gouffres*. Aptly translated as gulfs or abysses, they give access to the underground world the water has carved, with winding tunnels and precipitous canyons, rushing streams and plunging waterfalls, broad river beds and vast cathedral-like chambers set with giant stalagmites – wondrous places that until this century had remained in perpetual darkness.

The deepest and most majestic *gouffre* is the Gouffre Berger, which burrows 1200 metres below the *lapiaz* before emerging a few kilometres above Grenoble. The Berger, as it is known, offers one of the most potent lures in the sport of pot-holing. Named after the Frenchman Jo Berger, the first person to enter it in 1953, it was for a time the deepest-known cave system, renowned as the Eiger of the caving world. Now its reputation has receded a little; but every summer, when the plateau is clear of snow, parties of cavers make the descent to the bottom – a round trip of two or three days.

On 7 August last year Alex Pitcher, a seventeen-year-old caver from Derbyshire, was awaiting his turn at the Berger's entrance, a narrow gash in the *lapiaz*, overhung by pines. A short, muscular young man with a shock of fair, curly hair and a ready smile, he called a cheerful farewell and slid down a rope into the darkness. Two fellow cavers followed.

Before long Alex reached a section known as the Meanders, a twisting canyon where the water has sliced an exiguous path. There was a delay and Alex said, 'I'll go on.' He headed off into the Meanders, the beam of his headlamp flickering along the pitted grey walls. He was never seen again.

What happened to Alex Pitcher remains an utter mystery to this day. Although the Berger is an immense system it is also a finite one. There are no areas which have not been explored; and there was no area which was not searched, in some cases as many as six times, after Alex disappeared.

The searchers wondered if Alex could somehow have left the cave unnoticed, and so hundreds more people scoured the *lapiaz* for the best part of a week. They found nothing – no trace, no footprint, no clothing or equipment, least of all a body.

In the history of caving, the disappearance of Alex Pitcher remains unique. Mountaineers sometimes vanish without trace; but cavers, before last summer, never. Steve Marriott, the pot-holer who was the last person to see Alex before he set off along the Meanders, says: 'Nothing made sense. It seemed he had disappeared off the face of the earth.'

For Alex's parents, not knowing what happened to him is the worst aspect of their loss. His father, David, who spent a week on the Vercors plateau watching the search, says simply, 'We have nothing.'

His mother Norma adds, 'I do want to know what happened but there's no way we can get our questions answered. It would be much easier if it was finalised. The whole family – in the irrational part of our minds – thinks he might come back.'

Alex, born in 1970, was the second of the Pitchers' three children; his brother Michael was two years older, his sister Sara followed six years later. Alex, says his mother, was a 'handful' as a child. 'He had a very strong personality. He got into scrapes and did worse than the usual boyhood things. He presented problem after problem until he was thirteen.'

Alex's headstrong nature owed much to his mother's view of how her children should be raised. David Pitcher's work as a chemical engineer took him away for lengthy periods; when he returned he remained a withdrawn figure, unsure how to fit in. 'I think it is fair to say that Norma brought up the children,' he says. And Norma was determined that they, like her, would be self-sufficient.

Norma's own strength of character brought fierce confrontations with Alex, sometimes leading to impasse. But as he grew older Alex learned how to disarm his mother: 'He would always turn round and smile,' she says. That tactical skill evolved into a wisdom beyond his years, bringing a closeness with his mother that not all children enjoy. 'He was such a mature person,' she says, 'and he had an awful lot of charm.'

Michael Pitcher had much in common with his brother. 'I found it very challenging to be the man of the house and I grew up a lot stronger because of it – I think we both did.' Perhaps inevitably, given their similar temperaments, the brothers had frequent clashes, too. 'We had rows about *anything*. It was bloody noses and head locks.'

One cause of the rivalry was not hard to find. 'His brother got eleven O-levels at one sitting,' their mother says of Alex. 'His brother was taller than him, older than him, cleverer than him and Alex always brought up the rear.' Beneath his mature exterior was a surprising diffidence which she for one could discern. 'He had quite a low opinion of his ability. We did our best to boost his self-confidence but it was very difficult because big brother was always there as a shining example.'

But Alex found an escape route at hand. Although small for his age – at seventeen, when he disappeared, he was only five feet seven inches – he took a precocious interest in fitness and physique. From the age of six or seven he would remove his tee-shirt and flex his muscles whenever *The Incredible Hulk* appeared on television. 'He was impressive even then,' Michael says.

It seemed clear to his family that Alex had found a way of withdrawing from the competition by developing an interest of his own. He did press-ups on the kitchen floor, went running over the moors, took up swimming and tennis. Then Alex announced to his astonished parents that he intended to join the Marines, explaining that he would not need O-levels since he could leave school and enlist at sixteen.

His decision was all the more remarkable as there was no military background in the family. But his mother greeted it with the same tolerance she expected from him. 'We weren't over the moon about it,' she says. 'But if you love someone, you accept it.'

In 1978 the disruption caused to the family by David Pitcher's career was eased. Until then they had moved frequently, from Ellesmere Port to Holland, from South Wales to Burton-on-Trent.

That winter David took a job in Manchester and the Pitchers bought a house in New Mills on the edge of the Peak District. Next door lived the Heards: Chris, a primary-school teacher in his thirties, and his wife Caroline, who later had a son, David, and a daughter, Emma. The two families kept their distance at first. 'We got to know them steadily,' Chris Heard says, 'like all the best friendships.'

Gradually the families discovered their shared interests. Both liked the theatre, and bought adjoining season tickets at the Royal Exchange in Manchester. Both liked music, Norma teaching David Heard the recorder and piano. In return Chris Heard coached the Pitchers' children in maths. They enjoyed outdoor activities: the Pitchers went walking; Chris was a dedicated climber and pot-holer.

Michael and Alex first attended their local primary school, moving at eleven to New Mills comprehensive. 'Could do better,' was the uniform message of Alex's reports. 'He did only enough to get by,' Michael confirms. Alex was none the less a popular figure, friendly and approachable, and took part in an impressive range of local activities, playing in the school soccer team, joining the Cubs, singing in the choir at St George's Church and entering for the Duke of Edinburgh's award.

In the summer of 1984, when his father was away in Saudi Arabia, Alex told his mother that he wanted to take up a new sport: rock-climbing. She believes he had been attracted by seeing the adventures of Chris Bonington on television, and by the activities of Chris Heard next door. Chris recalls: 'Norma asked, would I take Alex out? I said, "Sure".'

Their first outing was to one of the Peak District gritstone edges, followed by trips to Wales and the Lake District. Later

Alex went with Chris and his family on holiday to Cornwall and climbed on the granite cliffs near Land's End.

Although Chris found Alex a clumsy climber at first, his compact physique gave him an ideal power/weight ratio which also compensated for his lack of reach. Chris found Alex especially good at 'finger climbing' – moving up on tiny handholds.

When Alex took up weight-lifting and circuit training Chris observed how his shoulders became broader too. Like many muscular climbers, Alex did not spend time pondering his next move: 'He liked to grab things and go.'

That winter Alex took up pot-holing as well. It may seem an unlikely activity for a climber, since there can hardly be a greater contrast between an open mountainside and the pot-holer's dark, claustrophobic world. But both convey a sense of excitement and exploration; and pot-holing is ideally suited to the winter, since the temperature underground stays in the low 40s and bad weather is no problem.

Alex's first trip was in Derbyshire, where the limestone is literally riddled with caves. At Christmas he and Chris spent a week in Yorkshire, eagerly descending two caves a day. Alex made himself a wet-suit, gluing together the spongy rubber pieces on the kitchen table; later his father bought him the array of technical equipment he needed.

Alex took to pot-holing as readily as he had to climbing. His build was ideal for the intimidating 'tight crawls', squeezing through tunnels often half-full of water. His stamina helped with tiredness and the cold; his maturity enabled him to combat the pot-holer's greatest enemy, panic.

Chris also believes that pot-holing and climbing, combined with his goal of joining the Marines, helped Alex contend with the cross-currents of his family: 'It was a way of doing something he wanted to do and opting out of the competition.' It is tempting in turn to see Chris Heard as a substitute father-figure for Alex. Michael, by contrast, had little to do with Chris: 'He sort of latched on to Alex and that was it.' Yet Michael believes Alex and Chris's relationship was more one of convenience, at least where Alex was concerned. Other cavers saw it as a partnership between master and apprentice. 'The way I see it,' Michael confirms, 'is that Alex was a very good climber, and that was all down to Chris.'

It so happens that the year Alex took up climbing and

pot-holing was also the time when his relationship with Michael began to improve. 'We did more together and we were friends,' Michael says. They spent hours in Alex's bedroom talking about school, girlfriends, music: both liked heavy metal, and Alex's favourite group was Slayer.

In 1986 an unexpected role reversal took place. Having led the way academically, Michael failed his mock A-levels. He promptly forswore university and said he would work in a bank. But Alex persuaded him to stay at school. 'Alex was saying, "Look Mike, you're going to regret it. All your friends are going to university and it will give you an extra three years to decide what to do."'

Four months later it was Alex who had to contend with a crushing disappointment. Exceptionally fit, he was as determined as ever to leave school and join the Marines. But after passing a medical with ease, an eye test revealed colour blindness and the Marines turned him down.

Alex responded with remarkable composure. 'He took a really bitter blow better than a lot of adults would have done,' Norma says. Within a few days he announced he would go to university and become a mining engineer. After barely three months' work he passed five O-levels: 'Absolutely incredible,' says Michael.

That autumn Michael began a degree course in biological sciences at Plymouth Polytechnic. With the separation his relationship with Alex deepened. They wrote regularly and spoke by phone at least once a week. 'I found him an absolutely terrific friend,' says Michael. 'You could talk to him about anything.'

Ironically it was now Michael who looked up to Alex. Following his rejection by the Marines, caving and climbing, according to his mother, had become 'his passion in life', and Michael envied his prowess. 'I found Alex better than me because although we were both mature he could have much more of a life than me.'

On a few precious occasions the brothers went climbing together, providing memories which for Michael have acquired a luminous intensity. In his bookcase he keeps a guidebook in which he has carefully marked the handful of routes they climbed at Windgather Rocks near New Mills. He also recalls their walks into the Peak District.

'One time we walked over to Edale, about ten miles. Another time we walked all the way up to the Mermaid's Pool on Kinder and then up under the Downfall and then we followed the river back down. It was an absolutely glorious day.'

Michael never went pot-holing: crawling around in semi-darkness getting wet and cold, he says, never appealed to him. But the sport prompted a conversation with Alex which Michael especially recalls: 'I said to him, "This is dangerous. If anything happens to you I want you to know I really love you." He said, "That's good, because if anything happens to me I want you to know I really love you, too."'

Caving, in fact, has a lower accident rate than climbing. Even so, the adrenalin buzz that comes from confronting risk is one of the attractions of the sport, as Alex acknowledged. The most dangerous incident to befall him in Britain came when a rainstorm caused a cave in Yorkshire to flood. He and Chris retreated through a tunnel with only a few inches of air-space left; shortly afterwards it flooded completely. 'It was no problem,' says Chris. 'We found it quite exhilarating.'

Alex did not mention the incident to his mother. He was usually non-committal about his activities, and if she ventured to ask what he had done would invariably reply, 'Not much.' 'I know now that wasn't true,' she says. 'I think we weren't told a lot of things because he thought we would worry.'

On one notable occasion, after he and his mother visited a show cave in Edale named Peak Cavern, Alex was more frank. Some years before, a young caver had been trapped in a remote part of the system and died despite intense efforts to pull him out. 'When we came back we talked about how that boy died,' Norma says. 'Alex said, "I know what I'm doing, Mum, and if it happens to me I will face it. Don't worry about me."'

Quite remarkably, Alex told his mother that if he was killed he wanted to be cremated and he wanted heavy metal played at his funeral. 'He knew the risks he was taking and he had them all worked out,' she says. 'He wasn't denying his fear or the danger. He had enough personal courage to overcome both. He was such a mature person and he looked things squarely in the face.'

Just as with Alex's ambition to join the Marines, Norma felt she too had to look the issue squarely in the face. And just as over the Marines, she adds, 'If you love someone you're prepared to let them go.'

In July 1986 Alex told his mother that he had been invited to join an expedition to the Gouffre Berger. It was an occasion, she recalls, of some pride. 'He was *asked* to go and he thought he was very privileged.'

The expedition had, in fact, been launched almost a year before, when Chris Heard and two friends, John Warburton, a printer, and Lance Davis, a computer programmer, decided to organise a descent. After applying to the local French authorities in the name of the North-West Pothole Club, they received an access permit for the first two weeks of August 1987.

According to Chris, Alex had been keen to join from the start: 'He was very turned on by the expedition.' They attended training sessions organised by the club, and Chris felt the Berger was well within Alex's capabilities. 'Fitness was the name of the game, and Alex was among the fittest five or six of the expedition.'

As the expedition neared, and Chris and Alex continued to climb and cave together, their partnership approached a crucial intersection. The moment when the apprentice overtakes the master is a poignant one, with the younger man looking ahead as if to a limitless horizon, the older consoling himself with his memories and wisdom. Chris accepted that Alex was already physically the stronger; and in technique he was close behind. By 1988, Chris foresaw, 'Alex would have overtaken me in terms of climbing standards.'

That moment came sooner than expected. In June 1987 they went climbing in Derbyshire: 'It was a sunny day and we were both climbing very well,' Chris recalls. But when Chris stepped on to a tiny foothold his knee splayed outwards in a way he had never seen before. In hospital Chris discovered he had torn several ligaments. 'I was getting old,' he says. 'I wasn't as fit as I should have been.'

Chris was also warned that he had no chance of being fit for the Berger. It was a double blow, for it deprived Alex of his caving partner. But Chris decided he should still accompany Alex to France. 'Alex was a quiet person and I felt it would have been a bit much to send him knowing only three or four people. He might have found it a bit lonely.'

Once at the Berger, Chris suggested, Alex should look for someone else to cave with: 'I gave him strategies for finding people, talking to them and getting to know them.' Alex, he adds, seemed 'quite happy' with this advice.

As departure day drew near, Alex was in a state of barely suppressed excitement. 'He must have packed his gear at least six weeks before he went,' Norma says. When his brother came home from Plymouth at the end of term he found Alex 'really excited – he couldn't wait.'

On 25 July, three days before he was due to depart, Alex said goodbye to his parents and sister when they left for a holiday in Yorkshire. Alex, says Norma, 'wasn't bubbling over with excitement because that wasn't his way. But he had a glint in his eye and a bounce in his step.'

Alex and Michael spent the last three days together, cooking for each other and going to the pub in the evening. For Michael it was a perfect time: 'Everything I thought and was feeling I told to Alex and he was the same. When he left we were such good friends.'

Alex left for France on Tuesday, 27 July, travelling in John Warburton's car with Chris and John's fiancée, Rosie. It was a leisurely journey – Alex sat in the back, reading and listening to his Walkman – and it was not until 31 July that they turned up the steep, single-track road that leads on to the northern edge of the Vercors plateau, ending at a campsite in a lush meadow named La Molière.

Half the expedition's two dozen members had already set up camp, and Chris and Alex pitched their tent close by. After a week's rain the clouds cleared, presenting a breathtaking view of the distant Alps – a fitting augury, they felt, of success.

The next day there was what Chris Heard terms a 'stampede' to the cave. The entrance is an hour's walk across the *lapiaz*, following a forest path that skirts fissures and outcrops, with arrows daubed on the rock at intervals to show the way. By midday fifteen of the cavers, eager for their first taste of the Berger, had reached the entrance, where they pulled on wet-suits, adjusted the lights on their safety helmets and set off down the first pitch.

As well as inspecting the cave, they had the task of preparing the way for the rest of the expedition. This entailed fixing ropes on the steepest sections, to be descended by the mountaineering technique of abseiling. They would climb back up by a method known as prusiking – pushing up the rope a clamp which locks in place instead of sliding down.

The expedition fixed a rope down the entrance pitch and another on the first true pot, a vertical, twenty-seven-metre, circular shaft named the Puits de Ruiz. More ropes were fixed on a broken forty-five-degree pitch named the Holiday Slides, and on a further twenty-five-metre pot, the Puits du Cairn, which leads to a chamber known as Cairn Hall.

Then come the Meanders, a passage so narrow in places that cavers can barely squeeze through. They negotiate the Meanders by the technique of 'bridging', bracing feet and arms across the gap, with the river that runs through the system bubbling along some ten metres below. However, only in a few places is there any real risk of a fall, and cavers dispense with a rope.

The expedition fixed ropes on the three pots that follow the Meanders, culminating in Aldo's, a forty-two-metre shaft that is the second deepest in the Berger. It is an intimidating place, where cavers have to launch themselves into the blackness without being able to see the bottom, and it marked the end of the expedition's progress that day. Alex went far enough to peer over the edge, returning to the campsite, Chris recalls, 'most impressed'.

For the next three days the senior members of the expedition continued rigging the cave. Aldo's, 250 metres down, is less than a quarter of the way to the bottom, but the angle eases thereafter, with a succession of caverns, waterfalls, canals and ravines between the pots. Finally, more than 1100 metres down, the river disappears in a series of flooded passages known as sumps.

For most cavers this marks the bottom, although divers using oxygen apparatus have swum through four of the sumps before concluding that further progress was impossible. Still rigging as they went, the leading pair of the British expedition reached the bottom on Tuesday evening.

Alex, meanwhile, was searching for new partners as Chris had prescribed, mingling with the other members who were climbing, swimming or merely lazing around the campsite while awaiting their turn to descend. By Wednesday Chris had narrowed the choice down to two groups; the first consisted of two cavers, Steve Marriott, a youth worker in his thirties from Bristol, and Phil Goodwin, a lecturer in his early forties from Southampton, who were due to go down on Friday, 7 August; the second, a younger team of three.

The trio had much to recommend it: by including Alex it could split neatly into two pairs. But Chris plumped for the older pair, feeling they offered 'a nice balance of experience and prudence'.

In fact, the pair was not quite as well-balanced as it seemed, as Marriott and Goodwin had only caved together once before.

But they had driven to France together and, according to Marriott, 'It seemed natural to carry on.' When Chris asked if they would take Alex with them, they readily agreed.

Alex, says Marriott, 'seemed very steady – a good solid person to have on the trip.' Nor did he view Alex as a novice or passenger. 'He had all the right equipment. He was really well set up and he knew what he was doing.'

At this point it is necessary to confront a question that causes pursed lips among expedition members even now. Just how far did Alex plan to go? The expedition's permit stipulated that no one under eighteen was to descend beyond Camp 1, 500 metres down. That indeed is what Alex had told his parents, as Norma recalls. 'He said, "I know I can't bottom the cave, Mum, but it doesn't matter – I can go to the bottom when I'm older." He was quite happy with that.'

Virtually everyone else accepted that Alex was intent on going to the bottom (although some say they did not realise he was only seventeen) and that was what Marriott and Goodwin had in mind. 'The plan,' says Marriott, 'was to go down to Camp 1 and stay the night there, go down to the bottom and back to Camp 1 and stay the night, and out the next morning.'

When 7 August came, Alex could scarcely contain himself. At breakfast, says Chris, he was 'hopping with impatience'. Chris helped pack his rucksack and at 11.30 they set off up the path. Marriott and Goodwin were already at the cave, as they had been taking their turn on 'entrance duty', checking other cavers in and out and serving tea from a nearby tent.

When Alex arrived he was, according to Chris, 'jumping up and down with excitement'. But, to Alex's frustration, Marriott asked him to 'hang on a bit'.

Marriott explained that since they intended to spend the first night at Camp 1, only three hours down, there was no point setting off yet. Besides, Marriott adds, he and Goodwin were in no particular hurry. 'We decided we would take our time and enjoy it. We were just going to go down and have a really good time.'

The effect on Alex was plain. 'He was stomping about,' Chris says. 'He was fed up doing nothing. All he wanted to do was to go down the cave.'

At 3.30 p.m. Marriott and Goodwin said they were ready to leave. By then all three had changed into their wet-suits, leaving their outdoor clothes, passports and valuables in the tent by the entrance, and Alex, says Chris, was 'raring to go'. He set off in the lead and swiftly reached the earthy floor of the entrance pitch. There he looked up at Chris.

'Take care, enjoy yourself,' Chris called.

'Have a good time – see you Sunday,' Alex shouted back, and disappeared from Chris's view.

Marriott followed Alex down the entrance pitch, with Goodwin bringing up the rear. The three men abseiled down Ruiz's and embarked on the Holiday Slides. But, after Alex and Marriott had reached the bottom, Marriott called up to Goodwin to wait.

The delay was caused by the arrival of another caver, Anthony Barnett, on his way back from the bottom of the cave. Barnett began to prusik up the Holiday Slides, which meant that Goodwin would not be able to start his abseil until Barnett reached the top. Meanwhile Marriott and Alex decided to continue down Cairn Pot into Cairn Hall and wait for Goodwin at the start of the Meanders.

It took Barnett, who was close to exhaustion, almost half an hour to reach the top of the Holiday Slides. When Goodwin began his descent he was not much faster. One of the more cautious members of the expedition, he liked to check his equipment carefully before each move, and there was a further delay caused by an awkward change-over between two ropes.

Down in Cairn Hall, according to Marriott, Alex was once again 'stamping around', not only from frustration at the prolonged wait but also from cold, as chunks of ice and snow linger in this section throughout the summer.

'He was getting very impatient,' Marriott says. 'He just wanted to get off, so in the end he said, "I'm going to go on now," and he went on down into the Meanders. I said, "Right, I'll wait for Phil."'

Marriott has often asked himself since whether he should have told Alex to wait. However, cavers – unlike climbers – do not consider it unusual to split up, especially as it is important to keep moving to stay warm. 'If I'd been down first,' Marriott says, 'it might have been me.'

Marriott adds that he felt no particular responsibility for Alex. 'I felt he was an equal and treated him as such. My concern was not with the front bloke but with the chap who was coming down – who was the slowest.'

Mariott believes that half an hour may have passed after Alex went ahead and before Goodwin at last joined him in Cairn

Hall. They lost further time in the Meanders because they were carrying a bulky rucksack which made it hard to perform the delicate bridging moves required.

Marriott and Goodwin duly reached the end of the Meanders, descended the next two pots, and approached Aldo's. Now, for the first time, they began to wonder what had happened to Alex.

They were surprised not to find Alex waiting at Aldo's, since it marked the limit of his earlier descent. They abseiled to the bottom and again found nothing. Next came an enormous chamber, the Great Gallery of the Starless River, 400 metres long and up to sixty metres high. Marriott was even more puzzled to find no sign of Alex here, but concluded that he had been 'keen to see the Gallery – he was obviously keen to get on.'

Expecting to find Alex waiting at Camp 1, they continued through the Gallery. After negotiating two waterfalls and picking their way through a monumental chamber strewn with giant boulders known as the Great Rubble Heap, they reached the site of Camp 1, a ledge beside the river, at 7 p.m. To their dismay, Alex was nowhere to be seen.

At first Marriott and Goodwin supposed that Alex must have missed the camp and carried on. But that theory contained an immediate flaw. Below the camp was the Salle des Treize which contains a spectacular cluster of giant stalagmites, some of them ten metres tall. Marriott was sure that Alex would have recognised them and realised he had gone too far.

Marriott also knew that two other cavers, Roy Blackham and Ian Brady, were on their way back up. Since the system narrows into a long canal below the Salle des Treize, it would have been impossible to miss Alex if he had indeed gone on. Marriott and Goodwin settled down into their sleeping bags to wait.

Blackham and Brady arrived at half past twelve. 'We asked if they had seen any sign of Alex,' says Marriott. 'They said no.'

The most common explanation for cavers going missing is that, for whatever reason, they have lost their light. The standard procedure is to wait for help to arrive. Supposing this is what must have happened, it was still without undue alarm that Marriott and Goodwin set off back up the Great Rubble Heap, calling and searching with their lights.

By the time they reached Aldo's they were more concerned. Their best guess was that Alex had fallen in the Meanders and was lying at the bottom, injured and/or unconscious. 'We looked very hard there but didn't see anything,' says Marriott. They reached the surface, tired and puzzled, to discover that it was already daylight. They woke the two cavers on entrance duty, one of whom ran down to La Molière.

At 8.58 a.m. – the time is etched in his mind – Chris Heard was woken by shouts outside his tent. Among them he discerned three chilling words: 'Alex is missing.'

Most of those involved in the events of the subsequent week account it the most dispiriting episode of their lives. 'It was a nightmare,' says Steve Marriott. Albert Oyhançabal, the head of the French cave rescue team for the Vercors region, who was summoned to the plateau that afternoon and remained there for six days, says: 'It surpassed logic. It was an absolute enigma.'

As the British and French cavers pondered on what could have happened, there appeared to be five distinct possibilities. In descending order of optimism, they were as follows:

1 Alex had damaged his light and was waiting to be found.
2 He had taken a wrong turning and was lost.
3 He was injured but was conscious and waiting to be found.
4 He had been injured and was lying unconscious.
5 He was dead.

The cavers were compelled to accept that if 1 or 3 were the case, it was surprising that Marriott and Goodwin had not found him already. The British none the less decided to begin the search anew. Four cavers were to look in the Meanders once again and seven in the Great Rubble Heap. Four more were to consider whether Alex had become lost.

The most likely place was at the entrance of the Great Gallery of the Starless River, where a white arrow has been marked prominently on a rock to show the way. If Alex had missed it he might have turned into one of two side passages, known as the Mud Gallery and Petzl's Gallery. It seemed improbable, as it involved climbing back uphill, but the last four cavers agreed to look.

When the British began their search at 11 a.m. they were still optimistic. John Warburton, who searched Petzl's Gallery, says, 'I thought he'd just be sat somewhere waiting for us.' As the passage became narrower and narrower, requiring ever more gymnastic moves, Warburton's hopes fell. 'Eventually I thought, "This is crazy. There's no way he'll have come up here."'

As the other British cavers reached the same conclusion, it was in a state of bewilderment that they gathered at Camp 1.

Although Blackham and Brady continued to insist that Alex could not have passed them unnoticed, three of the British decided to search as far as Camp 2, 740 metres down.

By now the French cavers, dispatched by Albert Oyhançabal, were descending too. In his fifties, orginally from the Basque region of France, Oyhançabal knew the Berger as intimately as any other caver. Like the British, Oyhançabal believed that Alex was certain to be found between the entrance and Camp 1.

Oyhançabal told the French cavers, including several who had carried out the original explorations of the Berger, to concentrate on the Meanders, the Petzl and Mud Galleries, and the Great Rubble Heap. The only moment of hope came when one found a glove that might have belonged to Alex. But it was far too old.

By the time the French reached Camp 1 they were as baffled as the British. Six of the British now set off back for the top, making yet another search of the Great Rubble Heap as they went. Oyhançabal met them as they came out. 'They were very tired,' he says. 'They said they had found nothing.' At 2.17 on Sunday morning the first French pair returned and presented the same bleak verdict.

Oyhançabal, meanwhile, had been endeavouring to learn more about Alex. He asked Clive Grummett, the most capable French-speaker among the British, if Alex would have attempted the long abseil down Aldo's by himself. Did he dislike water – and if so, would he not have turned back at the cascades in the Great Gallery? Was he impulsive? Or suicidal?

In reply to the last question, Grummett said he was sure that Alex was not. But even if Alex *had* hurled himself over the edge of a pot, for whatever reason, his body would be plain to see. And the blunt truth was that after almost twenty-four hours' searching they had found precisely nothing.

On Sunday Oyhançabal began again. He wondered if Alex could have been buried by a rockfall but no signs of fresh falls were to be found. When one team reported that it had searched a section, he sent another to repeat the process – in some cases up to six times. The French passed Camp 2 and pushed on to the bottom. A team of divers even swam through the final sumps, but it was all in vain. Quite simply, Alex had vanished.

For many who took part, the point at which the search for Alex became the search for a body cannot be precisely timed. Oyhançabal remained hopeful throughout: he asked a doctor how long it was possible to survive without food or water and insisted that, until Alex was found, he could be alive.

But for two of those most intimately concerned that moment can be fixed. Still unable to descend because of his injured knee, Chris Heard had waited at the entrance throughout Saturday, finally falling into a fitful sleep. In the small hours of Sunday he awoke with a jolt, and later wrote a description of the overwhelming sense of foreboding he had felt:

'Anguish scythed through my conscience, I snapped from dream to wake. Alex lay between two rocks, the silent cry had been his. He was gone . . . the time was 4:17. An immense sadness rolled over me, the ache in my heart was physical. I said goodbye to Alex, my friend, and quietly cried myself back to sleep.'

Although he did not say so at the time – it would hardly have been politic to do so – Chris realised in that moment that the search was pointless, at least in terms of finding Alex alive.

The same revelation came to Alex's mother almost simultaneously. At 10.30 on Saturday night Chris had telephoned his wife Caroline in New Mills and asked her to go next door to break the news. When Michael Pitcher heard that Alex was missing, he remained in a state of stunned incredulity: 'I simply couldn't believe it,' he says.

Alex's father was to retain a glimmer of hope throughout the following week, and flew to France on Monday to watch the search. 'I reasoned there was a possibility he was still alive and it was just a question of time until they stumbled on him,' he says.

Norma cherished no such hopes. 'I knew he was dead virtually straight away. We were told on Saturday night and at four o'clock on Sunday morning I knew. It was partly mother's intuition. But I knew that if he had been alive he would have made his presence known in some way or other.'

On Monday evening Albert Oyhançabal concluded that, alive or otherwise, Alex could not be in the cave. 'I was convinced of that,' he says. The only alternative was that he was somewhere in the *lapiaz*. One of the difficulties with this theory was that Alex's clothes and valuables had remained untouched inside the entrance tent.

Oyhançabal nonetheless advanced a possible scenario: after setting off down the Meanders, Alex had reached the foot of Aldo's without mishap. But there he had taken a wrong turning. By the time he had realised his mistake and returned to the main passage, Marriott and Goodwin had passed. Alex continued for a while but became apprehensive and turned back.

It was dark when he reached the surface and so he missed the entrance tent, while the two men inside remained asleep. Still wearing his wet-suit, Alex decided to try to reach the campsite and set off across the *lapiaz*. But he strayed from the path and then, Oyhançabal reluctantly concluded, must have slipped into a ravine or fallen over the edge of a cliff.

While Oyhançabal admitted that it remained a highly improbable hypothesis, it was none the less 'the most logical'. Certainly no one, British or French, could think of anything more probable or logical.

On Tuesday morning Oyhançabal asked the *préfet* of Grenoble to order a search of the *lapiaz*. The *préfet*'s secretary-general, Jean Gadbin, drafted in detachments of the police, army, fire brigade and CRS, reinforced by helicopters and tracker dogs. That afternoon, starting at the cave entrance, they fanned out across the *lapiaz*. At the same time Gadbin asked Oyhançabal to carry on the search underground. Guessing that the previous searchers might pursue their task with diminishing enthusiasm, Oyhançabal summoned fresh teams from neighbouring departments. The result, either above or below ground, was no different from before.

That night Oyhançabal held a meeting at the campsite with seven of the British cavers. Its purpose, according to one of those present, was a 'brainstorming session' – to consider every possibility, no matter how apparently unlikely or absurd.

Could Alex have suffered an attack of amnesia and be wandering somewhere across the *lapiaz*? Could he have faked his disappearance? Could he have been kidnapped? Could he even have met a French woman and eloped to the south of France?

The British replied that none of these fitted anything they had discerned in Alex's personality. That did not prevent one version from surfacing in the *Sun*, which reported that Alex was thought to be living a Rambo-like existence somewhere on the *lapiaz*, causing his mother intense distress through the callousness it attributed to Alex.

'I'm quite prepared to believe in the unbelievable,' she says. '*Something* happened. But I found the idea very offensive that he had run away, because my son would have *said* if he was going to run away and he wouldn't have done that to the rest of the expedition members either.'

With more than 200 people taking part, the searches went

on through Wednesday. On Thursday the British vice-consul, Brian Bubb, arrived from Lyon. He met David Pitcher and a helicopter was laid on to fly them over the search area, showing them the extent of the rescue effort and the difficulties of the terrain.

On Friday a new search of the *lapiaz* began, covering an area 100 metres wide and extending the entire length of the path. That evening M Gadbin told David Pitcher that he had no choice but to call off the search. 'By that time I had to accept the chances were nil,' David says. 'The guys had put their heart and soul into it and they were exhausted.'

That night Oyhançabal went home for the first time in almost a week. On Saturday he delivered his report to the police, concluding: 'It is impossible to believe this caver is still in the Gouffre.'

At 10.10 p.m. Oyhançabal had just reached home when his phone rang. It was Brian Bubb, the British vice-consul, who said he had some remarkable news. That afternoon a woman had telephoned the Foreign Office from Manchester to say she had seen a vision of Alex standing next to a figure clothed in white.

To Oyhançabal, the 'figure in white' sounded as if it could just be one of the giant stalagmites in the Salle des Treize. He also discerned what was in Bubb's mind. 'He didn't *push* me to go,' Oyhançabal says. 'But he asked me if it was possible to do something. He said, "What I am asking you to do is not rational." He was right. I don't believe in mediums. But as the person responsible I did not have the right to dismiss something, no matter what.'

Oyhançabal returned to the plateau and entered the cave shortly before 2 a.m. He and a colleague searched the Salle des Treize and descended for a further 200 metres before admitting defeat. 'Of course it was irrational,' he says. 'But we were no longer in the realm of logic. It was *une histoire de fou*.'

On 16 August Norma Pitcher arrived at the plateau with Michael and Sara. They visited the cave entrance and spent some time walking over the *lapiaz*. While Michael Pitcher says that he simply wanted to see the place for himself, Norma's main hope was to discover something final or absolute, some concrete verdict on Alex's fate. Four days later the family returned to Britain. 'We came away with nothing more than we had come with,' Norma says.

On 8 September there was a service at St George's Church at New Mills for Alex's 'everlasting welfare', attended by more than 200 people. 'We couldn't call it a memorial service because he hasn't been found,' Norma says. But – 'with or without a body' – she insists that she will have a funeral one day. 'I can't leave my son in limbo. I can't bear the thought of leaving him.'

When Michael Pitcher returned to Plymouth he took up climbing again out of a desire to relive his memories of Alex. One night he dreamed that Alex was standing at the top of a climb he had done that weekend. 'Somehow we had ended up climbing together and it was a very difficult climb and he said, "You've done really well, I'm really proud of you."'

Those venturing into the Berger after Alex's disappearance may also have cause to remember him, too.

Late in October two British cavers on the last expedition before snow once again covered the *lapiaz* were returning from the bottom when one, who was close to exhaustion, fell behind. As he struggled up the final pitches he was relieved to see his partner beckoning and calling encouragement from above, his wet-suit seeming to glisten in the beam of his light. When he reached the top he thanked his partner for his help.

'What do you mean?' asked his partner, who in any case was not wearing a wet-suit.

Sunday Times Magazine, 1988

Beneath a broad sycamore tree in the graveyard of St George's parish church in New Mills, Cheshire, is a simple tombstone. It bears a line from *Dr Faustus* by Christopher Marlowe: 'Cut is the branch that might have grown full straight.'

The line, with its implied lament for wasted youth, was chosen by Norma Pitcher in memory of her son Alex.

In August 1987 Alex Pitcher, a popular, good-humoured and impressively mature seventeen-year-old schoolboy, vanished in the Gouffre Berger, the deepest and most renowned cave system in the Alps. His disappearance set off the longest and most baffling search in the history of pot-holing.

His family – his parents Norma and David Pitcher, his older brother Michael and younger sister Sara – spent a week desperately hoping for good news. When the search was finally called off they were compelled to accept that he had died, but without any idea where, why or how.

For the family, the lack of any firm information had several traumatic effects. First, Mrs Pitcher said, the family succumbed to the 'irrational feeling' that Alex might still come back. 'It would be so much easier if it was finalised,' she said.

Second, Mrs Pitcher could not stop herself wondering what state her son had been in before he died. Perhaps, she says, 'he was alone, he was afraid, he was thirsty, he was hungry or he was injured – that bothered me a great deal.' Later, she adds, 'I virtually reconciled myself to the fact that I would never know – and I would never have him home again.'

Throughout that winter the mystery had also preyed on the mind of Albert Oyhançabal, head of the region's cave rescue team, who had directed the fruitless search. 'I really wanted an explanation,' he said later, 'for his family and for myself.'

Like the Pitchers, Oyhançabal had been angered by fantastical media speculation which proposed that Alex had abandoned his friends for a Rambo-like existence in the forest surrounding the Berger, or had eloped to the south of France. The authors of such stories, Oyhançabal said, were '*nécrophages*' – feeders on carrion. 'I wanted to demolish them.'

It was not until late May, when enough of the snow on the Vercors plateau had cleared, that Oyhançabal was able to return to the Berger's entrance. He hoped to find some animal tracks leading to Alex's body. 'There was nothing,' he says.

On 11 June Oyhançabal and three colleagues entered the cave. They decided to conduct yet another search of the Meanders, the section where Alex was last seen. Some 100 metres down they reached a chamber known as the Boudoir.

While the main cavern continues down, there is a narrow subsidiary passage leading out of the Boudoir three metres above the floor. This passage had been thoroughly searched the previous summer, when a caver reported that it ended in a barrier of stalagmites after 100 metres, but Oyhançabal decided to take another look.

As the cavers edged along the passage he noticed a faint breeze, suggesting that it was not completely blocked after all. When they reached the stalagmites their lights picked out a narrow aperture below the roof. They climbed up and saw that the passage continued beyond.

The cavers crawled through the gap and walked for another thirty metres before being halted by a broad, circular shaft or pot some eight metres deep. 'At the bottom,' Oyhançabal relates, 'we saw a greyish mass.' They saw a rucksack too and realised that the greyish mass was Alex – 'or rather,' says Oyhançabal, 'his corpse.'

Oyhançabal's first reaction was one of grief. Although Alex had clearly died through falling into the pot, Oyhançabal at first believed he must have lain there injured for some time. 'It looked as though he had died from exhaustion,' Oyhançabal says. 'We were heartbroken because this meant we had not looked hard enough.'

Then one of the cavers abseiled into the pot and saw a rock, apparently freshly fallen, lying nearby. Oyhançabal supposed that it had struck Alex on the head. 'We concluded he had not suffered,' he says.

Questions remained. Why had Alex strayed so far from the normal descent route? Why had he fallen into the pot, and where had the boulder come from? Only after several return visits did Oyhançabal deduce the answers.

It was already well known that Alex had disappeared after continuing along the Meanders alone, having become cold and impatient while waiting for his two partners to catch up. Oyhançabal concluded that Alex, using the technique of 'bridging', had climbed through the Meanders at too high a level, so that when he reached the Boudoir he was some distance above the normal descent route. Oyhançabal also believed that Alex was suffering from a crucial disadvantage. His helmet had been equipped with a lamp with a narrow beam.

In major systems like the Berger Oyhançabal considers it vital to carry *two* kinds of lamp: one with a narrow beam to pick out the path ahead; the other with a diffuse flame to illuminate a wider area. Otherwise, Oyhançabal explains, 'you don't get a general view. You can make a wrong judgment. It was probably the case for Alex.' That would help explain why Alex had strayed upwards in the Meanders – and why he had mistaken the subsidiary passage in the Boudoir for part of the normal route.

Here, Oyhançabal believes, Alex was handicapped by his youth. Experienced cavers would have realised they had strayed off-route. But Alex had never been in a large system before, nor was he accustomed to caving alone. 'He was very fit but he lacked the experience to evaluate the difficulties of a cave this size.'

Once past the stalagmites, the undisturbed mud and slime should have warned Alex he was on unknown ground. He should also have noticed the passage becoming steeper and more jagged, the signs of an imminent pot.

'When you arrive in such an area,' says Oyhançabal, 'you must be careful, as if on the edge of a cliff. Alex should have anticipated it. You can't blame him. It is a sign of lack of experience.'

Once at the pot Alex should have known conclusively that he was in the wrong place. The pots in the Berger are the landmarks of the system and are rigged with ropes and abseil points. 'Not seeing any ropes,' says Oyhançabal, 'he should have realised that he was lost. In a way, this is why he died.'

Instead of turning back, Alex began to descend the pot, taking hold of a boulder as he did so. The boulder was attached by a thin film of mud and gave way. Alex fell to the bottom of the pot, followed by the boulder.

When the Pitchers learned what had happened their immediate reaction, says Mrs Pitcher, was to think, 'Trust Alex to be so spectacular – he can't do anything by halves.' At first they, like Oyhançabal, believed that the boulder had killed Alex. But at the inquest they heard he had died from multiple internal injuries and a broken back. Although the pathologist reassured them, 'He wouldn't have known a thing,' Mrs Pitcher is prepared to look 'straight in the face' at how he may have died.

'We still don't know,' she says. 'I am haunted with the thought that he might have taken hours to die. It will continue to haunt me until I'm a little old lady.'

On 30 June a requiem mass was held at St George's Church, New Mills. It was, says Mrs Pitcher, 'the works. We needed a dramatic way of putting a full-stop to the chapter.'

For all her fears, Mrs Pitcher says, 'I feel a sense of relief and joy and peace. It's like the prodigal son. It's this overwhelming sense of him coming home. The wondering is over. Obviously there's sorrow and peace but there's joy as well.'

The family has moved from the house where Alex set off for the Gouffre Berger and where they last saw him alive. From their new home they can look across to the churchyard where his ashes lie.

'I can't express the feeling,' Mrs Pitcher says. 'But I know where he's going to be. He can't go any further. He's home and I can keep my eye on him now.'

7

SCOTLAND IN WINTER

I am glad that I knew Scotland in the pre-Motorway days, when it took two days to drive there from London in our Renault Dauphine, when much of the Highlands was still traversed by single-track roads and most of the loch crossings were by ferry. After twenty years, too, I still have intense memories of my first winter climbing with Tom Patey and John Cleare, even though I was usually fated to be sent back when they reached the crux of a new route in Tom's stamping ground of the far north-west. I did climb one new route with John, on Sgorr Ruadh, which was duly recorded in the SMC guide to the Northern Highlands. I am also immeasurably proud merely to have been present on the day when Tom made his breath-taking solo traverse of Creag Meagaidh and flattered to be included in his account of the climb, contained in *One Man's Mountains*, even though his description – as Hamish MacInnes also used to complain – sacrificed accuracy to wit:

> Peter Gillman, John's Press Colleague, announced that he had all the necessary material for his article, and that he ought to be getting along. Since this was the first time he had been within conversation range and had not yet started to climb, we were impressed by his talent for improvisation.

Sgorr Ruadh also represented my second Munro, and for almost twenty years I resisted their call; the article in the *Financial Times* from 1987 records the moment I succumbed. I am now *glad* that it is possible to drive to the Highlands from London in a day. Even so, I persistently dream of setting up anew in Edinburgh to bring them within closer reach.

*   *   *

Cold, hard, dangerous – and fun

Sunday Times Magazine, 1969

Winter on Quinag, a granite ridge running a mile north-wards towards Cape Wrath: a tongue of snow debouching into the scree at the distant end marks a gully burrowing into its stony innards. 'I don't know where it goes,' says Tom Patey, 'but we'll take a look.' The gully, its floor a basin of hard-packed snow, curves upwards between sheer walls, mounts a six-foot step of rock, then steepens into ice: Patey has cut steps with his ice-axe and we kick upwards, crampons biting with a crunch. Behind and below lies a tiny lochan, its surface troubled by the wind, and beyond it Loch Nedd, scattered with islets, opens to the sea: visual relief from our fissure's claustrophobic walls.

Above, the gully ends at a chimney boring vertically to the crag's top, dominated by a giant candelabra of hanging ice. Patey slithers upwards and hacks with his axe: slivers of ice catch the watery sun as they shower down, then die at our feet. Barring the way is a stalactite of ice, tree-trunk thick: impossible to believe it grew only that winter. Patey climbs closer, feet on nothing, slips, grabs, calls down: 'I think we'll have to give the mountain best'; continues nevertheless, bridging past the icicle and disappearing above.

John Cleare and I have watched with rising apprehension: it is only an hour to sunset, giving me an excuse to retreat. Precariously I balance down Patey's ice-steps, leaving Cleare to his fate. Head down to meet the wind, it takes me an hour to traverse the long dappled glen, a patchwork of snow and grey-green heather. Patey and Cleare arrive at the road in darkness, faces red and burning: on Quinag's top they scuttled to the descent gully between gusts of the easterly wind, throw-ing themselves to the ground and holding on with an ice-axe as they heard it approach like an express-train through a tunnel, hurling rocks past them in the air. It was 18 March, the day the Longhope lifeboat was lost in the Pentland Firth, thirty miles to the north.

Winter in Scotland: Tom Patey's world. For seven years he has been doctor at Ullapool, the herring-fishing village at the sea-end of Loch Broom. His beat, seventy miles from end to end, is one of the longest in the NHS; roads block with snow, and if the sea is too rough to cross Little Loch Broom to the crofting community of Scoraig, the only alternative route is a cliff-path five miles long.

Unlike some Highland doctors, he has a partner, and so is not tied to his practice twenty-four hours in twenty-four. He consumes his spare time voraciously, searching out unclimbed lines on the mountains round Ullapool: on An Teallach, Beinn Dearg, Liathach, Quinag. He has climbed in the Himalaya, but finds perfection in a long Scottish snow-and-ice route. 'Every winter route is an exploration: how difficult it is depends on how good you are at placing the steps. You need a lot of guile and cunning.' He also schemed the first ascent of the Old Man of Hoy in the Orkneys, climbing it (in summer) with Chris Bonington and Rusty Baillie – both Eiger men – in 1966.

Patey is thirty-eight, and for twenty years he has been at the forefront of Scottish winter climbing. Climbers' generations are brief, and past heroes are dismissed with ease after a season's inactivity: last winter Patey reasserted himself with the girdle traverse of Creag Meagaidh, one of climbing's 'last great problems', an 8000-foot route high across the face of one of the biggest cliffs in Scotland. Young aspirants had predicted a two-day climb, with a bivouac amongst the snow ledges halfway; starting almost casually at midday, Patey climbed it solo in six hours, and afterwards wore the widest grin his friends had seen for years. To some, solo climbing is the apotheosis: the greatest risk, the greatest sense of achievement. 'But I always climb as if I'm solo whether I've a partner or not,' says Patey. 'I tend to think that if I fall the rope will break anyway. There's got to be risk to bring the most out of you. It brings all your senses alert.'

Until the last war, winter climbing lagged a decade or two behind rock-climbing, confined mainly to the gullies that cleaved their way between the buttresses of a crag; then winter climbers turned to the crags themselves. 'We reckoned that any summer climb could be a winter one too,' says Patey. Postwar climbers used a short ice-axe for cutting holds: the traditional long-handled ice-axe (Alpenstock), first used by the Victorian pioneers, hindered more than helped. For a time Patey kept to nailed boots, which more stoical climbers still reckon the purest test of climbing skill – balancing on a hold on just one nail takes both confidence and strong calf muscles. Then belatedly Patey took up crampons, sets of detachable spikes: a climber wearing them on rock looks as ungainly as a turtle on dry land; but in their habitat of snow and ice the climber moves with rhythm and poise.

There came too a connoisseur's appreciation of ice conditions, like a surfer's of waves, their subtlety and infinite variability: from cascading waterfalls, frozen green and opalescent, perfect for cutting steps, to black ice, when snow has melted and frozen, treacly and resilient to an ice-axe blade. Snow varies too, from thigh- or chest-deep powder, agony to wade through; to packed snow with a surface crust, keen to receive the crampons' bite.

As winter climbing standards advanced through the 1950s, two major problems remained: Zero and Point Five Gullies on the north-east buttress of Ben Nevis. The word 'gully' was optimistic: they were mere ice-plastered scratches up the rock face. Patey had eyed them warily for several years; and so had Hamish MacInnes, an angular, idiosyncratic figure around whom the myths have clustered too. (Two – both true – are that he once embarked on a two-man expedition to climb Everest; and later returned to the Himalaya to find the yeti. He failed both times.) Earlier, MacInnes had waged a campaign against Raven's Gully, a cavernous slit high on the face of Buachaille Etive Mor, the pyramidical buttress that guards Glen Coe against travellers crossing Rannoch Moor. One of MacInnes's attempts had ended when, 100 feet above his partners, his rope froze solid to its carabiners. He undid the rope, continued solo, but was halted ten feet from the top by a chimney plastered with verglas – ice formed from running water, coated thinly across the rock. MacInnes, unable to move up or down, wearing only jeans and sweater, balanced there for eight hours of a winter's night before someone saw his partners' torch signals and came to the rescue. 'Aye,' says MacInnes non-committally, 'it was pretty cold.' MacInnes made the climb a month later in six hours, pulling a reluctant Chris Bonington, then only nineteen and on his first winter season, with him.

MacInnes had tried Zero several times, once retreating from halfway after an avalanche had all but swept him and his partner from their holds. In February 1957, Patey and MacInnes, putative rivals, both arrived in the climbing hut below Nevis at the same time, intending to try Zero; there was nothing for it but to climb together. Patey led the first pitch, 100 feet up an eighty-five-degree ice-trough; when Graham Nicol, the third man in the party, mistakenly dropped his ice-axe from the top, it fell clear to the ground. The last pitch of all, 100 feet of vertical ice, took MacInnes two hours.

The ascent of Point Five, nearly two years later, was a subject of the ethical argument of which climbers are so fond: Ian Clough led a seven-day siege on the route, climbing a pitch a day and retiring to the hut at night. An earlier attempt on Point Five had been made by the English rock-climbing master, Joe Brown – an audacious move, for Scotsmen guard their territory jealously. Once on Nevis, Brown and Don Whillans stole a 1200-foot rock route which for a time was the hardest in Scotland.

'English bastards,' yelled a Scottish climber when he saw them reach the top, and they retaliated by naming the climb *Sassenach*. The shame was expunged only when Robin Smith – later to die with Wilfrid Noyce in the Pamirs – and Dougal Haston put up an even harder route alongside.

Brown's Point Five attempt ended when a sheet of ice came away from the rock and he fell 300 feet, escaping with bruises. 'The process of learning is never-ending,' wrote Brown drily in his account of the incident, and it is true that English climbers often underestimate the seriousness of Scottish winter climbing, and take time to appreciate the way routes can alter from day to day.

Avalanches are a danger that have often gone unregarded, even though they have caused up to ten per cent of Scotland's mountain accidents each year. This year has been one of the worst: three climbers, all highly experienced, were swept away on Ben Nevis in January; then less than a month later four climbers survived and one died in an avalanche in Glen Coe. Even climbers in England are not immune: two were killed in an avalanche in Derbyshire in 1963.

Avalanches occur most frequently when fresh snow lies on the old, consolidated surface beneath. Conditions remain critical for twenty-four hours after a snowfall. 'If only climbers would keep out of the gullies and stick to the buttresses and ridges for those twenty-four hours, avalanche accidents would be cut right down,' says Hamish MacInnes, leader of the Glencoe Mountain Rescue team.

But an element of unpredictability is always there. The worst incident of 1968 was in the Cairngorms, when seven men in a party from the Scottish Council for Physical Recreation centre at Glenmore Lodge were caught on the slopes of Coire Cas, five needing hospital treatment. On this occasion there had been no fresh snow. The danger came from windblown snow, and the avalanche came down out of the mist, which had made it impossible to see the state of the higher slopes. 'I reckon only half a dozen people in Scotland could have predicted that avalanche, says Eric Langmuir, warden of Glenmore Lodge, who was away in Aberdeen that day, and got his first intimation of trouble when he saw RAF rescue helicopters overhead as he drove home.

Langmuir, an experienced winter climber himself, was the first man to make a thorough study of avalanches in this country: seven years ago a member of the Czech Mountain Service on a course at Glenmore Lodge showed him how to make a snow profile, examining the consistency of different snow layers to see whether or not they would adhere. Langmuir posts snow reports at the foot of the ski-lift in Coire Cas, but this is not one of his official duties and he doesn't always have the time. 'I think it's very necessary that there should be someone to do this properly,' says Langmuir. 'I'm sure it's only a matter of time before a skier going off the pistes gets avalanched.' If Langmuir's urgency has a personal emphasis, it's understandable: in 1967 he and three other men were avalanched in the Cairngorms while out looking for a missing climber. 'It's a terrifying experience, really terrifying. You just feel helpless – like falling into a heavy sea. The forces you are caught up in are enormous, and you realise that anything you might try to do is just a waste of time.' When the avalanche ran out, Langmuir's head was free, but the snow around him set concrete-hard within seconds. Unable even to breathe he lost consciousness before the two unburied men in the party dug him out.

Hamish MacInnes has been running courses in Glen Coe for four years to train dogs to search for avalanche and accident victims. The dogs can smell a man buried in thirty feet of snow, or one lying on the surface from half a mile away – so long as he is still alive. Last year MacInnes and the Glencoe team, the busiest in Scotland, were out twenty-five times – and many of the calls were not to climbers but to walkers or tourists lost or in difficulty. In September 1967 a party of eleven people – several wearing town shoes – had to be lowered 300 feet down a crag after they had strayed from the Aonach Eagach ridge on to difficult ground. Other calls have meant searches – often fruitless – for days on end, most hideously in the Cairngorms, where winds scour the moonscape plateau at more than 100 mph. 'It's like the Arctic,' says Hamish MacInnes. 'It's frightening, it's unbelievable. There's no shelter and you can't get out of the wind for a long, long time. You can't hear what anyone says and if it snows you can't see where you're going.'

A rescue call can come at any time. At 4 a.m. on 24 March last year a climber woke Hamish MacInnes to tell him that he and his partner had been forced to retreat from Raven's Gully: they had reached the bottom in darkness and unroped, but his partner had slipped on comparatively easy ground and disappeared. MacInnes phoned Ian Clough in Ballachulish, at the foot of the glen, and Clough went to the cottage opposite his own to wake Jim McArtney and Allen Fyffe, instructing that winter for Clough's winter climbing school. 'It's a rescue,' said Clough, and McArtney and Fyffe, who had been in bed for just two hours after a hard day's climbing, got dressed without complaint. Hamish MacInnes and his wife Catherine, a doctor, set out before dawn and found the man at first light. A long trail of blood in the snow showed them where: there was no need to look closely to see that he was dead. An experienced climber, he was himself a member of the Lochaber rescue team at Fort William; probably tiredness caused his slip, and his head struck rocks as he fell. 'What a shame, what a shame,' said Jim McArtney as he arrived back at the road with the stretcher party. The previous day two men had fallen, roped together, nearly 1000 feet down a gully on Creag Meagaidh, and survived unharmed. 'He was just unlucky,' said Catherine MacInnes.

Almost a year later McArtney was one of the three victims of the fatal avalanche on Ben Nevis.

Climbers readily accept their obligation to go out on rescues for other climbers. They are less enthusiastic about walkers or tourists who've got into trouble through stupidity, ignorance or inadequate equipment, but go out to rescue them all the same. But not everyone in the mountain rescue teams is a climber: the Glencoe team has shepherds and farmers who join in searches and rescues, though they're not paid even the pittance lifeboatmen receive. In August 1968 farmers in Glen Coe lost five hay days through going out. Civilian mountain rescue teams get no government or local authority money, and rely on collecting boxes in hotels and grateful contributions from people they've rescued. As it is, they are desperately short of money. 'We need about £8000 a year,' says MacInnes. 'In Glen Coe alone we urgently need £1300 for new radio equipment. We have sets but they are wearing out: it could be a matter of life and death, literally.' Insurance cover for death or disablement is only £1000.

Even MacInnes's dog training course next year is in jeopardy: he has only £80 towards the cost of £300. 'Young people are being encouraged to go out into the mountains but no one's worrying about how to get them out again when they're in trouble,' says MacInnes. 'We're not grumbling about going on rescues – but we just haven't got the equipment.'

Accidents usually have the effect of making climbers who have seen them evaluate the risks anew – but then carry on climbing just the same. 'For a month or so afterwards you look down and wonder what state you would be in if you fell,' says Patey. 'I'm used to it now,' says MacInnes. 'It makes me pretty careful when I'm climbing, but I'd never give it up. Winter climbing is the best there is.'

Scotland in winter has a rare, clean taste: melt-water from a burn appearing at intervals in the snow; the virgin smoothness of a frozen lochan; the lonely shrieks of a grey-white ptarmigan circling a whitened corrie; the sensuous fragility of a wind-blown summit cornice. A desolation to be savoured, the city's antidote; to those who know it, another world.

The lure of the Ben

Sunday Times, 1982

Ben Nevis was at its most seductive last Thursday. Beneath its giant North Face, fresh overnight snow had covered the floor of the Allt a'Mhuillinn glen, while confections of blue-green ice clung to the lower rocks. Above towered huge rock buttresses, plumes of spindrift billowing from their flanks, their tops disappearing into the swirling grey cloud that hid the mountain's 4406-foot summit.

Few readers of the *Sunday Times* would care to venture out into such a chill landscape. But it is precisely these conditions that lure Britain's winter climbers to Ben Nevis – with such fatal results. Slicing between the grey buttresses above Glen Allt a'Mhuillinn is a deep, snow-filled trough named Castle Gully, where four climbers have died in the past few weeks. A fifth was killed in Gardyloo Gully, further up the mountain beyond the aptly-named Coire na Ciste – Corrie of the Coffin.

These deaths form part of a grim pattern on Ben Nevis, which has claimed twenty-four climbers in the past four years: about a quarter of all Britain's mountaineering deaths.

Some mountaineers like to believe that climbing accidents are avoidable, and befall only those who break the safety rules. But, while most of the recent victims on Ben Nevis were young, the mountain has a sinister reputation for taking experienced climbers too.

Its sheer size, which renders it so irresistible to climbers, also attracts climatic extremes. The Victorian observatory on the summit – now in ruins – once recorded 240 inches of rain in a year, with snow lying twelve feet deep. The weather is also highly volatile. Ben Nevis, on the west coast, greets the frontal systems arriving from the Atlantic and, like the North Face of the Eiger, appears to collect the worst weather going, even when its less imposing neighbours are clear. 'There is no avoiding the fact that climbing is a risk sport,' says one leading Scottish mountaineer, 'and on the Ben, the risks are bigger than almost anywhere else.'

It is true that the first of the recent accidents occurred in classic avalanche conditions, when mountaineers are warned to stay out of gullies and away from steep snowslopes. But Ben Nevis has its own local rules, and Castle Gully is considered reasonably safe.

In fact, it was not the gully that avalanched the Monday before last, but a tier of snow that slid from a terrace of the giant Castle Buttress above. It swept a party of six to the foot of the gully. Two escaped unhurt and started digging their companions out, finding two injured and two dead.

Half an hour later, the second avalanche struck in Gardyloo Gully. This time, the climbers probably brought disaster on themselves by dislodging the loose snow as they climbed. Members of the Lochaber Mountain Rescue team, arriving by helicopter to attend to the first accident, hurriedly diverted to the second. Two climbers were found injured but alive, while the third was dead, almost certainly strangled by a climbing rope which had snagged over a rock in the fall.

Last Monday, two more bodies were found at the foot of Castle Gully, having lain there overnight. At first, it seemed that they too had fallen victims to an avalanche. But clues later suggested they were probably victims of a more conventional accident. A broken sling and a trail of blood on the rocks of Castle

Buttress suggested that one of them had slipped, dragging his climbing partner with him – an accident that confirmed the mountain's grim reputation for punishing mistakes.

Although most of the recent victims of the Ben were comparatively inexperienced, some of those who have died in the past have been among Scotland's most experienced mountaineers. In 1970, the leading ice-climber Jim McArtney set out with three companions in freezing conditions that seemed near perfect. But a warm front arrived, making the snow treacherously loose. When McArtney was a short way below the summit, a giant slab of snow slid away, killing him and two of his companions.

Two years ago, another party was descending into the Allt a' Mhuillinn glen by a path universally regarded as safe. But an avalanche broke away from the cliffs above, engulfing and killing the last man in the party.

Beneath Ben Nevis, the people of Fort William view the climbers' fascination with the mountain with puzzlement, but also some sympathy. A local undertaker refers to the first three months of the year, when both accidents occurred, as the 'silly season'. But, while the police compile their accident reports with the resignation of motorway patrolmen clearing away multiple pile-ups, few of them argue that climbing should be prohibited. They recall asking one survivor of the recent avalanches 'What will you do now?'

'Carry on, I suppose,' he replied.

Climb every mountain

Financial Times, 1987

B einn Sgritheall – pronounced Ben Scrioll, the scree mountain – is not one of Scotland's most celebrated peaks. It stands by itself on the northern shore of Loch Hourn, a lonely fiord on Scotland's jagged north-west coast. It is ringed by mountains of far greater renown, among them the Torridon peaks to the north and Skye's majestic Cuillin Ridge to the west.

Yet, Sgritheall has much to offer. The most enticing path to its summit begins a short distance above Sandaig, the tiny golden bay where Gavin Maxwell wrote *A Ring of Bright Water*.

As we laboured up Sgritheall's abrupt southern flank last month, we crossed a burn that tumbles down to Sandaig. As we looked back we could see where it runs into the sea – the very place where Maxwell's otters fished and played.

Sgritheall also has an eerie, isolated loch trapped in a hollow on its eastern ridge, and some satisfying scrambling as the ridge steepens towards the summit. For the most part, the ridge was wreathed in clouds as we climbed; but near the top they cleared to reveal Skye and the Cuillins, a misty blue in the evening sun, and beyond them the shadowy Outer Hebrides.

For us, Sgritheall had one more prize. As my son Danny and I reached the summit cairn, we offered the mountain a ritualistic incantation.

'That's twenty-nine,' I said.

'Twenty-eight,' said Danny.

Those readers who already know of the Munros will at once recognise our code. For the others, the term refers to the Scottish mountains which exceed 3000 feet in height. There are 276 in all, and Sgritheall is one.

There is a coterie of walkers and climbers who make it their goal to climb all 276 Munros. It is one of those essentially pointless and obsessional pursuits in which the British appear to specialise, and until this summer I thought I had managed to resist its call. As my exchange with Danny indicates, I might now have succumbed.

Thus, it can be seen that I was imparting the information that Sgritheall was my twenty-ninth peak, with Danny confirming he was still one behind. Implicit in my comment, of course, was the acknowledgment that I still had 247 peaks to go.

The person who I and fellow walkers can thank – or blame – for our obsession is an engaging Victorian eccentric named Sir Hugh Munro. After a diverse and colourful life, in which he was variously a professional soldier, King's Messenger, private secretary to the governor of Natal, Conservative parliamentary candidate and a collector of fossils, eggs and butterflies, he devoted himelf to making the first systematic list of Scotland's mountains.

In 1891, Munro published his *Table of Heights over 3000 feet*. He counted 283 in all – 'some,' as the fledgling Scottish Mountaineering Club declared in awe, 'perhaps never ascended.'

Munro next set himself the goal of being the first person to climb all 283. From his base on his family estate in Fife, a servant would transport him to remotest Scotland by dog-cart. There, he would stride off alone, carrying a long-handled ice-axe to assist his ascents and an aneroid barometer to check the heights.

By 1918, at the age of sixty-two, Munro had just two peaks to go. He was already planning the celebrations for his final ascent when tragedy struck. That summer, Munro joined the Red Cross and went to France with two of his daughters to run a canteen for the British troops. He caught a chill which developed into pneumonia, and he died the following year.

Munro's prize was taken by the Reverend Archibald Robertson whose parish of Rannoch, close to Ben Nevis and Glen Coe, was conveniently surrounded by Munros. Robertson did most of his travelling by bicycle and spent ten years at his task.

By 1939, only six other walkers had completed the full round. But in the 1970s, as outdoor pursuits boomed, the total soared. It has now passed 300 and is rising by dozens every year.

In the manner of obsessions, a remarkable range of records has been set. The longest time taken for the complete round is fifty-seven years. Until recently the fastest was three and a half months, by the redoubtable Hamish Brown. Now, a bespectacled former accountant named Martin Moran has done it in eighty-three days – a feat all the more extraordinary since it was achieved in winter.

It can also take a terrible hold. Far from being satisfied when he completed his round, Hamish Brown went on to make another seven.

Some when they finish go on to climb the Corbetts, the 223 peaks between 2500 and 3000 feet, and then the eighty six Donalds, between 2000 and 2500 feet. Others scour the rest of the British Isles for 3000-foot mountains – there are eight in Snowdonia, four in the Lake District and seven in Ireland.

Inevitably, too, where obsessions are concerned, arcane disputes have broken out. The most persistent concern what precisely constitutes a Munro: whether a peak can reasonably be called a separate mountain or is merely a 'subsidiary top'.

After several revisions, Munro's original list has been reduced by seven. The Scottish Mountaineering Club, while conceding many of Munro's original choices were 'random or irrational', has now decreed that further changes must be resisted – otherwise, 'the tables would no longer be Munros.'

For years I resisted all of this: the scrutiny of maps, the compiling of lists, the arguments over whether a mountain deserved to be a Munro. By this summer, at the age of forty-five, I had reached a desultory twenty-eight.

It is true that even this total brought me a gamut of rich experiences that left me wanting more. They include battling through a howling winter gale to the summit of Buachaille Etive Mor in Glen Coe; fighting heat and thirst on the Torridon peaks of Liathach and Beinn Eighe; crouching athwart the Inaccessible Pinnacle on Skye, the only Munro that requires pure rock-climbing techniques; and scurrying up Blaven one evening to see Skye's entire Cuillin Ridge rising majestically through the clouds as dusk arrived.

But still I thought I was immune to the Munros' call. I persisted in my belief even after climbing Sgritheall, our first outing during a fortnight's holiday this summer in Kintail. Then, I succumbed.

Virtually within sight of our cottage was the South Cluanie Ridge, which contains no fewer than seven Munros in its ten-mile switchback length. It was impossible to resist.

We set off for the first peak at the ungodly hour of 8 a.m. and spent the entire day in a world of our own, sometimes swathed in clouds, sometimes dipping below them to survey the desolate wilds of Kintail and Knoydart beyond. After eleven hours we stumbled back to the roadside, weary, parched but gratified, with the seven peaks under our belts. In one day, my total had been elevated to a staggering thirty-six.

Although our pace slackened thereafter, by the time we headed south at the end of our holiday I had forty-one Munros to my name. (Danny was on forty, having slipped out one morning to climb the peak that would bring him level; two days later, when his back was turned, I took it back.)

A map of the Munros now hangs on my wall, bearing forty-one marker pins; guidebooks are spread across my study floor; writing commissions that will take me back to Scotland are being sought. The arithmetic is daunting: twenty peaks a year would take me twelve years, by which time I will be fifty-seven.

With the insouciance of youth towards the practicalities of life, Danny says I should simply take a year off and climb them all. Once I would have laughed at the idea; now it no longer seems quite so absurd.

Small hill, big triumph

Sunday Times, 1988

T he wind had been an insidious presence all day, nagging at us, sapping our energy and spirits. Now, as we approached the summit of Cruach Ardrain, a 3400-foot peak in the southern Highlands, it seemed to redouble its efforts, scything over the mountain's icy flanks in a final bid to turn us back.

To compound our discomfort, clouds had descended around us like a clammy hand, making it impossible to see more than a few yards ahead. From above, four ghostly figures loomed out of the half-light, their faces turned against the wind. 'It's a complete white-out ahead,' said a young Scotsman from beneath an ice-encrusted balaclava. 'We're going down.'

It would, I suppose, have been logical and sensible for the three of us – me, my son Danny and his partner Rosie – to go down too. But winter hill-walking is not solely about logic and good sense. It is also about stubbornness and perversity. Rosie, who had never climbed in winter before, said she would prefer to go back. Danny and I, who had been in similar situations, were for going on, and the ayes had it.

It was not a moment to reveal inner doubts. I reassured Rosie that since our map showed that the summit lay due east, all we had to do was to follow our compass until we arrived.

We pressed on into the gale, now roaring around us like a turbine. I was intrigued to hear deep gasps emanating from somewhere inside me as I struggled to draw breath. But the adrenalin inspired by anxiety and excitement drove us on. Before long, the ground rose sharply and we found ourselves at the summit cairn.

Normally visible as a pyramid of stones, the cairn was totally encased in ice. We yelled congratulations into each other's ears, posed for the obligatory summit photograph – one of the last I obtained before my camera froze – then searched for somewhere to take a brief rest.

Beyond the cairn, the ridge fell away abruptly. Danny descended a few steps and carved a perch with his ice-axe in the lee of the wind. We nestled beside him and fumbled in our rucksacks for a celebratory piece of chocolate. Through rents in the clouds I glimpsed a frozen glen below and beyond it a mountain slope as white and barren as ours. Irresistibly, the words of Captain Scott came to mind: 'Great God! This is an awful place.'

While Scott's words captured the ambience of Cruach Ardrain, they were not entirely appropriate. Scott had just walked 800 miles across the polar ice-cap. We were barely forty miles north of Glasgow, and three miles from a road where cars passed oblivious to our mini-drama above.

Entirely of my own volition I had chosen to immerse myself in this thoroughly inimical environment – potentially dangerous, too. Of the thirty or so mountaineering fatalities each year, most occur in winter. Some climbers are caught in avalanches every bit as lethal as those in the Alps.

Yet walkers and climbers will still hasten into the frozen hills next weekend, with every likelihood that the mountain rescue teams will be in action once more. Why do they – and I – do it?

In summer, the rewards of hill-walking are plain to see. The ground is firm, the burns taste like nectar. I have traversed the monumental Beinn Eighe in Torridon on a day when its white quartzite rocks radiated heat, and stood on the summit of Stac Pollaidh in the far north-west at 11 p.m. to see a myriad lochs glinting in the extended twilight.

Winter brings glorious days too, when white mountain crests shimmer against an azure sky, beckoning you to their midst. Far more often, however, they seem to want to repel you before you begin. As you sit in your car watching snow lashing past your windscreen, the temptation to return to the last pub – especially in Scotland, where the pubs are open all day – can be all but overwhelming.

Therein lies the first, contrary satisfaction. Recent advances in winter clothing, together with the traditional mittens, gaiters and balaclavas, make you feel as snug as an astronaut in a life-support system. You positively relish defying whatever the elements can hurl at you.

Finding your summit presents a further challenge. On clear days this is straightforward, but the conditions we encountered on Cruach Ardrain were more the norm, calling for a measure of navigational skills. It requires a certain act of faith to put all your trust in a flickering compass needle, and our stiffest test came on Beinn Dorain, the 3524-foot whaleback peak above the Bridge of Orchy.

Clouds shrouded the entire ridge as Danny and I set off (Rosie said she wanted a rest and went for a quiet drive). We were following a course a few degrees off due south and a line of rocks helped us find our bearings.

We passed a crag where a frozen waterfall hung as if time itself had been suspended and we felt cocooned in an alien but self-sufficient world. But as we left the rocks behind, cloud and snow swirled around us, so that the ground and sky merged in one white, featureless mass.

This is the bewildering condition termed a white-out. As your eyes strain to focus, all you can see are specks of dust swimming across your eyeballs. You can see no more than a step or two ahead and the only way to locate the horizon – and a possible drop – is to lob snowballs ahead and watch their trajectory.

We momentarily neglected the compass and soon realised we had no idea where we were. The only recourse, when you discover you have been wandering in circles, is to find the last point where you knew where you were and start again. Suppressing a momentary shot of panic, we steered back down the ridge until we located our original tracks and followed them back up.

This time we stuck unswervingly to the compass and came upon a blade of rock protruding from the snow. At first we ignored it but then Danny hacked at it with his axe and found a marker cairn beneath. Our guidebook said the summit was 200 metres due south, and we headed into the murk.

We lost our bearing again, retraced our steps to the rock, set off once more and finally came upon the summit cairn. Our celebrations were the more joyous for being mingled with a certain relief.

To the outsider, it might appear that we had been playing a mixture of blind man's buff and Russian roulette. But we felt we had remained in control, extricating ourselves from our difficulties calmly and reaching the summit in safety. In short, we had kept to 'the rules'.

Danger, however, has a habit of coming upon you unawares. There are two incidents in my intermittent winter career which still give me cause for thought.

Once, after climbing in the lee of the wind, Danny and I reached the summit ridge of Buachaille Etive Mor near Glen Coe to find ourselves in a storm more violent than anything I have known before or since. At times the wind seemed to be about to lift us bodily into the air, so that we had to cling to the ground and scuttle between gusts to the safety of a corrie some 400 yards away.

And once, on the neighbouring peak of Buachaille Etive Beag, we turned back on becoming drenched and chilled by driving rain. Near the foot of the mountain a shock awaited us, for a burn we had jumped across on our ascent had become a torrent. It took us fifteen minutes to summon the determination to wade across, with the icy water surging up to our thighs.

It is hard in retrospect to estimate whether we were truly in danger – but it is a rare winter when at least one climber does not die on being caught in storms, or drown trying to cross a swollen river. For all the caution and safeguards, some irreducible element of risk remains.

But the risk has to be balanced against the potential rewards. The truth is that winter walking has provided some of my most scintillating sensations and memories, among them the day last month when the three of us climbed 3421-foot Meall nan Tarmachan in the Ben Lawers range. The wind, *leitmotiv* of the week, was there to greet us, driving squalls of sleet across the lower slopes. But as we came within the lee, it was replaced by an almost unnatural calm, made more uncanny by the roar we could still hear from the open glen beneath.

The mountain's Gaelic name means ptarmigan, and right on cue a female appeared in her milky winter coat, eyeing us from a patch of rocks. Long streaks of snow alternated with the grey heather, providing another inner refrain: the line from 'Pied Beauty' by Gerard Manley Hopkins: 'Glory be to God for dappled things . . .'

Our route now followed a pristine snowslope rising gently to a great cirque of rock and ice. There the snow afoot was lined with ripples like a frozen beach, presumably fashioned by the wind and casting shadows in the watery sun. We felt we were in some great sanctuary, a secret place that was our privilege, that afternoon, to know.

We now had the choice of making a rising traverse along a broad, snow-covered ledge, or making for the summit via a sensuous snow-filled gully at the very heart of the cirque. Emboldened by our surroundings, we decided on the direct approach.

As the angle steepened, our crampons bit with a satisfying crunch, with Danny in the lead. At a brief near-vertical section he sliced holds with his axe, showering Rosie and myself with shards of ice that glinted as they fell.

When we emerged from the gully we saw there was a last slope to surmount. The wind found us again but we ignored its ministrations as we kicked our way to the crest. The summit cairn was a few paces away: we unleashed yells of triumph and wonder as we strode towards it.

All around was a sea of peaks rising and falling like billows, a landscape of utter beauty and desolation. There were no cars, no roads, no signs of habitation: we felt immersed in a landscape that had existed thus for an eternity. How many others, we wondered, would know Scotland as we saw and felt it that day?

After five minutes, our eyes were brimming with tears from the wind and cold, and we turned to take the first reluctant steps back down. More lines from Hopkins ran through my mind, capturing our entire absurd enterprise.

O the mind, mind has mountains; cliffs of fall
Frightful, sheer, no-man-fathomed. Hold them cheap
May who ne'er hung there.

INDEX

Alvarez, Al, 114, 200–1
Anderson, Bob, 78, 89
Annapurna, 165
  1970 South Face expedition,
    45, 50
Antoine, Mo, 200–1

Baillie, Rusty, 42, 107, 113, 233
Barnett, Anthony, 214
Barry, John, 70
Bauer, Willi, 176–82
BBC, 53, 94–6
Beinn Dorain, 245–6
Beinn Sgritheall, 240–1
Bell, George, 153
Ben Nevis, 234–40
Birtles, Geoff, 99–100
Blackham, Roy, 221, 223
Boardman, Pete, 41, 55–65, 83,
  159–63, 164–8, 169–70
Bonatti, Walter, 122
Bonington, Chris, 13–23, 43–55,
  64–9, 75, 76, 98–9, 134,
  158–63, 164–8, 169–70, 200,
  202–3, 233, 234
Bonington, Wendy, 15, 46, 48,
  54, 66
Bourdillon, Tom, 84
Boysen, Martin, 23–32, 51, 54,
  56, 123, 159–63
Brady, Ian, 221, 223
Braithwaite, Paul (Tut), 159, 165,
  168
Brice, Russell, 73
British Mountaineering Council,
  195, 196

Broad Peak, 171
Brown, Hamish, 205–6, 242
Brown, Joe, 47, 73, 90–4, 94–6,
  96–9, 104, 150, 235
Brownley, Ron, 129, 131
Burke, Beth, 160
Burke, Mick, 23–32, 36–9, 43–54,
  62, 66, 75, 83, 85, 108, 123,
  146, 148, 150, 156–8,
  159–63, 167, 169

Casarotto, Renato, 174–5
Cerro Torre, 23–34, 37–9,
  119–28
Chang Bong-Wan, 176–7
Changabang, 55–64, 165
Charity, David, 144–7
Cho Oyu, 71
Chomolungma, see Everest
Chu Yin-Hua, 134
Clark, Beverley, 35–6, 107
Clarke, Charles, 170
Cleare, John, 90, 106–18, 231,
  233
Cliff, Barry 109
Climbing walls
  Altrincham, 196
  Bradford, 191
  Ebbw Vale, 190
  Leeds, 192
  Sale, 196
Clogwyn Du'r Arddu, 91, 92, 93,
  97
Clough, Ian, 19, 49, 66, 157, 167,
  235, 237
Clough, Niki, 157

Condict, Dave, 16, 108–18, 143–7
Corbetts, 205–6
Craig Gogarth, 90–4, 98, 128–33
Creag Meagaidh, 231–3
Crew, Pete, 23–32, 90–4, 95,
     98–9, 123
Croxford, Rosie, 244, 245, 248
Cruach Ardrain, 244–5
Culbert, Rae, 154
Curran, Jim, 172, 180, 182

Daily Mail, 14, 22
Daily Sketch, 14
Daily Telegraph, 13–23
Davis, Lance, 216
Desio, Ardito, 141
Desmaison, René, 157, 158
Desroy, Graham, 191–7
Dickinson, Leo, 101, 120–7
Diemberger, Kurt, 143,
     170–82
Donalds, 205
Dru, 157
Drummond, Ed, 198–9
Duff, Jim, 165, 167
Dunagiri, 56, 62, 64

Egger, Toni, 122
Eiger, 41–3, 49, 57, 203
   North Face
      Direct route 1966, 13–23,
      34–6
      voie normale 42–3
Eliassen, Odd, 67
Emery, John, 154–5
Estcourt, Nick, 50, 159, 165–8
Evans, Charles, 84
Evening News, 14
Everest, 55, 67
   1924 British expedition,
      134–40, 188, 197
   1972 British expedition, 43–55
   1975 British expedition, 159–63
   1988 British expedition, 72, 73
   1988 US expedition, 72, 74–89

Fanshawe, Andy, 71
Fawcett, Ron, 99–102, 104
Fawcett, Gill, 100–1
Financial Times, 119
Fonrouge, José, 28, 31
Fosse, Torgeir, 67
Fotheringham, Jim, 67
Frost, Tom, 50, 51, 156
Fyffe, Allen, 237

Gadbin, Jean, 225, 226
Gardiner, Alexander, 185
Giant's Pot, 206–9
Gilkey, Art, 153
Gillman, Danny, 241, 243, 244–8
Glen Coe, 234, 236, 239
Glencoe Mountain Rescue Team,
     147, 151, 235–7
Golikow, Karl, 20
Goodwin, Phil, 217–22, 225
Gordon, Adrian, 170
Gouffre Berger, 209–30
Gousseault, Serge, 157
Grummett, Clive, 223

Habeler, Peter, 79
Hamilton, Scott, 154
Haramosh, 153–5
Harlin, John, 13–23, 34–6, 146
Harlin, Marilyn, 15, 35
Haskett-Smith, Walter, 102–4
Haston, Dougal, 13–23, 40–3, 51,
     98–9, 107–8, 123, 143, 148,
     150, 157, 159, 235
Heard, Caroline, 224
Heard, Chris, 212–4
Hemming, Gary, 158
Hibberd, Gordon, 120–5
Hillary, Sir Edmund, 84, 135, 140
Himalaya, 70–4, 134–5, 141, 157,
     187
Hinkes, Alan, 71
Holliwell, Laurie, 130–1
Holliwell, Les, 130–1
Holzel, Tom, 119, 134–40

Hopkins, Gerard Manley, 247, 248
Howell, Ian, 112–18
Hunt, Lord, 54–5, 163

Imitzer, Alfred, 177–81
Irvine, Andrew, 72, 119, 134–40, 189

Jacquemont, Victor, 185
James, Ron, 149
Jillott, Bernard, 154
Jones, Eric, 120–5

K2, 70, 79, 140–2, 153, 164–8, 170–82
Kamajan, 166
Kamet, 55
Kangchenjunga, 153, 154
Karakoram, 153, 165
Keay, John, 182
Kilnsey, 104
Kor, Layton, 13–23, 107–8

Lang, Adrian, 112–17
Langmuir, Eric, 236
Leach, Mark, 104–6
Lehne, Jörg, 15
Livesey, Pete, 100–1
Longstaff, Tom, 58

MacInnes, Catherine, 237
MacInnes, Hamish, 147–9, 231, 234–8
Maestri, Cesare, 119–28
Makalu, 74
Mallory, George, 72, 119, 134–40, 188–9, 197
Marriott, Steve, 217–22, 225
Marshall, Jimmy, 41
Martin, Ian, 106–18
Mauri, Carlo, 123
Maxwell, Gavin, 240
McArtney, Jim, 237, 240
McCallum, Keith, 129–31

McNaught-Davis, Ian, 53, 94–6, 99, 100
Meall nan Tarmachan, 247–8
Mear, Roger, 70
Menlungtse (Qiao Ge Ru), 64, 71
Messner, Reinhold, 72, 80, 89, 204–5
Minks, Peter, 124
Moar, Isaac, 97
Moorcroft, William, 185
Moores, Paul, 73
Morris, Dave, 72
Moulam, Tony, 129
Mountain magazine 119, 129, 132, 133–4
Munro, Sir Hugh, 241
Munros, 205, 231, 240–3
Mustagh Tower, 97
Myhrer-Lund, Bjorn, 67

Nanda Devi, 55, 61, 63, 226
Nanga Parbat, 171
Napes Needle, 102–4
Nicol, Graham, 234
Noel, Captain John, 183, 186–90
Norton, Edward, 188, 189
Noyce, Wilfrid, 235

Observer, 18
Odell, Noel, 119, 136–40, 189
Ogre, 165
Old Man of Hoy, 94–7, 225, 233
Oyhançabal, Albert, 222–30

Parkin, Gordon, 206–9
Patey, Tom, 49, 95, 97, 108, 203–4, 232–4, 238
Peake, Steve, 198
Pertemba, 159–63
Phillips, Cliff, 120, 124
Pindisports, 44
Pitcher, Alex, 183, 209–30
Pitcher, David, 210, 212, 226, 227
Pitcher, Michael, 209–17, 226, 227

Pitcher, Norma, 210–17, 224–30
Pitcher, Sara, 211, 226, 227
Pot-holing, 206–30

Quinag, 230, 232

Renshaw, Dick, 56, 57, 59, 62, 169
Riley, Tony, 165
Ringdal, Helge, 67, 68
Robbins, Royal, 108
Robertson, Rev Archibald, 242
Robinson, Don, 192–7
Rogers, Nigel, 129, 132
Roskelley, John, 201–2
Rouse, Alan, 70, 79, 134, 141, 175–82
Rowe, Colin, 199

Salkeld, Audrey, 119, 134–40
Scafell, 103
Scafell, Pike, 103
Scott, Captain Robert, 70, 245
Scott, Doug, 46, 73, 74, 159, 165–8, 200
Sgorr Ruadh, 231
Shih Chan-Chun, 133
Shipton, Eric, 54, 56, 65, 69
Shoening, Pete, 153
Simpson, Joe, 202–3
Smith, Robin, 41–3, 235
Smith, Roy, 108–12
Smythe, Frank, 189
Somervell, Howard, 188
Stokes, Brummie, 73
Stott, Janet and John, 203
Strachey, Lytton, 136
Streather, Lt-Col Tony, 152–5
Sunday Times, 17, 30–3, 119, 144, 183

Tasker, Joe, 41, 55–64, 165, 166, 169–70
Taylor, Harry, 73
Teare, Paul, 78–89

Tenzing Norgay, 135, 140
Terray, Lionel, 122
Thompson, Mike, 46–7, 51, 156
Tilman, Bill, 54
Tirich Mir, 153
Tomalin, Nicholas, 17
Town magazine, 6, 133
Trachsel, Hans-Peter, 124
Traverse of the Gods, Swanage, 106–18
Tullis, Julie, 70, 79, 134, 141, 170–82
Tullis, Terry, 171, 172

Ullman, James Ramsay, 17
Unsoeld, Willi, 201
Unsworth, Walt, 16, 133

Venables, Stephen, 41, 72, 74–89
Vigne, Godfrey, 185

Walsh, Dave, 72
Warburton, John, 216, 217, 222
Watt, Donald, 151
Webster, Ed, 78–89
Weekend Telegraph, 16, 17
Westnidge, Peter, 147
Whillans, Audrey, 15
Whillans, Don, 13–23, 47–55, 65, 68, 93, 104, 150, 204, 235
Wieser, Hannes, 177–82
Willig, George, 200
Wilson, Ken, 119, 125, 129–33, 196
Wolf, Dobroslawa (Mrufka), 175–82
Wolff, Joseph, 185
Wood, John, 186
Wyn Harris, Percy, 136

Yates, Simon, 202
Yeti, 69, 71

Ziehman, Mimi, 88